MW01265360

The Journey of Anna Eichenwald

ISBN: 978-1-54396-503-2   ISBN eBook: 978-1-54396-504-9

Dedicated to

The Source

-

Who was…..Who is……and is to come

A C K N O W L E D G E M E N T S

Delia, my constant companion and encourager, provided excellent ideas for the manuscript, printing format and exceptional art work. A longtime mentor and friend, Bill Counts, was helpful in my research, proof reading the original text and giving me wise counsel. With her amazing computer skills, our daughter-in-law, Lisa Dianne Hunt, was invaluable to the process.

Authors of several history books proved invaluable in the research: they include, Otto Friedrich, <u>Before The Deluge, A Portrait of Berlin in the 1920's</u>, William L. Shirer, <u>The Rise and Fall of the Third Reich</u>, Michael Burleigh, <u>The Third Reich</u>, Richard Rhodes, <u>The Making of the Atomic Bomb</u>, and biographer Ronald W. Clark, <u>Einstein, the Life and Times</u>.

CONTENTS

The Journey of Anna Eichenwald

Whittaker Chambers, in his masterfully written account of his escape from Communism, espionage, and treason, describes a time when he and his family were in hiding and literally destitute. It had become brutally cold and their car radiator had frozen. They then discovered their home heating furnace was cracked. They had no money but called the repairman anyway. The furnace was beyond salvage so the repairman poured a 'mending liquid' in the tank with nothing else to do.

By a small miracle, the mending liquid sealed the cracked furnace, and the car suffered no permanent damage from the freeze. He and his wife began to view these and other events in their lives as 'Providential'. Situations out of their control seemed to be guided or driven by something or someone beyond themselves.

In reality we have no 'control' over the things we see as most important, especially life and death. It is true we can influence to some degree what happens, but we are certainly limited. Because man tends to view himself as central in the scope of things, he mistakenly believes he has control of history, remaining convinced that history is about him. Since the beginning of time, man has searched for truth and its source. There are not endless sources. In fact, there are in reality only two, God and man. Man's tendency to place himself as central in importance on the cosmic stage arrogates that he is the source of truth. But in this view, there are as many sources as there are individuals.

Placing God in his rightful position as Creator and Sustainer of the Universe confirms that he is the single source of *truth*, and that his truth is transcendent and immutable. In this model, all history is the working out of his eternal providential plan. What seems chaotic may not be chaotic at all.

In antiquity God had promised a 'national homeland' to the Hebrew nation. They occupied this land called Canaan, now modern Palestine, until their temple was destroyed in 70 AD. For almost 2000 years the Jews had no national homeland. In 1900 anti-Semitism was prevalent in American and European culture. With the exception of Zionism, no sentiment existed for the establishment of a Jewish homeland in Palestine. Yet in less than 50 years, circumstances stemming from two world wars would lead to the establishment of the nation of Israel in Palestine. Man could not have schemed nor predicted these consequences.

Anna Eichenwald was born of Jewish parents into a most chaotic time in German history. Hitler came to power in 1933 and predicted a 1000-year reign for the Nazi Reich. It lasted just over twelve years. Anna survived the Holocaust and in 1948 immigrated to her new homeland in Palestine.

We observe gravitational forces first described by Isaac Newton, but we do not understand the force or its cause, simply calling it Providential. We can observe history in a similar way, with limited understanding, and like gravity, should acknowledge it too is Providential.

CHAPTER 1
Eugenics

Walking briskly from her flat to work, Anna was apprehensive. Pulling her scarf more tightly around her neck, she headed up the steps of the University Hospital. A light snow was falling and there was no wind, but Anna felt unusually cold. She braced herself against the chill and began taking the steps two at a time, watching little clouds disappear and return every time she took a breath. Opening the door to the building she turned slightly to look back, pretending to struggle with her purse. She saw the parked car and turned away.

Monday mornings were always hectic. Anna was now an Associate Director of Surgery at the hospital, the result of her outstanding residency at the University Hospital, Berlin Medical School.

Today, her customary surgical rounds with resident physicians would have to wait. She was now a faculty member, and as such, she was scheduled to attend a meeting at 10:00 a.m. of the newly formed Counsel on Eugenics.

Anna had been informed of the meeting a few days earlier. It concerned her immediately. For all the accolades she was receiving for her professional accomplishments, trust was a diminishing commodity. She had already discussed the meeting with her surgical colleague, Christian Engel. She smiled to herself as she thought back to that conversation..... "There's something....ominous about it," she had confided in him. "I have a bad feeling. It can't be anything positive, and I feel trapped."

"You aren't superstitious, Anna," was all he would say.

"But Christian," she demanded. "Eugenics? I haven't thought about eugenics since I studied Plato." He stopped walking and turned to look at her. Several doctors rounded the corner he nodded toward them. Their conversation was still vivid in her mind.

"This isn't the place to talk about it, Anna. Besides, we will know soon enough what this is all about. Now weren't we headed for lunch? As I recall, you were going to buy me the best lukewarm meal the cafeteria has to offer."

She had smiled then and pulled out the inside of her coat pocket.

"Ah," he laughed. "Empty again. So I buy the lukewarm stew today." Christian could always get a smile out of her. They had gone through their surgical training together and had been both class-mates and friends. For years, Christian had been her most trusted ally. Now she was in love with him.

Like most surgeons, Anna had become a morning person. During her medical training, she and her fellow students learned more about quality naps than long hours of sleep, a habit that didn't change once she became a doctor. She was used to working extended hours with little rest. As she moved through the hospital's massive lobby she quickened her pace, her boots playing staccato across the gray, marble floor. She had arrived unusually early. And on this particular morning, she also felt something unusual. She was not prone to bad days or moodiness. She wasn't tired. But as she turned to head upstairs, she put the palm of her hand softly against her abdomen and took a deep breath. She recognized the feeling. Anna was nervous.

These were uncertain times. The advent of Adolph Hitler as Chancellor of the German Republic had changed much more than the political landscape. His appointment in 1933 had painted a new picture of Germany, one highlighted with bloodshed and political purges. Most of the country's citizens had initially welcomed a change. Even as the turmoil increased, they remained confident, lulled into believing that difficult changes required difficult measures.

Time would pass, and with it, the upheaval. In the end, Hitler would take them forward and the democratic process would take the country to a higher level.

Anna sat at her desk and poured a second cup of coffee. She still had plenty of time before the meeting. She stared out the window and allowed her thoughts to drift back to that crisp October day in 1934, when she and classmate Uri Avner attended a Nazi rally. The two had traveled by auto to Munich, where Hitler was to address the rally. Forty thousand people showed up, almost half in Nazi uniforms. Some held large banners displaying the Swastika. The colors were bold, the sounds were deafening and the air was electric. When Hitler spoke, he was mesmerizing.

Anna and Uri stood in the crowd, stunned at the power of this man who presented himself as a humble prophet, yet promised to commit himself to the task of improving the lives of all Germans. Whatever humility he brought to the podium died beneath the pounding of his fists and was resurrected as power personified. In apocalyptic language he spoke of a 1,000 year Reich, of social justice and reform. Like everyone else in the crowd, Anna and Uri were swept up in the oration and stirred by his passion and the content of his words.

That fall was ebullient; Anna and Uri and millions of other Germans could not know that they were subtly and carefully being lured into a web of deceit the likes of which the world had not seen. Anna, like so many others, was encouraged by the promises of this 'messiah' and elated at the prospects he laid out for her country. She believed she was witnessing a historic rebirth of Germany and that she would be a part of it. She would indeed be a part of it. Anna was a Jew.

The reprisals were already well underway. The Jews were the principle targets of the Nazi cabal, although many within the intellectual community had so far, been unscathed. Anna made every effort to pour herself into her work at the University. She was admired as a professor and teacher of surgery. She had recently received a coveted award as the outstanding teacher in the University system. Surely things would continue to go well for her.

Anna stood up from her desk and glanced out the window. She was looking for the car. Earlier that morning she had seen it during the four block walk to the University. For almost a month she had noticed the intermittent presence of a gray car parked at the corner of Meuerstrasse and Unter den Linden. It sat like a stone beside the Russian Embassy, a single occupant behind the wheel. The driver never moved. It had taken her several weeks to realize that she was being watched.

Anna was by nature, an optimist. As a child, she'd had little reason to resort to denial or force a positive attitude as a kind of defense mechanism. She had been raised in a loving home, with talented, generous and faithful parents. She believed in God and in the power of faith. Raised on such a firm foundation of values and goodness, it was natural for her to stand on this even on the few occasions when she had been troubled or upset. During such times, she would focus on the things and the people she loved. This morning was no different. Anna was troubled. So she turned her thoughts to Christian.

He had always loved her. Since their days in medical school, Christian had waited patiently for Anna to return his affection. She never did, so he was content to be her friend. He had met her parents and admired them. But he knew after that first introduction that his chances for anything more than friendship with Anna were even more diminished. They would never approve of a gentile who had a romantic interest in their daughter.

The National Socialist government had only complicated the issue. In 1934, the Laws for Protection of German Blood and Honor (known as the Nuremberg Laws) were passed. The first of the three laws abolished the citizenship of all Jews in Germany. They simply became 'subjects of the state.' The second law prohibited marriage or any sexual relationship between Aryans and Jews. The final law stated that no Jew could raise or lower the German flag. These laws were strictly enforced by the Gestapo. Anna had learned of a Jewish man who received a two-month prison term for just speaking to a 16- year old German girl.

Still, Anna and Christian spent hours together. They studied at school and as resident physicians. They had coffee together and took long walks. She knew that he admired her beauty. And she knew he was fond of her. But Anna thought of him as the brother she never had. That's why her sudden attraction to him after all these years had come as such a surprise. She loved to talk with him, laugh with him, confide in him. Then suddenly, she wanted his arms around her.

It had happened in an instant. One evening they were having coffee in the surgical lounge. Christian was laughing at something she said. He was looking away at the time and his eyes were smiling and sweet. Anna was overcome. She reached under the table and took his hand. His startled expression caused her to laugh out loud.

Anna had never been in love. And Christian had never dreamed she would return his love for her. As the evening grew late, Anna and Christian walked to her apartment and she invited him in. There was suddenly so much to say and so many feelings to express. Anna felt reborn as she listened to Christian pour his love into words.

"Anna, I loved you before I knew you. I always believed God had a girl for me. When I saw you, I knew you were that girl. You wanted friendship. I wanted your love. I knew you didn't really know how I felt about you. Besides, after I met your parents, I knew they wouldn't approve of me. But I still couldn't stop loving you. I tried. I spent time with other girls. But all I could ever think about was you."

"What other girls?" Anna snapped. Then she smiled. "Oh, so now you want to know," he laughed.

As the two sat in her tiny living room, Anna looked at Christian and began to feel warmth spreading across her stomach. It moved up her neck and into her face. She felt flushed. What would it be like to hold him? How would his lips feel on hers? She had never been intimate with any man.

"I never thought of loving you...this way," was all she could whisper. Christian stroked her face and moved closer.

"I was so busy with school, with my life. I just didn't...." Anna swallowed and struggled for the right words.

"I'm not sure how to move from where we were to what we are now. It's so new. It's like trying to get into a room...I'm already in.

Simultaneously they moved toward each other. Anna had been speaking so softly, Christian had moved closer to hear her. But Anna didn't speak. Instead, she kissed him. Christian closed his eyes, afraid that if he opened them he would see that it was all a dream. But her hands moved up to his face and he could feel her cool fingertips run lightly across his cheek.

"Pinch me," he managed to say.

Anna giggled softly and kissed him again. They remained in each other's arms, sharing kisses and talking until after 2:00 a.m. When he stood to leave, Anna wrapped her arms around him and leaned against his chest. They didn't speak for several minutes. Anna turned her head from side to side, as though trying to take in all of him. Christian ran his hands through her hair and breathed in the scent of her.

"I have to go," he finally said. "Remember, we're both working today."

One, long, lingering kiss later, and Christian finally pulled himself away from her. "I'll see you in a few hours."

"Not soon enough," she said with a smile as she shut the door behind him.

* * *

Anna forced herself back to reality and glanced at the clock. She looked around at her office, a private space on the building's third floor. Her position afforded a secretary, and Anna felt fortunate to have the services and friendship of Theresa Schmidt. Theresa arrived every morning at 8:30. They had developed a ritual. Over coffee, they would visit for a few minutes then move on to the day's schedule and administrative issues. In the last few months they had found time to discuss more important matters.

Other than Christian and her parents, Theresa Schmidt was the only person in all of Germany whom Anna trusted. Five years earlier, tragedy had befallen Theresa and her family. Theresa's husband, Dr. Willi Schmidt, was the eminent music critic of the Muenchener Neueste Nachrichten, the leading Munich daily newspaper. Their apartment was in Schackstrasse in Munich, and Theresa had made it a very comfortable home for Willi and their three children. On the evening of June 30th, Willi was in his study playing his cello while the children played in the living room. The doorbell rang and four SS men entered. Without explanation, they took Dr. Schmidt away. Four days later his body was returned in a coffin with orders that the family was not to open it. Dr. Schmidt had been mistaken for S.A. leader Willi Schmidt, who had been marked for assassination. The Gestapo later moved Theresa and her children to Berlin where she was given a job at the University and a small pension. Theresa never spoke of the Nazis and had grown fiercely loyal to Anna.

At 8:30 sharp, Theresa walked in the door. She and Anna talked for several minutes. Theresa was well aware that Anna's citizenship had been abolished by the Nuremberg Laws and that most Jews in Berlin were being forced to wear a yellow six- pointed 'star of David' on their coats. Jewish medical doctors and scientists employed by the University had not yet been required to do this. Anna and Theresa were extremely cautious in their conversations. They believed there were listening devices in the office.

Theresa knew about Christian. She was the only friend to whom Anna had divulged this information, and they had spoken of it only once. Theresa was well aware it was only a matter of time before the Nazis would remove Anna from her position. Jews were rapidly being removed from positions of authority.

The two women were silent for a moment and then Anna grabbed her notepad and her bag. "I'm off to the meeting," she said lightly. Theresa looked down at her notes.

"Yes, the eugenics meeting," she said aloud. "Good luck."

But Anna was already out the door. She took the side stairway down one flight and then across a long elevated corridor that led from the main hospital to the medical school building. The corridor was poorly heated and she walked quickly, drawing her white lab coat tightly around her chest. The main lecture hall was on the same floor. As she approached, two SS. sergeants stood at the door. They nodded, a gesture she acknowledged with a returning nod but without making eye contact.

Some thirty faculty members were already gathered in the lecture hall. Most were from the departments of medicine, pediatrics, anesthesia and surgery. Anna's eyes scanned the crowd until they found Christian. They looked at each other but neither one allowed their expressions to change. Anna took a seat near the front, the sole female and one of only three Jews on the faculty of the school.

Within minutes, one of three SS. officers stood to address the group.

"My name is Col. Gregor Papen. I am the deputy commissioner for the Counsel on Eugenics. We are here to inform the medical community of our program and to enlist your help in accomplishing our task. The Fuhrer understands and appreciates the dedication your staff has demonstrated in saving lives and fighting diseases. Our program is also a noble effort and will be carried out with the same dedication.

The program will have two components. The first will be research to aid our military. The second will aid our cause to purify the German people, something we must accomplish."

Papen went on to explain that there would be complete secrecy about the program. It would be administered by the faculty but would take place in various 'clinics' outside the main medical campus. Papen stressed that the 'subjects' would all be enemies of the state and would be moved from the prison system to the clinics. The research would be on living subjects to study gas gangrene, burns and the effects of hypothermia.

One group would be injected with Clostridia bacteria, the agent that causes myonecrosis or gas gangrene. The physiologic responses would be noted. The second group would be anesthetized and given scald burns on 30 to 50 percent of their bodies. He explained that the treatment of burns in warfare was critical to the welfare of German soldiers. The third group would be placed naked in ice water until their core temperature reached 88 degrees F. The patient's physiologic reactions would be observed. "The second phase of our program will be the cleansing phase," he said.

Papen's eyes showed no emotion. He did not appear angry or even stern. He may not have been gifted as an orator, but he was clever enough to know that there was no place for sentiment in instructions such as these. Sentiment could lead to failure. And his was a program that must succeed.

In clinical fashion, Papen carefully outlined the cleansing phase. It would consist of sterilizing children and young adults with birth defects and mental and emotional problems. Thus, the disabled would not be capable of procreation.

Anna felt herself sinking into her chair. The movement was imperceptible to others and she didn't make a sound. But from someplace deep within, she felt a weight settle over her like a blanket. What rose from it was an unfamiliar sense of anger and shame. She could no longer hear Papen. She was seeing in her mind, the 'program.' She had been taught to heal. She had taken an oath. Now she would have patients upon whom she was to inflict extreme physical harm and pain. This was not a medical program. This was a series of barbaric and sadistic experiments.... professional crimes; inhumane practices..... the antithesis of her profession.

Anna brought her lips together. Had anyone been looking directly at her, they might have thought she was about to whistle. Instead, she silently and softly exhaled, breathing out the fear and tension. She was going deeper into herself and into her chair. Anna looked just slightly to the left of Papen. She could not look directly into his face. She found a point on the wall just behind his ear and tried for a moment to find another image. But for the first time in her life, Anna could not think of pretty things or lovely people. She couldn't conjure images of stolen kisses with Christian. The man before her was fading. And in his place, Anna could see the definitive outline of horror.

The faculty was dismissed. They began to file silently out of the lecture hall. They were now, each of them, participants in 'the program' which would begin in one month. Anna forced herself to stand. She was still trying to find the strength to take a step when Papen approached her.

"Dr. Eichenwald." He said. Anna heard her name and drew in her breath again. She turned to him, unable to speak.

"We would like a few moments of your time," he continued. "You, Dr. Meitner and Dr. Richburg."

Anna and the other two Jewish faculty members were being detained. She looked around for Christian but he had already left the room.

Papen escorted them into a small filming room where there was a movie projector and seven chairs. They sat down methodically. In silence, they each asked themselves how their beloved country could have come to such a place or succumbed to such indignity and inhumanity. They also knew that it no longer mattered just how Germany had gotten there. What mattered was that it had. And they were trapped in it.

Papen dimmed the lights and started the projector. The first image on the screen was Berlin's Plotzensee Prison. The next image that came into view was an execution chamber. Six men were led in, hands bound behind them and black hoods covering their faces. They were forced to stand on a long bench, while piano wire, attached to a series of meat hooks, was placed around their necks. The bench was then kicked from under them. Their deaths took three to four minutes. The final minute or so found their bodies contorted with agonal convulsions. The projector stopped and the lights came on. Papen stood before them with a look of contempt.

"The Fuhrer expects this program to be implemented!" For the first time, he shouted when he spoke. Then he turned and walked out of the room leaving the three doctors to sit in stunned silence. Anna legs were shaking and she knew she couldn't stand up. The seconds ticked by. Still no one spoke. Finally, Dr. Meitner stood.

"Well..." he began. But he couldn't lift his eyes off the floor and his colleagues could not meet his. They left the room in silence.

CHAPTER 2

Anna & Erin

The 1920s ushered in radical changes throughout Germany. The Eichenwald family, though not politically active, was not exempt. Dinner table conversations increasingly centered on politics, and primarily, the terms of the Versailles Treaty signed after the Armistice ended World War I. With the war behind them, Germans wanted to get on with their lives. But the terms of the treaty were harsh and it was clear that the country was being punished. The Eichenwalds knew, as did every other German, that they were looking at an industrial recovery that could set the nation back 20 years.

One evening during dinner, Anna became animated in her discussion about the French.

"Father, they want to humiliate us," she exclaimed. "That's their only goal." An enormous problem was in the making for the democratically elected government. It was beginning to be viewed as the illegitimate child of the war. Five years earlier, two million front line defeated troops did not feel defeated, but were returning to a demoralized country spiraling into massive inflation and unemployment.

Despite this, not all of the radical changes in Germany were negative. In the miasma of defeat, the University of Berlin was establishing itself as the leading University in Europe. The 1921 Nobel Prize for science had been awarded to Albert Einstein for his 1905 paper describing the photoelectric effect. At least something in the country was going right.

Graduation ceremonies were routine for the faculty. But that was not the case for the graduates, and in particular, the Eichenwald and Nitschmann families. Daughters

Anna and Erin had both excelled and were now entering graduate school. Anna was beginning to build a reputation, as she was the first woman to be admitted to the medical school in the history of the institution. Her admission had been controversial. Three of the faculty had expressed opposition and threatened to resign if she were admitted. The Dean, however, was a progressive thinker. He realized that at some point, qualified female students would have to be admitted and he saw this time as the time to do it. Anna's parents, Hanz and Marlene, could not have been more proud. But as they made their way to the graduation ceremony on that Saturday in May, they were both lost in their own thoughts of this unique young woman, born to them 22 years earlier on a rainy Sunday in Munich.

"Hanz, remember how loud she was when she was born?" Marlene said with a quiet laugh. "I could not believe how something so small could make so much noise." Hanz chuckled and nodded. "I suppose she was trying to announce her arrival to the entire world."

The assembly hall was packed when they arrived, but Anna and Erin had been watching for them and met them as soon as they entered the doors. Best friends for more than a decade, the two had been inseparable though they were as different as night and day. Anna was all business. She knew what she wanted to do and set out with determination to achieve it. Erin was all passion. Music was her life and she had never lost sight of her goal to become a concert violinist.

The Eichenwalds were soon joined by Erin's parents, Paula and Isaac Nitschmann. They made their way through the assembly hall, the largest auditorium in Berlin, and found their places among the 4,000 seats. Situated on the campus of the main undergraduate college, the hall was an enormous gray stone structure with eight large paired Doric columns in front and three sets of massive 30-foot steel doors. Some 800 students were graduating so seating was limited to immediate family members. Both of the girls had received honors, not surprising their parents.

The ceremony was followed by a celebration dinner the parents had planned for the girls at the Romanische Café. It was a big unattractive building across from the Kaiser Wilhelm Memorial Church. Like a great barn, the Café seated 1,000 and was considered *the* place to go for Berliners. Up in the balcony, chess players sat at rows of small tables playing endless games late into the night. The only time Anna and Erin had been there before, they had seen two celebrities, Greta Garbo of the theater and Arthur Schnabel, the famous pianist.

Anna and Erin had both been awarded scholarships for graduate studies, Anna in medicine and Erin in music. They were sharing an apartment on Mittelstrasse, one block north of Unter den Linden and three blocks west of the main campus, in the center of the city. Their flat was on the second floor with two small bedrooms, a bath and a small front room with a stove and fridge. The fridge was essentially a wooden outer box covering an inner tin compartment. Ice, delivered on Mondays and Thursdays, was placed in a lower separate space keeping the compartment cool. Anna's room was sparsely decorated. She had a small desk and three book cases lined up against bare walls. This was a place to study. Erin, as the opposite of the two, had already adorned her walls with pictures of her family and favorite composers. She often put fresh flowers into vases and placed them decoratively on lace doilies. This was a room for an artist.

Despite their differences, the relationship worked. They often took breaks and sat across from each other talking about boys or Hebrew school or the latest fashions.

Runaway inflation had imposed a difficult time in Germany. Everyone felt the stress. Those with regular jobs got paid every day. Celebrated conductor, Bruno Walter, generally halted his symphony rehearsals for the mid-day rush. His musicians were paid with sacks of banknotes and they would dash out to exchange them for food. One day one of his trumpet players returned to rehearsal with a bag of salt, and a base player with two sausages. The wife of Henry Lowenfeld, a noted psychoanalyst, taught anatomy to three Chinese students. They could not understand German and she spoke no Chinese. So she used charts and diagrams and as a result, was paid with tea and 'the most wonderful rice cakes'. The machinations employed during times of extreme economic instability were most imaginative.

Most Berliners were managing to survive. Neighbors looked out for one another, working together through bartering and sharing. As bad as the economy was, it drew out the goodness of people and drew neighbors together. Oddly, there was an influx of foreigners to Berlin because of the inflation. One American writer who came with his family lived in a duplex apartment with a maid and a cook, something he never could have afforded in the U.S. He booked riding lessons for his wife, put his children in private school and he and his wife dined at the finest restaurants, all for his monthly salary of 100 U.S. dollars.

Anna's admission to medical school was unprecedented. And although that could have put her on a difficult pathway, there were three things working in Anna's favor. She was the daughter of an associate professor in the department of physics. She had achieved the highest score on the entrance exam. And the Dean had stepped in on her behalf.

From the start, both girls found the course work strenuous. Anna was taking gross anatomy, biochemistry, physiology, histology, and bacteriology. Erin was fully ensconced in music theory, advanced composition, violin, music history and classic composers. While Erin basked in her artistic studies, Anna was drawn to anatomy. As difficult as the course was, it would eventually draw her to the field of surgery.

Being the only female in her class did have its drawbacks. Gross anatomy lab was every Monday afternoon for five hours. She was frequently the first of four dissection partners to her cadaver, a 19-year-old boy who had died in a farm horse accident. Horses were used for plowing and riding and also for pulling logs, buggies, and stumps out of the ground. This unfortunate young man had been in the process of getting his horse into harness. As he walked behind the animal, a cat jumped from a loft in the barn and landed directly in front of the horse. Spooked, the animal kicked both hind legs and one hoof caught the boy flush on the left side of the head. The force of the blow caused massive brain damage and he lived only 36 hours. His grieving parents donated his body to the medical school hoping medical science might somehow benefit from his tragic death.

Anatomy is best studied from human specimens. The course was challenging, and it fascinated Anna. There were literally thousands of structures to dissect and Anna was more than willing to look to her sixty-year old bespectacled professor for the knowledge she was seeking. He was a grandfather several times over and delighted to have a young woman in his class for the first time. He went to great lengths to instill respect for the cadavers. They were human beings – deceased, but human.

During the months of work there were occasions when this fact was lost on some of the young men. Anna was not amused on one morning when she found her young male cadaver propped up and holding a magazine filled with pictures of nude girls. As her male counterparts burst into laughter, she coolly took the magazine to the rubbish bin and tore it in two. "Children," she said, in her best alto voice. "It's time to get to work."

Anna was tall, beautiful and bright, all attributes which enabled her to keep the respect of her classmates.

The rigorous experience of medical school produced a mutual respect and bond among the students. There was an unspoken understanding that the experience was not only unique but in a strange way, sacred. This may have been what appealed to Anna most during her course of study.

The Berlin Philharmonic was on a six-month tour of 20 U.S. cities and Erin's parents went with it. As musicians with the symphony, they were reimbursed in U.S. currency. This put Erin's family in the top 10 percent of wage earners in Germany. Simultaneously, Hanz Eichenwald was becoming internationally known in the new field of quantum physics. He was in demand as a speaker and being reimbursed in foreign currency stipends for his lectures out of the country. Sadly, most middle-class Germans were not so fortunate.

After the end of WWI, Germany was in turmoil. Campaigns of terror were being waged on the streets by both left-wing communist agents and right-wing extremists. The leading Catholic politician, Matthias Erzberger, was murdered by terrorists masquerading as patriots. He was the principle armistice signatory, and as such, was placed in an impossible position. He could only do his duty as a German diplomat to sign the document. The Allies had given the Germans no choice. Now he paid with his life. Another group threw prussic acid in the face of former Chancellor Phillip Scheidemann. The following year the highest-ranking Jewish official in Germany, Walter Rathenau, was shot to death while in route to his office. The assassin's slogan: *"Kill off Walter Rathenau now, that god-damned Jewish sow."* The anti-Semitism that was an undercurrent in all of Europe was now being openly displayed in Germany.

The political street thugs created enormous instability and chaos. But while murder and lawlessness were actively being used as instruments to acquire political power, the greater threat to the country's survival was inflation. Faith that the central government could turn the economy around was almost non-existent. The murder of Rathenau shook what little faith there was to the core.

One evening, Erin walked into Anna's study. "The Allies want the government to re-pay 130 billion marks for the war!" she exclaimed. "That is outrageous. It's going to be extremely difficult for Germany to honor this debt. Not only that, the Ruhr area of western Germany, which of course is being partially controlled by the French, is our most valuable industrial asset. How in God's name do they think we can pay all of that money? We don't have anything to pay it with!"

Erin was right. A year later, with no new resources, Germany defaulted on reparation payments. As punishment, France took complete control of the Ruhr area. Unemployment rose to 23% in only a matter of months. Even those with money found what they had evaporating. Families began selling things they didn't need, then moved on to trade away their most cherished possessions and heirlooms simply to buy food. But as the savings of the bourgeois were being wiped out, there were still those few individuals who had money. Café's with stylish ladies were available to foreign visitors in central Berlin, only a block away from the streets where starving children and the elderly languished in poverty. Along with malnutrition came other diseases; tuberculosis, rickets, and scurvy. One elderly writer, Max Bern, withdrew his savings of 100,000 marks for a one-day subway ticket he used to ride around the city. After taking in the ruins of his city, he went home, locked himself in his room and committed suicide.

The French occupation of the Ruhr industrial area was intended to humiliate the Germans. This spawned an undeclared war between the French troops and German citizens. German men and women could not accept their role as subservient to the French and the result was inevitable. The French did not use arms to wield their authority. They used arrests, deportations, and economic blockade to fight the German's opposing tactics - strikes, sabotage and dissent.

To compound the onslaught of humiliation, the French began using African colonial troops. Giving an African authority over the Germans created even more hostility. Over time, the need to survive forced some liaisons between these troops and local German women. The racially mixed children who came into the world as a result, were viewed as inferior 'Rheinlandbastarde'. As such, these children were accepted by no one.

Matters worsened. The majority of Germans had German Jewish friends and even relatives. But like the diseases spreading in the side streets, anti-Semitism was growing more contagious by the day. Germans were struggling and looking for someone to blame. Street talk and propaganda pointed to the Jews. Were they not controlling most businesses and banks? The economic problems brought on by the war were now being placed on the Jews. A new resentment was building against a group of people who were a convenient scapegoat.

Anna and Erin were not completely oblivious to this, but they were young and naïve, going about the business of being good students and fashionable ladies. They worked hard during class, studied hard afterwards, and lived for their weekends with friends and boys and family. The Sabbath was always a time of contentment. They attended Synagogue and spent the afternoon with their parents. The University was rife with ideologues whose tendency was to extol their personal viewpoints. So the Rabbi's commentary on the Torah was a welcome change. Anna and Erin were fluent in Hebrew, and their families stayed amused at their attempts to confound the Rabbi with questions that would even stump the great minds of Jewish history.

"Did the great flood in the time of Noah cover the entire earth?" "Was the Tower of Babel in Mesopotamia?" "Why did Joseph show compassion to the brothers who sold him into slavery?" The Rabbi was a humble man and was visibly grateful when Anna's father Hanz suggested the girls give him time to consider their inquisition.

Sundays were the only days that afforded the girls the luxury of sleeping-in. This was often followed by an afternoon at the Tiergarten or a performance at the opera. It was late May, a time of beauty in Berlin. Even the frequent thunderstorms were fascinating. The girls often donned their rain coats and umbrellas and stood outside to watch the lightning zigzag across the darkened sky in bold spears that hit the horizon and threw the city into silhouette.

The first Sunday in June was warm and the walking trails in the Tiergarten were lined with pink and white dogwoods. Rows of red and yellow tulips peeked out, surrounded by white daffodils, a fresco of tranquil colors. Strolling along the trails, thousands of Berliners sought to blot out the reprehensible forces surrounding them, if even for an afternoon.

Anna and Erin had gotten lost in the crowds. Anna, wearing a bare-backed sundress, absorbed the warm rays of the sun and the glances of more than a few young men in the park. She was aware of the dissonance in her country. But young people tend to live in the moment. It is difficult, historically, for them to denounce their feelings of immortality and instead, adopt an outlook that proclaims a bleak or frightening future. Nature does not seem to intend them to believe in the worst. So when they see it, they believe it will go away. It isn't denial in the truest sense. It is youth at its best.

On this sunny afternoon, time seemed suspended and Anna was in her own cloud of contentment. She had no interest in politics. University life kept her isolated from much of the chaos. While her homeland was being pulled into anarchy at a frenetic pace, Anna was lost in her books and the laboratory. When she did allow herself to dwell on the current situation, her deepest concern was that too many of her countrymen seemed to be going along willingly.

As evening approached, Anna and Erin walked past the Brandenburg Gate and down Unter den Linden. They turned north on Friedrichstrasse to the Weidendammer Bridge that spanned the Spree River. The street name changed at the bridge to Chausseestrasse. This was one of the centers of Berlin night life. University students often brought what little money they had to the bars and cafés, enjoying the freedom and entertainment, but mostly unaware that Berlin was being transformed into the 'Babylon' of the world. The collapse of the country's currency was leading to bank-rupt businesses, unemployment, food shortages, and loss of hous-ing. Marriage by middle class girls was accomplished by the paying of a dowry by the girl's family. Even maids saved and saved so they could get married. As the money became worthless, so began the decline of the cultural structure for marriage.

One of the many consequences of inflation was the discov-ery among young girls, that virginity was no longer valued. Berlin's prostitutes wandered up and down Friedrichstrasse and across the bridge to Chausseestrasse. Some strutted flagrantly in miniskirts and black leather boots. Others flaunted the image of youth and schoolgirl innocence, with pigtails and tight, white shirts. On occa-sion, a young girl turned out to be a young guy. They, too, needed fast money. When their physiques would allow it, make-up and effeminate moves could seal the deal as easily as any woman. Dimly lit bars often set the stage for hungry, high school boys to connect with government officials, financiers or any man prone to the affections of other men.

As Anna and Erin walked past the Kaiser Wilhelm Memorial Church on their way to the Romanische Café, one young girl caught Erin's eye. She was standing in a group of several other women. When her eyes met Anna's, she quickly looked away. She was tall and blonde, dressed in a low-cut orange blouse tucked into a tight, black leather miniskirt. Her high heeled boots hugged her thighs tightly, intended to draw the eye further up along her legs to the hem of her skirt. She carried an umbrella and had a jacket slung over her shoulder. She took a confident drag from the cigarette held in her right hand. A well-dressed man approached her.

"Na? Spazierengehen?" she asked with a smile. Her inquiry about where he was going and if he would like to take a walk was rebuffed.

"Noch eine zeit," he replied. Another time.

It seemed a harmless encounter. But Erin knew exactly what was going on. "Anna! That's Naomi Wiesner!"

Anna stared at Erin then looked back at the leather-clad blonde. Naomi had been a high school classmate. She had also played with Erin in the school orchestra. Anna had worked with her in student government. Without another word they turned to approach their friend.

"Naomi," said Anna. "Naomi."

Their friend turned toward them with downcast eyes. Her smile was gone. She had already recognized them and had tried to turn away before they saw her. "Come with us," urged Anna.

Reluctantly, Naomi left the group of women and began walking alongside Anna and Erin. They walked silently together and entered the Café where they found seats at a table in the back, in a quieter section of the mammoth building.

"Talk to us," urged Anna.

Tears welled up in Naomi's eyes. "Please, it's okay."

Anna took Naomi's hand and held it for a moment. Then Naomi took a deep breath and began her story. Her father had lost his job at the Deutsche Bank. He migrated to the coalmines of Ruhr, but there had been no word from him in three months. Her mother took a job as a maid in order to care for Naomi's three younger brothers. Then they were given notice they would have to vacate their apartment.

"So I must do this," she said. Her bottom lip quivered but her jaw was set. "Does your mother know?" asked Erin.

Naomi nodded. "It kills her," she said, steadying her mouth with her fingers. Her nails were painted a dark burgundy and they ran across her lips in quivering movements. Erin focused on this. It was too hard to think of what was really happening to her friend.

"Don't you worry about...?" Anna started to ask. Then she stopped herself. She was studying medicine. It was natural to think about things like pregnancy and venereal disease.

"And my choices are what, Anna?" Naomi asked defensively. "It may be killing my mother. But at least she and my brothers have a place to live."

This was a moment of reality for Anna and Erin. Here was a friend, a bright and gifted young girl, who had been forced into a dangerous and seedy lifestyle – in order to survive. She seemed to have no other choices. This was the most difficult part of the story to comprehend. Anna had always believed that having a good heart and strong values would lead to good things and a lifestyle that per-petuated good values. It is what her parents had taught her and what the Rabbi taught. How could the world be otherwise? How could it extract so high a price from so sweet a young girl? Naomi was good. She was now doing something bad – for the good of oth-ers. It was all suddenly upside down.

Anna and Erin ordered food so Naomi would eat. As they left the restaurant, they gave Naomi all the money they had and encour-aged her to go spend the evening with her family.

"I don't want to let go of you," Anna said as she embraced her friend outside the Café. She pulled away and took Naomi's face in her hands. "Be strong," she whispered fiercely.

Anna and Erin walked silently home together sharing a profound sense of loss. Each girl quietly said a prayer of thanksgiving. Such a tragedy had not befallen them. There were untold miseries in their country, but they had remained unscathed. They were safe. They were blessed. Two young women on the cusp of a promising future could not think otherwise.

* * *

Explanations as to the cause or causes of the inflation were complex. Some held a conspiracy theory that accused the German government of trying to perpetuate a gigantic fraud. This idea laid blame on a government that deliberately allowed the mark to fall to free the state of its reparations debt. German industry could decrease its indebtedness by refunding its obligations with worthless marks. This assumed that the average German did not understand complex economics. So when the idea hit the streets, most were outraged. One banker told one of his customers that in all of Germany there were only three men who correctly understood economics and two of them were out of the country. At least they were able to laugh about this tragic situation.

Karl Helfferich, the Imperial Treasury Minister proposed an idea for an economic solution. The plan, which eventually worked, was a National Mortgage Bank (Rentenbank). The bank began to issue 'Rentenmarks' backed by the nation's gold reserves, which were backed by a 'mortgage' on all of Germany's land assets. With these measures the German people accepted the value of the mark at pre-war levels - 4.2 marks to the dollar. This created an attractive situation for foreign investors. British and American loans were acquired to launch a new business boom. Within five years an American journalist observed, "businessmen were in business, generals were still generals, and the number of street prostitutes had dramatically dropped."

From time to time after Synagogue on Sabbath, the week-ends would find the girls going back home. As professional musicians, Erin's parents were usually performing on Saturday nights, opportunities that allowed Erin to go back stage at the symphony. Marlene Eichenwald especially looked forward to these week-ends. She did not work outside her home and was especially lonely because of Hanz's frequent travel and lecture schedule. She was delighted to spend time with Anna. Marlene had always been protective of Anna and tried hard not to show it. After all, Anna was grown and in graduate school. But every time she looked at Anna's sweet, innocent eyes, she could see nothing but a little girl.

On this particular week-end, Hanz was returning from a conference in Zurich. The train from Switzerland was arriving Sunday at 4:28 p.m. The previous day Marlene and Anna shared lunch after Synagogue in the Tiergarten. The garden paths pulled them away from the crowds to enjoy the flowers. Today, Marlene had a special surprise. In the midst of the inflation crisis, and to some degree because of it, foreign investment was pouring into the country. Many of the older department stores were being refurbished with lavish surroundings. One of the largest was Wertheim's on the Leipzigerplatz. It was only a fifteen-minute walk from the Tiergarten.

"Anna, I have been saving for this for weeks. I have a surprise! We are going to Wertheim's for a little shopping and then to the theater."

"And how did this come about?" asked Anna. She'd been so involved with her medical studies she hadn't taken much time for a social life much less shopping.

"It's time you had some new clothes and a night out. Your father makes plenty of money and I don't want him to be burdened with too much of it." They both laughed. "And the night out?"

"Well, Anna, we are going to a musical. It's called 'It's in the Air.' The cast is mostly unknowns. But one of the girls is getting very good reviews."

Marlene looked proud, as though she'd just received an award. "Sounds interesting," Anna replied. "What's her name?" "Marlene Dietrich!"

The following day, Marlene and Anna ate a late breakfast, then Anna tried on the new clothes. They laughed about times gone by, times that were less hectic, more tranquil. The train from Zurich was running two hours late, so Marlene dropped Anna at her flat so she could study. She waited at the bottom of the stairs until she saw Anna disappear safely behind her door. These were uncertain times. Though Marlene, careful as she was, had no real concept of the dangers from which her daughter would need protection.

CHAPTER 3

Einstein

Marlene returned to Central Station alone. The terminal was always busy but this evening seemed more crowded than usual. Eventually finding a seat, she tried to read for a few minutes to pass the time, but soon found herself mesmerized by the throng of travelers continually passing in front of her. She watched young mothers as they clutched their children's hands, somber faced men stiffly making their way through the lines of waiting passengers, old couples inching their way toward the stairs. A young girl walked past and glanced absently at Marlene. She was chatting with a friend, her face alive with an excitement and innocence Marlene had seen on Anna's face a hundred times. Her thoughts began drifting back to the days just before the war. Anna had been a gangly teenager and Hanz a promising young instructor in physics at the University. The world had seemed light.

The Eichenwalds had a Sunday tradition. They took the trolley from their home on Kaiser Wilhelm Strasse to the Kranaler Café on Friedrichstrasse. Marlene remembered the last time they had made the outing. That morning had started out no different than any other.

Hanz and Marlene had stepped to the edge of the street, protectively cushioning Anna between them. This had been their habit for years. But Anna was now almost thirteen years old and making a graceful exit from childhood. She seemed to be skipping adolescence altogether, moving from little girl to young lady without warning. She was already significantly taller than her mother, but that wasn't the only thing people were beginning to notice. Anna's dark hair caressed her face in waves, framing a porcelain complexion and striking, aquamarine eyes. Her smile seemed to be available for everyone. And there was no mistaking the new way in which she carried herself, the poise that had moved in overnight, replacing pre-teen awkwardness.

Anna Eichenwald was on the brink of womanhood. She was beginning to develop a sense of confidence in herself, studying the magazines for fashion photos and hairstyles, then mirroring them in her bedroom in the evenings. Occasionally she swept her long hair up on top of her head, securing it with combs that allowed a few dark tresses to escape. This gave her an older, almost glamorous image, and one that disturbed her father.

On this particular Sunday, Anna was thinking about the upcoming school year. Sporting a new outfit, a birthday gift from her parents, Anna moved easily, her long legs carrying her gracefully along the sidewalk. She seemed to float between parents, lost in her own magical world of clothes and boys and carefree dreams.

Hanz looked down at his daughter with pride, then flashed back to another Sunday, the one that brought Anna into his life. It had been raining when Marlene went into premature labor. Hans had rushed out of their home in Munich, heading first for the local mid-wife, then to retrieve the family doctor, who lived another three kilometers down the road. Dr. Baader had already expressed his concern about Marlene's elevated blood pressure and the swelling in her legs. Too often, he had attended women with Marlene's prob-lem, and the outcome had been disastrous for both the mother and the child. Dr. Baader did not like to give false hope and had shared his concerns with Hanz. He explained the complications and also the fact that the successful delivery of a child was sometimes out of his control.

Hanz had listened to the prayers of the rabbi in his synagogue, but he was not a man prone to prayer. That changed when Marlene went into labor. He prayed as he worked his way to the doctor's home, and he prayed as they took the harrowing buggy ride back to his house and charged through the front door. But they were too late. The mid-wife stood in the middle of the front room, sweat dripping from her forehead. She was holding a baby girl, a healthy baby girl.

Hanz stood motionless and stared. The tiny red face turned from side to side and her fussing quickly turned to wails loud enough to wake the neighbors. He looked at Marlene, who was pale but smiling and asking to hold her daughter. He felt the relief flood over him like the tears falling across his face and excused himself to step outside where he stood breathing in the night air and basking in what he believed was a miracle. The following day, Hans and Marlene named their new miracle, Anna Marlene Eichenwald.

Hanz looked at Anna and smiled as they turned into the café. Anna smiled back absently, lost in her dreams of the future. Neither she nor her parents could have known the truth. It was the summer of 1914, and this was Berlin.

A massive river of people pushed through the streets, ushering in what would become turmoil of historic proportion. The Archduke Franz-Ferdinand had been assassinated. The Hapsburg heir to the Austrian throne was dead at the hands of a Serbian national. As in most political assignations the reasons were unclear, and a volatile situation was now becoming an explosion.

Berlin was now a city of some four million people, a giant that had grown out of the marsh lands surrounding a once small Slavic settlement that cropped up during the middle Ages. Berlin had been given her name from the Slavonic words *birl*, meaning swamp, and *Collin*, a neighboring settlement. Conquered by Napoleon in 1806, the city was beset by revolution for the next 50 years. But by 1871, she had become the capital of the fledgling German empire.

On July 25, 1914, the *Berliner Tageblatt* and *Berliner Morganpost*, the city's two major newspapers, were both filled with reports of Serbia's refusal to comply with the Austrian-Hungarian ultimatum. The bourgeois seemed to come out of every corner of the city, furiously debating the consequences of a Balkan war with the German Reich. As Sunday dawned, the crowds continued to pour into the center of town. Some 10,000 made their way to the Schloss, the palace of Wilhelm II, emperor of all the Volk. In a patriotic frenzy, they were singing, "Deutschland, Deutschland Uber Alles," and the Austrian national anthem. Some marched together, some walked arm in arm. All made their way back down Unterden Linden to the Bismarck monument in front of the Reichstag. There was a sense of patriotic union, of common purpose.

That Sunday morning, there was also a collective sense of the inevitable….there would be war. Alliances were forming quickly. By early that afternoon youth clubs known as the Wandervogel were leading parades to the palace. Similar demonstrations began taking place in the outlying areas of Berlin and spread across the country. Patriotic revelers were banding together in Hamburg and Munich, in Cologne and in Mannheim. Hanover was no different. In every region, the populace was erupting in spontaneous and zealous support for the German cause. As the week passed, the idea of peace was being abandoned. The crowds were growing in size, their demonstrations becoming more robust. German pride was at its peak.

On August 1, 300,000 Berliners gathered in front of the palace, a testament to their readiness to defend the Fatherland. In those last days before the war, the fervor seeped from the streets into the German Foreign Office. A reckless diplomacy was being formulated inside those walls.

Hanz and Marlene had seen the beginning of this zealotry in the crowds pushing through Berlin on that Sunday morning in July. They had watched the throng as outsiders. The Eichenwalds had lived in Berlin for only two years, having left Munich when Hans received his appointment as instructor at the Kaiser Wilhelm Institute.

Hanz was a gentle, soft spoken man, an imposing figure who stood 6'4." He was handsome, with an angular face and thinning black hair. Despite his height, Hans was a modest, quiet man and for the most part, went unnoticed.

The Eichenwald family was of Jewish descent, and had a long established history in the community of Wasserburg in Southern Bavaria. The community sat on the edge of the Inn River, about 100 kilometers from the Austrian border. Hanz's father had been a chemist. He had handed down to his son, an easy grasp of science and an idyllic childhood. Hanz played with his friends, attended a Yeshiva school, and was embraced by a loving family and community. While Bavaria was predominantly Catholic, in Wasserburg the Jews retained their own distinction and held to their own heritage while blending seamlessly within the community.

By the time he was ten, it was clear that Hanz was intellectually gifted. Observant and verbal, Hans confounded even his father, asking incessant questions and offering insights beyond his years.

He seemed to question everything and had a particular interest in astronomy. "How is the moon able to hang in the heavens?" he asked his father one day.

"Gravity," his father replied, a bit taken aback.

"And what is gravity?" Hans asked.

Soon after, Herr Eichenwald visited a secondhand bookstore in Munich and bought his son a biography of Sir Isaac Newton. Hanz pored over the pages, devouring the content, fascinated by Newton's description of the concept of universal gravitational force. He learned that Newton and his colleagues developed the mathematics now known as calculus. Hanz marveled at the man's oft-quoted coda:

"This most elegant system of the sun, planets, and comets could not have arisen without the design and dominion of an intelligent and powerful being…"

The more he read, the more Hanz identified with this seventeenth century genius. He spent countless hours contemplating the mysteries described, and was awed by the movement of celestial bodies in time and space. The gravitational power that kept the earth orbiting regularly about the sun, also held its atmosphere in place while it hurled around the sun at unthinkable speed. Newton wrote accurate equations describing the force of gravity. But when asked to explain exactly what gravity was, Newton simply said, "I do not know."

In his *Memoirs*, Newton had provided a self-portrait of his contributions to the world.

"I don't know what I may seem to the world, but to myself, I seem to have been only a boy playing on the sea shore and diverting myself in now and then finding a smoother pebble or a prettier

*shell than ordinary, whilst the great ocean of truth lay all undiscov-
ered before me."*

The concepts Newton laid out had a powerful influence on young Hanz and sparked the beginning of his journey into the world of science and physics. He studied at the University of Munich, where he came under the influence of another great mind, the renowned physicist, Max Plank. It was Plank who had helped Hanz secure the appointment at the Institute. Young Eichenwald had distinguished himself in several areas, and under Plank's influence, had developed his principle field of interest in quantum physics. This was to Hanz, an entirely new way of looking at the subatomic world. The word *quantum* came from Plank's discovery in 1900 that energy exists in small discreet bundles called quanta. Quantum mechanics deals with the world of the very small. Thus, the quantum 'club' of physicists was a small one, as the theories were radically new and even to most physicists were beyond comprehension.

"I think I can safely say that nobody understands quantum theory," one of Hans' colleagues remarked one afternoon.

The only thing predictable about atoms and subatomic particles is that they are unpredictable. This, to classical physicists, was heresy because they worked in a world of predictable order, and they had become comfortable with that constant.

Like his father, Hanz was modest and quiet, but his demeanor belied his inner passions. He cared deeply for his family, his Jewish heritage and his country. Marlene hailed from Ulm, on the Danube, nestled in the foothills of the Swabian Alps. In 1805, this had been the scene of the Austrian's defeat by Napoleon. Ulm would later be noted as the birthplace of Albert Einstein.

Marlene's family had moved to Wasserburg when she was 12-years old. Within a year, she had attracted the attention of young Hanz, who was four years her senior. When he first saw her, he saw an angel. Petite, with strawberry blonde hair and blue eyes, Marlene had a delicate beauty and an engaging smile. Their courtship began as a platonic friendship and escalated slowly to long walks and holding hands. One evening as they walked together, they came to the simultaneous realization that they were in love.

As wonderful a realization as it was at the time, the love affair between Hanz and Marlene immediately presented itself as a crisis. Hanz had met the love of his life and at the same time had received acceptance to the University of Munich. Making a choice between Munich and Marlene never dawned on him. He wanted both, and without a second thought, he asked Marlene's father for her hand in marriage. The proposal was accepted. Once blessed by her family, Hanz and Marlene were also blessed by their community, all of whom were eager to participate in a traditional Jewish wedding celebration.

The date for their wedding held special significance for Hanz. It was to be just after Passover. In ancient times, the Jewish calendar was based on the lunar phases of the moon. A full moon occurred in the midst of the 28-day monthly cycle. The Passover celebration begins on the evening of a full moon, the first full moon of spring. It had been the moon's orbit around the earth that had sparked Hanz's quest for knowledge of physics. He had learned since, that the moon is held in orbit by the gravity of the earth, while conversely the gravity of the moon prevents the earth from spinning at an accelerated rate that would create constant gale force winds on its surface….such a delicate balance.

According to Scripture, the Hebrew nation had been delivered from bondage in Egypt some 3,500 years earlier. This deliverance had been accomplished by the marking of each Hebrew home with the blood of a male lamb. The Biblical account promised that the judgment of God would pass over the homes of each Jewish family, thus protecting the firstborn in each household. But this would not be so for the firstborn of each Egyptian family. The firstborn would be killed by the terrible tenth plague. The anguish forced Pharaoh to release the Jews from their Egyptian masters. It was the blood of a lamb that delivered the Jews from slavery. Some 1,400 years later, the blood of *the Lamb* would serve as the basis for Christianity.

The moon held great significance for Hanz.....the gravitational balance and order of the solar system, and his marriage to Marlene.

While having breakfast in the Kranzler Café that Sunday morning, Marlene and Anna ate and watched, their eyes constantly turning to the window and the crowds multiplying in the streets. They were witnessing the transition of German nationalism to a cultural rebirth. The sense of national purpose seemed to pull everyone together in a unity that would otherwise have been impossible with so many diverse political factions.

Hans was a patriotic man but not politically active. Germany had always been a splintered society. There was a working class and a middle class. There were socialists and conservatives, Protestants, Catholics and Jews. In the days that followed this quiet Sunday morning, the August days of this political transformation, a national unification process was begun. It was a process that would ultimately plunge the nation into war.

His patriotism was tempered with the reality of the true nature of war. He would not be taken into the military, and for this, Marlene was grateful. As an intellectual, he was aware of the existence of anti-Semitism. But from his own personal experience, he had not been confronted with it. The prejudice against his race and culture notwithstanding, Hanz could not have foreseen the diabolic events that would be triggered by these August days.

*   *   *

While political turmoil was growing daily, another significant event was occurring simultaneously in the scientific community. It began at the Solvay Physics Congress of 1911 in Brussels. Albert Einstein was in attendance, as was Max Plank and Walter Nernst, twin pillars of the German scientific community. Both men were deeply impressed with Einstein's ability. Their task was the recruitment of staff for a new series of research institutes in Berlin to be known as the Kaiser Wilhelm Gesellschaft zur Forderung der Wissenschaften – the Kaiser Wilhelm Society for the Advancement of Science. These men made initial contact with Einstein about the KWI at the Congress in Brussels.

The Institutes were being constructed at Dahlem, near the end of the new underground from Berlin. The first buildings were to be for physics and electrochemistry, headed by Fritz Haber. The Physics Institute, along with the others, would benefit from the magnetic scientific atmosphere of the German capital. It was believed that there would be few if any obstacles in attracting Einstein. But one possible problem was the fact that he had renounced his German citizenship 15 years earlier and was now a Swiss citizen. This was high drama. The two giants of the German scientific community were now traveling to Zurich to tempt young Einstein back to the Fatherland. They spent a number of hours pleading their case, but at the time, Einstein was not willing to give them a decision.

The two men took an excursion by train to await his verdict. They knew it was not unusual for Einstein to tweak the nose of authority, and he liked games. Einstein had explained that they would know his decision when they saw him. He would be holding a white rose if his answer was no, a red one if his answer was yes. As Einstein approached the men on the train platform, he was carrying a red rose.

Plank and Nernst returned to Berlin to prepare their draft presentation to the Ministry of Education. They proposed that Einstein serve as the director of the Institute for Physics with a salary much in excess of his present one in Zurich. They also asked that he receive appointment as full professor at the University of Berlin, where he would be given free rein to devote as much or as little time as he wished to his lecture schedule, and as much time as he wished on his research.

The draft was approved by the academy and the proposal was submitted to the government on July 28, 1913. On November 20th, the Kaiser approved the appointment, which Einstein formally accepted on December 7th. His acceptance was significant in several ways. First, there was the matter of timing. Einstein was scheduled to formally take up his duties on April 1, 1914. This was a benchmark for anyone, and for Einstein, it was achieved before his 35th birthday. But he was a pacifist, and would not have made this move if Germany were already in the midst of armed conflict.

A second significant aspect was the fact that Einstein's lecture schedule allowed him to devote his time to completing his Theory of General Relativity. And third, had he not immigrated back to Germany, he would not have been a target of the anti-Semites, and likely would not have moved to the U.S. in 1933. Einstein's presence in the U.S. in 1939 enabled him to use his enormous intellect and influence to encourage the effort which led to the development of the A-bomb which ultimately forced the surrender of Japan in 1945.

Hanz Eichenwald and his colleagues were brilliant in their own right, but like other scientists of their time, they stood outside the depth of Einstein's genius. But his genius was a gift few truly understood. After Einstein graduated from the Federal Institute of Technology in Zurich, he was refused jobs in academic institutions throughout Europe. Eventually, he found employment as a patent examiner in Bern, Switzerland. Working in obscurity, he devoted all his 'off time' to physics. In 1905, he published a number of papers that literally redefined reality. Collectively, these publications dealt with the nature of *time, space, light, mass and energy.*. In one of the publications, he proposed that light was actually composed of tiny particles called 'photons,' a concept known as photoelectric effect. For this, he was awarded the 1921 Nobel Prize. This was the only paper he felt was truly revolutionary. But in fact, it was his observations about relativity, the measurement of phenomena relative to one another, which changed the world's understanding of the universe.

Einstein was once asked by reporters to comment on the subject.

"When you sit with a nice girl for two hours, you think it's only a minute," he quipped. "But when you sit on a hot stove for only a minute, you think its two hours. That's relativity."

Most of the men in the institute were engrossed in trying to understand Einstein's reality. They knew that the speed of light had been established by Maxwell's equations as 186,000 miles per second. Einstein's work proved that nothing could exceed the speed of light. Out of the same equations came the understanding that velocity and time have an inverse relationship. As speed increases, time slows down. Finally, for any particle traveling at the speed of light, there is no passage of time. This leads to the conclusion that the only thing in the created universe that does not age is light. Relativity also established that energy and mass are interchangeable. Mass can be converted to energy and energy to mass, but neither can be created or destroyed. In a short time Einstein's conversion formula of E=mc2 (energy = mass x speed of light squared) became known worldwide.

When Einstein continued to expand his theories of relativity, he was forced to deal with the universal laws of gravity as demonstrated by Newton. He eventually came to understand that gravity and time are also related. As the force of gravity increases, time slows. So a watch will run faster on the top of Mt. Everest than at sea level. His ideas became more and more complex, and his colleagues at the Institute continued to marvel.

Nothing in Einstein's early history suggested dormant genius. In fact, he was slower than his peers in learning to speak, and he was socially withdrawn. His teachers and even his parents considered him a poor student and slow learner. When Einstein's father inquired as to what profession his son should adopt, he was told it didn't matter. Einstein, in the opinions of his teachers, would never succeed at anything.

His parents were Jewish but they were not religious. Since they didn't practice Judaism, sending their son to school was a simple matter of enrolling him in the school closest to their home, which happened to be a Catholic school. His home life was a happy one, and he recalled being confronted with the fact that he was Jewish only as an adult.

One of the great influences on Einstein was a young Jewish medical student, Max Talmey, who frequently visited the family. He gave 12-year old Albert a number of books on the physical sciences and mathematics. Within a few months, the boy had worked through all the elementary problems and was devoting himself to higher mathematics. Soon, the flight of his mathematical genius was so high that Talmey could no longer follow him.

Albert also enjoyed philosophy. By the age of 13, he was reading the works of Immanuel Kant, including The Critique of Pure Reason, an incomprehensible book to most. Kant became Einstein's favorite philosopher.

Another influence entered Einstein's life in his youth. He had studied the violin at the age of six, and motivated by Mozart, he became aware of the mathematical structure of music. He remained an amateur in performance, but that never diminished his enjoyment.

Before moving to Berlin, Einstein had developed a far more complicated concept he called general relativity. He was beginning to appreciate that gravity was not a force like other forces. Instead, he saw it as a consequence of the fact that space-time is 'curved' by gravitational fields. He continued to work on general relativity after moving from Zurich to Berlin in 1914. He presented his theory the following year, forcing yet another paradigm shift with his sheer brilliance. But he remained unobtrusive and was noted for his wit and humility. While at a meeting in Paris he predicted the following:

"If my theory of relativity is proven correct, Germany will claim me as a German and France will declare that I am a citizen of the world. Should my theory prove untrue, France will say I am a German and Germany will declare that I am a Jew."

Einstein – Official photo after winning Nobel Prize - 1921

Einstein and wife on SS Rotterdam – 1921 – Heading to America

*   *   *

Now hostilities were imminent. The declarations of war against Serbia and Russia were carried out on August 1st, exactly 117 days after Albert Einstein moved his family to Berlin. The following day, thousands of patriots filled Munich's Odeonsplaz to hear the declarations read from the steps of the Feldherrnhalle. Present in the crowd was an anonymous 25-year-old misfit who was trying to eke out a living as an artist. Adolf Hitler had recently moved to Munich after spending several years in Vienna where he had tried and failed to qualify for entrance into the Vienna Academy of Fine Art. His meager income came from selling his sketches and from a legacy left to him by his deceased mother. His father, Alois Hitler was an unsympathetic man who took little interest in his family. He was generally harsh with his children and frequently showed his disapproval of them. Adolf performed poorly in school and maintained a deep resentment for academia and teachers in general. In his later years he would remark that most of his teachers had something wrong mentally, and that quite a few ended their days as 'honest-to-God lunatics.'

The only subject that appealed to Adolf Hitler was Germany. Born in Austria, he had developed a passion for his adopted Fatherland. His presence that day on the Odeonsplatz was a personal liberation for him. For the first time he found a cause in which he believed. He gladly joined the army and his military assignment was to the Bavarian Reserve Infantry Regiment-16. Later, he referred to the years of the First World War as "the greatest and most unforgettable time of my earthly life." It was 'August Days', days that would encourage a demagogue who would in time establish another war machine – one that would rage against the entire world. Anna and her family would not be exempt from that rage.

CHAPTER 4
August Days

During the 'August Days' of 1914, the German society and its military presented a monolithic picture of devotion to its cause. Each opportunity for display of troops and armament was seized as if *esprit de corps* by itself would bring victory. While the Kaiser reviewed legions of troops at the Brandenburg Gate, the German High Command was drawing battle plans designed to use lightening troop movements. Properly executed, the German Volk would be rewarded with a stunning opening victory, but the victory never came, only a bitter defeat. The rapid victory became a war of attrition. Scarcely four years had passed, and the carnage had reached staggering proportions...8 million dead, including 1.9 million Germans, with 4 million wounded.

Mistakes and miscalculations are part of war. America was not directly involved in the war, but her ships were supplying the Allies. The German decision to begin naval attacks on American ships supplying England turned out to be a grave miscalculation. The United States was far removed from the problems in Europe, and the American economic machine was growing into a monster. A few years earlier, two brothers in the bicycle business had dazzled the world by flying a gasoline powered glider-like machine. It traveled 120 feet across a North Carolina beach – spawning the birth of the aviation era. Because of this and other accomplishments, American industry began to boom on every front, from automobiles to railroads to manufacturing.

The news that the German Navy was attacking U.S. ships was a shock to Americans. The common feeling in the country was that the Germans had awakened, what the Japanese would later call "a sleeping giant." Within weeks, tens of thousands of men joined the military. Within months, two million green but fresh American soldiers were injected into the fray in France. The American people had mostly passing interest in the European war, but attacks on U.S. shipping would not stand.

Early in 1918, Field Marshal Hindenburg had promised the Kaiser, "I will be in Paris by April 1st'." The conflict had long since degenerated into a war the Germans would not lose but could not win. Field Commander General Ludendorff was determined to change that. His spring offensive pushed through five French defense lines some 60 kilometers from Paris. It appeared the Hindenburg promise would hold until the advance was halted at the small village of Chateau-Thierry, where two regiments of U. S. Marines battled the Germans to a standstill. Using fresh American units, the Allies began a major counter offensive. Within days the Kaiser was urgently summoned to military headquarters where a despondent Hindenburg confronted him.

"The war is lost," he said. "Our forces are defeated and prolonging the conflict will be a monumental waste of life."

He insisted that an armistice be sought immediately. Although a man of enormous pride, the Kaiser could not and would not disagree. The defeat was bitter for the German High Command. Hindenburg and his staff would not view themselves as culpable. As the war dragged on there were, according to the High Command, "forces of defeatism and sabotage" in the homeland that could not be overcome. The German superior training and military skill not-with-standing, the loss of the war was beyond the control of the generals, at least in their view. But to many Germans the loss was not only shattering, but inexplicable.

The hardships of the following few years were predictable. A British Naval blockade in the North Sea and Baltic was especially devastating and caused serious food shortages. The principle home grown crop was turnips. Previously, many other types of vegetables had been available. Now instead of cabbage, spinach, potatoes, carrots, and beans, there were only turnips. The steady turnip diet was only part of the joyless German nadir. Berlin remained generally gray and overcast in winter, and a worldwide influenza epidemic was spreading to central Europe. This was a highly contagious viral illness that all too often was complicated by bacterial pneumonia, usually pneumococcal. As the patients were overwhelmed with fluid build-up in their lungs, they became weaker and more short of breath until the process would mercifully end their lives. At that time, there was no available treatment. On one particularly mournful day, the defeated city suffered 1,700 deaths. The German Volk, starving and dying by the thousands, was reeling between blatant despair and revolution.

The events of 1918 brought the people to their lowest point since Chancellor Bismarck had forged the German Empire in 1871. This was, however, not the case in the scientific community. Amid the chaos of the times, the scientists at the Kaiser Wilhelm Institute were working to develop an algorithm to prove the paradigms of Einstein's theories. Theoretical mathematics had been developed to demonstrate the principle that the speed of light is the same for all observers and that nothing can travel faster. If an object could be accelerated to that magical speed, its dimension would go to zero, its mass to infinity, and time would stop. His theory of general relativity was difficult to comprehend and even more difficult to prove.

Hanz Eichenwald and his colleague, Max Plank, spent endless hours contemplating the depth of relativity. Previously, they had thought that light traveled in a straight line. But Einstein's general relativity theory predicted that light should be "bent" by the force of gravity. Even with a war going on, Hanz had been in contact with Sir Frank Dyson of the British Royal Astronomical Society; the subject - proof of the effect of gravity on light. Sir Frank had suggested, "we have a chance to prove your colleague correct, or not, using the up-coming solar eclipse on March 29." On that day the moon would pass between the sun and the earth, and for a time, would block 99 percent of the sun's light. The darkened sun would be in line, simultaneously, with an exceptionally bright group of stars known as the Hyades. At that precise moment the light from the stars, passing close to the sun, could be observed and measured. An opportunity like this would not present itself for another 200 years.

As a physicist, Hanz had a unique understanding of the sun, a medium sized star in the Milky Way galaxy, one of a hundred million other galaxies. It is the principle source of energy for the earth. The publications of Einstein in 1905 established the understanding of the enormous energy production of the sun according to the formula $E = mc2$. In theory, this energy could be produced using the two most common elements in the universe - hydrogen and helium. Under certain circumstances, two hydrogen atoms might fuse, producing a different element - helium. The resulting helium would have less mass than the two hydrogen atoms, and the 'lost' mass would appear as energy in the form of both heat and light. It was now evident that a small amount of mass would produce an enormous amount of energy.

It was now becoming more apparent to Eichenwald, Plank and their colleagues that hydrogen fusion was not only the source of the sun's energy, but the source of light from all stars in all of the galaxies of the universe. General relativity predicted that light should be bent by gravity. Dyson, Eichenwald, Plank, and Einstein hoped to use the upcoming eclipse to prove it. The implications of relativity were so profound that they began to be viewed as spiritual in nature. Now, time was not seen as absolute, but dynamic. The assumption that the universe had always looked the same was also being called into question.

"The universe is changing," noted Plank. "This observation leads to the rather profound implication that it is finite...that it must have had a beginning!"

He and his colleagues simultaneously had the incredulous thought. *A beginning of the universe also implies an ending.*

Hanz's fascination with the sun had its genesis in childhood when he attended the Yeshiva Jewish boy's school. The ancient Egyptians, slave masters of the Hebrew nation for over 400 years, worshiped the sun as part of their polytheism. The sun was for them, the greatest wonder and thus, the most esteemed in their worship. The Hebrew Torah had been handed down over the millennia from ancient manuscripts. Tradition held that its author was the patriarch Moses. The question for Hanz was one of truth. Could he trust the accounts set forth in the Torah? The first phrase in the text is *bereshith,* which literally means 'in the beginning.'

This concept of beginning had always been abstract for Hanz. He was a scientist and always looking for concepts that could be proved. The Torah next mentioned *Elohim,* which means 'God,' who in a peremptory act, created all things. Though the universe could be observed as dynamic, the concept that it was 'willed' into existence by God was difficult to believe. Hanz clearly believed in God. But he remained skeptical that this God of the Hebrews was responsible for everything in the universe. The narratives in the Torah seemed to be just that - stories.

An atheistic view of the universe was based on the unavoidable element of unpredictability or randomness. But as Hanz had discussed with Einstein, "the observed universe is one of perfect order; there is nothing random about it." To this Einstein quipped, "and God does not play dice", meaning God is not arbitrary.

His theory of general relativity was, if true, clearly pointing to an event...a beginning. Hanz continued to ponder that first phrase of the Hebrew text, *bereshith.*

The planned expedition to view the solar eclipse in cooperation with his colleague Sir Frank Dyson, had implications far beyond his interest in physics. He was becoming convinced that God *could* have created the universe – but did he?

*　*　*

In 1918, Dr. Emil Leimdorfer was managing editor of Berlin's largest tabloid paper, *The Berliner Zeitung am Mittag.* On the morning of November 9th he received an urgent telephone call placed from the office of Imperial Chancellor Prince Max of Baden. The caller was frantic.

"His Majesty the Kaiser has abdicated!"

Within an hour the street vendors were shouting as they displayed the bold type tabloid, "KAISER ABDICATES! EBERT MADE CHANCELLOR!"

Two weeks previously, the Kaiser had left Berlin to join his military commanders in the Belgian resort of Spa. The news was devastating. The army could not hold out more than two more weeks. It was the opinion of his generals as well, that the government itself would not survive unless he abdicated the throne. The war was lost, and soon his country would be lost. His head was spinning as he attempted to absorb what he was hearing. After all, he was the *King*. His position was his birthright. Now his generals sought the power of the throne. Why would he abandon what was rightly his; why should he? A general strike had been called for the morning of November 9th to force the issue. The two largest political parties, the Independent Socialists and the Social Democrats, both supported the strike. Even as the Kaiser was refusing to abandon the throne, tens of thousands of striking workers were gathering outside the chancellor's office. The chancellery building was a massive structure with thick gray stone walls and two enormous lion statues on either side of the main entrance. This entrance was actually a driveway entering a large inner courtyard. A massive iron gate sealed the drive and a 24-hour guard occupied a small guardhouse to the right of the gate. The police had tried to seal off the entrance but were overpowered by the crowd. Even with the heavy draperies drawn on each of the twenty foot tall windows, their shouts were reaching the inner offices...a reflection of the violence of their mood.

Chancellor Prince Max, isolated and desperate, believed the strikers could and would execute him in a frenzy of mob violence. Fearing for his life, he decided to announce the Kaiser's abdication on his own authority. In this life-death struggle, he prayed the announcement would bring calm to the explosive situation.

Even as this drama was being played out, the Kaiser was formulating a plan to take back the country using the army. When Field

Marshal Hindenburg and his Chief of Staff General Groner were informed of the plan, Groner announced, "Sire, you no longer have an army." After further argument, the Kaiser reluctantly agreed to seek exile in Holland. Later that day he boarded a train for that country. Sitting alone in the special opulent railcar prepared for a king, his thoughts drifted back to the summer of 1914 when he proudly reviewed the military at the Brandenburg Gate. Now with no army, no country and no throne, the monarchy of the German people had come to an end.

By nightfall, there was great uncertainty about who was actually running the government. It seemed clear there was no desire to replace the monarchy. But the vacuum of leadership was unsettling. For the first time in more than 1,000 years the Germanic people had no king. After the rule of Charlemagne in 800 AD, Otto 1st had emerged in 962 to unite the eastern and middle kingdoms of Europe. But a stormy relationship existed between the Pope and the new German monarchy. The church/monarchy conflicts resulted in the spread of feudalism, a system in which landowners maintained a dominant stranglehold on the people. This dominance was ended by the Thirty Years War of 1618, a conflict that killed 30 percent of the population. The modern day succession of kings was begun by Friederich the Great and ended with the Kaiser. After more than 1,000 years, the people no longer had the will for a monarchy.

Revolution was in the air. The potential for violence was apparent, especially in the cities. People were angry and bewildered. Youth groups were seen almost daily in the streets. The leadership vacuum desperately needed to be filled. Two men emerged into the spotlight.

Karl Liebknecht was the son of one of the founders of German Socialism. He had started an anti-war movement in December

1914, being the first Reichstag deputy to abstain from voting for war credits. He was an outspoken critic of the war from the beginning. A rather short, austere man, he sported a black mustache which gave him a military presence. An isolated dissenter during the war years, his views had been vindicated by the German defeat.. Liebknecht had the full support of Lenin's new communist regime in Russia which had designs on spreading their doctrines to central Europe and even beyond.

A second man, Fredrich Ebert was the leader of the more centrist Social Democratic Party. Ebert had supported both the Kaiser and the war effort. He and the deputy director of the Social Democrats, Philipp Scheidemann, had encouraged Prince Max von Baden to succeed to the throne. Prince Max was the son of Wilhelm, brother of Grand Duke Frederick 1st and the former Chancellor, but Max had no stomach for injecting himself further into the conflagration of German political life.

In 1918 the country had seemed on the brink of civil war. But hostilities were narrowly averted by the abdication of the Kiser. In a bold move to advance the socialist agenda, Karl Liebknecht began driving around Berlin to rally the support of the thousands of striking workers out on the streets. At the same time, Philipp Scheidemann was in the Reichstag lunchroom when about 50 soldiers and workers stormed into the room. Word of Liebknecht's activities had reached the Reichstag and started a panic. The right wing supporters realized that there was significant danger of a Communist coup that could sweep them in to power and that they must be stopped at any cost.

"Philipp, you must come out and speak to the crowd," he was told. "Liebknecht is pushing for a Soviet style republic."

Thousands were waiting for some word, any word, unaware of the drama being played out. Scheidemann did not know what to say. Finally, he blurted out, "Workers and soldiers...the cursed war is over...the Emperor has abdicated. Long live the new Germany!"

A deafening roar went up from the crowd. In the state of excitement and confusion, his declaration was taken by the hopeful citizens as the beginning of a new government. A wild celebration ensued.

About 4:00 p.m., snow began to fall. As the winter chill of the evening set in, Liebknecht finally reached the palace with a small band of his rebel supporters. The tall palace rooms were mostly deserted. When he stepped out onto the main balcony, only about 200 people remained.

"The day of liberty has dawned..." he began.

But, in fact, he had missed the dawning of liberty, which had occurred a few hours earlier that day.

*　*　*

At this time, Anna Eichenwald was approaching her eighteenth birthday. She had passed quickly from her awkward teen years into a sophisticated young woman. She remained an excellent student, especially in math and science. She now stood at just under six feet in height. Her dark, auburn hair and blue-green eyes gave her a striking appearance and lured the frequent glances of admirers. Her mother had done an exceptional job of keeping Anna's values strong and her academic pursuits equally focused. Anna's interest in boys had been, for the most part, limited to flirting. With her looks and brains, she intimidated most of the boys she knew.

One of her father's friends was a medical doctor with a surgical practice at the Charite Hospital across the Spree River. Marvin Katz was in his early 50's. A robust man of some 200 pounds, he stood about six feet with a focused and intense decorum, and large brown eyes that penetrated whoever held his attention. He was a widower, having lost his wife in childbirth along with their only child. Now married to his work, his one hobby was as an amateur astronomer. He had become acquainted with the Eichenwald family after attending a lecture on solar eclipse. Marlene had been especially happy to have him for evening meals, hoping to fill the void of his lost family. Marvin was grateful for these gatherings, as he was especially fond of Anna and liked to think of her as the daughter he never had.

On an occasional weekend, Anna would arrange to go with him to the hospital emergency ward. It was on one such an occasion that Anna accompanied him for an urgent consult involving a 19-year old boy who had been brought to emergency unconscious following a car accident. The boy had been walking along Leipziger Strasse when a car jumped the curb and struck him. After arriving at the hospital, he regained consciousness but was pale and complaining of abdominal pain. His blood pressure was 90/60, pulse 120, lungs clear, and his abdomen was tense. Dr. Katz finished his evaluation and reviewed the lab work.

"He will need to go to surgery," Katz said in an urgent voice. "Call the blood bank and ask for four units of cross-matched and two unmatched units available. I'm going out to speak to his family."

Anna, who had never seen a major surgery, followed Dr. Katz to the waiting room where they found the boy's older brother. "Where are your parents," asked Katz, never glancing up from the chart.

"I have sent for them," the young man replied. "But we live ten kilometers from town."

"Good. Your brother has a serious abdominal injury and is bleeding. He is being moved to surgery."

The young man looked into Katz' large brown eyes and noted their concern. "Will he be alright?"

"He is a young, healthy boy. He will need blood, so I want you to go to the lab and see if you have his blood type. The nurse will show you the way."

Anna's heart was racing as she contemplated what was about to happen. As they walked to the surgical suite, her mentor seemed deep in thought and she was reluctant to speak. Finally, she broke the silence. "What do you think is wrong?"

"It's called a differential," Dr. Katz replied.

"Meaning, what are the possibilities?" she questioned.

"He has blunt abdominal trauma. The force of the injury seems to have been severe. My worst fear is a fractured liver or an aortic injury. It could be his spleen or torn vessels to the intestine. His urine is clear so I don't expect a kidney or bladder injury. He's shocky, so he has probably lost about half his blood volume."

Anna did not understand the term 'shocky' but did not ask. She was fascinated with the doctor's ability to evaluate the problem. She found herself feeling envy for his knowledge and skill.

"Surgeons are problem solvers by nature," said Dr. Katz as they parted for the changing rooms. "Solving this problem.... the challenge. Saving his life... the reward."

Anna, in her scrubs, cap and mask, stood on a short stool in the corner of the OR trying to absorb the drama. The boy was being put to sleep with ether. Dr. Katz and his surgical assistant entered, gloved and gowned.

"His pressure is 60!" the anesthetist called out as he turned both IVs to run as fast as possible.

"He has uncross-matched blood. Give it!"

One of the nurses had already prepped the abdomen with alcohol. Dr. Katz quickly draped off the field, and then in one quick movement with the scalpel, opened the abdomen through the midline. Immediately a large amount of dark blood gushed out of the incision and covered both surgeon and assistant. A large suction was placed into the wound and simultaneously Katz's right arm disappeared into the gaping wound. The liver felt intact. The bleeding was coming from the left upper quadrant. He quickly glanced up to see the blood running wide open, his right hand now blindly searching the left upper quadrant of the boy's abdominal cavity.

"The spleen is shattered," he said, keeping the others in the OR appraised of this life and death struggle.

With his left hand, he grasped what was left of the spleen. Using a long surgical clamp, with his right hand he placed the clamp on the vessels to the spleen and blindly divided the attachments holding the spleen to the surrounding structures, then delivered it into the wound still attached to the vessels

"Bleeding is controlled!"

"Pressure is up to 70...pulse is 120!" "Are you giving the matched blood?" "Second unit is running!

Katz placed a zero silk suture ligature on the vascular pedicle which had supplied the spleen to permanently seal it off, and divided the vascular supply to the spleen. He handed what was left of the spleen to the scrub nurse, then used saline solution to wash out the abdominal cavity and remove as much of the old blood as possible. Carefully, he inspected the liver again as well as the stomach, pancreas, and intestine. He could find no other injury.

"Pressure is up to 90. He's starting to make some urine," observed the anesthetist. "I'll use zero silk to close."

Dr. Katz glanced at Anna. He had been too busy to notice how she was dealing with the rather bloody scene. The look on her face did not betray her fascination.

He motioned for her to follow him and they entered a small lounge area. As they sat down he removed his sweat drenched cap.

"The boy's age probably saved him," he told Anna. "An older person would not have survived that much bleeding."

Katz relaxed for a moment and looked at Anna.

"Nothing like a little excitement on a Saturday evening, yes? So what do you think?"

"Pretty amazing," she replied. "Have you done similar cases?"

"Once in my training and another time about five years ago. A nine year old boy fell off his bicycle." Dr. Katz stood up. "I'm going to check on our young boy and speak with his parents. I'll meet you back here in 20 minutes."

Anna's eyes followed him out the door. She wondered if there was a place for a woman in this very male oriented world of surgery.

* * *

Fredrich Ebert was alone in the Chancellor's office. The building on Wilhelmstrasse was now abandoned. The events of the past 72 hours had made him the highest official in Germany. They had also shaken him to the core.

Ebert was a stout man with a raffish appearance, inconsistent with one born into poverty. The son of a tailor in Heidelberg, he spent his early years as a saddle-maker. Using inherent communication skills and fortunate circumstances, he had become a political party functionary in Berlin. Now at forty-eight years of age, he had been told by the departing Chancellor, "Herr Ebert, I now commit the German people into your care."

Sitting in the office in solitude, his thoughts turned sad as he considered his two sons, both of whom had been killed on the battlefields of France. They had been the joy of his life and he was still unable to get over their loss. He commonly experienced days of depression and bitterness. The loss of the war only compounded his feelings. Ebert was surprised and startled back to reality by the ringing of one of the office phones. The caller was General Groner, the deputy commander for Field Marshal Hindenburg. Ebert had spent little time in the office and was unaware the phone was a secret private line to military headquarters in Spa. He identified himself and warily asked how the army planned to deal with the crisis, and more specifically, how the Field Marshal would deal with it. Now that the Kaiser was gone, Hindenburg was in complete command. The answer was reassuring. The front line troops would be brought back to Germany and would support the Ebert-led government.

The following day, November 10th, a decree was released by a group of Social Democratic and Independent commissioners. It proclaimed amnesty for all political prisoners. This was being done in an effort to unify the government. There would also be freedom of speech, press, and assembly. All public officials would be elected by secret ballot. And the new government was committed to providing jobs, housing and food.

The majority of Germans were still very conservative. They remained orderly and compliant. Once, when a fire broke out around the royal Palace, the crowds running to escape did so paths observing the "keep off the grass" signs. In a few short years this sense of order in their lives would be obliterated. In its place would be chaos.

CHAPTER 5

'Mein Kampf'

History would record the years after the war as filled with turmoil. Because of the political crisis, a scientific event of monumental proportions was virtually ignored. The physicists at the Kaiser Wilhelm Institute were concerned with something much more fundamental than political turmoil - an imminent eclipse of the sun. This eclipse was significant. The opportunity to measure the gravitational force of the sun on the light from the Hyades group of stars would not occur again for several hundred years. Hanz Eichenwald knew this was not just a chance of a lifetime but of several lifetimes. To be working in the same Institute with Max Planck and Albert Einstein was something Hanz never could have imagined. Planck, in 1900, working on a theory to explain the relationship between radiation and matter, had postulated that energy existed in small discrete bundles he called quanta, taken from the Latin word 'how much'. And Einstein was opening his theories of relativity to the world. The depth of their discussions was beyond ordinary mortals. As they pondered the implications of general relativity theory, they were anxious for the breakthroughs of proof.

The law of energy conservation had been proposed in the mid-1800s. It stated that both energy and matter (mass) exist in a fixed amount. One can be converted to the other but the total amount of each will always remain constant in the universe. Man can convert mass to energy and energy back to mass, but is incapable of "creating" either one. And yet with the amount of mass/energy fixed, it was becoming more obvious that the entire universe was changing. The old idea that the universe was static and had always existed as such, did not fit what Einstein was observing. He began to reason that the universe was actually finite and at some point had a beginning. One day Einstein was discussing the topic with Hanz.

"If the universe had a beginning, what existed before?" "Nothing!" Einstein exclaimed. "Nothing existed before - void."

"So, we might assume there may have been an enormous black space full of nothing?" Hanz asked.

"No! An enormous black space is something - void is nothing. Void has no reference in human experience, no reference at all."

Einstein posited two conclusions about the origin of the universe. One, it came into being by chance. Or two, it was brought into being by a self-existent power out of nothing - ex nihilo. Chance, a random event, could not produce something from nothing. A universe of a hundred million galaxies did not come about by chance. But he also believed that a beginning event would necessarily require the concept of infinity. Mathematics, even theoretical mathematics, cannot handle infinite numbers. So the theory of general relativity itself predicted that there is a point, a beginning, where the theory breaks down.

"We can only know what has happened since the beginning, not before," Einstein reasoned. He was convinced of a genesis event. But as to what brought it about and how it occurred, he remained uncertain.

A few weeks after the armistice was signed officially ending the war, Britain's Royal Astronomical Society announced that it would send two expeditions to photograph the eclipse. The areas where it could be best observed were the town of Sobral in northern

Brazil and the island of Principe in the Gulf of Guinea. General relativity had predicted that light should be bent by gravitational field influence. So light from a distant star would appear to be in a different position to an observer on earth. During the eclipse the moon blocked the sun's light in such a way that the star's light could be photographed and measured. British teams were on both locations.

Einstein was asked to compute how much the light rays of the Hyades should be deflected by the sun's gravity. His computed answer was 1.75 seconds of an arc. Photographs were taken during the eclipse and during an ordinary evening. After several months the returned data showed the sun's gravity had deflected the light 1.64 seconds of an arc, almost exactly matching Einstein's estimate. When the results were disclosed at the next meeting of the Royal Society, one of the members later was quoted as saying, "The whole atmosphere of tense interest was exactly that of a Greek Drama. We were the chorus commenting on the decree of destiny as disclosed in the development of a supreme incident."

Hanz Eichenwald had been confident of what the findings would show, now for the proof. He had spent countless hours contemplating the implications of general relativity. Concepts that previously could not be proved, he now knew to be true. Nevertheless, he would spend years bringing this new found knowledge alongside all he had been taught as a student of the physical sciences.

As a child, Hanz had read, over and over, the first declaration of the Torah.

"Bereshith" - in the beginning, "Elohim"- God, "bara"- created, shamayin-ara all things." He had wanted to believe this as a child and dealt with it in his imagination. He viewed all he saw as mystical, all in the heavens and in the earth. To a great extent as an adult he still did. But now there was scientific evidence that seemed to confirm the ancient Hebrew manuscripts. His depth of understanding was still limited, but what had been mystical was now being proved reality.

The goal of Imperial Germany to dominate Europe by force was destined to fail almost from the start. German society was filled with deep fissures. The strains of war deepened those divisions. No adult citizen could escape intimate connection to the conflagration. The war belonged to everyone. A total of 13 million Germans had served in the military. Almost 2 million had died. From a world of peace and stability, the people were catapulted into a reality of death and destruction.

The German economy had been massively distorted by the industrialized warfare. The cost in financial terms was almost as devastating as the loss of life. Taxation covered only about 14 percent of expenditures. War bonds were used for the short fall. After the expected German victory, the bonds were to be redeemed through reparations from the defeated enemies of the Reich. But there was no victory, and no defeated enemies. Reparations would be paid *by* Germans not *to* Germans. To fund the war, the government simply printed more money. The resulting inflation was devastating. By 1918, the German mark had lost 70 percent of its pre-war value and was rapidly on the way to becoming worthless.

The war also contributed to what one observer called a 'moratorium on morality'. Crimes of all types increased. So did the rate of divorce, sexual immorality and the resultant venereal diseases. The numbers of fatherless children tripled. Some of the bitterest divisions in war torn Germany were racial. In 1916, the war ministry conducted a 'Jew-count' to shed light on who was actually doing the fighting. The survey was never published because it actually showed strong support for the war by Jews. They had been accused of prospering while others were dying. The strongest testimony of Jewish patriotism was the 12,000 war dead buried in Jewish cemeteries. The Eichenwalds, along with most Jewish families, had relatives who had died in the war. Jewish men had put their lives on the line along with thousands of other Germans.

*   *   *

Anna's world was a small sphere, one that swirled with school activities, friends and fashion. Her exposure to the war was limited. What she knew of it, she knew from her best friend, Erin Nitschmann. Erin's brother Peter had been in the war. Anna and Erin, as the only Jewish girls in their class, spent their time together. Although physically dissimilar, they were kindred spirits. Anna was tall, strikingly defined by the locks of dark hair that framed her aqua-blue eyes like a painting. Most of her physical traits were inherited from her father. But she had also received a good bit of his intellect. She tended to stay to herself focusing on academics. Erin, on the other hand, was assertive by nature and comfortable in confrontations. Her parents were professional musicians, both performers with the Berlin Philharmonic. Erin's father was the violin first chair and concertmaster. Her mother played the cello and was the stabilizing force in the Nitschmann family. Erin had studied violin since she was five-years old. With her pale skin, light blue eyes and long, strawberry blond hair pulled carefully into a pony tail, Erin appeared almost fragile. But those who came to know her discovered she was as willful as she was sweet, with a truly indefatigable nature.

Hans and Marlene were lovers of classical music. So the two families formed a natural bond that went beyond the friendship of their daughters. Each month, the Eichenwalds attended the symphony and frequently included Erin, whose parents were always performing. On occasion they would get together at one of their homes where they would be joined by Albert and Mrs. Einstein. Albert made no effort to hide his desire to play the violin, especially with the concertmaster. The two often played violin duets late into the night. These impromptu 'concerts' were a joy to all, but especially to the professor, who had often thought that if he had the talent, he would give up physics for a 'true profession.'

Before the war's end, Erin's mother had been unable to quell her concerns about the conflict. One of the darkest moments she had ever faced was the day she watched her son go off to war. She stood in the doorway overcome with sadness as she watched him leave. Since the morning she closed the door behind her, she had been unable to think of anything but his safety. The only respite she had from her worry were the moments in which she felt a sense of gratitude that he served in the artillery corps and not in the trenches. An activist in politics supporting the Social Democratic Party, she and her husband were well known in Berlin's music circles. Under normal circumstances, she would not have involved herself in the patriotic hoopla on Unter den Linden. But with Peter directly involved in the war, she now felt an obligation to involve herself. She joined the Nationaler Frauendienst (National Women's Service), the first and largest volunteer organization to mobilize German civilians. Working closely with the Red Cross, many Social Democratic party members joined socialists, Catholics and Jews to form Germany's most extensive welfare organization. The main function was to aid those families whose fathers had been mobilized to the front or who had become unemployed due to the downturn in business. The organization also ran day care centers, kindergartens and reading rooms. Anna and Erin greatly admired Paula's passion for the needy. Week-ends usually found them offering to help her by working in daycare centers and filling in at reading rooms.

During the post-war years, the German people experienced for the first time, life without a monarchy. For some, this was a time of sadness. For others, it was a time to become more independent. Initially there had been national solidarity. Now the society was fragmented – a state that would eventually determine the politics of the post-war era.

The abolition of reason for 66 million Germans was a process, a shifting paradigm. The transformation of this society from one having a moral basis of reason to an amoral one was subtle. If one places a frog in very hot water, the frog will immediately jump out. If the same frog is placed in tepid water and the water is gradually heated, the frog will remain in the water until cooked. This slow transformation could not fully take place without a leader. The Germans were now sheep without a shepherd. A cunning shepherd would come. And he would lead them to their own destruction.

Adolph Hitler served as a dispatch runner during World War I. He demonstrated little in the way of leadership and never rose above the rank of corporal. But he made up for it in courage. In November 1914, he narrowly escaped serious injury, possibly death. He was instructed to deliver an important dispatch to a forward command post. He arrived safely but declined an opportunity to stay for coffee. Within minutes of his departure, a French artillery shell hit the post, killing and severely wounding every man there. For bravery in the line of duty, Hitler was awarded the Iron Cross, second class. Two years later, a shrapnel injury from a British shell put him in a Berlin hospital. Returning to the front in 1918, he received a second injury. This time he was partially blinded by mustard gas. During his convalescence, the Armistice was signed. News of the defeat was emotionally shattering to him. Hitler became depressed and simultaneously began to cultivate an intense hatred for those he deemed 'responsible' for losing the war. This hatred would eventually be the driving force for his later attempt at European conquest.

With the Armistice signed, Field Marshal Hindenburg ordered a return of the army from the front. Within a month the difficult task of marching two million front line infantry from France to Germany began. The defeated military faced the march back home, only to arrive at a defeated and discouraged country. The mood of the German people could not have been lower, but President Ebert and the cabinet members were encouraged when they saw the vanguard of nine divisions marching down Unter den Linden. Hindenburg had kept them outside the city for a week of 'R and R.' Somewhat rested, their appearance belied the despair they all felt.

"I salute you," Ebert declared as he welcomed them at the Brandenburg Gate.

A crisis in governmental authority was looming, however, and while most of the soldiers returned to their homes, thousands more took to the streets adding to the frenetic atmosphere in Berlin. They had an underlying pellucid hostility about their "defeat".

Shortly after the army returned, the National Congress of Workers and Soldiers Council were formed. It represented a backlash against the military, with the goal of replacing the current military officers with 'elected' officers. Eventually the entire army would become the Volkswehr or people's army.

During the first post-war month, a military rally was held in the Berlin Philharmonic Hall in an effort to gain support for the Soldier's Council and the Volkswehr. A government spokesman had the floor and made the argument that 'elected officers would be accountable to the people.' Suddenly he was interrupted by a 25-year old Air Force captain named Herman Goering. This former commander of the Richthofen Squadron wore Germany's highest medal, Pourle Marite.

"I implore you to cherish hatred – a profound, abiding hatred of those animals that have outraged the German people," he cried. "The day will come when we will drive them out of our Germany!"

The meeting had been organized to bring discredit to the military, but the tone quickly changed as the anti-military supporters were shouted out of the hall. Lines of conflict were quickly being drawn and hatred began building among WWI veterans toward anyone who was anti-military.

Eighty miles north of Berlin, a half-blinded corporal confined to the hospital in Pasewalk, had already dedicated himself to that hatred. Several years later, Hitler would write in Mien Kampf the nature of his feelings the instant he learned of the German surrender in 1918.

"Everything went black before my eyes. I tattered and groped my way back to the dormitory, threw myself on my bunk and dug my burning head into my blanket and pillow…so it had all been in vain. In vain all the sacrifices…In vain all the death of two millions… there followed terrible days and even worse nights…in these nights hatred grew in me, hatred for those responsible for this deed. In the days that followed, my own fate became known to me…I, for my part, decided to go into politics."

In 1918 Germany was now a country of demoralized people seeking an identity. This once proud and united country was now fiercely divided. Radical right and left ideologies were growing. A society shattered by the consequences of military defeat was now splintered by classes, regions and religions. Their problems were of monumental proportions - inflation, unemployment, food shortages, reparations, and the threat of foreign invasion. Germany was now the 'whipping boy' of their enemies.

The ultra-liberal political left of 1918 was led by Karl Leibknecht. But the real source of this ideology was another German born exactly 100 years before - Karl Marx.

The son of a liberal Jewish lawyer, he studied law at the University of Bonn and eventually became an intellectual philosopher at the University of Berlin. But his radical views forced him to leave Germany within a few months of his teaching appointment.

He emigrated to Paris, then London, where he was befriended by Friedrich Engels, another German. On the anniversary of the French Revolution, in February 1848, they published the Communist Manifesto, a book that would bring them fame as well as infamy.

The war had long since lost the glory it once possessed. Government efforts to generate fresh enthusiasm for killing had failed. Bravery, honor and valor, imagined or unimagined, could not be sustained without cause in the reality of death and destruction. Working class men and women were realizing the war was being perpetuated by the military-industrial complex to serve class ends. War aims were proving divisive, especially in Germany and Russia. War weariness led to a surge of left wing militancy. As a result, Lenin's Bolsheviks seized power in Russia through violent revolution.

The goal of Liebkneckt was to duplicate the Russian experience. He was the first Reichstag member to actively work against the war. In his mind the plan could not fail; organize workers for strikes and demonstrations; publish a newspaper; control the streets by New Year's, 1919. The power of the people demonstrated with ruthless acts of violence in Russia would surely spread to central Europe. The time was ripe. Democracy would be seen as basically corrupt, and given the opportunity, the people would agree and rise up to overthrow the government.

Rosa Luxemburg, and old ally of Liebkneckt, had returned to Germany from Poland, deeply involved in the Socialist movement. She was a woman of great intellect, a gifted writer and orator and considered the equal of even Lenin. During the war, Luxemburg had spent several months in prison for her role in anti-government and anti- war demonstrations. While in prison, she penned a series of letters on socialist doctrine and the dogma of peace at any price. Now back in Germany and with the war ended, she helped the Worker's movement extend its power. Eventually the Worker's movement merged with the left wing of the Independent Socialist and the Revolutionary Shop Stewards. Liebkneckt and Luxemburg had decided the timing was right. Under their influence and leadership, the three merged groups formed a new political party - the Communist Party of Germany.

*　*　*

The school year was drawing to a close and not too soon for Anna. The last weeks dragged slowly. Exams were finished. Parties and ceremonies were on the horizon. Anna had the usual casual school friends and then her 'best friends'. She and Erin were more like sisters and were looking forward to entering University together. They had started looking for an apartment and the excitement of being independent was building. A young man of middle-eastern descent, Uri Avner, was another of Anna's 'best friends.' Uri had emigrated with his family from Egypt when he was twelve-years old. His father was a career diplomat at the Egyptian Consulate and for the past three years had been Charge d' affaires. His mother was a Coptic Christian and his father a non-practicing Muslim. Uri was living in spiritual no-man's land. He was bright, with dark brown eyes and jet black hair which he preferred to wear long but kept short because of school regulations. Berlin was very cosmopolitan so he did not draw attention in public places. He was not involved in athletics, but was in the chess club and spent much of his after school hours playing chess. He won several tournaments in the previous year. As a foreign student, he tended to keep to himself. This was largely the reason for Anna's attraction to him. In turn, Uri enjoyed the company of the girl who was the top graduate of the class, to say nothing of her extraordinary good looks. School was easy for him, and he excelled with little effort. Chess and girls aside, Uri's passion was politics.

When he was 15, Uri read and absorbed Marx's Communist Manifesto. He had followed the post-war political turmoil of his adopted country with intense interest. Even though Arabic was his first language, Uri was fluent in German and had mastered it with virtually no foreign accent. He also spoke a fair amount of English. The prison letters of Rosa Luxemburg had found their way into his hands and he was keenly aware of the slightest changes in the political atmosphere. He observed that personal liberties had significantly diminished during the war and the war-time propaganda was especially egregious to him. The slogan *love your country and defend it* had morphed into *hate your enemy and kill him.*

Although Anna had no serious interest in politics, she spent hours listening to Uri's observations. He pointed out that escalation of the war had translated directly to increased profits of the upper class. The war had become a self-perpetuating monster, feeding on itself and governments had become prisoners of their own propaganda. The Volk were fighting the war and the Volk were bearing the hardships created by it.

"Anna, it will be 1,000 years before that changes," he once told her.

"I don't doubt what you say, but it's hard for me to relate to it," she replied. "I suppose we are a bit isolated from all this. Our government must put the war behind us and move on to rebuild. Don't you agree?"

Uri raised his gaze and gave her a penetrating look.

"The critical question remains this. 'How IS that going to happen?' Fundamental changes are needed, sweeping changes."

The week before their graduation, Uri and Anna spent a Saturday afternoon at the Berlin Museum of Natural History. After touring the museum, they made their way to the basement coffee shop.

"Anna!" Uri suddenly exclaimed. "Everything that's taking place in Russia could happen here in Germany. The workers have forced an end to Czarism and now there's an apparent Bolshevik victory."

Anna was aware that changes were taking place in Russia. But she was unaware that the Czar had been overthrown. Uri's information had come from some of his underground socialist connections, something he was unwilling to share even with Anna. She was now more interested and decided to press him for more details.

"How do you know the Czar has been overthrown? I haven't read anything about it."

Uri avoided her gaze and said softly, "Well I just know."

They enjoyed going to the coffee house and sampling the varieties of coffee, tea, pastries and pate`. They usually sat in the corner away from the counter. Anna's favorite treat was the lemon cus-tard pastry with the buttery flavored crust. Taking a bite, she thought about their conversation. She hadn't sensed anything unusual in it, since Uri's passion for politics was always on the surface. University students were always keenly interested in the process of change. The idea of revolution only heightened the excitement. Uri had decided the day before that he would not share with Anna an event that was dominating his thoughts. On May 17th he had secretly joined the newly formed German Communist Party. Now another woman was getting his attention - Rosa Luxemburg.

* * *

The default candidate to spearhead the new government, Friedrich Ebert, was a thoughtful and resourceful man. Although normally non-confrontational, he was distressed by the bravado of the socialist movement. The military had pledged their support to the new Ebert-led government, but he desperately needed a can-didate for defense minister. A man named Gustar Noske had been suggested by General Groner. After a meeting with Noske, Ebert felt he was a man he could trust. That trust quickly paid dividends when Noske learned of a secret plan to organize a new kind of volunteer force known as Freikorps (Free Corps). They would be highly mobile "storm battalions" comprised of only the most loyal and disciplined war veterans. They were organized with great flex-ibility having short, eight week tours of duty. Over several months they developed into about 200 frenetic units, with a loyalty to no one except their own unit commanders. A number of brigades were comprised of soldiers who had fought in the Baltic, and they brought with them their traditional fighting symbol, *the Swastika.*

Originally the Freikorps represented their officer's passionate desire to rebuild an effective military. Wartime forced men into a polarity - friend or foe. Through the activity of the Freikorps, this polarity was being displayed in the streets of most German cities. It would soon become clear that these men had no scruples about killing political enemies. The Freikorps principal enemy was the socialist left and their desire to impose their Russian style ideology on German society.

As the new government was evolving in the post-armistice confusion, a number of bizarre events occurred. One of the strangest involved the Berlin Police Department. On one Monday morning, Emil Eichorn, the leader of the Independent Socialist Party, walked into the central station and boldly announced that he had been authorized to take over the Berlin Police. The whole thing was a fabrication, but there was no one to contradict the claim, and so he did. In December, the new Ebert government dismissed him, bringing on a major confrontational crisis. Outside police headquarters in the Alexanderplatz, restless Berliners mobilized by the thousands. Eichorn appeared on the balcony vowing he would not give up the post. Inside, ten top left-wing political leaders were meeting. Karl Liebknecht, head of the German Communist Party, was the most influential. They made a momentous decision which was unanimous. Now was the time for revolution. Liebknecht addressed the crowd outside. His words were greeted with thunderous approval as red flags waved, hands and hats rose into the air.

When night fell, word quickly spread that a general strike would begin the following morning. Working men and women felt that finally they had the power to shape their future. The strike succeeded in closing most of Berlin's factories, stores, and public transportation. Electricity was lost in most of the city as more than 200,000 demonstrators surged through the streets. They seized rail stations, newspapers, and even controlled the Brandenburg Gate for a time. The attempted liberal coup was given the name Spartakus, and involved some 250,000 unemployed who were desperate and ready for change. Both liberal and conservative sympathizers took to the streets. Over the four-day strike and confrontation, the death toll approached 1,000. Unfortunately, the conflict would not be resolved without further violence.

Within 48 hours the Freikorps began hunting for Karl Liebknecht. He had vacated the street battleground and decided to go into hiding in the slum district of Neukolln. Mostly ignoring the ruin of the revolt he had started, he was informed his own wife and son had been arrested. Still, he chose to stay in hiding. The Freikorps intensified their search. From the second floor apartment window with curtains closed, Liebknecht was watching the patrols below. Soon they would be going door to door. On the night of January 14, he decided to flee to the middle class district of Wilmersdorf. A communist sympathizer offered his apartment and Liebknecht was joined there by two other fugitives, Rosa Luxemburg and Wilhelm Pieck, a communist party operative. Earlier Pieck had secured false identity papers for the two leaders to aid their escape effort.

The situation grew desperate and the three fugitives discussed their strategy. Liebknecht and Luxemburg were the main targets.

"We should move in the next 48 hours," Rosa said in a hushed voice. "I feel we should go by auto because they'll be watching the train stations."

"I can be in contact tonight with someone who can get an auto," said Pieck. "The identity papers we have are very authentic. The key is to get out of Berlin and get to the country-side."

Liebknecht knew but did not say that he had great fear of the Freikorps. Rosa felt they would be sent to prison and the movement would be set back for as long as three to five years. Liebknecht feared they would not get to prison alive.

On the evening of the following day an informant notified the authorities of their location. Freikorps troops quickly surrounded the apartment and took them into custody. Freikorps headquarters had been set up in the Eden Hotel next to the Berlin Zoo. Liebknecht and Luxemburg were placed in separate rooms for 'interrogation'. The beatings were severe. Of note, Wilhelm Pieck was kept in a hallway escaping harsh treatment. Colleagues later came to the conclusion that he was the informant who had given them up. The following day they were placed in separate cars for transport to Moabit Prison.

The first car carrying Liebknecht detoured to the Tiergarten and stopped in one of the dark by-ways. Stunned and bleeding, he was pushed from the auto and shot multiple times. It was later reported that he was shot while trying to escape. As for Rosa Luxemburg, she was riding in the back seat of the second car and was told she was being transported to prison to await prosecution. Instead, she was forced to bend over in the seat and was shot in the back of the head. Her body was dumped in the Landwehr Canal.

With their leaders murdered, the communists lost virtually all of the momentum they had seized in their attempt to gain control of the new Republic.

One week after the murders, 30 million Germans went to the polls. Political violence had become all too common and the voters welcomed the opportunity to confirm the democratic process. For millions of Germans, this squalid chapter of their history was being closed. Friedrich Ebert and the Social Democrats were given a solid majority. The man who had been the de facto president was now Germany's duly elected Chief of State. With little formal training he faced the monumental task of trying to save this sinking 'Ship of State.' His country had no guiding paradigm. His mandate was to draft a constitution and establish a legitimate parliamentary government. A constitutional assembly would be held, but Berlin was still unsafe. Ebert decided to hold the assembly in Weimer, some 200 kilometers southwest of the capitol. The assembly convened in the National Theater where Franz Liszt had once conducted Wagner's Lohengrin.

Ebert was overwhelmingly elected the first president of the new Republic, a formality of the assembly. Then the delegates began the task of considering the new constitution. A rough draft had been completed by Hugo Press, a liberal professor of law at the University of Berlin. It contained features borrowed from the American, British, and French constitutions. Specifically, the president would have broad powers and be elected by popular vote. Proportional representation would protect minority interests, and the provincial state governments would have a great deal of autonomy.

The delegates spent weeks debating every detail, from protection of local interests to a new design for the flag. The final draft was met with approval. But the document was flawed and would prove to be greatly beneficial to the Nazi cabal to come. The provincial autonomy would allow Hitler and his group to flourish in their early days in Bavaria. Article 48 specifically gave the German president the power to rule by decree. It was this provision that paved the road that Hitler would travel to become Chancellor in 1933. The genesis of the Nazi Third Reich was, to a great extent, made possible by a document which had been very carefully crafted by men who did not see how it could be used to take over their country.

The development of the Nazi oligarchy was almost exclusively a reflection of the decadent mind and machinations of Adolph Hitler. Cunning and deception served as a shield, masterfully covering his personal hatred and resentments which would, in time, codify into national policy. In Vienna, he had been influenced by the Mayor, Karl Lueger. His desire was to maintain a Catholic-German dominated monarchy. Anti- Semitism was central to this goal and Hitler was particularly intrigued by this strategy.

After the signing of the Armistice, Hitler began to analyze Germany's defeat, and in his malevolent thought process, began to connect the defeat with covert plotting of Jewry. Well on his way to developing a hatred for Marxism as well, he then associated communists with Jews, something he called 'the Jewish Doctrine of Marxism'. Much of the development of his rabid anti-Semitism was kept to himself. He became obsessed with the idea of an eternal struggle between two hostile forces. The 'Aryan' represented a wandering creative angelic force; 'the Jew,' a counter force he viewed as Satanic. The survival of the planet was hanging in the balance. In his paranoia he saw the Jews as being engaged in a conspiracy to achieve global domination. Reflecting on his earlier time in Vienna, he later would write:

"Vienna appeared to me in different light than before. Wherever I went, I began to see Jews, and the more I saw, the more sharply they became distinguished in my eyes from the rest of humanity. In a short time I was made more thoughtful than ever by my slowly rising insight into the type of activity carried on by the Jews in certain fields. Was there any form of filth or profligacy, particularly in cultural life, without at least one Jew involved in it? If you cut even cautiously into such an abscess, you found, like a maggot in a rotting body, often dazzled by the sudden light – a little Jew."

Post war Munich was fertile soil for the nourishment of such perfidious ideas. An army political indoctrination course was a platform to develop his oratorical skills. Bavarian political life needed scrutiny and this became his first salaried job outside the military. He was attracted to one of the groups he was to monitor, and in September, 1919, he joined the German Worker's Party (Deutsche Arbeiterpartic – DAP). By 1921, he had developed a significant influence with the membership. He was soon able to persuade the majority to abandon the committee-style leadership in favor of himself as 'chairman.' The DAP was also given a new name: The National Socialist German Worker's Party (Nationalsozialistische Deutsche Arbeiterpartei – NSDAP). The final party name was an acronym for National and Sozialist – NAZI.

Hitler's view of recent events was aggressively stressed at party meetings, namely that Germany's defeat and economic problems were the result of international Jewry and Marxists. Most Germans were bitter about the Treaty of Versailles and angry with the resulting economic downturn. How quickly they had forgotten that they had supported the policies that had plunged their nation into a war of aggression. Now, just as quickly, they were buying into the deception about Jews and Marxists.

The new Nazi party quickly acquired a newspaper, then formed its own strong arm squad, the Storm Detachments or SA. By December 1923, the membership had grown to 55,000.

At year's end, Hitler decided on a bold move and led an attempted coup in Munich. It failed and he and others were arrested and put on trial for treason. The trial and Hitler both drew national attention. He was convicted and given a five-year sentence of which he served only ten months. While in prison, he wrote most of Mein Kampf (my struggle), a narrative of his political awakening.

The seeds of political hatred had been sown. Cultivation of those seeds would result in a cataclysm not experienced in the history of the world.

CHAPTER 6

Surgical Training

Anna was in a deep sleep when the phone call came. It rang six times before she could rouse herself enough to answer it.

"Dr. Eichenwald, you are needed in the VIP suite immediately," said the operator uncharacteristically abrupt.

Anna glanced at her watch. It was 4:30 a.m. She still held a book in her hand, having fallen asleep after reading for half an hour. Momentarily disoriented, she opened her eyes, blinked several times to shake the sleep, then realized something unusual was happening. She had never been to the VIP suite. Located on the top floor of the hospital, most staff members had no access to it. The suite was reserved only for the very wealthy or those of high political position.

Anna went into the bathroom and splashed her face with cold water. She grabbed her coat and bounded up four flights of stairs. There, on the seventh floor, was the VIP suite securely tucked behind two massive oak doors. She paused a moment wondering if she should knock, then entered trying to imagine why a first year surgical resident would be requested here. She immediately recognized Dr. Karl Scheidemann, president of the University of Berlin, and Dr. Hierholzer, chairman of the Department of Surgery, both standing at the end of the hall. She slowed her pace and searched for more familiar faces. She saw Gregor Schracht, chief surgical resident and met his eyes. He began walking in her direction.

"Hello, Anna," he said. His face was stern. "President Ebert has been admitted to the hospital, and he's dying."

* * *

Charles Dawes was an American banker who frequently traveled to Germany. He was involved in an effort to rescue the German economy, having realized the potential for enormous investment profit if the inflation could be controlled. He had attended a reception for Professor Einstein in America in 1921 and had met Hanz Eichenwald. It was at that time he began to see what Germany could become.

Dawes' plan was straightforward. He suggested fixing a reparation payment schedule at 2.5 billion marks per year. In addition, he proposed that all allied troops be removed from the Ruhr area. His plan was implemented in 1924 - the Dawes Plan for Economic Recovery.

During his weeks in Germany Dawes had been invited to the home of Hanz and Marlene Eichenwald. The other guests that evening included Albert Einstein and Max Planck. After dinner, the men retired to the library for cigars and brandy. Hanz and Max watched in amusement as Einstein questioned Dawes about international economics and Dawes questioned Einstein about relativity. Later, they agreed to a draw. But in reality, Einstein understood far more about economics than Dawes knew about relativity. In future years, Dawes would admit being pleased with the plan he had 'master-minded.' But his conversations would always come back to the event of what seemed to him, a magical evening spent with the famous Nobel Prize Laureate.

Whatever upswing the economy took, it did not improve the political fortune of President Ebert. The economic turmoil had brought out hostility from both the left and right. Ebert was attacked in the press and publicly accused of everything from treason to bribery. Rather than ignore the falsehoods, he became obsessed with defending his honor. Knowing none of the charges could be proven, he filed lawsuits for slander and mounted a campaign in his defense.

Late one evening after one of many stressful days, Ebert began having abdominal pain. The following morning he was examined by his personal physician and given a diagnosis of acute appendicitis. But Ebert refused to go to the hospital. "My honor is at stake," he told his physician. "I cannot possibly leave my office." His condition worsened by the day. Finally, he had no choice but to enter the hospital. By that time he had developed massive peritonitis for which there was no effective treatment. In the VIP suite, he was given IV fluids and morphine. Anna was told that a team of first year surgical house-officers would attend to Ebert, each working eight-hour shifts. She would assume the first.

Anna entered his room and saw Mrs. Ebert sitting in the corner. She was pale and drawn. "Good morning, Mrs. Ebert," said Anna. "I'm so sorry about what you and your husband are going through."

Ebert was 54-years old. He was an honest man, one who had never sought political power. But as is historically the case with some leaders, they are forced to step into such positions.

Anna noted Ebert's blood pressure. It was barely audible at 90, and he was not responsive. She felt he was in septic shock. He died before Anna even completed her first shift.

The State Funeral was extravagant. He had, in fact, been loved by his people. Bands played and politicians gave eulogies, each hoping to get into the spotlight. Workmen wearing black armbands marched in mourning. Bewildered Germans nationwide were suddenly confronted with the fact that once again they had no leader.

The German constitution had not provided for a successor, a significant oversight. So an election was held with seven candidates but it did not produce a clear winner. A second election was to be held with new nominations. This time retired Field Marshal Paul von Hindenburg was persuaded to run. He was 77 years old. In a bizarre turn of events, the Nazis abandoned their candidate for Hindenburg. Moderates supported ex- Chancellor Wilhelm Marx, and the communists stood behind their leader, Ernst Thalmann. Hindenburg won a close race over Marx. Had the communists joined the other left-center parties for Marx, Hindenburg would have been denied the Presidency and the opportunity to appoint Adolph Hitler as Chancellor - which he did in 1933.

*   *   *

Excitement was building for Erin Nitschmann. She had completed her graduate studies in May of 1927. Her mother and father had been on a second tour with the Philharmonic, this time for six weeks. They traveled to London, Brussels, Paris, Athens, and Monti Carlo. The Nitschmanns were about to arrive home at Central Station. Erin could hardly wait, her excitement doubled by the fact that she had a scheduled audition in a few weeks with the Berlin Symphony. She was vying for one of two positions as apprentice violinist and her father had been appointed as one of three examiners. Some 60 musicians had sent application from throughout Europe.

Erin had matured. She now had two degrees, one in violin and the other in music theory. When she saw her parents step out of their train car, she abandoned all self- composure and began running down the platform. She threw her arms around her parents.

They had hardly finished the formalities of reunion when Erin grabbed her parent's hands and blurted out the news.

"Dr. Stoller has been enormously helpful in my preparation for the audition," she said excitedly. "He's been pushing me harder than usual."

Ernst Stoller had been Erin's instructor in advanced violin performance for the past year. Her father was a longtime friend of Stoller and was pleased Erin was working with a man of his stature. "So, how is it going?" he asked his daughter. "Are you making any progress?" A broad smile came across her face.

"You'll see for yourself, pops."

The three walked together arm in arm as if they were barely touching the ground. The audition was in Symphony Hall. Each candidate was required to play a series of musical scores by sight, and then a series of compositions played back after hearing them only once. The third segment included performing a brief composition written by the candidate. Finally, each would perform the first movement of Beethoven's Concerto for Violin in D major, Op. 61.

Erin had been working on her performance for the entire year. Her father, due to his relationship to Erin, would not take part in judging the competition. Her mother had been too nervous to stay in the hall so she waited in the foyer with Erin's brother, Peter.

During the first segment, Erin's technical skills reflected her solid instruction and preparation. Her composition was a light work which lasted only three minutes. She performed it beautifully. If one could have seen the music, one would have looked upon a dancing butterfly on a spring day.

The concluding piece, considered one of Beethoven's finest, had first been performed on December 23, 1806, by Franz Clement, principal violinist of the Theater and dier Wien. The work was dedicated by Beethoven to the friend of his youth, Stephen von Breuning. The concerto had grown in popularity and was regarded as the touchstone of the violinist's art.

Erin's performance was a virtuoso. She played with an unusual degree of lyric expansion. In pure sound terms, this performance was unprecedented for an apprentice. A generating force was maintained throughout the movement, ending with mystery and suspense. The three examiners looked at each other in amazement. From his chair in the back of the hall, Erin's father sat stunned. He could not believe what he had heard. He thought back to her fifth birthday, the day she received her first violin. The time had passed so quickly. She had been a little girl in pigtails. Now she sat poised, passionate in her performance. How could such a level of talent have evolved leaving him unaware, as though he had missed it?

Paula and Peter entered the hall and sat down next to Isaac. He was at a loss for words. How could he describe what he had witnessed?

"Well?" demanded Paula.

"Yes," said Isaac. "She did very well. Very very well."

Erin approached her parents and Paula threw her arms around her daughter, crying. Peter was all smiles.

That evening the family celebrated over dinner. Relieved to have the performance behind her, Erin was buoyant. She looked around the table and captured the faces of each member of her family. It was etched in her memory, a shining, still moment of incandescence.

It took almost three weeks before Erin received the letter stating that she had been chosen as one of the two apprentice violinists for the Berlin Symphony. Within two weeks she would begin preparation for the fall season. Her one-year apprenticeship would then transition into her professional career as a violinist. Erin's goal was to become a concert violinist. No one doubted she would achieve it.

Berlin was a city that loved music. One of its legendary figures was an Italian, Ferruccio Busoni, who had moved to Berlin in 1894. It did not take him long to become known as a master pianist. Small in stature, Busoni had a somewhat stooped appearance. But he was strikingly handsome with long flowing hair and a chiseled face. Busoni's greatest accomplishment was the revision of much of the piano literature of Bach. He also created transcriptions of Bach's organ music, still considered classics.

A number of promising young pianists followed Busoni to Berlin; most notably, Vladimir Horowitz, Wilhelm Backhaus, and Claudio Arrau. All of them were admired. But the standard of excellence was set by Arthur Schnabel. He was a stocky man with a thick grey moustache. Although not a true virtuoso, Rudolf Serkin had once stated of Schnabel, that "he was the greatest influence on us all."

Professional jealousy is common, and among musicians it is no different.

"How is your friend, the great adagio player?" Rachmaninoff once sneered to a member of the Schnabel circle. Rachmaninoff was a showman and very popular in his own right. But he was not held in the same regard as Schnabel. His concerts with the Philharmonic were stirring. But he played to the crowd and thus, could not reach the level of Schnabel, considered the foremost interpreter of Beethoven and Schubert. In 1927, the world marked the 100th anniversary of the death of Beethoven.

Arthur Schnabel had studied the life and music of the great composer, and had great compassion for him. An account of an opera rehearsal by Beethoven had never left his mind. In one or Beethoven's last efforts at conducting, the singers and orchestra members were very focused on their conductor, but were having great difficulty following his gestures. Finally the music became chaotic…then silence. Beethoven seemed confused, and seemed not to understand the reason for the breakdown. It was then that he realized he could no longer conceal his deafness.

As Beethoven was gradually becoming deaf he had written, 'it was impossible to say to others; speak louder…shout! I am deaf!' Schnabel desired to honor this genius composer and do it in Berlin. To accomplish this, he planned to play the cycle of all 32 Beethoven Sonatas. A series of seven consecutive Sunday concerts was scheduled all at the Volksbuhne (People's Theater) in Berlin's working class district rather than in Symphony Hall. Schnabel was a modest man and did not like calling attention to himself.

Among the nearly 2,000 Berliners in the Theater were Paula Nitschmann and her friend Kathe Kollwitz, the artist They both had a love of music, but their bond of friendship was based on another reason. They each had sons named Peter who had gone to war. Kathe's Peter had not returned.

Almost a year had passed since Paula had accompanied Kathe on a pilgrimage to the Belgian village of Reggevelde. It was there that her 18-year old son had lost his life, just three months after the start of the war. Kathe had received information of the possible burial site for her Peter. They found the cemetery with the entrance blocked with barbed wire. Circling around to the side they found a narrow, little used path, then entered and began their search.

"Paula! Look at this," cried Kathe.

There were what appeared to be several thousand white crosses set in a geometric pattern throughout the cemetery. In the panoramic view, the appearance was one of order and serenity. What had been the chaos of a murderous war had been transformed into a beautiful and spiritual display of remembrance for those who had not survived. The two women walked silently and separately, meandering in no particular pattern, searching. Kathe's eyes moved slowly from cross to cross. Almost half of the crosses were inscribed with 'unknown soldier.'

In this area of Belgium, the Germans were said to have lost 200,000 men in the course of only four years. Kathe began to worry that perhaps her Peter was lying in one of the 'unknown soldier' graves. She did not want to be denied the final chance to be near him. An hour passed. Then suddenly, Paula cried out to Kathe. "He's here! Right here!"

Kathe took a deep breath and slowly moved to the cross. The midday sun was warm and a gentle breeze caressed her hair as she stood motionless; her beloved son, at last. Kathe whispered, "He would have been 31 this July."

Paula placed her arm around her friend and they stood in silence as the minutes passed. Paula had found wild flowers near the entrance to the cemetery. She broke off three stems and handed the flowers to Kathe, watching as her friend placed them on the grave of her son.

Kathe paused and looked at her own fingers as they released the flowers. For a moment, she was lost in the memory of Peter's tiny fingers as they had once held a small bouquet of wildflowers he had picked for her. She remembered his sweet face as he had smiled up at her. She remembered everything. How he felt in her arms as she rocked him to sleep. How warm his skin had been as she bathed his tiny body when he had a fever. She recalled taking him to school on his first day and staring back into his anxious eyes as they followed her out the door. She had left him there and her heart had ached.

The pain in her heart was now so great that she knelt because she could no longer stand. A senseless war had robbed them both. She would carry only his childhood, his early years in life. His future as a man was lost to her forever.

Standing side by side, the two friends had similar thoughts. One son had been spared and one was lost. Peter's cross was distinguished from the others by only one thing - his name. In history, his name would be a statistic, but as Kathe walked from Peter's grave, she believed that God would always know his name.

The following morning during the auto ride back to Brussels, the winding tree- lined road was a comfort to Kathe. The beautiful countryside and flowered meadows brought serenity and a graceful closure to her anguish.

"Paula, I had a dream last night. I dreamed there would be another war. In the dream, I imagined that if I and others would drop all we were doing and devote all our efforts to speak out against it, we could prevent it."

Kathe was intuitive. But she was wrong. The Second World War was looming, still more than a decade away. But there would be no individual, no group capable of preventing it.

On that Sunday afternoon in the Volksbuhne in 1927, the two women, friends and mothers of sons, were stirred by Schnabel's performance and his tribute to a creative genius, composer Ludwig Van Beethoven.

*   *   *

Anna was finally feeling settled in her new appointment as a surgical house officer at the University Hospital. Since her days of anatomy she had dreamed of becoming a surgeon. There were only a handful of female surgeons in all of Europe. Her determination and direct approach to problem solving assured her of success, at least in her own mind. She had observed her male counterparts and seen how they tackled problems head on, looking for a cure rather than a way to manage the disease process.

Anna's favorite rotation as a student was on the surgical service, with pediatrics a close second. She would go to the emergency ward as often as possible in the hope of finding a laceration to suture or a fracture to set. Her fellow resident for this rotation was Christian Engel. The chief of the service was Gregor Schracht. Anna admired Dr. Schracht. He had an intuitive sense about sick people - the more difficult the problem, the more intense he became. He was a very skilled surgeon and Anna remained infatuated with his ability to make difficult procedures look easy.

Of all of Anna's medical colleagues, Christian Engel was her favorite. They spent long hours together on student rotations, and now as house officers on surgery. Christian was the brother she never had. Although born in Germany, his parents were from the Ukraine and had emigrated in 1894. Christian's father was an engineer and was employed initially in dam construction projects. He had moved on and was now in road construction. Christian was easy going and enjoyed teasing Anna, taking advantage of her gullible nature. He had been the ring leader in the cadaver prank. Tall, with angular features, Christian had dark hair much like Anna's, although he perpetually looked as though he needed to shave. Women found his most attractive feature to be his large, brown eyes. He resembled Anna's own father, but unlike Hanz, he was sardonic and sanguine.

Surgical call was every third night. Christian and Anna were paired for this rotation and they alternated first call. The first call had responsibility for evaluating any new problem or emergency. The alternate person was back up if the first call got tied up in the operating room. Gregor Schract was the senior resident in the house and evaluated any patient being considered for surgery. The early evening was spent rounding on the post-op patients. Anna and Christian generally did this together so both would be aware of any potential problems during the night.

"Hey, Anna, hope all's quiet!"

"Probably won't be, knowing my luck," she replied with a grin. As Christian disappeared into his call room, he called back to her.

"Let me know if you get swamped. Otherwise, you know I need my rest." He smiled at her and closed the door.

Anna planned to do some reading as was her custom on call. She changed into fresh scrubs and got some coffee. She checked in with the hospital operator and opened her surgical textbook. edited by an American surgeon, William Halstead. In the introduction, Halstead made it clear that the greatest influence on his surgical philosophy had come from German surgeons. On several tours of German speaking countries, he had noticed the overwhelming success of the German educational system in training surgeons of the highest order. Anna had been reading for about 10 minutes when the phone rang. "Dr. Eichenwald, you are needed in the emergency bay."

Anna generally took the back stairs three flights down to the emergency area. She knew the charge nurse well.

"Dr. Eichenwald, the patient is a three week old with two days of vomiting. The pedi resident has been called and is on the way."

As Anna entered the nursery area she observed a young couple. The woman seemed to be in her early 20s and tried to smile as she held her son. The baby was listless and Anna immediately noted that he appeared dehydrated. This was the couple's first child, and the first grandchild in the family.

"I'm Dr. Eichenwald," she said, taking the child into her arms. "Any problems with your pregnancy?"

"None," the young mother replied. "He was delivered at home by a mid-wife. He was fine until two days ago. He started to be fussy and then he would vomit my breast milk. He hasn't held anything down for the past 24 hours."

"Has he had any fever or diarrhea?"

"We don't think so" said the father. He remained standing beside his wife, who now sat down wearily.

Anna placed the little boy on the exam table. She noted his mouth was very dry and eyes sunken. His heart rate was 154, high for a three week old. His chest was clear and he had no abdominal distention. She placed the end of her little finger into his mouth and he immediately began to suck on it. His abdomen was soft. Gently, she pressed into his tiny abdominal cavity and felt a small lump in the upper abdomen. It was firm, like an olive. The pediatric resident entered the room.

"I'm going to ask Dr. Schracht to have a look at him," she said to the resident. "I'll be back in a second, and I'd like to know what you think."

Anna called Dr. Schracht and related the history and her findings. "What do you think?" he asked her.

She went through several possibilities.

"I'll be right down," he told her.

Blood work had been drawn and a scalp IV started by the pediatric resident. Gregor Schracht had a good idea of the diagnosis but said nothing until he had examined the child. His exam confirmed his suspicion - hypertrophic pyloric stenosis. Anna had considered this but was unsure, never having seen a case. She stayed in the background.

Dr. Schracht turned to the parents.

"Your baby has developed an obstruction just at the end of his stomach. It is from a swollen muscle. The treatment is surgical. If not corrected, he will not survive. If corrected, he should be fine."

The mother's eyes filled with tears and her husband placed his arm around her shoulder. "He's so small. Will he be able to get through surgery? How dangerous is it?" The baby's mother looked up with imploring eyes as Dr. Schracht took her hand.

"He is my responsibility and he will make it. It's true he is very small, but the problem is straight forward. He will need some fluids and then we need to get started." Surgery was set for 4:00 a.m. The anesthesia used for children and most adults was open-drop ether. Although an explosive agent, it was extremely safe when properly used.

Anna and Schracht scrubbed while the baby was put to sleep. Operating on a three week old did have significant risk, but the hydration would help him tolerate the anesthetic and surgery.

After a sterile prep, a small transverse incision was made in the upper abdomen just to the right of the midline. Schracht quickly placed his index finger into the abdominal cavity and located the enlarged muscle mass. He then allowed Anna to do the same.

"Now try to grasp it and bring it into the wound," he said.

Anna was able to get the mass between her index finger and thumb, then pulled it just to the surface of the wound. Schracht grasped it with a non-crushing clamp. Using a scalpel he divided the muscle until the inner lining of the stomach was bulging through the divided muscle. He carefully showed Anna each step and then helped her close the abdominal cavity. The entire lifesaving procedure, a pyloromyotomy, had taken about 45 minutes.

As Anna wrote the post-op orders, Gregor Schracht went to talk with the family. Later, he gave Anna the references for the original publications describing the procedure. They were published in 1910 and 1912 by Fredet from France and Ramstedt from Germany. The procedure had become known as the Fredet-Ramstedt operation. As Anna reviewed the publications, she thought it ironic that these men were developing a lifesaving procedure shortly before their countries became bitter enemies on the battlefield.

She slept for two hours, then met Christian for breakfast. She shared in detail, the events of the night. He was envious.

"Why didn't you call me?"

"I knew you needed your sleep," she replied with a smile, never looking up. Christian sighed and Anna continued. "You're the one who taught me the surgical motto."

"I know…I know. Eat when you can, sleep when you can, and don't touch the pancreas!"

Anna finished her rounds about 11:00 a.m. Her last stop was by the nursery. Her patient had already taken one ounce of water with no problem and would resume nursing later that day. His mother, holding and intermittently rocking him, looked up at Anna.

"How can I thank you?"

"Well, he'll go home tomorrow," she said. "That's all the thanks I need. It was Saturday and she was ready for some sleep.

＊　＊　＊

In 1921, Albert Einstein made his first trip to the United States. He was received as a hero although almost no one understood his theory of relativity. He met with President Warren G. Harding and was involved in fund raising for the Hebrew University in Jerusalem. Now, in 1927, he was returning to deliver a series of lectures on the east coast. His colleague, Hanz Eichenwald, was invited as well to deliver talks on quantum mechanics. On April 1st, Professor and Mrs. Einstein, along with Hanz and Marlene, boarded the train at central station for the trip to Amsterdam, then on to the SS Rotterdam to New York.

Hanz had a growing interest in aviation and in New York he indulged his interest reading multiple articles on the subject. The most intriguing was the April 8th edition of the *New York Times* about hotel owner Raymond Orteig and his offer of a $25,000 prize to the first man to cross the Atlantic from New York to Paris, or vice versa, in a heavier- than-air machine. A flight had been made in 1919 from Newfoundland to Ireland, a distance of 1,900 miles. But the distance between New York and Paris was more than 3,500 miles - a much greater challenge.

There were several contenders. One of the most interesting was listed as 'C.A. Lindbergh, Air Mail pilot from St Louis!' This man had flown as a 'barnstormer' in Texas. He was known for landing in any field that took his fancy and for taking locals up for joyrides.

For the attempt, he persuaded Ryan Airlines to allow him to use one of their aircraft. The plane was modified for the 4,000-mile flight with several extra fuel tanks. It carried no radio, only minimal instruments, and had a single engine.

Three attempts for the prize had already been made. Commander Byrd and two companions crashed their aircraft on a test flight, but no one was seriously injured. Davis and Wooster took off from New York in a critically overloaded plane, crashed and died. A week later, a Frenchman named Nungesser departed from Paris with a co-pilot. They were never heard from again. As the German physicists were preparing for their return sail, Hanz noted that Lindbergh had scheduled his attempt for May 20th.

On the voyage home, Hanz began to consider the excitement of the Lindbergh attempt. "I have always wanted to fly an airplane," he confided to Marlene. "What bravado. What courage Lindbergh is showing. Why not go to Paris? He just might make it!" Marlene had a good sense of humor and was spontaneous by nature. She responded with a twinkle in her eye, "Let's go!"

Anna needed a break from her routine and was thrilled with the idea. The day after the Eichenwalds returned, Hanz had his secretary purchase three train tickets to Paris departing on May 18th.

Their first day in Paris was for sightseeing and relaxation. This was mostly decided upon for Anna's sake, given her rigorous call schedule. The next day, they had an early breakfast and headed off in a taxi to the airport landing strip at Le Bourget. By 5:00 p.m. there were thousands of Parisians on the grounds waiting. At 6:30, the American Ambassador arrived. By 9:00 p.m. the excitement began to change to apprehension. They didn't know that at that time, Lindbergh was about to cross the English Channel. Precisely at 10:12 p.m. the faint sound of an engine could be heard. Everyone grew quiet until the lights on the wing tips could be seen. Then 20,000 Frenchmen, along with a few Danes, Swedes, and Germans began cheering wildly. The plane circled once and made a final approach. As it touched down, the crowd swarmed the runway. Lindbergh was hoisted on the shoulders of two men. He made a few remarks to the crowd and then was rescued by the American Ambassador.

A week later, he and his plane were returned to the U.S. on a navy warship. His famous flight had taken 33 hours and 39 minutes. His return trip took approximately ten days. He was given a hero's welcome with a New York tickertape parade. His place in history was established and the modern aviation industry was launched. The Eichenwalds had been witnesses to one of the most extraordinary events of aviation history.

"I would not trade the excitement of this experience even for a chance to pilot my own plane," Hanz said to his girls.

* * *

While the Berlin Philharmonic was giving concerts, surgeons were being trained and the world was captivated by the daring of an American aviator, something else was happening, as well. Adolph Hitler was instructing the Nazi faithful, including Joseph Goebbels and Heinrich Himmler.

"The receptivity of the masses is very limited, their intelligence is small, but their power of forgetting is enormous. In consequence of these facts, all effective propaganda must be limited to a few essential points. These slogans must be repeated until every last member of the public understands what you want him to understand."

Hitler had been released from prison in December 1924, having served 10 months for an attempted coup of the local government in Bavaria. For the next two years he was barred from speaking publicly. His immediate problem was a split in the ideology of the Nazi party. The northern segment, run by Gregor Strasser in Berlin, was presenting the party as favoring a socialist agenda. While the mission of the southern segment of the party, based in Munich, seemed to be just the opposite.... to fight against communism.

Anna's longtime friend and classmate, Uri Avner, had continued his studies at the University of Berlin. He also continued his friendship with Anna, seeing her occasionally on weekends, usually for lunch in the Tiergarten. Still unknown to Anna, Uri was becoming more deeply involved with the Communist Party. Most party meetings were held late at night and were clandestine in nature. After the murders of Karl Liebknecht and Rosa Luxemburg, the party was forced to go underground but they continued to aggressively recruit new members. They were well aware of the ideological split in the Nazi party. If the northern segment remained socialist in orientation, in time, they could be a conduit for the communists to dominate Berlin and central Germany.

Uri was involved in a plan to infiltrate the Nazi party in Berlin. Inside information would prove invaluable for the communist cause. The Nazis were still small in number and were delighted to have any university student. Gaining traction with youth was central to their strategy for political success. Uri had become a weekly attendee at

Nazi meetings. It was at one of those meetings he first met Joseph Goebbels. Each large city was designated as a 'Gau', or district. A Gauleiter (leader) was appointed for each district. Goebbels had been designated the Gauleiter for Berlin.

Joseph Goebbels was a 29-year old follower of Hitler. He stood only five feet tall and limped badly because of a withered leg from childhood polio. He had graduated from the University of Heidelberg in 1921 with an ambition to become a writer. Raised in a lower-class family as a Catholic, his mother longed for him to become a priest. At the university his advisor in literature was a Jewish professor named Friedrich Gundolf, who was not fond of Goebbels. The goal of young writers was to gain access to the inner circle of established writers. Goebbels attempted to do this with the noted poet, Stefan George. When he failed, he blamed Gundolf.

One evening after a Nazi Party meeting, Goebbels asked Uri to join him at a nearby pub. This was a unique opportunity for the communist sympathizer to get to know Herr Goebbels. The pub was a five-block walk from the warehouse where the meetings were held. Because of Goebbels polio disability, they took a taxi. Goebbels was clearly anxious to know more about Uri.

"Tell me about your studies. What's your major?"

"I am most interested in political science and will earn a minor in history." Goebbels looked at him quizzically. "You aren't native to Germany, are you?"

"No, I was born in Egypt. My father is a career diplomat with the Egyptian embassy. We came to Germany when I was 12 and I have decided I want to live in Germany and work in politics."

"Very interesting. The party is looking for students to help us organize student groups."

As they reached the pub, Goebbels paid the fare and gathered his coat and briefcase. Once settled inside, he spoke again. "I had a dream of being a writer. In fact I wrote a novel called *Michael*. It was, in effect, the diary of a heroic soldier. It was rejected for publication by a Jewish company, Ullstien and Mosse, the bastards."

Uri could hear the bitterness in Goebbels' voice and did not pursue the issue. He was becoming more aware of the hatred of Jews, especially in the Nazi party. Goebbels continued. "I have now dedicated myself to the Party."

He explained that he had written many articles for the *Berliner Arbeiter Zeitung* (Berlin Workers Newspaper) attacking the capitalist system. Uri also knew that he was becoming noted as a speaker for the Nazi cause. Their conversation continued late into the night. Uri came to see that Goebbels was not only a tireless worker; his intention was to become a leader of the highest order in the party.

The following month Hitler called for a debate of the differing viewpoints of the party. The meeting was to be in the Bavarian city of Bamberg. It was planned in the middle of the week so that a limited number of members from Berlin could attend. In fact, Gregor Strasser and Goebbels were the only representatives. Hitler dominated the meeting. The two men from Berlin were intimidated, then humiliated. Later in the day, in private, Hitler confided to Goebbels.

"I want you in my 'confident group' in the Party." Goebbels was overwhelmed and later wrote in his diary:

'April 13, 1926…Hitler speaks for three hours…brilliant…we are moving closer. We ask…he replies. I love him…I am reassured all round…I bow to his greatness, his political genius!'

Gregor Strassor felt betrayed. He was stunned by the turn of events. An obvious outsider now, he returned to Berlin and is reported to have said: "My heart aches. I can no longer believe in Hitler absolutely."

The Bamberg meeting was a defining moment for the Nazis. Strassor could no longer stand up to Hitler. The Party could now show its true malevolence. The brown- shirted street thugs called the Sturmabteilung or SA, were gaining strength under the direction of their leader, Ernst Rohm. They were now involved in the dirty work in the streets for the party. As the communist party became stronger, they usually supplied the opposition for street violence.

When Uri went to the next Nazi Party meeting he saw the dramatic changes. Over the next two months he gradually dropped from attending and eventually stopped going at all.

At this time, the SS or Schutz Staffel was formed. This was the personal protection squad for Adolph Hitler. Headed by Heinrich Himmler, it eventually grew to be an army within an army, with multiple branches and even some business enterprises. Ten years hence, the SS would be charged with the organization and management of the 'Race and Resettlement Office' of the Nazi Reich. Himmler would go on to mastermind the organization that created the concentration and death camps, stamping Nazi Germany in infamy.

CHAPTER 7

Lise Meitner

In many ways, the past 25 years had been a magical time for Lise Meitner. The Austrian born physicist was drawn to Berlin in 1907 to continue her post-doctoral studies with the eminent physicist, Max Planck. She was only the second woman to earn a Ph.D from the University of Vienna and had already published outstanding work on alpha and beta radiation. She was petite, with beautiful dark features. Given the aggressive environment of physics, she remained remarkably shy.

Once established as a research fellow, Lise was befriended by the prominent radio-chemist, Otto Hahn. He had moved to Berlin a year earlier after a year of study in Canada. He had come to work with another distinguished chemist, Emil Fisher. Hahn admired attractive women, but soon found that Lise had great intellect to go along with her beauty. He and Lise each needed a collaborator, so the physicist and radio-chemist made a natural team. Her beauty notwithstanding, their relationship was totally professional. They did not eat lunch together or even go on walks; yet they became very close friends.

The Kaiser Wilhelm Institute had opened in 1912, and offered a place for research and study for a large number of world-class scientists. The main buildings were located in Dahlem, a beautiful section of Berlin somewhat removed from the hustle and bustle of the city. The setting was pastoral. But in time, it would produce monumental advances in science and technology.

Lise lived in an apartment at the Institute. She loved music and enjoyed the symphony as well as the theater. But for the most part, her life was the world of physics where she could, in her own words, "pursue truth." She was indefatigable at the task.

Although the KWI, as it was known, was the epicenter of much of what was going on in the world of science, another world class institute was being established in Denmark. Niels Bohr, a Danish atomic physicist, had opened his own Institute for Theoretical Physics in Copenhagen in 1921. The following year he was awarded the Nobel Prize for his explanation of the structure of the atom. The term 'atom' was derived from a Greek word meaning 'indivisible.' For centuries the atom was thought to be the smallest unit of matter. Now, with the work of Ernest Rutherford in England and Bohr in Denmark, the structure of the atom, its central nucleus and orbiting electrons, was all coming into focus.

Lise Meitner had enduring relationships with many of the world's leading physicists, including Hanz Eichenwald and Albert Einstein, who often referred to her as 'Germany's Madam Curie.' Each of these relationships was important to Lise, but none more than her friendship with Niels Bohr and his wife Margrethe. Lise was Jewish by birth. But in early childhood her family had become Christian and she had been baptized. She remained single and kept close ties to her family in Austria and her sister, a concert pianist. Even so, she occasionally opted to spend the Christmas holidays with the Bohr family in Copenhagen. The Christmas of 1932 was one such occasion.

Lise boarded the train at Central Station on the evening of December 21st. It was a gray, overcast season. Christmas tradition in Germany was an important time of celebration. Even with the pressure of inflation, many were doing their last minute shopping and traveling, crowding the train station to greet and send off loved ones. The station's central area hosted a 50 foot Yule tree, the boughs of which could barely be seen behind hundreds of balls and crystals glittering as the light bounced around their bright red and green splendor. It was a fresh tree and Lise could smell a scent of pine as she passed by. By nature, she was a caring, thoughtful person and had spent the previous two days scurrying around for presents for the Bohr's five sons. Her train arrived only a half-hour late. There on the platform to meet her, was Margrethe Bohr and her 17-year old son, Christian. She could not walk fast enough to greet them.

Lise Meitner, distinguished scientist, was also a loyal friend with maternal instincts. She and Margrethe had become extremely close and Lise cherished the times she could abandon scientific pursuits in favor of those more feminine. She had made this trip to forget the world of atoms, neutrons and protons. She wanted, if only for a few days, to twirl in front of full length mirrors, feel the smooth, elastic texture of bread dough between her fingers, and spend hours at the kitchen table with Margrethe, clad in house coats and poring over this carefree time.

Once they arrived at the Bohrs' home, Lise spent a few minutes freshening up, then joined Margrethe for afternoon tea in the sitting room. This was their time to catch- up on their separate worlds. Margrethe was an outstanding cook and served pastries filled with candied fruits and warm buns with frosting, all made fresh that day. But despite the pleasure and anticipation of this visit, Lise could not hide her concern about the events taking place in her homeland. Margrethe could sense that her friend was troubled.

"Tell me of your work at the Kaiser. How are things in Berlin?"

Lise said nothing at first. She looked across the tea set directly into Margrethe's eyes. It took Margrethe a moment for the sadness to register.

"Please," she said softly.

"The work is fine. Germany is not." "Talk to me," Margrethe persisted.

"I will," Lise replied, nodding. "But it is complex. I think we should talk about it later. It's Christmas. I want to feel the joy of it…"

She sipped her tea and forced a smile. "Later, we will talk," she said.

The next morning Margrethe took Lise on a tour of their new home. "At least it is new to us," she laughed.

Her husband was now considered a Danish national hero. His 1913 publication "On the constitution of atoms and molecules" made him a Nobel laureate. In the summer of 1932, the Danish Academy had bestowed on him lifetime occupancy of the Danish House of Honor. Now he and his family were living in a palatial estate originally built for the founder of Carlsberg Breweries and subsequently reserved for Denmark's most distinguished citizen. The main house was built of native granite. The home had 24 rooms and 20-foot ceilings. The estate was built on 20 acres of land with tall pines and evergreens. It was a haven for raising five sons.

After touring the house and the grounds, the two returned to the kitchen. "I know you want to

spend some time with Neils," said Margrethe. "Let's make some tea. I have a few things I need

to take care of for the boys and this will give you two a little time to catch up."

Niels was a physically imposing man. He was tall for his generation, with a large head and hands. He also was a marvelous athlete, enjoyed sailing and skiing and routinely took the stairs two at a time. Parenthetically, he spoke with a soft voice, not much above a whisper. He had met Lise several years earlier at the annual Solvay conference in Brussels. For some reason he had felt a responsibility to look after her. She had seemed fragile and alone, as one of only two women in the physics 'club.'

Over tea, he asked about his friends Einstein, Eichenwald and Planck, and inquired about Lise's associate, Otto Hahn. For three hours they were lost in the question about whether the liberation of energy from the atomic nucleus was achievable in the next ten years. Finally, they relived events of the 1927 Solvay conference where Bohr and Einstein were "in the thick of it." The issue central to the discussion was the recently formulated 'uncertainty principle' that stated the velocity and location of an electron could not be measured simultaneously. One measurement always made the other measurement uncertain. Einstein refused to accept this idea repeating his famous quote, "God does not play dice." Lise and Bohr laughed as they recalled that at breakfast every morning, Einstein would make up a challenging theoretical problem to try to disprove the uncertainty principle, only to have Neils solve it by dinnertime.

"I had finally heard enough of the dice business and told Albert that he could not decide for God how to run the world," Neils laughed.

The Institute's annual Christmas party was held that evening in an enormous basement room. Inside, was an old, dry well originally intended to house spectrograph equipment. The well was covered with a large metal lid which served as a platform for the Christmas tree that had been decorated by the wives of the staff. The room was filled with scientists and their families as well as the staff of the

Institute. The gathering was made up of an exceptional group of physicists, several of whom would go on to become Nobel winners.

After refreshments of roast turkey and beer, Neils' oldest son Christian entered the room dressed as St. Nicholas and bearing gifts for all the children. Finally, Niels got up to review the accomplishments of the past year and to thank everyone for their hard work. Lise was lifted up in the joy of Christmas, at least for this one evening. She was happy to be away from the miasma that was Germany, and happier still to be with her dear friends.

Late Christmas Eve, Niels and Margrethe were able to be alone with Lise. Neils had avuncular warmth toward his colleagues and especially toward Lise. The three enjoyed after dinner cider and basked in the warmth of the fireplace. Lise sighed and looked around the room. She realized that she envied Margrethe and the life she enjoyed with her family in Denmark. Niels broke her reverie.

"Tell us about Berlin," he said quietly.

Most of the scientists at the KWI were not political and Lise was no exception. But virtually all of them were deeply concerned with events occurring in the government. Things seemed to be spiraling, like an out of control fire, bearing the potential to bring great destruction. Yet millions of people were becoming willing participants in the conflagration.

Lise tried to gather her thoughts before she spoke.

"I am afraid for the country," she finally said. "I am afraid for Einstein. I'm afraid of the Nazis. There is still wide spread unemployment and people are angry. The Nazis have gained strength with every election and now they control the legislature. Hitler has made Hermon Goering the Reichstag parliamentary chairman. Just five years ago this man was in a Swiss mental hospital. Now he's running the legislature? As if that is not enough, they are sowing seeds of political hatred. They are blatantly showing contempt for the rule of law. Those brown-shirted 'storm troopers' are nothing more than street thugs. They fight with the communists almost on a nightly basis."

"And what of Albert?" asked Margrethe.

"As we all know, Albert is an enigma. He dislikes publicity and yet he cannot help but create it. The Nationalists hate him and shout 'Jew science' when they see him in public. A group of right-wing activists rented the Philharmonic Hall to hear lectures against the 'Einstein hoax' and he showed up and taunted them! He is almost inviting trouble. Still, I know all of this hurts him. Someone in the crowd actually stood up and shouted "cut the throat of that dirty Jew." Otto and I continue our work and it is going well. But I can tell you that many people are going to leave the country if the Nazis come to power."

"So there is serious risk to his life?" asked Neils.

"Very much so. First of all, Albert is an outspoken pacifist. But the German people are in a violent mood. Another thing that concerns me is his involvement in Zionism....this is a subject that only stirs more anti-Semitism. You know he denounced his German citizenship once. And he'll do it again. He'll leave Germany."

Lise paused. "Dear God, he must leave Germany!"

Tears welled up in her eyes and she wiped them away. "I don't know what is to become of us."

Neils moved to the sofa where she sat and placed his massive arm around her. He knew they would have to put her on the train back to Germany in the morning. With all of his brilliance, he was at a loss as to how to help her.

The train was almost empty when Lise boarded. It was Christmas Day and few people were traveling. The 'uncertainty principle' formulated by Werner Heisenberg, stated that an observer could determine either the position or the velocity of an electron but never both simultaneously. Now she faced her own uncertainty. Although a converted Christian, Lise was Jewish. She knew her position at the KWI would not be secure if the Nazis came to power.

Lise was adept at fragmenting her thoughts. Rather than focusing on her fears, she forced herself to concentrate on her work. She was excited to have Leo Szilard, a Hungarian theoretical physicist, working with her for a year. James Chadwick at Cambridge had just discovered the neutron, another component of the atomic nucleus. It had the same mass as a proton but no electrical charge. Already those in the field of nuclear physics were considering using the neutron to unlock the massive energy of the atomic nucleus. In his mind, Szilard had worked out a scenario in which a neutron could be used to split an atomic nucleus, thus releasing other neutrons. They would in turn, split more nuclei, causing a chain reaction. This could result in a massive release of energy….a bomb; A bomb capable of causing mass destruction.

The leading physicists of the day were skeptical. Rutherford described harnessing nuclear energy as 'moonshine,' and Einstein compared it to shooting in the dark at scarce birds. Szilard, who was Jewish, also worried about the changing political landscape in Germany. He had discussed the problem with an old friend from Hungary, chemist Michail Polanyi. "The Germans are too civilized to let the Nazis do anything really stupid," said Polanyi.

But Szilard was not so sure.

Since the eclipse of 1919, when Einstein's theory of General Relativity was proven true, he had been catapulted into an orbit of fame experienced by few other men in history. At the time, Arthur Eddington was secretary of the Royal Astronomical Society. Along with E.T.Cottingham, he made eclipse observations on Principe Island. The veracity of the complex theory hinged on proof that light was "bent" by gravity. In this case the gravity of the sun. Following his return to England at a dinner of the Royal Society, Eddington shared his eclipse experience with a parody of the *Rubaiyat,* using the final verse.

The Clock no question makes of Fasts or Slows, But steadily and with a constant Rate it goes. And Lo! The clouds are parting and the Sun

A crescent glimmering on the screen- It shows! It shows!

Five minutes, not a moment left to waste, Five minutes, for the picture to be traced – The stars are shinning, and coronal light

Streams from the Orb of Darkness – Oh make haste!

For in and out, above, about, below

'Tis nothing but a magic Shadow show Played in a Box, whose Candle is the Sun Round which we phantom figures come and go.

Oh leave the Wise our measures to collate.

One thing at least is certain, LIGHT has WEIGHT One thing is certain, and the rest debate –

Light rays, when near the Sun, DO NOT GO STRAIGHT.

In the fall of 1932, Lise Meitner began seeing a crescendo of anti-Semitism and jealousy of Einstein. She was anxious to see him protected in some way and made an appointment to talk with him in his office. It was only a few days before he was to go to America's

Cal-Tech for a visiting professorship. All of the professional staff in the department referred to him as 'prof.' He was not only their leader and one of the great minds of modern science, but he was their mentor and friend. Lise pleaded her case.

"Prof...you know the Nazis are gaining strength. There is already so much jealousy of you. You surely understand that for some, you are a hated symbol and it is impossible for you to be above this battle."

While she was pouring her heart out to him, he stood up and began to search his pockets for something. First he tried the side pockets of his jacket, then his trousers. They were the pockets of a school boy, containing bits of string, wads of paper, and a pen knife, cookie crumbs, bits of tobacco dropped from his pipe, an old train ticket and finally a card with shredded edges. Written on the card was a verse of a poem by Bert Leston Taylor which had been given him by a friend. He read it aloud.

"When men are calling one another names and making faces, and all the world's a jangle and a jar, I meditate on interstellar space, and smoke a mild segar.'"

She buried her face in her hands and began to laugh. "You are impossible!"

He smiled at her.

"When do you think you and Otto will be ready to attempt bombarding a nucleus with neutrons?"

On his 50th birthday, in 1929, the Einsteins were presented a city-owned villa on the Havel River. It was to be known as the 'Einstein house' but the transfer of title never happened. Then he was promised a beautiful lakeside plot in the suburb of Caputh, near Potsdam, but that gift was also never received. There were clearly political factions working against anything that would bring honor to Germany's most famous citizen. Finally, Einstein bought the property himself and built a villa using his own savings. This was especially pleasing to his wife Elsa, because it gave her a sense of security. Now in the fall of 1932, the world travelers were off to his teaching fellowship at Cal-tech in Pasadena. Privately he was devastated by the 1932 election results showing the Nazis gaining power. Several months earlier, Elsa had been given information that he had been targeted for assassination, much like his friend Foreign Minister Walter Rathenau, 10 years earlier. Without the professor's knowledge, she hired private bodyguards for him. As their taxi pulled away from their villa, he told Elsa to turn around.

"Take a good look at our villa before we leave this time," he said. "Why?"

"Because it will be the last time you will see it!"

* * *

January is not the coldest winter month in Berlin, but it is usually the wettest. Anna Eichenwald knew this and always went out prepared with rain gear. Late Saturday afternoon, the first one in the new year, she found herself walking down Unter den Linden from her apartment to the main University campus. The street was crowded with trolley cars and traffic lights. In spite of this, Unter den Linden was a beautiful tree lined boulevard and Anna always enjoyed her walks. A cold mist was falling and she picked up her pace. She welcomed the break from the confinement of the hospital.

Anna was on her way to meet her friend, Lise Meitner. Despite the 20-year age difference, they had much in common. Both were exceptionally intelligent, loved music and believed politicians were fallacious. The two had met years earlier because Lise and Anna's father Hanz were colleagues at the physics institute. Every few months they managed to carve out time from their busy schedules to have dinner together. Tonight was special because both were invited to Anna's parents' home. Lise had taken a taxi from her apartment at the KWI to the University. Then they would walk together down Neue Friedrich Strasse, past the stock exchange to the townhouse of Hanz and Marlene Eichenwald.

Lise's taxi pulled up to the University administration building at almost the same time Anna was crossing the street to meet her.

"Anna!" Lise called out, in an uncharacteristically loud voice. After smiles and hugs, Anna took Lise's hand.

"How have you been? It's so good to see you."

"I'm well," said Lise. "And very rested! I spent Christmas with the Bohrs in Copenhagen and it was delightful. They are such wonderful people. What about you? How is the world of surgery?"

"Well, pretty much the same. It's definitely not for the faint hearted!"

The two were happy to be spending time together again; Anna because she had great admiration for this woman of science, and Lise because being with Anna seemed to take her back in time. With Anna, Lise could forget that she was 52-years old.

They slowed their pace as the cold mist put a refreshing coat of moisture on their faces. They needed this time to catch-up and break away from the tedium in their lives. It had been more than three months since their last visit.

The Eichenwald's townhouse was an old structure with character. It was a grey stone building with an elevated first floor. The stairway up from the street was framed with large Doric columns. A family crest carved from the same grey stone rested above the massive oak front doors. The building had been constructed in 1848 and the original owners had occupied it for almost 60 years. The Eichenwalds were the third owners of record. A three story home with a basement, the main living area was on the first floor with a bedroom and sitting room on the second floor. The top floor held a third bedroom and study. Each floor was built with a dark, rich oak, as was the massive stairway leading to the second level. The ceilings of the first level were 12 feet in height, giving the home a palatial feel.

Marlene was anxious to see her guests and opened the door before they had reached the top stair. Hanz was right behind her, entering the front room just as the two women did. There were warm greetings and a convivial atmosphere matched by the glow of a blazing fire in the large, front room. Hanz handed each woman a glass of brandy and received via Lise, greetings from their friend Niels Bohr. Hanz had always found it interesting that in the European physics 'club' there was indeed, competition - but no professional jealousy. The conversation remained light hearted throughout the evening. And even though it was still three months away, the upcoming concert of Arthur Schnabel, to repeat his cycle of thirty-two Beethoven Sonatas, was discussed at length. This was to be the first nationwide radio broadcast of a concert. Radio was new and had become wide spread in Germany. With the gradual improvement of the economy, there were hopes the Berlin Theater could be revived, although many stars like Greta Garbo had left Germany for the U. S. or England. The Theater offered great escape from pressures of work and life. These four would welcome it back to society.

In time, the mood of the evening became more somber. Hanz had little interest in politics, but he did have a deep devotion to his country and paid close attention to political news. After the dinner plates were cleared he moved his chair away from the table.

"The most recent moves by Chancellor Papen may prove to be disastrous," he said. Papen had dissolved the Reichstag and lifted the ban on the Nazi storm troopers. Hanz continued.

"I think it is possible the Nazis might try to take the government by force. They are desperate for power, and I do not believe they will be able to gain control democratically." He looked directly at the women.

"Hitler hates us. And he hates us only because we are Jews. In Mein Kampf, he wrote 'the personification of Satan as the symbol of all evil assumes the living shape of a Jew.'"

The weight of those words hung in the air. The group, gathered around the table, sat quietly and tried to absorb the impact of what it would mean for this maniac to be running their country. And yet thousands, possibly millions of Germans saw him as the person who would bring Germany back to prominence or even dominance in the world.

Lise asked a rhetorical question intended for Hanz. But she looked at Anna when she spoke.

"Would we all lose our appointments at the Institute?" Hanz' response was both sensible and laconic.

"All of the leading physicists at the KWI are Jews."

Hanz, now becoming a world leader in the field of quantum mechanics was unaware that the world's most original physicist had decided to leave German soil and would not return. Indeed, two months after this dinner at the Eichenwalds, Einstein renounced his German citizenship for a second and final time.

Beryl Nussbaum was a distinguished 80-year old Rabbi who had immigrated to Germany in 1901, the year Anna was born. Over the years she had spent at least a dozen afternoons with him after Synagogue discussing Jewish history. On several occasions she had asked about his understanding of the problem of anti-Semitism. Most of her life Anna had been sparred overt hostility, but she was well aware of what was lying just beneath the surface. She recalled with ease the stories the Rabbi had shared with her, beginning with the Torah and the Prophets.

"Rabbi Nussbaum always explained that the stories of our forefathers in the Torah center on our covenant relationship with God. Initially it was unconditional, between *Yahweh* (Jehovah) and our patriarch Abraham. God promised to make Abraham and his descendants a great nation. God directed Abraham to the land of Canaan, which today is modern Palestine, and said *'to your off-spring I will give this land.'* After our people were delivered from bondage in Egypt, they traveled to Canaan and remained there until 70 AD, when the Romans destroyed the Temple in Jerusalem. Hundreds of years earlier, Moses was assured by God that if our people remained faithful to him, we would be his 'treasured possession.' But we have not remained faithful and I fear that once again God will abandon us.

In the middle ages, through the influence of the Church, the Jews were expelled - first from England, then Normandy and finally France. But they flourished in Eastern Europe. This was especially true in Germany, a region of multiple sovereignties and one from which they could not be expelled. In the 18th and 19th centuries the Jews began once again to flourish. They became merchants, bankers, university graduates and leaders in academic society. Now it seems they could be, once again, subjects of extreme persecution."

Anna paused a moment, wondering if she should continue. But she was unable to do anything but pursue her thoughts.

"Rabbi Nussbaum stressed that in ancient Israel it was indisputable that God was almighty, perfectly just, and that no human was completely innocent in his sight. But there were many upright. Nonetheless some of the upright underwent suffering. Their suffering was not pleasing to God. In time, the people returned to their covenant relationship with God. So in a sense he used the suffering for the good of his people.

There were times when those who were governing the Jews attempted to destroy all copies of the Torah and the Prophets. Multiple times our people were taken into captivity and cut off from the Temple. During those times we turned back to God and Synagogue worship. During one of those times the prophet Jeremiah spoke for the Lord saying, '*I know the plans I have for you…plans to prosper you and give you a future. I will gather you from all the nations and places where I have banished you, and I will bring you back to the land which I promised you.'*"

Lise looked intently at Anna, her brow furroughed. Being a Christian, she saw the problem from a different perspective. She believed God was pursuing the Jewish people - not persecuting them; that God desired them to know him and trust him. She knew there were times when many of her people had turned their backs on Jehovah. She knew this because she was a Jew.

"These times may be difficult, extremely difficult. There is no way to predict what might happen. In the end our scholarship and positions of influence, important to this country, may not save us."

Marlene searched for the hand of her husband. She was thinking of their lives together, their exceptional daughter, and Hanz's academic influence in Europe. Their world could come crashing down simply because they were Jews. The room remained still. The only sound was the crackling of flames from the fireplace in the next room.

*   *   *

The intellectual giants of the universities, institutes and the arts had little or no understanding of the dark side of Berlin. Salka Jenschke was a Polish girl of 22, who had come to Berlin hoping to land a job in theater. She had come with enough money to live for a few weeks and was sure she could get some bit parts and hopefully be noticed by a producer or director. She was pretty in an ordinary sort of way. When she auditioned, she was noticed more for her figure than her acting abilities. As a result, by the end of her first two months she had no job, no money and no prospects. In desperation she became a topless waitress in a cabaret a block from the famous Aldon Hotel on Unter den Linden. It didn't take her long to overcome her anxiety over being bare breasted in front of leering strangers. She even began to realize she was being admired by both the men and some of the women escorting the men. Soon she realized she could earn much more than her wages in tips – so she registered as a prostitute. Salka was intelligent and made herself available at only certain times of the month, and only with men staying at the Hotel Aldon. Occasionally she would accompany a man and his female companion, but of course for more money.

A frequent visitor to the cabaret was a man named Karl Gropemann. He was a large man standing 6'4" with partial balding. He was soft spoken and had a kind face. Over a six month period he had asked Salka several times if she would accompany him to his apartment. She finally consented, breaking her own rule about the Aldon Hotel. Gropemann had been nothing but kind to her over the months and had given her numerous tips. She asked him to wait outside while she got dressed. In the dressing room her friend Heidi Denke was also getting dressed. When Heidi learned where Salka was going her smile faded.

"Be careful, Salka. Six months ago, a girl working here disappeared and was thought to have been involved with that man."

Salka began to have a foreboding feeling. She asked the club manager to inform Gropemann that she was feeling ill and would not be able to go with him. Gropemann only returned to the cabaret once after that and Salka was not working that night. About a year later Salka recognized his picture in the *Berliner Tagblatt*. A young woman was found murdered in his apartment after neighbors heard a commotion and screams. He was indicted and convicted of that crime and later linked to seven other murders of young women.

Later that year, Salka became romantically involved with a young man named Fritz Keppler. Fritz worked for a construction company. His wages were above average and soon she moved in with him and gave up the cabaret and prostitution. Unfortunately for both, they became involved with using and selling cocaine. These two young people with so much potential, so much promise, were consumed by the sewer of Berlin street life.

The political street violence was the direct result of the action by Chancellor Franz von Papen to lift the ban on the Sturmabteilung (Nazi Storm Troopers). Papen followed this by dissolving the Reichstag and finally dissolving the government of Prussia which contained 60 percent of the land mass of Germany and almost 70 percent of the population. This move was unprecedented in the history of the country and provided an avenue for the Nazis to gain control of Prussia, which they did. These events also allowed the Nazis to gain control of the national Reichstag in Berlin. The Nazis now held control of the majority of seats and the presiding chairman, the corpulent ex-pilot, Hermann Goering.

Hitler decided the time was right to take over the government. He traveled to Berlin for a meeting with General Kurt von Schleicher and President Hindenburg, now 85 years old. Accompanying Hitler was Ernst Rohm, who had been made head of the SA- Storm Troops. Rohm was a squat, ugly man whose face was scared from old war wounds. He was an active homosexual, a trait Hitler was willing to overlook for the time being. In the meeting, Hitler demanded he be made Chancellor. Only minutes later, Hindenburg dismissed the Nazis as though they were errand boys. He had an intense dislike of Rohm and later told General Schleicher in reference to Hitler that he might appoint 'that Bohemian corporal' as postmaster, but never Chancellor.

This enraged Hitler. His greatest fear was that he had lost his chance for power. To further confirm his fear, Papen resigned and General Schleicher was appointed the new Chancellor. His plan was to try to divide the Nazis and thus, significantly weaken them politically. Somehow Hitler was able to hold the party together. It was Christmas and most Germans preferred shopping to politics. The four weeks of Advent were peaceful as the streets were filled with the sounds of "Stille Nacht" and "O Tannanbaum." It was the calm before the storm.

In January, Chancellor Schleicher appeared to be at the height of power. He had the support of both the President and the military. The Nazi party was bankrupt and in despair. Hitler and his inner circle of Joseph Goebbels, Heinrich Himmler and Hermann Goring met nightly. They were anxious to be present for any opportunity, even an unexpected one. Ernst Rohm was not included in these gatherings because Hitler hated homosexuals and no longer trusted Rohm. Hitler and his cronies feared they would be forced to go through another round of elections at a time when the party was in debt thirty million marks (five million dollars). President Hindenburg had repeatedly stated that he would never appoint 'that Prussian misfit' as Chancellor of Germany. On the first day of January, 1933, Goebbels wrote in his diary, 'there are only dark days ahead, all chances and hopes have quite disappeared.'

By the 7th of January everything had changed. Former Chancellor Papen made a speech in Cologne urging the Nazis be included in any new government. A Cologne banker, Kurt von Schroder, arranged a meeting for Papen and Hitler with the underlying idea of overthrowing Chancellor Scheicher. Essential to Papen's plan was that he be made Co-Chancellor with Hitler, and Scheicher be dismissed from the war ministry. This was not Hitler's plan. He was determined to be the sole German Chancellor and told Papen he would settle for nothing less. Papen was still very close to the President and set off for the Presidential palace. There, he persuaded Hindenburg that the Nazis must be made a part of the government and that Hitler, as Chancellor, could be controlled.

By now Hindenburg had become weary of resisting. The following morning Hitler was summoned to the palace from his headquarters in the Kaiserhof Hotel across the street. As Hitler entered the Chancellery his staff, now including Rohm, watched intently from the fourth floor of the hotel. A large crowd began to gather in the street between the two buildings as they sensed that something important might be happening.

Joseph Goebbels later recorded in his diary, 'a few moments later, he is with us. He says nothing, and we all remain silent. His eyes are full of tears. It has come! The Fuhrer is appointed Chancellor!'

CHAPTER 8

Ernst Bishoff

January, 1933. It was the beginning of the final six months of surgical training for Dr. Anna Eichenwald. She was completing an exceptional time in her life and had been rewarded with an appointment to the teaching staff in the Department of Surgery at the University of Berlin. She would be doing what she loved in the city she loved. The time had passed quickly. She was now the administrative chief resident and was running the surgical service for both charity and private patients.

Monday, January 30th, was a clinic day, affording Anna the chance to leave the hospital a bit early. She left at 5:00 p.m. The weather was fairly mild for January, and she changed from her scrubs to a light woolen dress and gray rain slicker with her favorite red silk scarf. She stepped out onto Unter den Linden. The traffic was unusually heavy and became more so as she walked east toward her apartment. She was unaware that four hours earlier, Adolph Hitler had been appointed Chancellor of Germany.

After the radio broadcast of the ceremony, curious sightseers began jamming the area around the Brandenburg Gate. Newsreel trucks were parked up and down the wide boulevard and by evening, Nazi paramilitary formations composed of the storm troopers and newly formed SS were assembled for a full dress parade down Wilhelmstrasse into the old core of Berlin. The throng of well-wishers was not anticipated. It was later reported that close to one million Berliners took part in this extraordinary demonstration of allegiance to a party that promised a new Germany. Hitler observed the parade from his balcony in the Kaiserhof Hotel, already intoxicated with the power that had so suddenly been placed in his hands. Thousands of Germans brandished torches and formed a river of fire from the Tiergarten through the Brandenburg Gate where the 'goddess of victory' lashed her stone horses forward. The crowd sang with gusto as bands played and flags waved. One of the war-songs was "Siegreich Wollen wir Frank Reich Schlagen" - *We mean to defeat France*. Thousands were carried away with enthusiasm from the song which brought back to mind the Treaty of Versailles.

The next few weeks brought with it, almost daily acts of violence. The weekends were even more dangerous. The violence took place most often under the cover of darkness as the Nazis and Communists ambushed each other. It was also widespread in Dusseldorf, Hamburg, Munich, Mannheim and as far north as Kiel. Still, the majority of the people remained neutral, shocked and dismayed at what was taking place.

On February 1st, Anna received the sad news that her friend and classmate, Uri Avner had been killed in a riot in Mannheim. She recalled earlier times when they met in the museum coffee shop and remembered listening to his political rhetoric. She had not seen Uri for two years, but she was not surprised that he had gotten himself involved.

The Nazis were determined to remain in the public eye. Joseph Goebbels had been appointed the party chief for propaganda and took full advantage of the violence. A riot on February 2nd cost the lives of an SA officer named Maikowski and a policeman, Joseph Zaunitz. Three days later, an enormous state funeral was held for the two slain 'heroes' at the Berlin Cathedral. The service was attended by a number of dignitaries including Hitler, and was carried live on national radio. Outside, 40,000 SA and SS troops stood in cold drizzle. The funeral procession moved from the Cathedral along Unter den Linden, up Friedrichstrasse to the Invaliden Cemetery where the two were laid to rest next to two prominent 19th century generals, an honor that far exceeded their status in German military lore.

Ernst Bishoff was a 29-year old SS officer who had joined the Nazis four years previously. He was from Nuremberg, in Bavaria, and had come to Berlin with dreams of becoming a military officer. His political views were strongly anti-Marxist so he was attracted to the National Socialist German Worker's Party (NSDAP) where he first met Hitler. Bishoff was clearly Aryan, with blond hair and blue eyes. He was quiet but keenly observant. Hitler had taken an immediate liking to him and considered he might eventually be a suitable replacement for the undesirable head of the SA, Ernst Rohm. Hitler was scheduled to address the nation on February, 10th. The address was to be broadcast on national radio. The first radio station began broadcasting in 1923, and by 1933, most Germans had radios. Another of Goebbels ideas was to have the address broadcast by loudspeaker at the busiest intersections in Germany's 10 largest cities. Communists were still trying to thwart the Nazi momentum and had organized to try to disrupt the broadcasts. The address was to originate from the Sportplast at 6:00 p.m., a time slot designed to ensure it would reach the foot traffic on the streets, which peaked at that hour. Brown-shirted Nazis congregated throughout all of the areas in which the speakers were set up, tasked with keeping order and to demonstrate the competence of the new regime. More than 100 SA and SS personnel were in Berlin under the command of Ernst Bishoff. As commander, he was dressed in an all-black SS uniform with a red Swastika arm band. He stationed himself at the busiest intersection in Berlin.

Hitler began his address at 6:07 p.m. Thousands stood in rapt attention as he spoke. He focused on a national sense of purpose and his predictions of a 1,000 year Reich. The Communists desperately needed something to disrupt the speech. Suddenly a single shot was fired. The target was Bishoff who was hit in the chest. The force of the shot knocked him back several feet, and his comrades caught him as he fell. Screams, panic and confusion gripped the crowd. By the hundreds, people began ducking and running from the area. The gunman disappeared into the crowd despite the frantic search that followed. Bishoff was quickly placed in a Nazi sedan and was sped away for the 25 kilometer ride to the University Hospital.

Anna Eichenwald had experienced a quiet day. She had supervised two surgeries in the morning and clinic in the afternoon. As chief resident on call, she was available for emergencies and consultations requiring surgery. Anna rarely paid attention to political matters. But the events of the past two weeks were much on her mind. She had stopped by the emergency area to see if things were quiet before heading to the cafeteria and then her call room. As she was visiting with one of the nurses, Captain Bishoff was brought in on a stretcher. One of the SS officers was shouting,

"He's been shot! He's been shot!"

Anna followed the stretcher into the trauma room, along with two nurses and a junior resident. Bishoff's blood pressure was 80 systolic and his pulse was barely palpable. Anna grabbed a pair of bandage scissors and quickly cut off his uniform and underclothing.

"He's got a single entrance wound in the left anterior chest," she said aloud. "Get me a chest tube tray!"

Almost simultaneously she turned him on his right side to look for an exit wound. She could find none. She then felt his abdomen and quickly looked for any other areas of injury. He was becoming unresponsive but did have some spontaneous movement of his lower extremities. This told her that he likely did not have a spinal cord injury. She quickly prepped his left lateral chest and placed a chest tube with a trochar. Five hundred ml. of blood filled the vacuum bottle.

"Chest x-ray, stat!"

Anna turned to the junior resident.

"Call the OR and tell them we are coming up… then call your back-up."

Bishoff's pressure was still in the 80s with a weak, thready pulse. Anna turned to the nurse.

"Set up six units of matched blood and get three units of un-matched."

The anesthetist was now in the room and the chest x-ray completed. As Anna evaluated the film she saw something unexpected and disturbing. The film showed an expanded lung but a very large heart shadow, twice as large as would be expected.

"He's got a cardiac injury," she said to the anesthetist. "Let's take him up now or we're going to lose him."

The resident ran out to get the elevator. When Anna and the anesthetist got there with the captain, the elevator was waiting. The OR was on the fifth floor and the ride seemed like an eternity. The OR was ready and the patient was wheeled in with a pressure that had dropped to the 70s. Bishoff was quickly put to sleep and turned up at a 60-degree angle. The nurse prepped around the chest tube as Anna and the junior resident scrubbed. While scrubbing, Anna stuck her head in the door.

"Where is the blood? Get it!"

Just as she had said this, the blood arrived and one unit of unmatched was started in each arm. Anna and the resident gowned and gloved.

"Call my staff and tell him we have a GSW to the left chest," Anna yelled as she draped out the chest. "I'll call him when I get the chest open. Knife!"

Anna opened the chest through a left anterior-lateral thoracotomy. The pericardial sac around the heart was bulging and tense. As she opened the pericardium, blood exploded out of the sac. There was a tangential hole in the left ventricle that was actively bleeding. With each heartbeat, blood was forced out of the heart about 3 centimeters. Anna placed her left index finger over the hole to control the bleeding.

"Suture!"

She carefully placed three mattress sutures in the heart muscle to close the hole. As the resident controlled the bleeding she tied the sutures.

"Bleeding is controlled. How's his pressure?"

The blood pressure was up to 100. He was stabilizing. She inspected the chest cavity for any further injury or bleeding and found none. She then helped the resident close the chest and called her staff.

Anna glanced at the wall clock in the post-anesthesia area. It showed 10:55 p.m. Orders were written and he continued to look stable. But she decided to stay with him for a few hours in case of further problems. Another bleeding episode would likely be his last. He remained stable and Anna dozed off about 4:30 a.m. She woke up 20 minutes later and checked with the floor nurse. Then she was off for a shower and breakfast. She had a full day ahead.

That evening Anna finished rounds with the surgical team then swung by x-ray to check his film. It showed the lung fully expanded and a normal sized heart silhouette. She walked wearily by his room to find him sleeping and glanced at the chest tube bottle...no bleeding. Sensing someone in the room he opened his eyes.

With a faint smile Anna said, "Captain Bishoff, I'm Dr. Eichenwald, your surgeon."

* * *

Joseph Gobbels, though the smallest in stature of Hitler's lieutenants, was now the Fuhrer's 'attack dog.' As head of the Propaganda Ministry, he now had access to the state controlled radio network. He was a former broadcast journalist and had a keen interest in print media as well. Goebbels had a plan. The Nazis would gain control of Germany's almost 500 daily newspapers. Within the short time span of six months, they would control both the airwaves and the print media.

Now they needed a legitimate avenue for controlling the lives of ordinary German citizens. Gobbels provided that avenue on the night of February 27th, when SA storm troopers set fire to the Reichstag and blamed the arson on the Communists. There was outrage in the newspapers and in all the news accounts. The following day, because of this 'emergency,' Hitler produced a presidential decree that placed severe restrictions on personal liberties. These included the right of free expression, freedom of the press and the right of assembly. In a single day, with little understanding of the consequences, all German citizens lost their most basic, constitutional rights.

In the March elections, the Nazis garnered 52 percent of the vote. It was still far short of the two-thirds majority needed to alter the constitution. The legislature was now meeting in the Kroll-Opera House. The delegates were debating a statute known as the Alleviation of the People's and the Reich's Misery, otherwise called *The Enabling Law.* This law would permit the government to pass budgets, promulgate laws, alter the constitution, and essentially run the country without parliamentary approval. There were 81 Communist delegates in the Reichstag. All were placed under house arrest.

Following that event, new rules were adopted so that any member absent without excuse would be counted as present – thus a quorum could always be achieved. Uniformed SA and SS men then took up positions lining the hall, looming over the shoulders of the delegates who were not Nazis. The Enabling Law passed by 444 to 94 and representative democracy in Germany was gone.

The rule of law was now replaced by police terror. The new Enabling Law was quickly implemented by Wilhelm Frick, the Director of the Interior Ministry. On the 7th of April, he issued a decree that affected everyone employed by the civil service and educational system. The decree stated that every individual of non-Aryan origin was to be terminated.

The following month, Goebbels announced that German culture and politics would be united. He created the Reich Cultural Society. Artists, writers and performers would now be required to join the society in order to work, and non-Aryans were excluded from belonging.

Goebbels had an abiding hatred for most of his professors and the publishing houses who had refused to publish his novel

Michael. On May 11th, in the largest cities across the country, SA troops and bands of German youth raided libraries for the purpose of destroying books deemed 'not German' or 'tainted by Jews.' In all, some 200,000 volumes were burned. The bonfire in Berlin was on Unter den Linden between the Opera House and the University. Goebbels later proclaimed the following:

"The age of Jewish intellectualism has now ended, and the success of the German revolution has again given the German spirit the right of way. The past is lying in flames. The future will rise from the flames within our hearts..."

Somewhere in the pile of burning volumes was a book by poet Heinrich Heine who had once observed, "Where ever books are burned....in time, people are burned!"

*   *   *

Erin Nitschmann had exceeded even her own expectations as a violinist. This was her eighth year of performing with the Berlin Philharmonic, counting her time as an apprentice. She was a rising star in the concert world but still played second chair behind her father who remained concertmaster for the orchestra. Still very close to her family, she was encouraged to pursue her career in the concert world. For this reason, she was spending more time traveling, and had recently returned from a trip to the United States where she performed with the Philadelphia Orchestra.

It had been almost eight months since Erin had seen her best friend and old classmate, Anna Eichenwald. Erin's travel and Anna's call schedule had caused the cancellation or postponement of several of their efforts to get together. Finally, a time together was materializing. Erin had arranged for two tickets to hear Arthur Schnabal, who was repeating his earlier performances of the cycle of thirty-two

Beethoven Sonatas. This was the fourth in the series...the same series that Erin's mother Paula had attended several years earlier with her friend Kathe Kollwitz.

Erin and Anna met in the Tiergarten for an early dinner and planned to walk to the Metropel Theater for the concert. It was a beautiful spring evening, rather warm for mid- April. Anna was anxious to hear about Erin's travel to the U. S.

"Tell me about the trip, all the details...from the beginning!"

Erin covered the travel in detail, beginning with crossing the Atlantic. She described Philadelphia, her hotel, the concert and her host family.

"Anna, I must hear about your job," she said excitedly. "I can't wait any longer. Tell me everything!"

"I've accepted a position as a surgical instructor in the department starting July 1st. I'll have primary teaching responsibilities, which I like, and no research, which I don't like."

The two talked non-stop and ate very little. In the course of the evening, Erin shared that she had met a young man in Philadelphia.

"Who?" Anna demanded. "And how did you meet?"

Erin explained that David Natanson was the business manager for the Philadelphia Orchestra and his family was her host family. "What is he like, tall...short...how handsome is he?"

Erin smiled and replied, "Well, he is handsome and very funny."

The time had gotten away from them. On their walk to the concert, Erin shared a concern about her family. Arnold Schoenberg was a professor at the Academy of Music and a longtime friend of her father. He was working on an opera in Paris when he learned that he had been dismissed from the Academy and was told not to return to Germany. Erin also told Anna that her family was seriously considering leaving the country. They believed their positions with the symphony were no longer secure.

"Have you heard about the Reich Cultural Society?" she asked in a low voice. "All writers, artists and performers must belong, but Jews are excluded. If we stay, we will be forced out."

Anna processed this information as they headed into the concert hall. It was almost more than she was able to digest. She squeezed Erin's hand as the music began, then both young women, each gifted in their own right, were swept away by the sounds of Schnabal's performance. It was again, a flawless interpretation of Beethoven's sonata in E flat, Opus 81A, known as 'Les Adieux." It was an appropriate title. After that evening, Schnabal's performance schedule was abruptly cancelled by the Nazis.

Lise Meitner had always kept quiet about her Jewish heritage. She was not ashamed of it. In fact, as a 'Hebrew Christian' she took pride in her Jewish ancestry. But at the same time, she did not feel connected to Jewish tradition. When anti-Semitic sentiments were activated, she kept silent at first. But when Hitler moved to legalize anti-Semitism and abolish the civil rights of German Jews, she felt obligated to discuss the issue with her colleague Otto Hahn. One afternoon in early June, after he had returned from lecturing at Cornell in the U.S., Lise opened the conversation.

"You know, I am really Jewish. I don't want to be an embarrassment to you." He took her arm.

"Lise, you could never be an embarrassment to me no matter what happens. This so-called non-Aryan policy will cause many of our colleagues to leave. But I am going to do all in my power so you can stay. You are not just my associate...you are family to me."

Otto Hahn had become the director of the KWI when Einstein left. He knew only too well what might happen in the next few months. He also realized that political changes were out of his hands. By September, his fears were realized. Fully one-third of the KWI faculty was forced to emigrate. But for reasons that were not clear, nothing had been said to Hanz Eichenwald, and he decided to remain, along with Max Plank, who was not Jewish. Most of the others left, including Edward Teller and Leo Szilard. As for Lise Meitner, she was allowed to remain to do research but was not allowed to lecture at the University. Because she was an Austrian citizen and not German, she was allowed to continue her work with Hahn. She always suspected that he somehow intervened on her behalf. By the end of the year, some 1,600 scholars had left teaching positions in Germany. Several who left the KWI would go on to become Nobel winners.

The members of the 'physics club' took care of their own. Niels Bohr turned up in Hamburg. He was traveling throughout Germany to see who needed help. One individual rescued by Bohr was Otto Frisch, the nephew of Lise Meitner. Frisch was an extraordinary scientist with a genius for apparatus design and was working for Otto Stern on a cyclotron design. Stern, shocked to learn that Frisch was Jewish, simply said, "So am I," and the two left Germany together. Frisch had received a one-year Rockefeller Fellowship. But the fellowship was withdrawn because it was contingent on each scientist having a job at year's end. The crisis ended when Bohr came to the rescue.

"Come work with us," he said to Frisch. "We like people who can carry out thoughtful experiments."

Three months later, tragedy struck the Bohr family. Niels was sailing with his eldest son Christian and two friends. They were on the Oresund, the sea passage between Sweden and Denmark. With little warning a squall blew up placing their sloop in very rough seas. Eighteen-year-old Christian was swept overboard. They circled the area as long as there was light, but the seas remained stormy and the water cold. Lise Meitner received the news by cablegram. When she read it, she sat down and wept. It had been only nine months since her Christmas with the Bohrs. Just as Niels Bohr had felt powerless to help her with the Nazi pogrom, she now felt helpless to alleviate their grief. The next day she sat down to try to express her feelings. She wrote the following words:

"Through deep and rushing waters with my Savior, mid firey flames he walks just at my side;

I'm welcomed and counted in his favor, behind me lies the world and foolish pride.

I feel the Spirit's breath upon my shoulder, a caring touch to wipe a tear stained face;

He sheds his light to make my faith grow bolder, amazing love to share with me his grace.

Her cable was sent the next day. Bohr retreated for a while into his grief, but found healing in his efforts to help those who had lost their work and homes.

Kathe Kollwitz received a call from her longtime friend, Paula Nitschmann. They had a number of things in common, including a love of music and sons named Peter, both who had fought in the Great War. Many months had gone by since their last visit. Paula asked Kathe if they could meet for lunch.

It was September and the Nitschmanns were busy rehearsing with the Berlin Philharmonic for the fall concert season. The two friends agreed to meet on Saturday at the Romanische Café across from the Kaiser Wilhelm Memorial Church. Paula was a few minutes early and stood to greet Kathe as she walked into the enormous entry hall. They requested an upstairs table for more privacy and began to review some of their times together. The last was a concert, the debut of the 13-year old prodigy, Yehudi Menuhin, playing concerti of Bach, Beethoven and Brahms.

After placing their orders, Paula lowered her voice.

"Kathe, I'm so happy to see you. And I have to tell you that we are leaving Germany next week. Isaac has found a teaching position at the London Conservatory of Music and Erin is going to America to join the Philadelphia Orchestra."

Kathe looked away briefly.

"Paula, that's wonderful…when did you decide? And how can I help you?" "Last spring, we could see there was no future for us here. In fact, we know we will be dismissed from the orchestra. It's just a matter of time. Isaac is excited to be teaching rather than performing. And America will give Erin the opportunity she deserves in the concert world. Our lives will change. We no longer have a country. But we have work and we will be safe."

Kathe smiled back at Paula.

"You know how much I love you, Paula, and how much I admire you. I will always be grateful for our friendship. I don't think I could have survived losing my son without your support. I mean that. I will miss you more than you know. As for myself, I'm going to explore how I can get to London in the next year or so. Promise you will write and let me know how you are. I promise I will stay in touch too."

They finished lunch and said their good-byes. They smiled as they parted. The smiles served to veil the unspoken thoughts of each woman – thoughts that this could be their last time together.

*   *   *

For most German citizens the early years of Nazi control were orderly and tranquil. By the summer of 1933, there was no organized resistance to the new government. The Communist Party had been outlawed and there were no more street riots. Unemployment was dramatically down as the world began to pull out of the Great Depression. For the first time since the war's end in 1918, there seemed to be order in the land. Everyday German life was significantly improved, not only financially, but also by the new Nazi program, Kraftdurch Freude - Strength through Joy. It allowed, for the first time, extended holidays of one to two weeks for ordinary citizens. The goal was to improve productivity. The KdF program organized trips to Naples, the Alps, Spain and Norway. It brought large profits to the state railway system as well as rural hotels. This helped the German people to overlook the fact that they had lost their constitutional freedoms. The Enabling Law gave Hitler dictatorial power to run – or ruin - the country. Since the print media was controlled by the Nazis, there was no avenue to challenge his actions. Also, information kept from German citizens was the five year plan to re-build the German 'war-machine.' There could be no objection to activities by the government being kept from the people. To the average German, 'Strength through Joy' was proof that the Nazi goal of increased prosperity and abolition of class status was working.

But there was a dark side to this new moon. The National Socialists, with their newly acquired power, quickly moved to settle old scores with political opponents and Jews. On the first day of April, a nation-wide boycott of all Jewish businesses was held. This was only the beginning. In May, a prison camp had been opened in the suburb of Munich. It would later be known as Dachau. The concentration camp was located in an old power plant with a capacity of 5,000. Any man considered an enemy of the state could be sent there. Offenders included criminals, gypsies, Jews, homosexuals, and communists. The camp was run by a former mental patient, Theodor Eicke, and quickly evolved into a place of licensed brutality. Minor infractions resulted in solitary confinement. Hanging was the consequence for those who committed acts of major disobedience or those held for political reasons. The 'rules' and the consequences for breaking the rules evolved daily, routinely invented by guards. Obedience was impossible.

If and when released, inmates were required to sign a pledge of silence. They were forbidden to discuss prisoner treatment. The penalty was re-incarceration. In spite of the fact that Germans were aware that opposition to the regime resulted in imprisonment, most saw the practice as a means to restore order and voiced no objections.

The following year in April, SA/Storm Troopers numbered some 300,000. They were loyal to their Commander, Ernst Rhom, and a number of high ranking Nazi officials including Heinrich Himmler, Commander of the SS, felt that Rohm had become too powerful. He and others convinced Hitler that Rohm planned to betray him. And in fact, Rhom had aligned himself with Gregor Strasser, the former director of the Berlin segment of the party. Strasser remained a socialist and wanted to lead a workers revolution, something anti-thetical to the goals of the Nazi party. Hitler's solution was to turn violent. In early June he ordered a purge. It became known as the

'Night of Long Knives.' Rohm was arrested and Hitler ordered that he be given a pistol to end his own life. Rohm refused. "If I am to be killed, let Hitler do it himself."

Rohm was stripped to the waist and two SS officers emptied their revolvers into his chest. In all, 150 'enemies of the state' were eliminated. Other scores were settled as well. Goring was jealous of the rank and influence of General and former Chancellor Kurt von Schleicher, so the retired General and his wife were shot. Finally Gregor Strasser was imprisoned and murdered in jail. Within days, the Reich Minister of the Interior, Wilhelm Frick, framed a law that declared the murders 'legal.' Hitler declared the matter closed with the chilling words:

"In this hour I was responsible for the fate of the German people, and therefore I became the Supreme Justice of the German people....Everyone must know that in all future time if he raises his hand to strike at the state, then certain death will be his lot."

Hitler's rise to power was one of modern history's remarkable stories. In 1928, the retiring British Ambassador to Germany finished his memoirs titled...The Diary of an Ambassador. A series of historical notes were added by Maurice Gerothwohl, diplomatic correspondent of the *London Daily Telegraph*. His footnote about Herr Hitler was as follows:

"Rose to notoriety in 1922 shortly before the Mussolini coup d'etat in Italy...founded the so-called German National Socialist Workmen's Party. Concentrated on exploiting the Semitic and Bolshevik bogies...in the autumn of 1923 he joined with General von Ludendorff in leading the insurrection in Bavaria, but after a temporary escape, was arrested...he was finally released after six

months and bound over for the rest of his sentence, thereafter fading into oblivion."

By 1933, millions of Germans believed in Adolph Hitler. History would show him to be semi-literate and incompetent, a man who had failed at everything he had attempted save his time in the military when he was a dispatch runner. He did not possess the skills and intelligence to run a country. But he had an uncanny ability to persuade his country. More than anyone, he believed in his own myth. And he managed to convey his power utterly. On one occasion, when told by an assistant that he was mistaken, Hitler bluntly answered, "I cannot be mistaken…what I do and say is historical."

CHAPTER 9

Exodus

By now, Anna had settled nicely into her position. She had lecture assignments for senior medical students and was running the monthly morbidity-mortality conference for the surgical house staff. Anna felt like a bird that had been let out of her cage. She was also pleased that Christian Engel, one of her favorite people and a surgical colleague, had been added to the staff. Still, she remained concerned about the political turmoil surrounding her, and more directly with the upcoming move of her best friend, Erin Nitschmann. They had known each other since they were both seven years old and had started Hebrew school together.

The Nitschmanns were cautiously developing their plans to emigrate. There had already been a one-day boycott of Jewish businesses and a few Jewish men were being detained for reasons that were unclear. But the Nitschmanns had something in their favor; Erin and her parents occasionally traveled to perform outside of Germany. Their passports and travel documents were in order.

The plan was to leave on a Friday evening after rehearsal and take only clothing they could pack. Erin had arranged to see Anna at her apartment the evening before their departure. The next evening they would board the train for France, catch a ferry and cross the English Channel. Anna knew this. For their last evening together, she prepared sandwiches and a pot of tea and waited for her friend to arrive for what could be their last visit together for some time.

Erin showed up with her usual smile and an appetite. The conversation was light hearted and filled with laugher as they recalled their early years together - playing 'dress-up' and devising pranks to play on Erin's older brother, Peter. One memorable day during high school biology class they chased a hamster in the school hallway for half an hour.

"Erin, you would never touch your frog! I had to do all of your dissection." "And that's when I decided you were going to become a frog doctor," Erin laughed.

They lost track of time as good friends do. Finally, it was time for Erin to go. They two wrapped their arms around each other and could not stifle their tears.

"Anna, God will take care of you. I have prayed that he will keep you safe." Anna couldn't speak. She knew the bond they had formed was a tightly wound mix of history, friendship, trust and deep love. Time and separation would never break it.

Erin's taxi pulled up.

"I love you, Anna" she said quickly. "And I love you."

Anna watched from the window as the taxi pulled away. From the back of the vehicle, Erin stared up at the building searching for her friend. The silhouette of Anna's face disappeared into the night.

The following Saturday, Anna joined her parents for lunch at their home after Synagogue. She hoped to speak with her father about any plans he might have to deal with the political situation. She knew that many prominent members of his department had left, but he had decided to stay. Most Jewish lawyers had already been disbarred and many Jewish physicians had been dismissed from their hospital appointments. So far, no one had approached Anna about her position at the University. She had learned of the sad case of Heinz Moral, a Professor at the School of Dentistry. When he was dismissed from his teaching position, he committed suicide.

Anna's mother brought her a cup of tea. She thanked her and looked back at her father. She wanted to tell him about her experience after the surgery on the SS officer. "Do you remember the soldier who had the gunshot wound to the heart?" "Yes. Wasn't that in January or February?"

Anna nodded.

"He had a critical injury with bleeding into the pericardial sac around his heart. He was near death but came through the surgery and had an uneventful recovery. The day he was discharged something odd happened. I got a call that afternoon to come to his floor. When I got there, two men in uniform were standing over by the nurse's station. Dad, one of them was Hitler. I was stunned. He didn't extend his hand but he said he wanted to thank me for saving his comrade's life. He didn't have any expression on his face...it was like he was looking through me. Then he just said, 'you may go' as if I was one of his officers. The whole thing was bizarre." "What do you make of it?" her father asked.

"I don't really know. I think he wanted to see me...to see if I was a real person. But it was frightening...he was frightening...just staring at me."

Her father said nothing.

"So you have not been contacted by anyone about your teaching and research position?" she asked. "I know that Lise was told she could no longer lecture but could continue her research with Dr. Hahn."

"I have not been contacted by anyone, nor has Otto Hahn. It's almost as if I have been singled out as the one Jewish physicist they want to keep."

Hanz, like every Jewish professional, was deeply troubled by what was happening. But he felt relief that Lise was being allowed to stay and that he was able to continue his association with his friend and mentor, Max Planck. His decision was courageous given the fact that so many Jewish people were being excluded from the fabric of German society. This government position was codified with the passing of the Nuremberg Laws, also known as the Law for the Protection of German Blood and Honor. Under this statute, Jews fortified their citizenship, becoming 'state subjects' and were prohibited from marrying or having sexual relations with non-Jews. In spite of these egregious laws, Hanz felt that Jews had no future anywhere in Europe. He also did not believe the ancient Hebrew concept that a person's suffering reflected his guilt in the eyes of God. This made no sense to him.

One thing Hanz did appreciate was that there seemed to be no racial machination within the physics community. It was true that most, but not all of the members in the 'physics club' were Jewish. The subject of race had never come up and he could not remember ever having thought about it. Social issues were simply not discussed. Their focus was on science, such as the atomic nucleus and neutron bombardment of that nucleus. Bohr's concept was that neutrons and protons were so closely packed that the nucleus would simply absorb any energy from bombardment. So he had no enthusiasm for tapping into that potentially enormous source of nuclear energy. Bohr's close friend and colleague, Ernest Rutherford agreed and had called the idea "moonshine." Hanz was not so certain. He was closely watching the progress of Lise Meitner and Otto Hahn, who were delving into the complexities of uranium, the heaviest of all naturally occurring elements. It had been discovered late in the 18th century by a German chemist and was named after the then newly discovered planet, Uranus. Most uranium existed in the isotope form U-238, but a very small amount occurred as the isotope U-235, which seemed to be the form of uranium that could most likely be used in energy production. Hanz and other physicists were intrigued with the concept because of Einstein's formula $E = mc2$, which stated that a very small mass could be converted to an enormous amount of energy.

During the course of the pursuit of uranium bombardment, Lise Meitner's status changed. In July, 1936, an agreement was reached between Austria and Germany. Germany would not interfere in Austrian affairs and in return, Austria would acknowledge being a 'German State.' Using backdoor diplomacy, Hitler gained assurances from Britain and Italy that they also would not oppose peaceful alternatives to the status of Austria. Then on February 12, 1938, a face to face meeting between Hitler and Austrian Chancellor Schuschnigg provided the fireworks and intimidation that led to Germany's total annexation of Austria. After exchanging pleasantries, Hitler began screaming at the Chancellor.

"I have a historic mission and I am going to fulfill it because Providence has appointed me to do so," he cried. "You certainly aren't going to believe that you can delay me by so much as half an hour. Who knows? Perhaps I'll turn up in Vienna overnight like a spring storm. Then you'll see something."

The next day as the Chancellor was considering his position, Hitler began to mobilize troops along the Austrian border and the annexation was accomplished. This meant that like every Austrian, Lise Meitner was no longer considered an Austrian citizen. She was now German and the German anti-Semitic laws applied to her. She was trapped.

Max von Laue, a theoretical physicist and friend of Lise's, had heard that Heinrich Himmler, head of the SS, had issued a decree forbidding any further emigration of academic faculty. Von Laue contacted Lise who quickly concluded that she would soon lose her research position at the KWI and be vulnerable to the Nazis. She contacted colleagues in Holland for help. Her Austrian passport was now just a souvenir. If she left, it would be with no valid visa or passport. Her Dutch colleagues were able to persuade the government of Holland to accept her without documents.

On July 16th, Dirk Coster, a Dutch colleague, traveled to Berlin to help her. She told friends she was going on holiday. Only Otto Hahn knew the truth. The two men spent that night helping her pack. Hahn gave her a very valuable diamond ring he had inherited from his mother for her to use in the event she would need it. On Saturday morning she boarded the train with Coster. She was beginning to feel more comfortable until the train approached the border. At that point, Nazi military officials began checking all travel documents. Her invalid Austrian passport was taken. For 20 terrifying minutes, Lise sat frozen in her seat, her heart pounding in her chest. She was certain she would be arrested. Then suddenly an official approached her and handed the passport to her without a word. A few minutes later, the train passed into Holland and safety.

Lise traveled to Copenhagen the following day for an emotional reunion with the Bohrs. Niels Bohr had found her a position in Stockholm and a Nobel foundation grant to support her.

Three years before Lise left, a young German chemist named Fritz Strassmann had joined their team at the KWI. Now it was left to the two men to sort out all of the substances which might come from the bombardment of uranium. Hanz Eichenwald would also be involved as a technical consultant. Hahn tried to keep in touch with Lise about the work. She was safe, but in a strange country with a strange language. She had become depressed. A marvelous scientist who had spent more than 20 years working with Hahn, Lise was now alone.

In his letter, dated December 19, 1938, Hahn related that he and Strassmann were spending sixteen-hour days in the lab. They were seeing something 'very strange' in the way of results. The substances from the uranium bombardment were expected to be isotopes of radium but had the characteristics of barium.

Lise spent Christmas with her nephew, Otto Frisch, in the Swedish village of Kurgalv. He was working with Bohr in Copenhagen and took the ferry to Sweden. He was close to his aunt, especially since they both worked in the same field of nuclear physics. They discussed at length, the unusual results being reported by Hahn. On the day before Christmas, she and Frisch continued to discuss the 'problem' even though they were on holiday. If the large uranium nucleus were split into two smaller nuclei, combined, they would weigh less than the original one uranium nucleus. The 'lost mass' would be changed to energy. Lise had the packing fractions in her head and calculated the expected amount of released energy. They also determined that for every neutron absorbed, at least two neutrons were released.

Lise turned to her nephew suddenly.

"Otto, they have split the atom! Hahn and Strassmann have split the uranium nucleus and they don't know it!"

This incredible breakthrough in nuclear physics was not the only thing to celebrate. Two months previously, a German diplomat in Paris was killed by a Jewish teen and violent rioting in Germany had resulted. Thousands of Jewish men were arrested, and among them was Otto Frisch's father. After returning to Copenhagen the first week in January, Frisch received a cablegram that his father had been released unharmed.

Lise Meitner – theoretical physicist who worked with Otto Hahn on nuclear fission. – sketch by Delia Hunt

CHAPTER 10

Kristallnacht

In March of 1935, the dominos would begin to fall for Europe and its millions of Jewish citizens. Under the Treaty of Versailles, Germany was forbidden to build a military of more than 100,000 men and also prohibited from having a General Staff. Joseph Gobbels, head of the Nazi Propaganda Ministry, had been admonished never to allow the term "General Staff" to appear in print. But Germany was building a substantial Army as well as a Navy and an Air Force. Hitler gambled that Britain and France would not interfere. On March 16th, he announced a law establishing universal military service that would build a peacetime force of roughly half a million men. His gamble paid off. Britain and France protested with diplomatic posturing but took no action. The Versailles Treaty was dead. The following day, Sunday, there was great rejoicing across the country. Most Germans felt their honor had been restored. Two months later the Fuehrer followed up with a speech to the Reichstag assuring the world that the German people wanted only peace and understanding based on justice for all.

At the end of World War I, a segment of German territory on the French border had been set up as a neutral demilitarized zone. This was done under an agreement called the Locarno Treaty. Now, twenty years later, France was divided by internal strife. Hitler deemed the French government to be impotent and seized the moment, brazenly moving troops into the neutral zone. Simultaneously, he made new proposals for peace. After this, he calmly declared that the Locarno Treaty was now invalid. By international law the French had every right to retaliate against the Germans, and Britain was obligated by treaty to support her. But both countries shied away from the risk of hostilities.

It was a bold move by Hitler to parade three German battalions across the Rhine River bridges, and one that changed the strategic situation in Europe. But Hitler and Winston Churchill seemed to be the only two paying attention. For France, this was the beginning of the end. France possessed military superiority but would not stand up to German aggression. Later in the year, Hitler invited the Italians to join him, declaring privately to Mussolini that together they would conquer Europe, including England. In a speech in Milan in October, 1936, The Duce, as he was known, declared that Italy and Germany were the "Axis" around which the other European countries would revolve. England, France, nor the German people realized that Hitler's singular goal was to prepare for yet another war.

November 5, 1937, was a watershed moment for the Nazi Third Reich. A meeting was held in the nerve center of the Reich in the Wilhelmstrasse in Berlin. Attending were six important individuals: Field Marshal von Blumberg, Commander-in-Chief of the Armed Forces; General Baron von Fritsch, Commander-in-Chief of the Army; Admiral Dr. Raeder, Commander-in-Chief of the Navy; General Hermann Goering, Commander- in-Chief of the Air Force; Baron von Neurath, Foreign Minister, and Colonel Hessbach, adjutant to the Fuehrer. The meeting lasted just over four hours. As that fateful day darkened, Hitler made it clear to those in attendance that he had made an irrevocable decision. His goal - to persevere, make secure, and enlarge the German Aryan Race. It would be done in the heart of Europe, and it would be done with violent military aggression.

There was dissent from three of the commanders, but their objections were unrelated to the immorality of the plan. Their concern was that the military was unprepared. Within three months the three commanders were replaced. Early in 1938, the bloodless annexation of Austria occurred, an event viewed as a 'family affair' by its neighboring countries. Austria was strategic to the Hitler war plan. Now the German military flanked Czechoslovakia on three sides, and Vienna, the communication and trading center for Central Europe, was in German hands – all without a shot being fired. Perhaps more important to Hitler was the demonstration once again that Britain and France did not have the will to oppose him.

* * *

On the first of January 1939, most notables in the world of physics were trying to grasp what Otto Hahn had accomplished, including Hahn himself. Lise Meitner and her nephew Otto Frisch had calculated the energy release from splitting a uranium atom to be about 200 million electron volts. They now had a better understanding of the energies involved, but the physics were still murky. Then on January 3rd, Frisch returned to Copenhagen. He explained the findings to Bohr, who struck his forehead.

"What idiots we have all been! This is wonderful. This is as it should be!"

A few days later, Frisch was describing his findings to an American biologist named William Arnold who was visiting Copenhagen for a year on a Rockefeller Fellowship.

"What do you call the process of one bacterium dividing into two?" Frisch asked Arnold.

"Binary fission," Arnold replied.

"Could you call this process of dividing uranium nucleus fission?" "Of course!" Arnold said, smiling.

Later that month Meitner and her nephew published two papers in *Nature* on the disintegration of uranium by nuclear bombardment. The term "fission" was used in both articles.

Amid the excitement of this discovery, a number of the world's most gifted physicists were leaving Europe because of the political unrest. Two of the most gifted were Szilard, the Hungarian who had worked in Berlin, and Enrico Fermi of Italy, whose wife Laura was Jewish. Both men were concerned that the potential for a nuclear weapon should be kept secret from the Germans. However, Fermi's concern did not rise to the level of Szilard's.

At this time, many of the scientists were headed to the Washington Conference on Theoretical Physics, a conference patterned after Bohr's annual meeting in Copenhagen. Szilard, Fermi, Teller and a number of others were preparing to take new jobs in the U.S. Fermi's 1938 Nobel prize money had provided financial security for their move.

"We have founded the American branch of the Fermi family," he laughingly told his wife.

Initially, there was elation within the world of physics. They had discovered what might be an endless source of energy. But the elation was short-lived. The dominos were falling in Germany. For the millions of Jewish citizens of Europe, it began with the sound of breaking glass – *Kristallnacht*.

On November 7, a 17-year old German Jewish refugee in Paris shot and killed Ernst von Rath, the third secretary of the German Embassy. The teen's father had been among the 10,000 Jews deported to Poland in box cars the previous week. Two days after the shooting, Goebbels issued instructions for "spontaneous demonstrations" to be carried out in the night. And it was indeed, a night of horror. Throughout Germany, 119 synagogues were set on fire along with Jewish homes and businesses. Men, women and children were shot trying to escape the flames. Thousands were arrested. There were cases of rape, crimes considered more egregious than murder, as they violated the Nuremberg racial laws forbidding sexual relations between German Aryans and Jews. By the time the sun came up, 800 Jewish businesses were destroyed and several thousand damaged. The cataclysm of November 9th was further multiplied when Hermann Goering met with a dozen cabinet ministers and determined that the State would confiscate all the insurance monies owed to the Jews for damages, and levy a collective fine of one billion marks for "the abominable crimes."

Thousands of men and some women were taken to the concentration camps. Most spent the night standing on the parade grounds. They were stripped of all clothing and their heads shaved. They were then dressed in blue and white striped jump suits. Many were assaulted by SS guards and those who struck back were beaten senseless. Deaths were officially listed in the records as suicides. Trips to the latrines could be fatal. Some who fell into the three meter deep pits could not get out and died in the excrement.

There was significant international condemnation of the Nazi pogrom. The American ambassador was recalled from Berlin. But the reality was that the civilized world was generally indifferent to these Jewish problems. Most countries had highly restrictive Jewish immigration laws and humanitarian rhetoric did not alter that fact.

By now, Germany's Jews were living on nerves. They were officially banned from public schools and universities and forbidden from practicing trades or owning shops. Isolated in their homes, they would hurry along the streets, not bothering to rest on the segregated park benches painted yellow to ensure that only non-Aryans sat on them. The Nazi goal at this stage was forced immigration. But the 500,000 German and Austrian Jews remained highly vulnerable. Immigration as a solution could turn at any time to extermination.

Anna Eichenwald was keenly aware of what was happening around her. She had no call obligation for the last week-end in January and planned to spend the afternoon after Synagogue with her parents. She had been involved with the care of some of the victims of the murderous violence of Kristallnacht, and felt that she must be certain that her parents understood the gravity of the situation.

Anna and Christian were quietly devising a plan that would keep her from being trapped by the Gestapo. They had deliberately kept their romance a secret. Only Anna's secretary, Theresa Schmidt was aware of it. Anna had yet to share her secret even with her parents.

To the Eichenwalds, Anna was magic. They could not look at her without being struck by her beauty, her intelligence and her grace. Time and again, she surprised them. Given the temerity with which she accomplished her goals and her oblivion at what others would perceive as challenges, the Eichenwalds were not surprised that she had become the rising star of the University Surgical Department.

Optimistic themselves, the Eichenwalds had passed on to Anna an unwavering hope. Even during the onset of the political turmoil, the Eichenwalds had remained calm and positive, watching her successful endeavors with pride. She had a golden touch and was clearly admired and noted for her abilities. They were proud of her. They believed in her future, until the Night of Broken Glass. At dawn, the Eichenwalds looked out upon the crystal drops that littered the streets of Germany. They saw in those tiny shards, a reflection of the future of the Jewish people.

"I think it is over," Hanz whispered from the window. "I think my daughter's future...."

From behind him, his wife reached up to touch his mouth. "Don't say it, Hanz."

The two stood quietly together. They had given their daughter hope. And it was being stolen from her. Anna, the young girl who carried sunshine with her, the one whose smile could light the dark, whose hands could heal the sick – had one great mark against her – she was Jewish.

Late in the afternoon, Anna went to see her parents. As though nothing in the world had happened, Marlene poured tea and the three sat comfortably in the main room of the townhouse. Then Anna did something uncharacteristic. She scribbled words on a piece of paper and handed it to her parents.

Is your home secure? Are you sure there are no listening devices?

Hans read the note and looked at his daughter.

"I have had an engineer from the Institute come and look over the house. He believes it is clean."

"Good," said Anna. "I actually considered meeting you in a public place. But I wanted to come here. I just wasn't sure if it was safe. I need to share some things with you...things that have happened in the last few months."

"Well?" asked her mother with a smile.

"Well…I'm in love! Actually, love may not be the best choice of words…I am committed and irreversibly bound to Christian Engel."

"Anna! Is he Dr. Engel, the one we met last year?" asked Marlene. "He's the one."

Anna smiled and felt herself blushing. She felt suddenly giddy and silly. Here she was at 37 years old acting like a little school girl.

"Anna, this is wonderful for you. But…he isn't Jewish, is he?" Anna took a deep breath.

"No, mother. But I didn't exactly plan this."

Marlene smiled and glanced at Hanz. This was bringing back memories of their early years when Hanz began courting her as a teen. Hanz decided it was time to speak, despite the fact that he didn't like the subject. "Anna…it's against the law. Who knows about this?"

"Nobody. We are extremely cautious. Our call schedules and long hours in the hospital give us time together. We have not spoken of marriage. We know it is impossible with all that is going on…but possible maybe someday. We take each day as a gift. Soon we will be separated."

"What do you mean, separated?" asked Marlene. "Let me finish."

Anna sat back in her chair.

"May I have a little more tea? I want to talk about Christian. But first, I have to talk about something else. I need to explain about the Eugenics meeting. The Nazis are beginning a program of medical experimentation for the military. I can't go into detail but I will tell you that it's barbaric and completely immoral. I will not do it. The other program is just as bad but I won't be involved in that either.

The Reich Criminal Office and The Law for Prevention of Progeny with Hereditary Diseases are involved. They have classified certain individuals as 'asocial.' It's a catch-all term that can mean anything from beggars to gypsies or homosexuals and even the mentally ill, or anyone with an inherited defect. Large numbers of children are being involved. There is a three physician panel for review. Each case is scored with colors. Red for death, blue for survival, and white for further assessment. Most children get red. The defective children, like those with Downs Syndrome or some with just physical defects like a club foot are sent to camps. Then one by one they are selected for 'immunization.' The children who are immunized..."

Anna closed her mouth and shut her eyes tightly. The tears fell as she spoke again.

"They are never seen again."

She opened her eyes and looked at her mother. Marlene was gazing down at the floor with a bewildered expression. Hanz fixed his eyes on Anna. It was worse than he had thought. He was trying to imagine the torment his daughter was enduring.

"The program also includes adults who are considered defective," Anna went on. "I have met a retired physician from Stuttgart who had a grown daughter with epilepsy. She was sent to an asylum. He fully understood that his daughter had been selected out for extermination. He tried to have her removed from the list and she was removed. But not in time. He brought me her last letter."

She reached into her bag and brought out an envelope, then unfolded the pages and began to read.

Dearest beloved Father,

Unfortunately it cannot be otherwise. Today I must write these words of farewell as I leave this earthly life for an eternal home. This will cause you much, much heartache. But think that I must die as a martyr and that this is not happening without the will of my heavenly redeemer, for whom I have longed for many years. Father, good Father, I do not want to part from you without asking you and all my dear brothers and sisters once more for forgiveness, for all that I have failed you in throughout my entire life. May the dear Lord God accept my illness and this sacrifice as a penance for this.

I embrace you with undying love and with the firm promise I made when we last said our goodbyes, which I will persevere with fortitude.

Your child Helene.

On 2 October 1940. Please pray a lot for the peace of my soul. See you again, good Father, in heaven.'

Anna folded the letter and carefully replaced it in her bag.

"I have been made aware of the diabolical procedures to rid society of these people. They are placed into the hands of uncaring people and transported to extermination centers. They are then shepherded through rehearsed procedures that result in their being locked into hermetically sealed gas chambers disguised as showers. Some are even given bars of soap. Death comes in the dark. I expect that many finally realize what is happening to them." Anna looked into the faces of her parents. They were ashen.

"The corpses are disposed of in crematoriums. Helen's father was notified of her death from 'breathing problems.' This country is headed down a dark, dark road and there is no turning back. Fortunately, physicians are not being forced to participate in the exterminations. I feel I still have my position at the University because I saved the life of the SS officer, but I know I am being watched by the Gestapo. If I do not participate in their barbaric experiments, I will be arrested. None of the non-Jewish physicians are being forced to participate in the experiments; that is voluntary so Christian is safe." Anna took a deep breath. This would be the hardest part for her.

"Christian and I have planned my escape. I can't give you any details. The less you know the better. I will contact you through Christian. Also know that I completely trust my secretary Theresa Schmidt. You will not be given any information about where I am or what I am doing. If questioned, your response can only be that I have left the country. Any message that contains the word 'complete' or any form of that word will mean that I am well. Do not try to contact Christian. He will contact you."

As startling as Anna's words, they were not unexpected. The Night of Broken Glass had changed all perspective for the Eichenwalds. The political situation had deteriorated even since Hanz had decided to remain at the KWI.

Anna stood up to leave. She stressed again, the critical importance of secrecy. Then she hugged her parents. Marlene began to sob quietly.

"I love you both more than I can ever express to you. The Lord Jehovah will take care of me. And I will see you again."

Anna left with one last smile and shut the door behind her. She did not break down until her parent's townhouse was out of sight.

* * *

The code name for the surprise attack on Czechoslovakia was *Case Green.* The plan was originally devised in June 1937. Czechoslovakia was made up of several minorities including one million Hungarians, one-half million Ruthenians and three and a half million Sudeten Germans. The plight of the Sudeten Germans would be the pretext for military action. But defending them was only a ruse. Hitler's goal was the destruction of the Czechoslovakian State and the occupation of the entire territory. Despite what had just happened in Austria, France and Britain were blind to the plan. It began with the High Command of the Armed Forces – Oberkommando der Wehrmacht, or OKW. In May, the Goebbels' propaganda machine put out multiple stories of 'Czech terror' against the Sudeten Germans. On May 19th, a Leipzig newspaper ran a front page report of German troop movements. But British and French intelligence could not confirm this. In the meantime, the Czech military mobilized. Hitler was at his mountain retreat in Berchtesgaden and felt humiliated by the Czech government. He had been accused of an aggression he had not committed, but fully intended to. He swallowed the humiliation and sent messages to the Czech, French and British envoys that there were no troop movements and there would be none. Most liars become angry only when caught lying.

By September of '38, two critical developments had occurred. First, several high-ranking officers decided to overthrow Hitler. Second, invasion plans had been re-set for October 1st. The Generals in the conspiracy sent a secret emissary to London for assurances that Britain would stand against the invasion, but there was no concrete answer. A September 7th editorial in the *London Times* suggested the Czech government give up the Sudetenland to Germany for the cause of peace.

There was dark, almost unbearable tension gripping each of the capitols of Europe, except of course, in Germany. The Nazis were holding a five day party rally in Nuremberg. Goering made one of the final speeches with these closing words:

"A petty segment of Europe is harassing the human race... this miserable pygmy race (the Czechs) is oppressing a cultured people, and behind it is Moscow and the eternal mask of the Jew Devil."

Hitler's closing remarks were more of the same, demanding the Czech government give 'justice' to the Sudeten Germans.

With mounting pressure, British Prime Minister Neville Chamberlain decided to visit Hitler personally. He flew to Munich and boarded the train for a three-hour trip to Berchtesgaden. Chamberlain did not fail to notice the dozens of train cars loaded with German troops and artillery passing on the opposite track. Hitler demanded a right of self-determination. Chamberlain agreed in principle - and another domino fell. Hitler gave him assurances that no military action would be forthcoming. While Chamberlain returned to transmit the good news to his Cabinet and to the French, the Germans prepared for the October 1st invasion as planned.

A second meeting was set up between the two heads of state, this time in the small Rhine town of Godesberg. Chamberlain was bringing everything for which Hitler had asked. At the meeting in the Dreesen Hotel, Chamberlain talked for an hour, carefully laying out the planned agreement to the German Chancellor. Then Hitler spoke.

"Do I understand that the British, French and Czechoslovakian governments have agreed to the transfer of the Sudetenland from Czechoslovakia to Germany?"

"Yes!" Chamberlain exclaimed with a broad smile.

"I am sorry," Hitler replied, "but after the events of the last few days, this plan is no longer of any use to us."

Chamberlain had been deceived. He was bitterly disappointed and withdrew across the Rhine to consider his options. A final meeting occurred the following evening and an ultimatum for October 1st was given to Chamberlain for German forces to occupy the Sudetenland. Frantic diplomatic efforts by Britain and France were to no avail.

September 28th was called 'Black Wednesday.' War seemed inevitable. To the officers who had considered removing Hitler, the time had come. But there was one major reason not to implement the plan. At least two of the Generals involved suspected that London and Paris had secretly told Hitler they would not go to war over Czechoslovakia. The only reason for a planned coup was to prevent a European war which seemed unlikely under any circumstance.

At noon on Black Wednesday, Hitler received an urgent message from Mussolini asking him to hold off another 24 hours. Hitler acquiesced.

"Tell the Duce that I accept his proposal," he responded.

With this, Hitler sent invitations to the heads of Britain, France and Italy, to meet with him at noon in Munich the following day. The Czechs were not invited. The meeting would seal their fate.

There was more than a little irony to the fact that within the baroque, Bavarian city of Munich where Hitler made his start as a lowly politician, he was now greeted like an emperor. The talks with the heads of state were anticlimactic, rendering to Hitler exactly what he wanted when he wanted it. Unknown to Chamberlain, Hitler and Mussolini, had vowed two days earlier to fight 'side by side' against Great Britain.

Churchill was not in the government at the time. Yet he alone seemed to understand what had happened. On October 5th, he spoke to the House of Commons.

"We have sustained a total and unmitigated defeat...We are in the midst of a disaster of the first magnitude. The road down the Danube...the road to the Black Sea has been opened...

All the countries of Mittel Europa and the Danube valley, one after another, will be drawn in the vast system of Nazi politics... radiating from Berlin...And do not suppose that this is the end. It is only the beginning!"

Even as Churchill spoke these words, German troops were occupying the Sudetenland. His words, for the most part, went unheeded.

CHAPTER 11
Germany invades Poland

As a young man in Hungary, Leo Szilard had dreamed of saving the world.

"If we could find an element which could be split by neutrons," he would muse. Otto Hahn had now found the element to be uranium. As a result, many physicists in Germany as well as the U.S. began to believe that a bomb of massive proportions was possible using the U-235 isotope. This is not exactly what Szilard had in mind when he thought of saving the world.

Szilard had ideas about how to proceed. He shared them by letter with Enrico Fermi who was teaching the summer session at the University of Michigan. Szilard's idea was to mix the uranium with carbon in the form of graphite. The graphite would slow the neutron bombardment which might lead to a chain reaction and possibly to a bomb. But Fermi did not share those views. Szilard saw a need for urgency because he realized that his German counter-parts would eventually come to the same conclusions about a chain reaction and a weapon. So he decided to contact two Hungarian colleagues, Edward Teller and Eugene Wigner. They knew that Belgium was mining large quantities of Uranium in their African colony of Congo. Teller and Wigner feared that the Germans might be able to get their hands on it and wanted to contact the Belgian government. Then they were reminded that Albert Einstein, the world's most influential physicist maintained a close friendship with Elizabeth, the Queen of Belgium.

Einstein was spending the summer at a cottage on Long Island. Wigner and Szilard called him and arranged a meeting. On Sunday, July 16th, the two drove to Long Island and after some difficulty, found the cottage. These men knew Einstein only by reputation and were surprised at his physical appearance. Later Szilard would recall the following.

"He was a muscular man with a magnificent furrowed forehead and enormous brown eyes. He was most cordial, but seemed a bit puzzled as to why we were there."

Szilard explained about the secondary experiments toward the chain reaction with Uranium and graphite. Surprisingly, Einstein said he had not considered the concept, but quickly visualized the implications of this technology and that it might be developed by the Nazis.

He was reluctant to approach the Queen directly, but said he would help in any way possible. He dictated a letter to the Belgian Ambassador as Wigner took it down by long-hand in German. That letter was taken back to Princeton, translated and typed in English. Wigner was then off on holiday to California with his family.

The letter went to Szilard for review. During that time, Szilard was put in contact with Alexander Sachs, a Russian emigrant and economist who had become a consultant to President Roosevelt. Sachs convinced Szilard, who then convinced Einstein that the matter should by-pass the Belgians and go directly to the White House. The letter was revised and the plan was for Sachs to meet with Roosevelt. All of the issues with a weapon of this magnitude could only be imagined. The Hungarians had their own agenda and hoped it would lead to world peace and possibly even a world government.

Sachs was scheduled to see the President the first week of September 1939. However, history did not cooperate. Hitler had already taken over Austria, the Rheinland neutral zone on the French border, and Czechoslovakia, all with no armed opposition. On September 1, 1939, he boldly invaded Poland.

Sachs did not see Roosevelt the first week of September, nor the second, third or fourth week. Britain and France declared war on Germany on September 3rd. The Germans were throwing 56 divisions plus nine tank battalions and full air support against 30 thinly spaced Polish divisions that were using WWI armament and artillery. The invasion was a colossal mismatch.

As Europe was being thrust into yet another conflagration, a debate was going on in the U.S. Congress concerning the bombing of innocents. Long range bombers had been developed since WWI and the fear was that thousands of women and children would be killed or injured as a result. The previous June, the Senate had passed a resolution condemning "inhumane bombing of civilian populations." Six months before the resolution Roosevelt had requested funds for long range bombers. The drama and debate spread nationwide. *Scientific American* had the most accurate evaluation, saw the dark truth and put it in print:

"Although aerial bombing remains an unknown intermediate quantity, the world may be sure that the unwholesome atrocities which are happening today are but curtain raisers on insane dramas to come."

Finally, late on Wednesday afternoon, October 11, Alexander Sachs got to see Roosevelt. His aid, General Edwin Watson reviewed Sachs' agenda then opened the door to the Oval Office.

"Alex", Roosevelt said with a broad smile. "What have you been up to?"

Sachs had copies of Einstein's letter and the introduction letter from Szilard, but decided to explain them in his own words rather than read them. His version of the fission story emphasized the goodness of atomic energy, power production and in medical treatments, then the potential of a weapon. He purposefully juxtaposed the potential 'good and evil' of atomic power. He ended the presentation reading from a 1936 lecture by Francis Aston titled, "Forty Years of Atomic Theory".

"Personally I think there is no doubt that sub-atomic energy is available all around us, and that one day man will release and control its almost infinite power. We cannot prevent him from doing so and can only hope that he will not use it exclusively in blowing up his next door neighbor."

Roosevelt was listening intently.

"Alex, what you are after is to see that the Nazis do not blow us up." "Exactly," Sachs replied.

Thus, with the help of a letter from Einstein, the effort to build an atomic bomb in the U.S. was launched.

* * *

"Danzig is German, will always be German, and will sooner or later become part of Germany."

These words of Adolph Hitler were spoken to Polish Foreign Minister Jozef Beck during the first week of January 1939. The old port of Danzig had been made a free city by the Versailles Treaty, along with a corridor giving Poland access to the Baltic Sea. Now Germany wanted it back. Beck's reply was that an attempt to take the city by force would lead to armed conflict. Fresh reports of an imminent attack on Poland prompted the British and French governments to pledge support to Poland if attacked. Now a line had been drawn in the sand. For Poland, the wolf was at the door.

For the first time, the U.S. government made an effort to influence the European process. On April 15, President Roosevelt sent a telegram to Hitler and Mussolini. It was a simple request that those two leaders give assurances they would not attack their European neighbors. Hitler replied in a Reichstag speech on April 28th, filled with ridicule and sarcasm. Soon after this, Hitler retreated to his summer home at Berchtesgaden to supervise the final military plan to invade Poland at summer's end. A last minute letter to Hitler from Chamberlain gave assurances that an attack on Poland would be considered an attack on England.

At daybreak on September 1, 1939, German troops poured across the Polish border to attack Warsaw. In support, the German Luftwaffe attacked targets from the air bringing for the first time in world history, swift death and destruction of unimagined magnitude. While people were dying by the thousands in Warsaw, people in Berlin were mostly apathetic. They were dazed to find their country in a war they were sure their Fuehrer would avoid. After all, they had taken Austria and Czechoslovakia without firing a shot. This was a stark contrast to 'August Days' of 1914 when the Kaiser and his troops had been cheered with wild enthusiasm. Once again, Germany began a major military action in 'response' to a faked attack on a German instillation. During the night of August 31st, German *SS* men dressed in Polish uniforms attacked the German radio station at Gleiwitz. From the outset, the German invasion was referred to as a 'counter attack'. It was now of little consequence that the most brutal and destructive war in history was started by a diabolical plot of deception.

Hitler and Himmler viewing map of troop movements – 1939

Hanz Eichenwald knew the world of violence and anti-Semitism was closing in around him. He had made a decision to remain in Germany based on two factors. One, he felt that anti-Semitism was pervasive throughout Europe, and any move would be of no benefit from that standpoint. And two, he felt that intellectuals in Germany could remain above the political turmoil. He was correct on the first count but dead wrong on the second. His own daughter, an associate professor of surgery at the University of Berlin, was being watched by the Gestapo and was in danger of being "detained".

In April of 1939, Frederic Joliet in Paris published a paper in *Nature* that documented 3.5 secondary neutrons per fission of uranium. It concluded that if a sufficient amount of uranium were immersed in a suitable moderator, a chain reaction could perpetuate itself. This information had reached the Reich Ministry of Education who, in turn, set up a meeting with the Wehrmacht's ordinance department. In attendance were Eichenwald, Paul Harteck, a young physicist working in Hamburg, and Kurt Diebner, a nuclear physicist who was working in the ordinance department. Otto Hahn had been invited but in an effort to avoid the issue, arranged to be elsewhere. These three men were asked to evaluate the evidence to date on the possibility of developing a nuclear bomb in Germany or anywhere else. After three hours of discussion, the three men drafted a letter to the German War Office concluding it was possible, perhaps probable, that a nuclear weapon could be produced with explosive potential many orders of magnitude greater than conventional ones.

By September the War Office Department had consolidated German fission research under its authority and determined the director of research would be Hanz Eichenwald. It was now clear to Eichenwald why he had been allowed to stay in Germany without persecution. The project would be centered in Berlin at the KWI.

Other physicists involved included Otto Hahn, Walter Bothe, and Hans Geiger, as well as Harteck and Diebner. It was a strong team. Given the resources and funding, they might just pull it off.

The first person Eichenwald wanted to talk to was his friend and mentor, Max Planck. Planck had been responsible for bringing Hanz to the KWI, and the Nobel Laureate had been like a second father. The morning after the meeting with the War Department, Eichenwald stopped by Planck's office. His secretary was accustomed to Dr. Eichenwald's drop-in visits.

"He's in his office," she said with a smile.

Max Planck was a physicist of the classical school. At the turn of the century he outlined what was to become known as Quantum Theory. It stated that light and energy do not move in continuous waves but in small 'bundles' he called quanta. As a young physicist he had believed that atoms existed only in theory. Now in his 80's, he was still very bright and enjoying the rapid fire discoveries in the world of physics. As the two old friends shook hands Planck got right to the point. "So, Hanz, you have agreed to head our bomb project." Eichenwald smiled as he took a sip of his coffee.

"I'm not so sure the position is voluntary. This seems to be the reason I was not forced to leave the KWI three years ago. At any rate, from a technological standpoint, I'm not sure it can be done; at least not in the four year target date."

Planck was a loyal German but no Nazi supporter. Privately he thought Hitler was a mad man. His loyalties were with his country, war notwithstanding. Hanz continued, "I find it strange that the War Department would put a project of this magnitude in the hands of a Jew, especially in view of what this country is doing to the Jews."

"You are the best qualified and most of the others have left," replied Planck. "A number of men who were forced to leave including Teller, Szilard, Fermi and a half a dozen others, are now helping the Americans build their bomb. Hanz, I'm sure you realize you are in a vulnerable position. They may decide to cast you off like so many rotting fish off of a fishing boat. You must remain valuable to them."

Hanz did not speak at first. He clearly understood what Planck was saying, made eye contact with his old mentor and nodded his head.

"I would like to stop by from time to time just to visit," he finally said. "Anytime," Planck replied. "I won't be much help with the physics, but…as a friend."

"Thank you."

Hanz had gotten the information he needed. He closed the door as he left.

On the evening of September 20th, Hanz and Marlene Eichenwald faced life issues they could not have imagined three years earlier. A megalo-maniac had plunged their country into a war many Germans neither understood nor wanted. Their daughter was in danger of being arrested. And Hanz had been made director of a military project to support a regime he now hated.

They picked at their food and tried to finish their meal. Finally, Hanz spoke in a muted voice.

"Marlene, we must give Anna over to God. She is a treasure to us and I believe a treasure to God as well. We are powerless to protect her. Thousands of Jews are being arrested, but so far Anna has been spared. She is very intelligent and the man who loves her will help her."

Marlene looked at her half full plate.

"I pray you are right. I feel like someone in a boat being swept along by a raging river with no oars and no rudder. We all may survive or we may be dashed on the rocks by the rapids. We have no control."

Hanz then shared with his wife that he had no intention of helping the Nazis develop a weapon so they could dominate the world. He had developed a deep and abiding hatred for the Nazis and their pogrom against the Jews. Both of their parents had died and for that they were grateful, but they had a number of relatives who had been placed in ghettos and were being moved to concentration camps. His plan was to remain 'valuable' to the War Office at least until he could plan their escape. Now it would be much more difficult and dangerous. Like Anna, he would be watched carefully by the Gestapo.

The previous year at Bohr's Copenhagen conference, Hanz met Chaim Weizmann. This fascinating man, a biochemist, was working on fermentation products. He had become good friends with Ernst Rutherford, the legendary New Zealander now working in England. Rutherford had won the 1908 Nobel Prize for unraveling the complex transmutations of certain radioactive elements. Hanz wanted to know more about Rutherford as well as Weizmann. The two men spent an entire afternoon in conversation. As for Weizmann, he was a Zionist and always looking for converts. Born in western Russia and raised the third of 15 children, his family lived in a section that had been cordoned off for Jewish families, the Pale of Settlement. When Weizmann was only an eleven year old, he had written a prophetic letter. He had stated that "the Kings and Nations of the world are plainly set upon the ruin of the Jewish Nation; the Jews must not let themselves be destroyed; England alone may help them to return and rise again in their ancient land of Palestine."

By the age of 18 he had worked his way to Berlin and earned a PhD at the University of Fribourg in Switzerland. He and his wife immigrated to England where he worked as a research chemist and discovered an anaerobic bacteria that decomposes starch. In the process, he found that one of the decomposition products was acetone, a critical ingredient in the manufacture of cordite, the explosive used in heavy artillery. This led him to a meeting with Winston Churchill, who at the time was the First Lord of the Admiralty. The British were in dire need of cordite and were short because of the shortage of acetone. The Weizmann process could produce an almost unlimited amount of acetone. Thus, Weizmann played a major role in the evolution of WWI and contributed significantly to the Allied victory. The government of Great Britain wanted to honor him is some way, but Weizmann declined any award and simply stated that at sometime in the future England "could do something for my people."

Weizmann had become acquainted with Arthur Balfour, the British Foreign Secretary and had made him aware of his dream of the establishment of an Israeli nation in Palestine. In 1917, the Balfor Declaration was issued by Foreign Secretary Arthur J. Balfour endorsing the idea of establishing the idea of establishing a "national home" in Palestine for the Jewish people. Weizmann was indeed grateful and saw this as a beginning for his dream.

Hanz was curious about Rutherford. The two had met at the Copenhagen conference.

"Tell me about Rutherford," he said to Weizmann. "He seems an exceptional man."

Weizmann replied, "He is… he really is. His work on alpha particles was elegant, plus he is a very charismatic person. Frequently he has friends and students for dinner on the weekends, followed by long hours of discourse about almost anything, even if he knows nothing about the subject. All in all, he is one of the brightest and most delightful fellows I have met."

"And what of politics," asked Hanz.

"That's the one subject he will not discuss and one in which he seems to have no interest."

Hanz had taken an immediate liking to Weizmann. As they parted, he turned solemnly to him. "My situation in Berlin is tenuous and there might be a time when the risk reaches critical mass. I would like to stay in touch about my situation."

Weizmann reached out his hand. "I look forward to hearing from you. You can always reach me at this number." He handed Hanz a card. As he turned to leave Hanz said, "Count on it,"

Chaim Weizmann (to right of Einstein) SS Rotterdam – 1921

In London at 11:15 a.m. on September 3, 1939, Lord Halifax handed the German charge d'affaires a formal note that stated, "I have the honor to inform you that a state of war now exists between our two countries from today, September 3rd". An ultimatum was issued by the government of France later that day. This was, in fact, a technicality. There was much more going on behind the scenes. Days before, Mussolini had backed out of any military action. So early on the morning of the 3rd, Hitler sent an urgent letter to try to draw him back into the alliance. In a much more significant development, the Nazis entered into highly secret negotiations with Russia to join the attack on Poland. In turn Russia would get Lithuania. When the agreement was made public, Stalin was the clear winner, receiving almost half of Poland and control of the Baltic States. In his first encounter with Hitler, Stalin was the clear victor.

An internal struggle was also brewing in the German Naval High Command. They felt strongly they were not prepared for the war but were forced by Hitler to commit to the action of September 1st. At 9:00 p.m. that same day, the Nazi submarine U-30 torpedoed an unarmed British ocean liner, *Athenia,* carrying 1,400 passengers.

112 perished, including 28 Americans. The French armed forces, although superior to the Germans in overall strength, failed to act, and the British were simply not prepared. By October 15th, Poland had been swallowed up and no longer existed as a country.

Marlene Eichenwald had many acquaintances but only two close friends. Victor and Paula Herzog were owners of a small family bakery and pastry shop on Konigstrasse just east of the main post office. When the Eichenwalds first moved from Munich, Marlene had walked past the shop and noticed the front door and sign. The entrance was wooden and in the form of a pumpkin with a glass door in the center. The shop was called "The Pumpkin House." She met Paula Herzog and they became fast friends. Paula was four years older than Marlene, with short, light brown hair and large hazel eyes. She tended to smile most of the time and was always eager to inquire about the state of affairs of the patrons. She treated regular customers and newcomers in the same, congenial way. Victor did the baking. While everything was good, the pumpkin bread was their specialty. Twice a day, at 9:00 a.m. and 3:00 p.m., hot pumpkin bread made its way to the shelves. In the back of the shop was a courtyard with an arbor covered with wisteria and honey suckle. A series of six wooden tables filled the courtyard for coffee, tea and conversation. The Herzogs closed on Shabbat for Synagogue and opened an hour late on Sundays. They did a brisk business.

Marlene's other close friend was Laura Knochen. Laura was employed as a librarian at the University on the main campus. She had worked there for 10 years. Her husband, Gerhard, was killed in France in 1918, about six months before the war's end. Marlene visited the library usually one or two mornings a week to fill her appetite for reading. Laura was very proficient in her position, and not accustomed to idly chatting with library patrons. But she quickly gained an appreciation for Marlene's unique qualities. Eventually the women set aside Tuesdays for lunch. Sometimes they went to the Pumpkin House for pastries and tea. As the head librarian, Laura loved her work. She had been married five years when the war robbed her of Gerhard. Now a widow, she immersed herself in her work, took no interest in men and refused to succumb to self- pity. She felt she could endure the loss of only one husband, one broken heart, so she vowed to remain single. A Catholic, Laura had several friends in the church and at the University, but Marlene became special to her.

The events of 1939 were disturbing to both women. Laura was an avid reader of history. During one of their Tuesday lunches that September, she couldn't help but make comparisons between Hitler and a Greek general in antiquity.

"About 350 BC, a Greek general, Philip of Macedon, began a military domination of the area," she said to Marlene. "His smaller war-like neighbors could not stand up against him. As he would conquer one country he would propose peace to another. Sound familiar? By 338 he had conquered all of Greece. But two years later he was assassinated. His son was Alexander the Great, who continued his father's conquests but to a much greater extent. Much of the world became Hellenistic in cultural orientation. They even adopted a common language called Koine Greek that was used to write the Christian New Testament. Interestingly, Alexander died at age 33 in Babylon under mysterious circumstances. He died in the palace of Nebuchadnezzar."

"So, you see a parallel between the Hellenistic culture of 300 BC and the Nazi Aryan race?"

"Absolutely, Marlene. But Alexander's world of conquest was short lived. Hitler has proclaimed the Third Reich will last 1000 years. Well, I doubt it!"

"One thing seems clear though, Laura. Nations will not oppose Hitler for what he is doing to the Jews. They will rise up only when they are directly threatened by him."

"I'm afraid you are right," she said sadly.

They were sitting in the courtyard of the Pumpkin House. The entrance was no longer as inviting as it once was. Now there was a large, yellow six-pointed Star of David painted beside the door.

As the two women sat quietly, Paula Herzog appeared with a fresh pot of hot tea. She and Victor had been devastated by the Night of Broken Glass. They were fortunate to have avoided being arrested or beaten, but many of their neighbors and Jewish friends had been taken to camps and their businesses damaged or destroyed. The Herzog's escaped with only the yellow star. They had been instructed to add "Israel" as their middle name and now each wore a yellow star on the left upper corner of their coats.

Paula smiled weakly.

"You are both a balm to the spirit," she said with a forced smile.

Setting the pot of tea on the table, she turned to hug each woman, then pulled out a chair and sat down. Marlene smiled at her and felt a sense of guilt seep into the well of relief she'd been harboring for having been spared the abuse the Herzog's had experienced. As suddenly as the guilt came, it was replaced with a wave of anger. She said nothing. Instead, she wondered in silence how God could allow such a degree of evil and inhumanity to flourish.

Laura was the first to acknowledge these unspoken feelings.

"You know that we hate what is going on in Germany," she said, taking Paula's hand. "At least men can rise up in defiance against tyranny while we can just watch. But there are those who will not just watch."

"The love of friends is about all we have," said Paula. "Our business will not sustain us. The future is frightening. In fact, I don't think there is a future." Paula stood up and thanked both women for coming. "I have to get back to the bakery," she said quickly.

Laura and Marlene sat in silence for a few moments. "It's such a helpless feeling", Marlene moaned.

"And you're in a more difficult position than I am," Laura replied. "But I'm not going to just watch this happen. My husband died for this country. He died for Germany not for the Aryan Race."

Within a few short weeks of the Nazi victory in Poland, radical changes in the cultural landscape were initiated. Just before the invasion began, Hitler had warned his Generals that they should not interfere if they witnessed immoral or tasteless activities. Reinhard Heydrich, chief assistant to the director of the SS, drew up a directive for what became known as 'housecleaning'. In this memorandum, the concept of a 'final solution' was established. Within months, more than one-half million Polish Jews were deported east of the Vistula River into what would become known as 'ghettos'. Over the next year, the focus of the war moved to Denmark, Norway, and finally France. Thousands of Polish intellectuals were murdered by the SS. Thousands more froze to death in the 'resettlement'. The winter of 1939 to 1940 was unusually severe. The Nazi goal was to ensure there would be no professors, lawyers, doctors, politicians or Jews left in Poland…. no one who could potentially lead a resistance movement.

In February 1940, *SS* Oberfuehrer Richard Gluecks was looking for a suitable site for a new 'quarantine camp'. He informed Himmler that he had found an area near Cracow, Poland. It was called *Auschwitz.*

The previous Christmas of 1939 was unusually bleak for Germany. Normally the high point of the year, the cold was severe and the celebrations were few. Hitler felt it appropriate to exchange holiday greetings to the Russian Head of State. He sent a wire.

"Best wishes for your personal well-being as well as for the prosperous future of the peoples of the friendly Soviet Union."

Stalin sent a reply. "The friendship of the peoples of Germany and the Soviet Union, cemented in blood, has every reason to be lasting and firm."

After many weeks of secret preparation, on April, 9, 1940, the German envoys to Denmark and Norway delivered an ultimatum that those governments immediately accept, without resistance, the protection of the Third Reich. Specifically, the protection was against Anglo-French 'occupation'. Although there was virtually zero threat of an Anglo-French invasion.

The Danes were in an impossible situation. Their little island nation was indefensible. The Danish King capitulated and by break-fast the next morning, Denmark was in German hands. Norway was a different story. Some of the northern ports fell easily to the German Navy, but Bergen in the south, connected to Oslo by rail, resisted. The British Navy became involved and a British Sub sunk the German light cruiser *Karlsruhe.* German warships ran into stiff resistance along the 50-mile Oslo Fjord. But when Nazi para-troopers captured the Oslo airport, the Germans got the upper hand. Although Norwegian and British forces slowed the advances, within about six weeks the entire country came under German control. On June 7th, the Norwegian King and his government were evacuated to London on the British Cruiser *Devonshire.*

The quick conquests of Denmark and Norway were important victories for the Reich and discouraging for the British. But the German Navy had taken heavy losses. This fact would be vital in the months to come, although the depleted navy was not considered an issue for the German High Command. Their singular goal for the next year was victory in the west, the conquest of Belgium, Holland, and France.

*   *   *

In 1940, Hanz Eichenwald found himself in a profound moral dilemma. He had been selected to head a military project to develop a nuclear weapon. If successfully produced, the weapon would help Hitler dominate the world. It had been made clear to him that if uncooperative, he and his wife Marlene would be deported with other Jews. They would likely be sent to Poland. His colleagues on the project were not pro-Nazi. But they were pro-German. They would work diligently for the cause and hope the political issues would be resolved. Hanz felt that none of the men with whom he worked were anti-Semites. But he didn't feel comfortable discussing their thoughts about what was happening to their country. The initial goal of the group was to develop a strategy to successfully produce a controlled chain reaction in uranium or a similar element. All of their other research projects were placed on hold to focus on this one project for the military.

Hanz had shared with Marlene that he thought a bomb could be successfully produced in five years if every decision made was the right one. He told her there could be no blind alleys. And he also told her of his intention to begin the planning of their escape. He foresaw a plan that could unfold in one to two years and was certain that the Gestapo could intervene at any moment and for any reason, and remove him from his highly sensitive position. Hanz did not tell his wife that he would die before placing a weapon of mass destruction in the hands of Adolph Hitler. He knew that the energy production of even two pounds of U-235 would be devastating. It would kill large numbers of civilians and spread radioactivity for hundreds of kilometers. He also knew there would be no effective defense from such a weapon. For the maniacal Fuehrer of the Third Reich to have such a weapon was unthinkable.

Hanz suspected that his appointment to the bomb program had been hotly debated, and on this, he was correct. The War Ordinance Department wanted him involved while the Gestapo wanted to arrest him. In the end, it had seemed foolish to waste his talent. It might also have been a propaganda nightmare to place a man of his international reputation in a ghetto. So the decision had been made at the highest levels to keep him onboard and to watch him closely. If there was any evidence of sabotage, he and his wife would be killed.

Hanz didn't have to know the details of this decision to know why and how it was made. He was no fool. In those early months of 1940, the nuclear arms race took off. And strangely, the director of the German effort was determined that his side would not win and that he would live to tell the tale.

The German team had decided that fast-neutron fission of U-235 was the best way to achieve a bomb. This meant their initial focus had to be on acquiring a large amount of uranium and then finding a suitable method of separating out the U-235 from the U-238, which was the dominant isotope. Getting the needed quantities of uranium was possible. But isotope separation was the problem. In addition, acquiring a suitable moderator might prove difficult. Hanz favored heavy water or deuterium. The only source of significant amounts of heavy water in the world was an electro-chemical plant 90 miles west of Oslo in southern Norway. Earlier in the year, the management of the plant had been approached by German officials regarding buying all of their available heavy water. But the Norwegians had refused. By May of 1940, German forces occupied Norway and the plant was now in German hands.

The military activity in the early months of 1940 had been dubbed the 'phony war'. With overwhelming force and almost no meaningful resistance, the Germans had occupied Denmark and Norway. Now on May 10th the 'phony war' abruptly ended as Germany invaded Belgium, Luxembourg and the Netherlands. This paved the way for their planned invasion of France.

CHAPTER 12
An Expression of Love

It had been almost a year since Anna had attended the meeting called by the Counsel on Eugenics. Images of that horrific film and the executions of the six men in Plotzensee Prison had drifted into her mind on dozens of occasions. She made every effort to dismiss them. But she still had the nightmares. In her dreams, she would stare at the dangling bodies and almost feel the piano wire tightening around her throat. Then she would wake up, gasping for breath, her fingers tugging at her nightgown in the darkness.

So much had happened in her life and the life of her country since that first meeting at the hospital. The barbaric experiments designed for the eugenics program had been postponed indefinitely. This was primarily due to the intensity of military activity that followed the invasion of Poland. For every day that the program was delayed, Anna was grateful.

She remained extremely busy at the hospital. While most of the wounded soldiers were being cared for in field hospitals and centers in Stuttgart, Dusseldorf and Hamburg, a number of war casualties were beginning to trickle into Berlin from the front. She and Christian found themselves caring for more and more each month. Mounting casualties notwithstanding, the German Wehrmacht was experiencing victory after victory with their Blitzkrieg tactics.

The passing of the Nuremburg Laws and the violent hours that made up the Night of Broken Glass, together formed the perfect atmosphere of fear and helplessness among Jews and other minorities. Vast numbers of businesses were lost. Women saw their husbands arrested. Given the Gestapo surveillance apparatus, resistance was pursued with extreme caution. Anyone found trying to subvert the war effort or protect the 'enemies' of the Reich was shot or hanged.

In spite of the military successes, enthusiasm for the war among the German Volk was almost non-existent. It had been only 20 short years since the end of WWI and the Treaty of Versailles. The memories of dead husbands, fathers and sons were still fresh. It was a crime to openly criticize the war effort. For all these reasons, no one did. But many harbored their misgivings silently.

Christian and Anna, too, were hiding something. They conducted a masterful performance in hiding their relationship. When their paths crossed in public, they remained professional and polite, hardly daring to make eye contact. Fear of discovery was a constant threat and both worked diligently to keep it from showing in their behavior. At times, Anna felt that she was holding her breath through most of her hours at the hospital.

In May of 1940, something unexpected happened. Despite the rapid collapse of French resistance, the German High Command feared that the British Royal Air Force would resort to bombing raids. Because of this fear, nightly blackouts were begun in Berlin and other major industrial cities. Until this point, only far western areas had been bombed. But the High Command wasn't taking any chances. In addition to blackouts, major cities were ringed with massive anti-aircraft instillations. Beginning May 15th, no electric lights were allowed on the streets or in buildings without black curtains or drapes. Street traffic was limited to walking or short auto rides requiring no headlights. All emergency facilities such as hospitals and police stations were equipped with heavy black window coverings.

Anna continued her work as a surgeon and had not allowed herself to follow the progress of the war. That began to change. Suddenly, she found herself looking at the newspapers, keenly interested in the 'air war.' While others associated the blackouts with the possibility of attacks and bodily harm, Anna looked at the situation almost as if it were an adventure. People who find themselves in love have an odd ability to overlook bombs and explosions.

For three months, Anna paid no attention to the Gestapo vehicle parked near her apartment. Like many others at that time, she knew the Gestapo conducted surveillance. She just wasn't sure how it was done or if she was on the watch list. The threat of the Gestapo seemed like a thing of the past. She didn't dwell on the idea. Instead, she concentrated on her love for Christian and her work. She spent long hours in her office, reviewing charts and talking with Theresa. They had looked diligently for listening devices but had never been unable to locate any. Still, they spoke confidentially and only in a small hallway between their offices. Anna regularly altered her schedule so that she had no real pattern to her comings and goings. She did not want to be easily observed. She kept unusual hours, even when she had no call obligations. Now, with the blackouts, she and Christian had almost total freedom of movement at night. Their fears of being detected simply vanished.

Theresa Schmidt had a three bedroom flat about ten blocks from the University. One of the bedrooms had a separate back entrance in case the renter wished to sub-let the room. She was aware that Anna and Christian had no place for privacy and when she mentioned this to Anna, the couple felt that God had provided them a gift.

They set up an elaborate schedule to meet once each week. They always arrived at least an hour apart and left the same way.

They never walked together, never took the same route. But they had no trouble remembering specific dates and times.

Theresa always tried to place a bottle of wine in the room. She and her husband Willi had always set aside one evening each week for dinner and a bottle of wine. The murder of her Willi robbed her of so many things. But their weekly dinner dates were what she missed the most. Perhaps this was why she took such delight in helping Anna and Christian find a time and a place to be together.

They kept the only two keys to the outside door. The room was on the ground floor of a two story flat so they felt somewhat secluded. But they continued to remind each other to stay quiet.

Anna tried not to think about a private time with Christian. They had been in love for more than a year but had never spent more than two hours together alone. Most of their contact was still at the hospital. Anna hated the war and the squalid Nazi Reich responsible for keeping her away from an open relationship with the man she loved. But she was grateful for the blackouts. They seemed a gift of fate. The Hitler oligarchy that was putting her at greater and greater risk now provided her with the one thing it had attempted to deny her.

It was now early June. The blackouts had continued for the past month. Anna was in love. But as yet, she had no lover. Their first meeting was this very night. She felt nervous but excited. The wait in the surgical lounge seemed like an eternity. She read journals and fidgeted. Finally, it was nine o'clock. She took a back stairway down to the hospital basement then out a little used back entrance. It was very dark outside with low cloud cover. She proceeded to walk quickly the three blocks east on Behrenstrasse, then turned south on Freidrichstrasse and walked the last four blocks to

Theresa's flat. Anna had taken the route a dozen times in different ways and knew every kilometer. The streets were deserted. She put the key in the lock. As it turned, she was suddenly startled by the loud 'click'. It sounded like a gunshot in the still night. Then she was inside, the door locked behind her. Heavy drapes were pulled closed against the window and the room was lit only by a small bulb in the bathroom. The door was slightly ajar and projected a small stream of light from the bathroom to the opposite wall. The wall appeared as if a white line had been painted on it. She could make out the bed, the table and two chairs. Theresa had placed the wine and glasses on the table. Anna smiled, grateful for Theresa's friendship. She tossed her lab coat across the bed and stared at it. Somehow, in the dim light, she could see her embroidered name on the white fabric. It was oddly comforting. Even in these dark and troubled times, she still had a name.

Anna placed a chair in the corner and sat down in the dark. Her emotions turned inside her as though they were sailing along on some kind of inner roller coaster. She thought of leaving the door unlocked then changed her mind. She waited, aware of every sound. There were muted conversations across the hall and she could hear footsteps on the street as people made their way to their destinations in the night. When the footsteps faded, the silence was jarring.

She heard the sound of a key being inserted into the lock. Her heart began to pound in her chest. Dear God, could everyone hear it? The door quickly opened and closed, then she heard the click of the lock a second time.

"Anna?" Christian whispered. "Over here."

He moved toward her voice as his eyes searched for her. She stood to meet him. As his arms found her soft shoulders, he said more to himself than to her,

"Thank God you're here!"

He kissed her gently, then again, slowly. They had always had stolen kisses in the hospital, always hoping no one would see. Now, he had her alone. Her lips met his and he breathed her in as he continued to kiss her. His arms encircled her and he lifted her up to him, holding her tightly. She put her head against his shoulder.

"We need to talk…before anything else," she whispered.

Christian waited while she poured two glasses of wine. He took his glass and sat down. As she moved across the room, he lit a cigarette and deeply inhaled.

"I have been working on the plan for your escape," he said softly. "It's too dangerous now for you to get out of the country. We can make it look as if you have left the country, then change your identity."

"I don't want to just go into hiding, Christian. The war could last for years. I want to work against the Nazis."

Christian took a deep breath. He tried to digest what Anna had just said. "My sister lives in Leipzig. She works at a bank. She can arrange proper documents for you. She has been smuggling Jews out of the country but it's now too dangerous. I already sent her your picture. She's going to create a new name for you and a proper I.D."

Christian put his cigarette to his lips and inhaled again. He was nervous. "She is very resourceful, my love. She will find you work."

Anna walked back toward Christian and slid onto his lap. She placed one long kiss on his lips.

"You think she will need about a month or so?" "More like six."

Anna held his head on her chest and began running her fingers through his hair. Christian now had the opportunity to pour out his heart to her.

"I observed you, first at a distance, then up close. You have eyes that sparkle and are so honest. When others speak, you never look away. To have you now is an unspeakable gift. I have longed to be with you, to hold you close. Where ever you are is where I want to be. I am incomplete without you. Just to be near you like this is something I had only imagined."

He spoke softly to her for what seemed like just a few minutes, when he realized she was asleep. The stress of her life and work had taken its toll. Anna was physically and emotionally exhausted. Deep in the recesses of her mind was the anarchic Nazi Reich, now implementing the 'final solution' for the Jews of Europe.

She lay quietly, wrapped up in the down quilt in a paradigm she had not experienced since her childhood. In this night, in the arms of the man she loved, she had escaped the horror of being Jewish in Germany.

She had not realized Christian's move from her arms to leave. Suddenly, he was above her, whispering in her ear and kissing her as he spoke. "It's five o'clock. I have to leave now. I'll see you later at the hospital." "Be careful," she demanded. "I love you."

Anna locked the door behind him and went into the bathroom. She couldn't walk to her apartment as yet. She decided to shower. As the warm water ran across her face and body, she remembered Christian's hands. But instead of the ache she might have felt for him, a sense of anger overtook her. She was in a trap set by her own country. She was in love with a man who could be arrested for loving her back. Instead of losing herself in love, she would have to work to survive.

Anna began to cry. She might never have children. She might never be able to live with Christian. There would be no home in their country. No chance to grow old with the man she loved.

Anna let the water wash over her face. She kept her hands tightly against her mouth. She cried silently until the water turned cold. As her body cooled down, she stepped out of the shower and stood without moving.

I will stay alive, she mouthed. I will work for their defeat..... work against these monsters who want to destroy my life and my people.

It was an abrupt ending to their night together. She dressed quickly and left the apartment. There were no tears now, no emotion. Nothing. Exactly what they wanted of her.

*   *   *

The first week of May, 1940, displayed for the world, a new kind of military tactic. The German tank divisions had their own self-propelled artillery and a brigade of motorized infantry. The tank commanders were bold in their decisions and skilled in execution. One young Brigadier General, Erwin Rommel, was especially daring. At the same time, the British Government was resolving a cabinet crisis of leadership. On the evening of May 10th, Winston Churchill replaced Lord Chamberlain as Prime Minister. He was a leader determined to keep Europe out of any plan that would master them by the Germans.

In the meantime, the German Luftwaffe ruled the skies. Although the Belgian army fought valiantly, they were overrun in a matter of weeks. They were near collapse in the north and German armor was advancing up from the south on the coast of France. Caught in a trap at Dunkirk, were nine divisions of the British Expeditionary force, ten divisions of the French First Army and the remaining troops of the Belgian Army. A crisis of inestimable scale faced the new Prime Minister.

On May 29th, with the Germans closing in rapidly from the south, they suddenly halted their advance. The order to stop was given by Hitler himself, though the reasons were unclear. Goering may have had some influence so he could steal the glory from the army and allow his air force to finish off the allies from the air. There was also the possibility that Hitler decided to spare Britain a bitter humiliation thus increasing the chance of a peace settlement. There were actually some in the British aristocracy who were sympathetic toward Hitler. He had information that these sentiments might even be shared by some members of the royal family. Another possible reason for his action, Hitler was aware that the American Ambassador might be more favorable toward the Nazis if they acted with some restraint. As a last resort, the Germans could always use the trapped soldiers as bargaining 'chips'. But in their arrogance, it did not occur to the Germans that they might not be in total control of the situation.

Unknown to the Germans, the British had been planning for days to attempt a massive evacuation. They dubbed it *Operation Dynamo*. The German High Command viewed the British and French as trapped rats waiting for destruction by the cat – the German army. But the Allied troops were not waiting; they were leaving…. by sea. By the time the stunned German High Command realized what was happening, more than 300,000 British and French troops had been safely evacuated across the channel to England. The last four days of the operation were accomplished in weather bad enough to ground the Luftwaffe. The last day of the evacuation, June 4th, Churchill delivered a stirring speech in the House of Commons.

"Even though large tracts of Europe may fall into the grip of the Gestapo and all the odious apparatus of Nazi rule, we shall not flag or fail. We shall go on to the end. We shall fight in France; we shall fight in the seas and oceans; we shall fight with growing confidence and growing strength in the air; we shall defend our island, whatever the cost may be."

The Germans were unfazed. They swept across France like a forest fire on parched ground. June 16, 1940, an armistice was signed by France. Hitler was so sure the British would agree to his terms, he made no plans for crossing the English Channel and continuing the war on English soil. In his view, why should Britain fight alone against hopeless odds when it could get peace and remain intact? This question was asked everywhere except at the residence of the British Prime Minister on Downing Street. There, surrender was never considered. England had an 'inflexible resolve' to continue the war. And not just for themselves, but for Norway, Denmark, Poland, Czechoslovakia, Holland, Belgium, and above all, France. Churchill boldly declared that if the British Empire and its Commonwealth should last for a thousand years, men will say....... "This was their finest hour."

The Chief of Operations at the OKW (High Command of the Armed Forces), General Jodl, wrote on June 30th..."the final victory over England is now only a question of time." The invasion plan for England was *Operation Sea Lion*. But there really was no enthusiasm to implement it. The Germans didn't have the naval strength to take on the British Fleet and simultaneously transport an invasion force across the English Channel. By September Hitler gave up the idea completely and turned to Goering and the Air Force to destroy the R.A.F.

The air offensive was launched on August 15th. That day, more than 1,500 bomber and fighter sorties were flown, but the British Fighter Command, using Spitfires and Hurricanes, inflicted severe damage on the attacking Germans. One rather stark advantage employed by the out-numbered British was something new in warfare - *radar*. The attacking German planes could be tracked from the moment they left their bases in western Europe. This paradigm shift in technology puzzled the Germans who were far behind the British in the field of electronics.

Adding to the Nazi problems in what history would call 'the Battle of Britain', was Goering's decision not to attack the radar instillations. As the Germans continued to pound Britain with their superior number of aircraft, the attrition was beginning to take a toll on British planes and pilots. Now Goering made a second major tactical error. He stopped attacking the battered R.A.F. and shifted to massive night bombings of London, apparently in the belief that the bombings would destroy the will of the British people. He was wrong.

On August 23rd, German bombers were ordered to target factories and oil storage tanks on the outskirts of London. They missed their targets and dropped their bomb loads in the center of the city killing some 30 civilians. The following night, in retaliation, R.A.F. planes bombed Berlin. This was the first time bombs had fallen on the German capital and it was a major psychological blow. The Nazis were outraged, in spite of the fact they had been bombing other countries for months. Nazi controlled newspapers cried "brutality" in their descriptions of the British. The Luftwaffe intensified its bombing runs over England, but continued to lose more and more aircraft. By mid- September the Battle of Britain was a stalemate. With no real winner, thus Germany was essentially the loser.

Even before the plans to invade Britain were completely abandoned, Adolph Hitler had come to a decision. In the spring of 1941, he decided to turn to Russia and complete the conquest of the European Continent. Where Napoleon had failed 130 years ago, Hitler was determined to succeed.

* * *

As the Battle of Britain was drawing to a close in May, 1941, the race for building a bomb was becoming more intense. Germany had access to the world's only heavy- water factory and to thousands of tons of Uranium from the Belgian Congo. The only thing it did not have was a cyclotron. Eichenwald and his associates had decided that their biggest problem was isotope separation of U-238 and U-235. This was a very expensive proposition, but necessary. They were going to bank on a 'physical separation' technique. To move the process forward, a large wooden laboratory was being built on the KWI campus to house a breeder reactor. To keep espionage agents from becoming too curious, they named it the Virus House.

The German and U.S. efforts to manufacture a bomb were both affected by the Nazi Wehrmacht, but in opposite ways. In the U.S., the program was beginning to bog down in bureaucratic doubt. It was dramatically rescued by *Operation Barbarossa*, the German Blitzkrieg invasion of Russia that began at dawn on Sunday, June 22nd. The American program, in danger for its life in May, was now back on track. Aiding the U.S. effort was their British counterpart, the MAUD Report, which in October was terminated and transferred to the U.S. At the time of the transfer, the British were convinced of the success of a Uranium bomb, possibly by 1944. The collaboration of the two programs added significantly to expectations.

The invasion of Russia was now a reality and the German bomb program was being de-emphasized. This change in posture was worrisome to Hanz Eichenwald, but not for military reasons. His safety depended on his role as program director. But just as there appeared to be serious doubt about the future of the bomb, Fritz Houtermans became involved.

Houtermans was a tall, raw-boned Austrian. Half Jewish, he had also had links to the Communist Party. His father was Dutch, his mother Austrian. He was proud of his mother's Jewish origin. His PhD. in experimental physics was earned in Gottingen. He had brilliant ideas. One he developed in Berlin with a visiting British astronomer, Robert Atkinson. Together they worked out a theory about the expenditure of energy in stars. At the extremely high temperatures in stars (in excess of 10 million degrees) nuclei could penetrate other nuclei and cause reactions, releasing enormous amounts of energy over billions of years. Because of the extremely high temperatures, they called these events *thermonuclear reactions.*

In 1933, he had immigrated to the Soviet Union but ended up in prison, a victim of one of Stalin's purges. His wife and two small children managed to escape to the U.S. It appeared he would languish in a Soviet jail. But when Hitler made his temporary pact with Stalin, Houtermans wound up being part of a prisoner exchange and in 1939, was handed over to the Gestapo. He was then saved from the fate of a concentration camp by a physicist colleague, Max von Laue, one of the few German scientists who would stand up to the Nazis. Von Laue got him a job in private industry where, by August, 1941, he had worked out all of the basic ideas necessary for a bomb. Although kept private, his ideas moved the process along.

About a month after the 'miracle at Dunkirk', Winston Churchill sent a personal letter to Stalin warning him of the danger of Nazi hegemony in Europe. The Soviet dictator did not bother answering. Instead, he actually showed the letter to the Berlin government. Britain wanted to maintain a balance of power. As later would become evident, Stalin possessed incomprehensible ignorance of the drama that would soon engulf his country. In fact, at the moment of Stalin's complacency, Hitler was making his final plans to launch his attack against Russia. With the fall of France and the prospects of a British demise, he felt free to turn his Wehrmacht from West to East. In June of 1940, Hitler announced to his generals his intention to 'turn to Russia' and asked them to begin preparations for the invasion. Hitler believed Britain had weathered the storm partially because the English thought Russia would throw them a lifeline, as a man on the shore would do for a drowning man in the water. This sophistry led to his conclusion – "The sooner Russia is smashed the better!" He obviously believed he could neutralize the British by taking out the Russians. The course of the entire war would hang on this judgment.

His aim was to shatter the Soviet Nation in one great blow. He would use 120 divisions in two great armies. One would move south to Kiev and the Dnieper River, and the second north up through the Baltic States to Moscow. The attack would begin in May 1941, and the operation completed in five months.

In the fall of 1940, the Germans began troop deployments in preparation for the spring offensive. Ten infantry and two armored divisions were sent from the west to Poland. The panzer tank units were given the mission of protecting the oil fields in Rumania. The

Russian General Staff was informed that the troop movements were strictly replacements of older men who were moving out of the military into industry. They apparently believed this fabrication, at least to some degree.

As a matter of clarification, the Russian foreign minister, Molotov, was sent to Berlin in November of 1940. Bilateral talks were held but the discussion started on the subject of the four powers: Russia, Germany, Italy and Japan. The focus of the discussion centered on how to define their individual 'spheres of interest'. Hitler assured Molotov that they would "finish off" England as soon as the weather broke. He also briefly touched on the problem of America, feeling the U.S. had no business in Europe, Asia or Africa. Molotov agreed, but that was the only thing about which the two men agreed.

The following evening the Russians held a banquet in their embassy. Molotov had just proposed a friendly toast when air-raid sirens began to blare. The roar of British bombers and the thunder of the flack guns could be heard overhead. The two foreign ministers scurried to shelters and continued their dialogue. His German counterpart, Ribbentrop, pulled out a draft of a mendacious agreement, attempting to draw the Russians to their side. It was based on the position that the war with England had been won. In response, Molotov retorted, "If that is so, why are we in this shelter and whose bombs are falling on us?" In the final preparation for *Operation Barbarossa*, the so called 'Commissar Order' was issued by Hitler. The commissars were any individuals in Russia who opposed the ideology of German National Socialism. The order was that they all should be killed including women and teens. Any German soldier guilty of breaking international law would not be prosecuted. It stressed that Russia did not participate in the Hague Convention and therefore, had no rights of international law. The implication was that any soldier could decide guilt or innocence and meter out instant justice. In reality, that meant execution. Hitler intended for the German foot soldier to be a killing machine – and not just of enemy troops.

Heinrich Himmler, commander of the *SS*, was entrusted with special "tasks" for the preparation of the political administration of Russia. Occupied areas were to be sealed off and no one would be allowed to observe the actions of the *SS*, which would act independently from the military. Hermann Goering was given the task of securing Russian economic assets for use by German industry. The Russian economy and her natural resources would become the 'slaves' of the Nazi Reich.

Alfred Rosenberg, born in Russia and an early mentor of Hitler, was made Commissioner for Central Control of the East European Region. His many directives included the intention to export virtually all food stuffs in southern Russia to Germany. He saw no obligation to feed the Russian people. This policy was intended to systematically starve millions of Soviets. Rosenberg said, "It was a matter of priorities."

In spite of all of the evidence of an imminent attack - the presence of one million Nazi troops in the Balkans, the conquest of Yugoslavia and Greece, and the occupation of Rumania, Bulgaria and Hungary - Stalin and his associates in the Kremlin hoped there would be no attack. Germany was under a British Naval blockade and in need of raw materials. Inexplicably, the Russians were actually supplying Germany with the raw materials they needed for a military build-up. The Kremlin obviously believed the rumors of invasion were just that, rumors.

The official start date of 'Barbarossa' was June 22. An all-day meeting was held on June 14th by the German High Command to go over last minute details. The task ahead was enormous, the largest military operation in history. The front stretched some 1,500 miles from the Arctic Ocean to the Black Sea. During the lunch break, Hitler gave a comprehensive speech stressing that he was forced to attack Russia because her fall would force a British surrender. Once again he stressed the need to deal with the Soviets using "brutal means".

On Sunday morning, June 22, the same day Napoleon had crossed the Niemen River in 1812 to capture Moscow, the Nazi Wehrmacht poured across that same river into Russia.

* * *

The task of producing a chain reaction with Uranium was proving to be as difficult as Hanz Eichenwald had feared. His value to the Reich depended on the success of a project he did not want to succeed. He was trapped and had to find a way out. Isotope separation could not be achieved by chemical methods or gaseous-diffusion. What the German physicist desperately needed was cyclotron technology. Isolated by the war, this would prove difficult to get.

The British-American team had more physicists and significantly more resources. Arthur Compton, an American on the team, had drafted a report to the third annual National Academy of Sciences meeting, and it was very brief.

"A fission bomb of superlative destructive power will result from bringing quickly together a sufficient mass of element U-235. This seems to be as sure as any untried prediction, based upon theory and experiment, can be."

At almost the same time, German physicist Werner Heisenberg, a devoted protégé of Bohr's, was visiting his old mentor and showed him a drawing of the experimental heavy water reactor he was working to build. Bohr was fiercely anti-Nazi and interpreted this information to mean the Germans were making significant progress towards a bomb. Even though this was not the case, Bohr passed along this information to his British and American colleagues. Denmark was Nazi occupied territory, but Bohr had maintained complete academic freedom because he was a world-renowned physicist.

As 1941 was drawing to a close, Hanz Eichenwald felt his time was running out. His options were limited. While in the KWI, his activities were unrestricted. Outside the KWI, the Gestapo knew his every move. He was convinced that any escape plan must involve deception and that he would need help from a trusted person in the University. Two men came to mind. One was Max Planck, his mentor and friend. A realistic analysis of the situation revealed that Planck might be too old. Someone involved in a plot would have to be tough and bold, willing to take risks. Planck might crack. The only man left was Max von Laue. He was one of the few physicists who had the prestige and courage to stand-up to the Nazis. He had done it before when he helped Lise Meitner leave the country, and more recently, he freed Fritz Houtermans from the Gestapo.

One evening, Hanz arranged to see von Laue after hours in his lab. All of the lab assistants and graduate students were gone.

"Max, good to see you," Hanz said, extending his hand.

"It's been a few weeks, how are you? And how is the project coming along?"

Hanz smiled, "Oh yes! The bomb. It's a challenge. All we need is maybe another 100 million marks and a giant cyclotron."

Both men laughed. Max von Laue was an outstanding physicist and an even greater individual. Just being in his presence decreased Hanz's level of anxiety.

Max took Hanz by the arm. "Let's go back into my office where we will not be disturbed."

He was well aware of the circumstances his friend faced. Even before this encounter he had been considering ways to help the Eichenwalds. He would not speak out against the war effort but he felt nothing but contempt for the Nazis. He had many scientific colleagues who were Jewish and friends outside of academics as well. As they entered his office, he closed the door.

"I have been working on a plan to get you and Marlene out of Germany."

Hanz felt as if a huge weight had been removed from his shoulders. "Why am I not surprised! We really need some clear thinking. When your life is at stake, you are too close to the problem. What are your thoughts?"

Max was the clear thinker. "I have a mountain retreat where I go to write and be alone. Only my wife and I know about it. Not even my secretaries know. If I'm writing a paper or just need to get away, it is ideal. If we can get you there, then to France, the French underground can get you to the English Channel. Then...I don't know."

Hanz picked up the conversation. "I have a friend in England named Chaim Weizmann. He knows Churchill." Von Laue was astonished.

"Churchill! You're not going to do any better than that! I will begin laying some ground work and you start thinking about timing and contacting Weizmann. When will you be ready?"

"Sometime in the next two months."

"Alright," said von Laue. "I'll contact you in about three weeks. If the plan is for some reason at risk, I will get you a message with the word *fission*. You do the same. I have worried for months about your situation. The Germans have sold their national soul to the devil. I believe history will reveal this time as the nadir of our 1,000 years of existence."

As Hanz started to leave he gave Max a long gaze but could not speak. Von Laue did.

"I understand what this means to you. My thanks will be your safety in England."

*   *   *

In the same month that Max von Laue and Hanz Eichenwald were secretly plotting an escape for the Eichenwalds, Hitler believed Russia was finished. Field Marshal von Brock's northern Army group had pushed to within 200 miles of Moscow along the same route Napoleon had taken. Farther south, von Loeb's 21 infantry and six armored divisions were almost to the Dnieper River and Kiev. After months of combat, Hitler gave a radio address to update the country.

"I declare today, and I declare it without reservation, that the enemy in the East has been struck down and will never rise again."

But the conclusions of the German High Command were not only premature, they were wrong. The farther the German troops advanced into Russia, the more determined the Russians became. They were throwing fresh troops into battle almost weekly, and the German Panzer tanks were found to be no match for the Russian T-34. With the swift advances and the lack of suitable air fields, the German infantry was losing its air support. Finally, a theory that heavy Russian losses would result in an overthrow of Stalin proved to be inaccurate. The Russian people might have feared Stalin, but they were convinced that he was superior to the Nazi boot on their throats. The success of the Russian invasion was now a race against time. The brutal Russian winter was in the air. At this point Hitler made a major tactical error. He could center his effort on Moscow, the prize goal, or Leningrad in the north and the Ukraine in the south. His generals urged him to take Moscow. It was the major transportation and communications center and contained most of Russia's armament facilities. Hitler decided to focus on the industrial areas and oil fields of the Ukraine. The strength of the Russian Army was positioned to defend Moscow. They expected the attack to come there. Even with this decision, the central Nazi forces were within 40 miles of Moscow when the mid-October rains came, followed quickly by snow. The biting winds froze more than the ground. They penetrated the German troops like a barbed wire fence. The German generals began to re-read accounts of the disastrous winter of 1812 that led to Napoleon's defeat. The stark reality was that the same winter that had defeated Napoleon was going to defeat them.

On December 6, 1941, Russian General Georgi Zhukov began a counterattack across a 200 mile front against an enemy bogged down in six-foot snow drifts and minus 35-degree weather. For the first time since the invasion of Poland, the Wehrmacht was in retreat. The bitter reality of the Russian winter was staring the German High Command in the face. The picture they were seeing was the collective, frozen corpses of thousands of German soldiers.

The following day, Sunday December 7th, was an infamous day in American history and in the history of the world. The Japanese Navy, using carrier based planes, attacked the U.S. Pacific fleet at Pearl Harbor in the Hawaiian Islands. For more than nine months Hitler had been trying to get Japan into the war, but not against the

U.S. He wanted the fight with Britain. Japan's seizure of Singapore and other British bases in the Far East would greatly weaken England. He also felt it was important to steer away from provoking the U.S. into abandoning her position of neutrality. But the Japanese had bigger fish to fry. On November 25, 1941, their carrier task force set sail for Pearl Harbor. Hitler had never mentioned his intention to attack Russia, and the Japanese felt deceived. Now they were taking things into their own hands. Preceding the attack on Pearl, Japan had invaded parts of Manchuria and China. In the process, some 200,000 women and children had been slaughtered. The U.S. response was to freeze Japanese assets in America and embargo oil and iron ore to Japan. The Japanese could survive no more than 18 months without access to Asian Oil and iron. This forced their hand. The commander of the Japanese Fleet, Isoroku Yamamoto, had studied in the U.S. and had an intimate understanding of the potential strength of the American military. But if war was to come, he intended to "give a fatal blow to the enemy fleet." In reality, he visualized a conflagration that might become uncontrollable, burning everything in its path.

At 7:00 am in Hawaii on that Sunday, two U.S. Army privates were manning the mobile radar station on the northern most reach of the island of Oahu. They noticed an unusual disturbance on their screen. They plotted the radar signal at a northeast bearing of 130 miles. They called the information center at Fort Shafter on the other end of the island. The lieutenant who took the call decided it must be a squadron of B-17's coming from California.

"Well, don't worry about it!"

The following afternoon, Franklin Roosevelt addressed a joint session of Congress. He requested and was granted a declaration of war against Japan, Germany and Italy.

* * *

December of 1941 brought almost a sense of relief in London. The nightly bombings from German aircraft had slowed to about one episode a week on average, and since the British air defense radar systems were active and accurate, there were no surprises. The German sorties were mostly harassment efforts. They were not interested in continuing to confront the British fighter squadrons since they had been losing two planes for every one lost by the British.

The British people had the sense of confidence that comes with having a big brother. America had officially joined the fray. Things did not seem nearly as bleak as they had in the spring when Londoners endured nightly pounding from the Luftwaffe. British citizens were supremely confident in their leader, Winston Churchill. His 'bull dog' determination had become contagious.

Chaim Weizmann was in his office at Cambridge where he served as adjunct professor of biochemistry. He had no lecture responsibilities because of the Christmas holiday. The undergraduate students were on break and his doctoral candidates were off as well. His secretary, Mary Casterbridge, was trying to tie up last minute details before the ten day break between Christmas and the New Year. She knocked softly on his door and entered.

"Dr. Weizmann, you have a cable-gram from the Swiss Embassy. It is marked urgent and confidential."

"Thank you, Mary. Hold any calls for the next hour."

He waited to open the sealed envelope until she had closed the door. It read as follows:

To: Chaim Weizmann, PhD. - Cambridge University – England

Form: Hanz Eichenwald PhD. - KWI – Berlin

Explosive situation rapidly reaching 'critical mass'. Anticipate movement in next few weeks. Can pick-up rendezvous in English Channel be arranged?

If affirmative…reply enzyme studies going well. If negative… reply enzyme studies failed.

Hanz

Switzerland, the only neutral country during the war, provided a reliable way of information transmission as long as it was of a non-military nature. Cables could be sent from their embassy in Berlin to any Swiss embassy in the world. In wartime the only other way of communication was by short-wave radio, which was used by the French and Danish underground.

Chaim Weizmann buzzed his secretary and asked her to get him a line to the department of the Navy. He was still well known for his work during WWI and had actually been awarded the Queens Medal, the highest award given to a civilian in England. He was a renowned scientist and a Zionist. Since his childhood in Russia he had believed that the Jewish Nation was destined to settle back in the land they had been promised in antiquity. There were many who denied that the Jews were a nation at all. But Weizmann believed that not only were they a nation, but one deprived of their national territory. They had been driven out of Palestine in 70 AD, this was the second Diaspora or scattering of Jews. The first was their exile to Babylon in 605 BC.

Now his dream of the returning of his people to Palestine seemed more of a reality with the Balfour Declaration of 1919. He had helped resettle hundreds of Jewish intellectuals from occupied

Europe. Now he was in a position to help his friend Hanz Eichenwald and wife, Marlene.

"Dr. Weizmann, I have the Navy Department."

Weizmann spoke with an undersecretary to the Admiralty and made an appointment for the following afternoon. He then dialed a secure direct line to Churchill. This number was known to only 10 men in England, including the Lords of the Admiralty, Army and Air Force. Weizmann felt it a high privilege to be included in the group. He never expected to use it. The phone was answered by a Colonel Branch. About one minute after Weizmann identified himself Churchill was on the line. "Chaim, nice to hear from you...how can I help you?"

Churchill was a warm, iconic man. He also knew Chaim Weizmann would only contact him on business of some urgency. Weizmann briefly explained the situation with Eichenwald. When hearing that the directing physicist of the German nuclear bomb project was trying to defect, Weizmann had his full attention.

"Chaim, we will pull out all the stops to get your man to England, you can be sure of that."

The following day Weizmann met with officials of the British Navy. They had already been briefed by Churchill's office. A plan was devised to use a submarine to pick-up the Eichenwalds under cover of darkness, four miles off of the coast of France. The British had short-wave communication with the French underground and would set the coordinates. There was a four day window with no moonlight during the third week of January, weather permitting. They would have to be transported in a row boat. A motorized boat might draw attention from German shore patrols. The French underground would have the responsibility of getting the Eichenwalds to the rendezvous point.

Two days after Christmas a cablegram was delivered from the Swiss Embassy to the KWI for Hanz Eichenwald. It read:

To:Hanz Eichenwald PhD. - KWI – Berlin

From: Department of Biochemistry - Cambridge University – England

Enzyme studies going well…expect completion week of January 20th.

Department Chairman

Chaim Weizmann was a champion of Judaism. He had worked tirelessly in the resettlement of Jewish academic refugees and was active in recruiting faculty for the Hebrew University in Jerusalem. He now had the opportunity of delivering a giant in the world of physics. But he was not thinking of the University. This was a deadly game. If it was lost, the Eichenwalds would end up in an incinerator at Auschwitz or some other death camp. Weizmann was in fact a minor player on the team. The major players were those in the occupied territories willing to risk their lives for faceless souls trapped in a capricious world.

The military setbacks in Russia were not the only negative news for the Third Reich. It was clear in Berlin that the German economy had reached its limit of expansion. The Minister of Munitions now had made it clear to the nuclear bomb team that progress must be clearly seen in the next six months or the project might be scrapped. A high level meeting was called for the third week in January to present evidence of progress towards a bomb. It would also include concrete expenditure estimates and a timetable. Hanz decided to ask Werner Heisenberg to make the presentation.

It would be a crucial meeting in the German effort to produce a weapon of mass destruction. The strain of the war effort and the recent setbacks was taking the focus off of the bomb project.

With the New Year behind him, Hanz was finding it almost impossible to focus on physics or bombs or the Nazis. He had lunch on two occasions with Max von Laue and the plan for their escape was taking shape. The key hurdle was to be able to leave Berlin without arousing suspicion of the Gestapo. He was scheduled to deliver a lecture on Quantum Theory at the University of Munich on January 12th. His office at the KWI had made his travel arrangements for the train to Munich for the 11th with return on the 13th, a Saturday. This time, Marlene would accompany him as she did on occasion.

Hanz and Marlene had decided not to inform Anna, although she had been aware for months that there was something in the wind. She knew they had to leave. In all of Berlin, only von Laue was aware of the plot and details. Once they were safe in England, he would inform Anna. He had connections to the German underground, run mostly by Communist sympathizers and Christians who were strongly opposed to the Nazi war and pogrom. The risk was always there. Even a man of his stature could be brought down. His hideaway in the Harz Mountains, west of Berlin, would be used as a stopover.

Beyond that, he had no knowledge of the operation. Von Laue had only sketchy details of the resistance work. The less he knew the better. He was aware that the Gestapo had informants everywhere. He even knew of teens who had informed on parents. Betrayals were not uncommon. Complicity was a death sentence.

* * *

Since the controversy over the appointment of Hanz Eichenwald to head the bomb project, Heinrich Himmler had in mind to end the controversy. His authority had been challenged and he was determined to end the career of this Jewish physicist. His Gestapo surveillance had informed him of the planned trip to Munich. This would be an ideal time to detain the professor, then quickly transport him to Poland. Arresting him away from Berlin would effectively cut off any support he might have from the KWI. Himmler also wanted to prevent him from attending the upcoming meeting to discuss the bomb project. The head of the SS thought it reprehensible that a Jew would be involved in any military effort, especially this one. Himmler was a lugubrious sort, and more so when he did not get his way.

On Wednesday, January 10th, Hanz finished his work in his office an hour early. He gathered his most important documents and placed them in his briefcase. He hoped, rather, he believed that he would never see his office again. There were many memories but no time to ponder them. As he looked around one final time his thoughts briefly drifted back to his long visits with Einstein and their discussions on the Universe. It truly had been a phenomenon to sit for hours talking to this most unique man. Einstein wisely had left Germany when the Nazi Reich came to power. Now Hanz was going to place his life and the life of the only woman he had ever loved in the hands of complete strangers. It was a deadly gamble. He pulled his office door closed and looked at his secretary Heidi.

"I won't be in tomorrow. Our train leaves in the evening and I have some work to do at home. I'll see you on Monday."

"Have a safe trip," she replied.

The following morning, Thursday the 11th, was an unusually bright day. It was crisp and cold but beautiful. Hanz walked the 10 blocks to his bank. He planned to withdraw 1,000 marks for the trip; he knew he could use five times that much but was fearful of calling Gestapo attention to a larger withdrawal. The train departure time was 6:06 pm from Central Station. It was an overnight trip with two stops in route. First, they would go to Leipzig and the second stop would be Nuremburg, then on to Munich with arrival at 8:15 am. His lecture was at 1:00 pm. He had been told he would be contacted in Munich before the lecture. That is all the information he had, and he had no choice but to trust his colleague Max von Laue.

As the time progressed, Hanz and Marlene were silent, each trying to contemplate leaving their home of the past 25 years. Marlene was taking a final walk through to see their pictures, allowing her mind to wander. There was one old grainy photo of their marriage and her favorite picture of Anna at the age of six, holding up the first tooth she had lost. Marlene removed it from the frame and placed it in her bag. They would leave it all; every possession, every photo, every link to their lives. But they would not leave their memories.

Packed with only what they would need for an overnight stay, the Eichenwalds embarked on a journey they hoped would yield them a lifetime. Many of their friends had been forced to leave; now they were joining them. Marlene allowed herself one last look at her flower garden in the rear of the house. Now dormant in winter, she could visualize the roses and marigolds, the geraniums and tulips. The beauty of her garden was a stark contrast to the cold, emotion-less men whose ambition was to enslave millions by military might. And for what reason? And what sane person would understand it anyway? Marlene was brought back to reality by the voice of her husband. "Marlene. It's time to go."

With two small suitcases and one briefcase, Hanz and Marlene closed and locked their front door. Their taxi was waiting.

"I don't know if I can leave without speaking to Anna," she whispered. "Max will get word to her soon enough. We can't make any mistakes."

On this same day, Heinrich Himmler had given final instructions concerning the arrest of the Eichenwalds.

"They are to be arrested in Munich and immediately transported to the ghetto in Cologne," he said to his adjuvant. "Then the train to Poland, and to Auschwitz, understand? If they resist shoot them."

He loomed in front of the adjuvant like a dark pit of anger and hatred. The adjuvant quickly left the room and contacted the Munich Gestapo office. The orders were clear.

Berlin Central Station was an enormous gray stone structure. It was the transportation hub for all of Germany and now all Europe. Since it was used for public transportation only, it likely would never be bombed. The inner central area was almost the size of a soccer field with an arched 100 foot ceiling. On average, 11,000 passengers passed through the main terminal every day. Hanz and Marlene quickly found their platform and boarded. It was 5:17 pm.

Their small state room was comfortable and private. Upon entering they noticed a Nazi soldier. The military was everywhere. Germany was at war. Hanz locked the door and pulled the shades.

"I would rather not see anyone," he said to Marlene. "This trip can't end soon enough."

Marlene sat staring at the floor and said nothing. Her feeling of hopelessness was starting to overwhelm her. Without looking up she reached her hand out to Hanz. He sat beside her and placed his arm around her shoulders. He knew what she was thinking.

"Anna will be fine. I know she will be fine."

When the train slowly began to pull out of the station, they still had not moved. There was a slight jolt, and then another. The steam engine struggled to change the inertia of the cars from stationary to moving. Once moving, the acceleration was steady. Within 20 minutes they were in the countryside.

It was getting dark and Hanz opened the window shade. Lights at the road crossings whizzed by in a blur. He then lowered the shade. Marlene had no appetite so Hanz went to the dining car and returned with a pot of coffee. Marlene looked up as he entered.

"Do you have any idea what's going to happen?" she asked.

"We will be contacted by the underground before the lecture or possibly before we board the train to return to Berlin. The plan is to get us to the Harz Mountains. That's where von Laue's hideaway is located. Then we go to France and the Channel."

"What are our chances?"

Hanz wanted to be optimistic.

"I think they are good. There is no question that we will be taken to a ghetto or worse if we stay. I think the bomb project will be dropped. It's just a matter of time." He was not a man prone to fear. But for reasons he did not understand, he felt unusually confident. Perhaps because of his trust of Max von Laue. Or perhaps because he was an optimist by nature.

The train gently rocked along with the ever-present clickety-clack, clickety-clack of the steel wheels crossing the rail joints.

Marlene fell asleep sitting on the sofa. He decided to let her sleep. Sleep was the only escape she had from her apprehension.

The next two hours passed quickly. Hanz must have drifted to sleep himself but came awake as the train began to slow. He glanced at his watch. It was 9:50 pm. The scheduled 20 minute stop in Leipzig was at 10:00 pm. After that, they would change for bed and hope to get some sleep. Sleep had not come easily the last few weeks. Too often it had been brought on by exhaustion and too often interrupted by worry.

When the train came to a full stop Marlene woke up. All was quiet.

"As soon as we leave Leipzig, why don't you get a hot shower," Hanz said, taking Marlene's hand. "It will help you relax."

They heard distant muffled conversation and paid no attention. Then suddenly there was shouting. It was coming from the rear of the car. Rapid steps in the hallway were followed by loud pounding on their compartment door.

"Open! Open! Police!"

At first Hanz was frozen. He was startled that someone would be pounding on the door. The sound became louder.

"Open up, now!"

Hanz unlocked the door and two *SS* officers entered. "Dr. Eichenwald, you are under arrest!"

Marlene opened her mouth to scream but nothing came out. "For what?" Hanz demanded. "What is the charge?"

The officer glared back at him.

"You should know, Jew bastard." He turned to the other officer. "Cuff them. Get their luggage."

The railcar attendant, pale and stunned, looked like an apparition. The officer shoved him against the wall slamming his head against the glass window. "Move aside. Keep all of the compartment doors closed."

The Eichenwalds were quickly taken off of the train to a waiting car with military markings. The car sped off into the darkness. After a brief time, the officer turned to face Hanz and Marlene.

"Dr. Eichenwald, I'm sorry. We work in the underground resistance. We must be convincing."

As he removed their handcuffs he continued.

"We have an informant in Himmler's office. They had planned to arrest you as you left the train in the morning. We found out just in time."

Hanz reached for Marlene's hand and held it tightly

"Thank God!" he whispered.

CHAPTER 13
Werner Schmidt

Laura Knochen stopped by the Pumpkin House Bakery to see if Paula Herzog had seen Marlene. Laura had not heard from her friend in over two weeks. She greeted Paula with a hug. "Wondering if you have seen Marlene? We were going to have lunch last week, but she didn't come by. I called her home and stopped by, but no one is there."

"No, I haven't heard from her either," Paula replied with a downcast look. "I suppose she is on some kind of travel with her husband. Jews are prohibited from traveling, but that might not apply to professors."

Laura could see the fatigue in Paula's eyes. She was sallow and looked thinner. "Can we go in the back?" Laura asked.

The two women made their way to the back of the store. It was empty of customers but they had already acclimated to the need for secrecy. Laura had been contemplating for weeks, the idea of becoming involved in the defeat of the Third Reich. She didn't consider anything of a military nature, but she wanted to do something. Laura pulled Paula close to her.

"You and Victor are in danger," Laura whispered.

"We know that," Paula said, her eyes on the floor. "Our son was working with us here. Now he's disappeared. We haven't had a word from him in a month now. We think the Nazis have taken him to a ghetto or detention camp. We are waiting ourselves. Our turn is coming. Most of our friends are already gone…taken. Our Synagogue was burned."

Paula was silent a moment, then said again, "We are waiting."

Laura placed both hands on Paula's shoulders. "Look at me, Paula. You and Victor come stay with me at my flat. I insist. I have an attic. You can sleep there. I have no family. This is your only hope."

Paula smiled faintly. "Laura, if they catch you at this they will kill you. No question they will kill you. And Victor and I will still be deported to a work camp."

"Get Victor," Laura went on. "I must talk to both of you."

Paula went to the kitchen and returned with her husband. They had locked the front door and displayed the 'closed' sign.

"You both must understand. The war the Nazis have brought is more than a war of conquest. It is for racial cleansing. Their intent is to exterminate every Jewish man, woman and child from Europe. The Synagogues in Germany have been destroyed. Almost all of your friends are gone. Your son has disappeared. Where are these people? Thousands of them, gone! I am begging you. Come to my home, tonight. Get your things. After the blackout begins, say about 11:00, come to my place. Paula, you have visited, you know my place, remember?"

Victor had listened intently. "We will come," he said. "You have obviously thought this through. You are willing to risk your life?"

"My husband is gone. This is my way of fighting the Nazi madness. I will expect you at 11:00. The door will be unlocked."

By 1942, 90 percent of Jewish Germans had been moved to ghettos or placed in concentration camps. Virtually all of the Polish intellectuals and social elites had been murdered. The remaining two million Polish Jews were placed in labor camps. There was horrific overcrowding with tens of thousands sequestered into insalubrious ghettos. Most were used as forced laborers, given limited food and poor treatment. This attrition by forced labor was planned. In time, thousands would disappear into a legendary vanishing point. Even before the fall of Poland, the concept of deporting Polish Jews had been debated. One idea considered, was the movement of a million Poles to the French colony of Madagascar, off the coast of east Africa. The plan was never implemented. Another consideration that had some American and British interest was the deportation of Jews to Ethiopia, which was then controlled by Italy.

Prior to 1942, mass deportation of Jews seemed to be the answer. After 1942, the 'Final Solution' had quickly evolved into a massive extermination strategy, one that included forced labor or gas chambers – both of which were designed for death.

* * *

The day of the scheduled lecture on Quantum Theory at the University of Munich found Heinrich Himmler in a rage. He screamed at his adjuvant. "What do you mean they were not on the train? Did they just vanish?"

The captain, ashen faced, tried to explain. "Herr Commandant, they were arrested and removed from the train by *SS* officers at the Leipzig stop, but *SS* has no record of the incident. They were taken off of the train by imposters."

Himmler sat down behind his massive desk. His office, lined in dark mahogany, held several Renaissance paintings pilfered from occupied France. The office was an extension of his enormous ego. The lush room with its dark rich leather furnishings was in fact, a horror chamber. In this room, insidious plots were devised and cruel decisions settled to seal the fate of hundreds of thousands of people. In this one small space, a scheme was designed that would have permanent and devastating impact around the world. Here, Himmler and his deputy-in- command, Reinhard Heydrich, hammered out the details of the 'Final Solution' of the Jewish problem – their existence.

Himmler had become second only to Hitler. He shared Hitler's view that Jews were 'subhuman' and that Europe should be "Jew free". Germans would become the master-race. All other occupied peoples, particularly those in Russia and the Slavic countries, would be slave labor to the Reich. Hitler himself placed his stamp of approval on these policies. He emphasized as much in a memoranda in July, 1941.

"As for the ridiculous hundred million Slavs, we will mold the best of them to the shape that suits us, and we will isolate the rest of them in their own pig-sties; and anyone who talks about cherishing the local inhabitant and civilizing him, goes straight off to a concentration camp."

Given such dark sentiments and an agenda set in stone, Himmler was more than irate that the man he most wanted to eliminate had been allowed to escape right from under his nose. This was more than an insult. It called for swift retaliation. But to whom should he direct it? He had been outsmarted.

"Get me the *SS* Commandant in Munich and get me the files of all of our staff. We have a traitor in our midst! He or she will be found and dwelt with."

"Yes Commandant."

"And get Colonel Scheidemann immediately. I want this Jew Professor found!"

"Yes Commandant."

The ride in the military vehicle had been quiet. Hanz and Marlene Eichenwald were drained, although the four hour trip to Halberstadt in the Harz Mountains was uneventful. The road was winding and the gentle moving of the car back and forth finally took Marlene into a restful sleep as she leaned against Hanz' shoulder.

The men of the underground resistance rode silently with them. They had introduced themselves by first names which Hanz understood to be aliases. Every day in the resistance was lived at great risk. These men and a few women were suspicious of everyone they did not know and even some they did. Any person could be an informant for the Gestapo or *SS*, so anyone coming into the underground was watched carefully and given almost no information until it was clear they could be trusted. Almost all those involved were ethnic Germans. A few Jews from the rural areas were also involved.

The retreat of Max von Laue was very remote, about four kilometers north of the village of Halberstadt. The road was gravel but the snow had been plowed. The cabin was well maintained, but principally used in the summer. It had electricity and a wood-burning stove, a bedroom and a large living area with a hearth. Max had an office in a loft above the bedroom.

One of the resistance members had been to the cabin earlier in the day. He had built a fire and brought coffee, bread, bacon, beans and eggs. They arrived around midnight and the fire had burned low, but the cabin was warm and inviting.

Approaching the door, two of the men gave the Eichenwalds brief instructions. They should stay inside the cabin. There was plenty of firewood. Someone would contact them the next evening after dark. The men were aware that the time line projected them to be at the French coast by the 20th. As the men left, Hanz added wood to the stove and locked the door. Sleep was welcome for the two weary travelers.

At that same time, Himmler was sitting quietly in his office reviewing the files of the men on his staff. He explained the situation to the Munich office. The mole must be found and Eichenwald must be found as well. At first glance he did not notice anything unusual in the files of his office workers, but he remained suspicious. All 12,000 *SS* personal in Germany had been placed on 'high alert' for the Eichenwalds. The search was headed by Colonel Scheidemann and the focus would be along the western border. The couple likely was headed for England. They needed to be stopped at the German border. It would be more difficult to find them in France. All border points had been notified.

The following evening about 9:00 p.m., a man who appeared to be a farmer, came to the cabin on a motorcycle. He was brief. He told the Eichenwalds they would be picked up the following evening and gave no further details. Hanz and Marlene spent the next day resting. They ate a late breakfast of boiled eggs, coffee and bacon. The secluded cabin was comfortable but they were asked not to build a fire during the day. Smoke would call attention that someone was there. They wrapped themselves in blankets. That night, again around 9:00 p.m., the same man returned to the cabin.

"About 4:00 a.m., you will be placed in a truck for the journey to France," he told them. "What kind of truck?" asked Hanz. "Is it safe?"

"You will see. It's our best chance."

He climbed on the motorcycle and looked at Hanz and Marlene. "Good luck," he said as he pulled away.

The resistance was well organized. They had improvised an elaborate escape plan for a high profile target such as Dr. Eichenwald. A quick decision had been made to execute the plan for him. It involved a truck driver who transported a load of beer and ale once a week into occupied France for German troops. The route was from Heidelberg to Paris. The truck carried 32 barrels of beer. A carpenter had modified the bed of the truck and built a concealed compartment large enough for two adults lying flat. It had not been used previously. The major problem would be getting past the checkpoint at the border, then dealing with the consequences when the beer was not delivered in Paris on schedule. The Eichenwalds needed to be in Calais by January 20th. It would be too dangerous to deliver the beer with them concealed in the truck since the delivery warehouse was run by the German military. The driver had a choice. He could defect to England or take his chances of getting caught if he returned to Germany. There were no trials for those in the resistance. They were tortured for information and then shot.

Werner Schmidt was not a complex man. Raised on a farm, he had a ruddy complexion, light blue eyes and muscular shoulders and arms developed from years of plowing behind a mule. His father had sustained severe war injuries in 1917 and was an invalid who existed on a modest pension. Werner quit school in 1919 to help support the family. He married Maria Strobel, a girl he had known since childhood. As a teen Maria idolized Werner and now loved the simple life he provided. They lived on the family farm outside Heidelberg. Werner's mother had died during childbirth and he was the only surviving child in his family.

He was not taken into the military because he was the only son of an invalid war veteran. He despised Hitler and what he had done to Germany, and as a result, joined the underground in 1939.

He had never confided this to Maria. Although she never questioned him about his activities, she suspected his involvement. Werner lived a dangerous double life. A man living very much on the edge, he had been making the weekly beer runs for over a year, crossing back and forth across the border at Strasbourg, France. He had limited information about underground operations, but knew code words and the names of several operatives. His truck had not been used in any previous clandestine operation; now it was time.

Since joining in 1939, only two men had been caught by the *SS*. Both died without giving up vital information. Families were never involved in the resistance and wives never participated. They were simply too vulnerable. Rape and torture of wives in the presence of their husbands was an *SS* specialty. Men with children at home were never in the underground for the same reason.

Werner had spent the afternoon with Maria. She sensed something different in his behavior. He sat with her in his arms, stroking her hair and kissing her forehead. As he looked down his eyes filled with tears.

"Werner, what is it?" she pressed. "I'm going to Paris tomorrow." "You go every week."

"I won't be returning...at least not for a while. If anyone inquires about me, you expected me back in two days as usual. Do you understand?"

"Do you have to do this? I mean, why? Why do you have to go?" "This is my way....our way...." He could not continue. Maria looked into his eyes and nodded her head. She shared his contempt for the Nazis. Now she was being called on to do her part and was resolved to do it well. She did not understand exactly what he was doing, but she now understood he would not return. He was not afraid to die and even believed he could stand up to torture. But he knew his limits. He could never endure seeing his Maria in the hands of the *SS*. He would give them what they wanted and still be killed. The underground carried even more risk than fighting at the front. At least he believed in his cause. Many at the front did not.

Werner and Maria Schmidt were among the hundreds, perhaps thousands of heroes of the war. They clung to each other and cried. Finally, he pulled himself away from her. "Be brave Maria," he said. "I will see you again...I don't know when. I love you."

He left about midnight for the three hour trip to Halberstadt. He had filled the truck with petrol and soaked several rags in it as well, then placed them in a metal container. It was a cold, clear night. Trucks traveling on rural roads did not raise suspicion. There were no known check points between Heidelberg and the Harz mountains. He took back roads and by-passed Frankfurt. The truck arrived at the von Laue cabin about 3:45 a.m. on Monday 15th. The Eichenwalds heard the truck and were ready.

As they walked out of the cabin Werner greeted them with handshakes. "I am your ride to France. You'll need blankets."

Hanz inquired about the truck and how they would be concealed.

"There is a compartment built into the bed of the truck big enough for two adults," said Werner."If you did not know it was there, it would be difficult to detect. The border guards at Strasbourg will likely have dogs that can detect human scent. Petrol confuses their sense of smell. As we approach you will open this container filled with petrol soaked rags to confuse them."

"Will it work?" asked Hanz.

"It should," Werner replied. "But we haven't tried it. Now our lives depend on it."

"And if it doesn't work?

"Then I will be shot and you will be arrested," he said.

Anna had not talked with her parents in almost a week. Her custom was to see them at Synagogue. Now there was no Synagogue to attend. She had phoned on two occasions without success. She was unaware of any travel plans. Jews were barred from travel although she seemed to recall a planned trip to Munich for some type of lecture. It was Monday morning, January 15th. Anna had finished staffing the surgical clinic and was doing chart review in her office. She had planned to work late and kept thinking of the time she would have later in the day with Christian. Then her secretary Theresa knocked on the door and entered. Anna noted a confused expression on her face.

"Dr. Eichenwald, there are two officers to see you."

Almost simultaneously, two *SS* officers walked into her office, one moving Theresa aside on entering.

"Dr. Eichenwald, sorry to bother you. Are you aware your parents have disappeared?" Anna was clearly startled.

"Disappeared…no…when?"

She felt her blood pressure rising. She stood facing the men, her mind racing to try to recall their conversation about the bomb project. But she had known almost nothing about her father's work. The senior officer continued.

"Your father was scheduled to deliver a lecture at the University of Munich on Friday. He and your mother boarded the train to Munich

on Thursday evening. They were not on the train when it arrived...
and you do not know of their where-abouts?"

"No, I have no idea."

The officer would not divulge the information that they were
removed from the train, but he was convinced Anna was being truth-
ful, and he would report that to Himmler. As they left, he handed her
a card with the *SS* headquarters number.

"Please call us if you hear from them...." He knew she
would not.

That evening Anna was more than anxious to see Christian.
Their routine was to meet in the surgical lounge and talk briefly about
surgical issues, then leave separately and meet again in his office
using a back entrance. When Anna approached Christian he smiled
and gave his usual warm greeting. Anna did not return the smile.

"My parents have disappeared," she said quietly. "I'm sure
they have left the country or they're trying to leave. I'll see you in 20
minutes in your office."

As Anna left the lounge, Christian's head was spinning. He sat
down to gather his thoughts. None of the medical staff had heard
from the Counsel on Eugenics, but he was aware of the Nazi programs to eliminate mentally and physically handicapped children.
He was concerned that the escape of the Eichenwalds could trigger
the arrest of Anna. He had mailed her picture to his sister in Leipzig,
but had no word from her. Now he felt a greater urgency. He knew
that Anna was at greater risk.

The two met in his office and sat on a sofa. Anna agreed that
she could be arrested at any time as a reprisal.

"This is looking more dangerous for me by the day. I know my
parents were at risk, just like me. Something may have triggered

their leaving. I think the *SS* believes I did not know anything about it. That seemed obvious, I think. But it won't protect me. They may be deciding while we speak when to make their move."

"I'm afraid you're right," Christian agreed. "I'll contact Sarah tomorrow. She has been working on your identity papers and looking for a place for you to live and a job for you. If need be, you can live in her flat for a few weeks."

"Well, we knew it was coming. Now it's here."

* * *

Werner Schmidt had decided it would be safe for Hanz and Marlene to ride with him in the truck cab until daybreak, or until they approached Heidelberg. Once in the concealed compartment, they would have to remain there until well past the checkpoint at Strasbourg. That would be a tiring six hours. During the ride he was able to get some information about his 'VIP' passengers. After hearing about the KWI and the nuclear bomb project, he knew he had made the right decision to risk his life for them.

"Can you tell us anything about yourself?" asked Hanz. "The other resistance workers have said nothing. We are grateful for those who are risking their lives for us. If you cannot speak, we will understand."

After a long silence Werner finally spoke. "I can tell you about myself if you like, but only because of this special circumstance."

"You mean our trip to the English Channel?"

"Let me explain," said Werner. "I have worked in the resistance for three years. My wife is not involved and knows nothing of what I do. We have no children and my father was left an invalid by the first war. That's why I am not in the military. I chose to resist the

Nazis. I drive this beer truck to Paris once each week. We have prepared for one year for an important person or persons who need out of Germany not knowing who that might be. Now we have names and faces."

"So, this truck is the special circumstance?"

Werner continued. "Partly. If we get by the German border, then we will be joined by someone from the French underground. We will by-pass Paris and drive to Reims, then to Calais. When I do not arrive in Paris on schedule, the SS will begin to look for me. They may go as far as connecting me to your escape. At any rate, we will dump the beer in the ocean and burn the truck. The French underground is in contact with the English by short-wave. That's all I know. If I am caught they would torture my wife in my presence to get information from me. For this reason I am going with you to England. My other option would be to go back and work in another part of the country and if caught, end my life. Either way, I would not see my wife again."

Marlene was moved by the story.

"So, you are giving up your family for us?" "No. I am doing this to fight Nazis."

Daybreak approached. Werner turned off of the main road onto a gravel road that led to a farmhouse. He turned into the lane to the house.

"The occupants have left. They do not want to see you nor you them. Go inside and use their toilet. If we get by the border, you will be in the compartment for the next six hours. In one-half hour we will load the beer. Then to the border. You must not speak or make any noise at the border."

He handed Hanz the metal container with the petrol soaked rags.

"I will tell you when to open it and place the rags around your bodies. There is a small passage from the truck cabin to the compartment for ventilation and communication."

The Eichenwalds disappeared into the farmhouse and returned in five minutes.

The flatbed truck had wooden side rails. The ones in the rear could be removed for loading and unloading. Hanz helped Marlene up onto the bed platform. He was searching for the compartment opening but could not find it. Werner then stepped onto the platform and used a small steel pin to pry open two side by side doors that opened like barn doors. Their borders were cleverly concealed in the slot margins of the platform. Hanz and Marlene lay down in the compartment with the canister between them. As Werner closed the doors, it occurred to both that this compartment could be their coffin. Neither mentioned these thoughts to the other.

After the 30 minute ride, the truck pulled into the distribution dock. Thirty-two kegs of beer and ale were loaded. The Eichenwalds were both thinking the next few hours would end their lives or send them on to freedom and safety. They could see very little. Hanz searched for Marlene's hand. They set off again for another 90 minute journey from Heidelberg to the German border. Werner spoke with them through the ventilation passage. They were cold. Then truck began to slow.

"Open the canister and place the rags around you," Werner said calmly. "We are approaching the checkpoint."

Marlene began to feel nauseated. She swallowed to try to keep from vomiting.

Werner had made the trip weekly for about a year. He knew a number of the soldiers by name. As he pulled up to the guardrail blocking the road, he saw no familiar faces. All of the men were SS. He was not waved through as usual, but was directed to pull off of the road. An SS lieutenant walked to the truck.

"Good day. Please get out of the cab."

As Werner stepped down the lieutenant continued.

"We are looking for a couple trying to escape the country, a Jew and his wife. Have you seen them?"

"I have no knowledge of them," he replied, looking directly at the lieutenant. Werner could see that the lieutenant did not believe him.

"Step aside!" he yelled sharply. "We are going to unload the truck."

Four SS soldiers then unloaded each barrel of beer, carefully rocking each one to feel the movement of the contents. They were 50-liter containers and could easily hold an adult. One by one, the barrels were checked. The lieutenant watched carefully as the troops finished checking all of the barrels. He began to be agitated and glared at the soldiers.

"Are you certain?" he demanded. "Ja, Leftenant!"

The lieutenant then stepped up on the platform. "Get the dogs!"

He walked across the truck bed. Hanz and Marlene lay terrified below. Neither could move a muscle. They could feel the force of the lieutenant's boots as he stood on the wood over them. Standing directly on the doors, he looked down.

"Herr Leftenant...a call for you," said the sergeant.

The lieutenant stepped down to take the call, but gave an order as he walked away. "Have the dogs inspect the truck."

Two German shepherds circled the truck and as they crawled under the truck they seemed confused. The petrol rags were doing their job. Then one of the dogs began to bark at something in the undercarriage. The sergeant looked under the flat bed, then back up at the lieutenant as he returned.

"What is it?"

The sergeant saw a dead bird that had been caught between the petrol tank and the iron frame of the truck.

"A dead bird," said the sergeant. "Load the beer."

Hanz had been silently praying. He was convinced more than ever that God could hear him. As they listened to the sounds of the barrels being reloaded, he squeezed Marlene's hand. He wanted to shout. He did so in silence.

The back rails were put in place and Werner climbed into the cab. He started the engine and rolled the window down. As the truck began to slowly move onto the road he heard a sound he had dreaded.

"Halt!"

The lieutenant had thought of one last thing. "How about one barrel for us?"

Werner smiled. "Of course, Herr Leftenant. Of course."

* * *

Laura Knochen had worked all evening to prepare her home for the Herzogs. Her apartment was on the top floor of a three-story building. There was a front and back entrance to the main hallway on the ground floor. The ground units were two stories and the two top units were one level with an accessible attic space. The attic spaces were large but poorly insulated. They were comfortable in the winter because of heat rising from the coal stoves. The summer was a problem. Access to the attic was by a very narrow stairway at the end of a hallway. The small door was only four feet high. Laura had taken a mattress, one table, one chair and a lamp into the space. Fortunately, there was also an electrical outlet.

She had lived in the flat for six years, longer than any of the other four tenants. She knew each renter but none well. Below her lived an elderly couple. He was a retired druggist and they stayed in most of the time. The other two were women whose husbands were in the Army. They both worked in munitions plants. As far as Laura knew, both women supported the Nazis and their anti-Semitic policies. She did not know about the couple below her.

Laura instructed the Herzogs to come to the rear entrance where she would meet them. They arrived promptly at 11:00 p.m., each with a small suitcase. She quietly took them to her apartment and then to the attic. They had embarked on a journey from which there was no return. They had lost all of their family, all of their possessions, all of their friends, and given up their livelihood for a chance to live. They were enormously grateful to have Laura Knochen to help them. But they knew that Laura was doing far more than helping them. She was giving her life for them. This was an effort that could result in a death sentence. In her mind, Laura had already sacrificed herself for them. She was confident she could conceal her 'guests' from her neighbors who worked in the munitions factory but the elderly couple was another matter. The Herzogs would have to use the toilet during the day while Laura was at work. The couple would know someone was in her flat. Laura decided to introduce Paula as her sister-in-law who had moved in when her home in Düsseldorf had been destroyed by R.A.F. bombs. Victor would be non-existent to the outside world. Her fear was that someone in the complex would suspect Paula was Jewish and notify the authorities.

Laura now needed food for three. Anyone who observed her shopping habits would know this. Did anyone ever pay attention to what she did? She did not think so but couldn't be certain. She decided to keep to her usual routine as much as possible, attend mass every Sunday and have Sunday lunch with friends. She missed her time with Marlene but had decided the Eichenwald's had escaped the country. This was at least what she wanted to believe.

Victor and Paula spoke very little to each other. When they did, it was only in a whisper. He remained in the attic almost all of the time except for personal hygiene and meals. As much as possible he and Paula tried to act as one. They took showers together twice a week, a ritual that became the highlight of the week for Victor. Laura was kind enough to bring him reading material from the library. He often read and afterward, took a nap, which also became part of his routine. This was difficult for a man who had been so active all of his life. But he had to do it for Paula.

Victor Herzog was the third of five children in a Jewish family. He was born in Prague in 1883. His father owned a flourmill near the outskirts of the city. Vic worked in the mill as a youngster and became interested in baking. He met Paula in school and at age 20, asked her to marry him. Their first child was stillborn. Two years later she gave birth to a son, Julius.

The German economy in the 1920s was recovering from inflation and Victor recognized Berlin was becoming a thriving center of culture, transportation and entertainment. He and Paula moved there in 1924, and he used his savings to buy the building to start the Pumpkin House Bakery. Now trapped in a Nazi gulag, they lived day to day in the reality that each day could be their last.

As time went on, Vic began to believe they would survive. He reflected on his life and recalled times as a child when his father would take him and his older brother fishing. His parents told their children repeatedly that they were valued and unique. He had been exceedingly happy with Paula and he cherished their business and working with Julius. He had always been able to overcome any discrimination he had experienced. His parents had stressed to their children that the Jews were 'God's Chosen'. He sarcastically thought to himself that Hitler had failed to get the message. Now the conundrum - Laura Knochen, a Christian, was risking her life for him and for Paula. Day after day, he sat in the attic and tried to unravel the mystery.

They were now settled into a routine. The Herzogs ate break-fast with Laura but spoke only in low whispers. From time to time, Paula would talk in normal tones to validate her presence. Their evening meals were the same. Victor looked forward to the reading materials and an occasional newspaper. One of his greatest fears was that he or Paula would become ill. Laura assured them that she knew a physician who would help if needed, although it had been over a year since she had seen Anna Eichenwald.

* * *

Travel in the French countryside was more relaxed. Hanz and Marlene tried to sleep but the wooden compartment was less than comfortable. It was cold but they clung gratefully to the blankets and to each other. After four hours, both were hoping for a break soon. Werner informed them that they would take a detour about 100 kilometers past the German border. They turned east off of the main road onto a gravel road. After another ten minutes the road took them north to a farm house. Werner pulled the truck behind the house into a clump of trees. He was joined by a French National and they moved the beer kegs so the compartment doors could be opened. The bright sunlight temporarily blinded the couple. They were helped out of the compartment to stretch their legs. Marlene looked at the Frenchman.

"Toilette?" He pointed to the farmhouse. Hanz shook hands with the Frenchman. "Merci!" He followed Marlene into the house.

Hanz had picked up a significant amount of French in his travels and spoke with the resistance worker. He learned that the major concentration of the German occupying force was in Paris and along the coast of the English Channel. It was mid-morning and the four took time for cheese, salami and bread, along with a glass of wine. There was much less danger of detection, especially since they would not come within 100 kilometers of Paris. Their route would be to Reims, Saint-Quntin and on to Calais with one stop on the way. The Frenchman rode with Werner in the cab to trouble-shoot. Werner felt he could handle any German patrols as long as they were not *SS.*

With each passing day Himmler knew the chance of finding Hanz Eichenwald was diminishing. Hanz had simply disappeared like a thief in the night. Himmler had interviewed the men who had talked with Anna and was convinced she was not involved. She was another story and he intended to deal with her soon. His men had questioned Hanz's secretary. She clearly expected his return. It would be a bold move to question any of his colleagues. Max von Laue had a history with Jews but was too distinguished to approach.

Any inquiry would be an accusation and there was no hard evidence that any of them were involved. The only neutral country in central Europe was Switzerland, and they had refused political refugees to maintain their neutrality, keeping the floodgates closed.

Himmler believed the Eichenwalds would go to Holland, Belgium or France and then to England. To have the director of the German Nuclear bomb project successfully defect would be more than an embarrassment. It would give the Allies vital information. But with Himmler, this was personal. He had been made a fool, and it would not stand.

He sent word to the *SS* office in Paris that this man would be trying to leave Europe across the English Channel. Patrols along the coast from Amsterdam to Le Harve, France would be placed on high alert for the next two weeks. The break would come at night and probably in a motorized craft of some type. Fishing vessels were strictly forbidden to sail after sundown. Any vessel of any type would be stopped or fired on. This would also be a good opportunity to catch and kill some French resistance fighters.

Thirty kilometers southwest of Calais, on the coast, was an isolated fishing house with a small marina tucked into a cove. The beer truck pulled into the gravel drive and the Frenchman was greeted by two men who came from the house. They were discussing what to do with the beer and the truck. By morning, the *SS* would suspect that Werner Schmidt was involved when the scheduled delivery was not made. The *SS* would be looking for the truck all over France. The men drove the truck inland to an abandoned barn where they unloaded the beer. The Eichenwalds were relieved to be out of the container. A resistance worker named Trey had followed the truck and transported Hanz and Marlene, exhausted, back to the coastal house. It was now just past midnight on the 17th. The truck was driven twelve kilometers westerly just past the village of Wissant where it was pushed off of a sheer bluff into the ocean. The resistance fighters knew well the German patrol schedules and stayed off of the main road to avoid them.

The house being used for the operation was well off of the coastal road. It was only a half kilometer from a marina. The fishing vessel at the marina was still in use but would not be used for the rendezvous boat. Hanz and Marlene were given the only separate room and both fell into deep sleep. It was a clear, cold night with stars in a black sky. The time window for the pick-up would begin in three days.

The following morning bright sunlight was streaming through the single window. Hanz woke and for a moment did not realize where he was. His mind quickly adjusted and he rolled over and kissed Marlene on the forehead. She did not stir. He quickly entered the small bathroom, showered and dressed, then went to the main room where a crackling fire welcomed him. Werner was already sitting at the table enjoying his coffee.

"Good morning. You look rested."

"I slept so hard that when I finally woke up, I did not remember where I was." Werner laughed.

"A good rest indeed."

Unlike Hanz, Werner looked tired. He had tried to get some sleep in a chair without success because his thoughts were with Maria. He knew that sometime today she would be forced to confront the *SS* looking for him.

"So, you are coming with us?" Hanz asked.

Werner explained that if he returned and was caught, the SS would torture Maria in his presence for information and then kill him or both of them. Hanz stood motionless, his coffee cup in his hand. He realized how completely war could obliterate the morality of some men, but knew the Nazi bastards had none to start with. He was stunned that an entire generation of men had lost all sense of human value. His thoughts went back 40 years to a time when he studied the Torah and the Prophets. He remembered the story of Joshua. God had brought the Hebrews across the Jordan River to Jericho. The city was well fortified with high walls. The Hebrews had no way to attack the city, but God had promised it to them. The Lord instructed the people to take the Ark of the Covenant, the symbol of the presence of the Lord, and march around the walls seven times. Then they were instructed to sound a trumpet blast and shout. When the people did this, the walls collapsed and the Hebrew Army streamed in. They destroyed every living thing with the sword… men, women, young and old, cattle, sheep and donkeys. God destroyed the city because it was evil, and Hanz now understood that the evil of the Nazi Reich was no different.

He walked over to Werner and laid his hand on his shoulder. He could say nothing to comfort him. He had no words to convey his gratitude to this simple man who had sacrificed so much for two total strangers.

Hanz moved to the table and sat down. He was still thinking, still struggling with the realization that in a strange way, the sacrifice of one man of honor could balance the treachery of millions of his countrymen who were only too glad to band together in their hatred of the Jews.

*   *   *

Maria Schmidt had spent the day staying busy with chores. This was her first day without Werner. She did not understand. She only knew that Werner had left and she was alone with his invalid father. War brought heartache, but she had not expected this.

Dusk came early in January. The long evening shadows crept across the front yard, casting images that resembled prehistoric animals. Still, it was a peaceful scene. She was startled to notice a gray auto rapidly approaching the house along the gravel road. She stepped onto the porch for a better look, then was gripped with terror. She could make out a Swastika emblem on the side of the auto. Two Nazi officers in black *SS* uniforms stepped from the car.

"Good evening," said one of the men. "We are looking for Werner Schmidt." Maria's heart was pounding.

"I am his wife. But he's not here." "Where is he?"

Maria recalled what Werner had said. She tried to stay calm and do exactly as he had instructed her. "He drives a beer truck once a week to Paris. He should return tomorrow."

The officer in charge gave her a smirk. "Can we go inside?"

"Of course, come in. Werner's father is an invalid from a war injury and stays in his room most of the time. Can I offer you hot tea?"

"No, thank you. We wanted to inform you that your husband did not make the delivery in Paris. We think you know where he is."

Without realizing it, Maria raised her voice.

"Why would he not make the delivery? Has he been in an accident?"

She was clearly shaken.

"There was no accident. He has disappeared. We believe he is involved with the underground."

Maria had not allowed herself to think Werner might be involved in anti-Nazi activity. Now she had to try to convince them. As she faced these men she began to see an ugly change in their demeanor. The Junior officer drew his revolver and began shouting. Then he pushed her against the wall.

"Open your mouth!"

Maria was frozen. She could not think. "I said open your mouth!"

He had the revolver barrel in her face. As she opened her mouth, he placed the gun barrel into it. "Do you want your brains splattered all over this wall?"

She shook her head and tried to back up but there was no place to go. She shut her eyes and began to cry.

"Genug! She doesn't know where he is."

With that, the men disappeared. Maria slumped to the floor. Just at that moment, Werner's father opened the door.

"Maria, was someone here?"

It was critical that no unusual activity be observed about the fishing cabin. The trawler went out as scheduled. There had never been a land patrol near the house, but German patrol planes were seen every few days. Time began to drag for the Eichenwalds. Two more days with nothing to do but wait. Hanz found an old chess set and he and Marlene played a few games. They had not done that since Anna was a baby. It was difficult to concentrate.

"This is a lost cause," Marlene finally said.

She had questions Hanz could not answer. Would they live in London? Would he work on the allied bomb project? Would it be difficult to learn English?"I'm sorry Marlene. I don't know. I don't know and I don't know!"

The evening of the 19th, Trey brought a team member they had not met. Pierre was a large man of about 60. He had a thick white mustache and looked like a sailor, with weather beaten skin and a wrinkled face. He had a prominent limp to the left when he walked. He shook hands with Hanz and Marlene, then asked Trey if there would be language problems. He was assured Hanz could understand and translate his French into German for Marlene and Werner. Pierre had been in contact with the British Navy and their weather service for two nights. He explained the escape effort.

"We have a 12-meter open boat with oars and a small outboard motor. We must make a rendezvous point bearing due west four miles from shore. A British Submarine, H.M.S. Aberdeen, will surface between midnight and 3:00 a.m. They will stay at periscope depth until they see our signal. We have four nights to make our connection, but the first is the best. The shore patrols are on high alert looking for you. The weather looks favorable, at least for the first two nights. We will row the boat for the first mile to get out of shore range, then we should be able to use the motor. I will drive the boat with Trey. Any questions? Good! We will leave at 10:00 o'clock tomorrow night."

Tomorrow could not come fast enough for the Eichenwalds. Marlene had not really had time to think about Anna. She wanted to get to England so they could get word to her. Both Hanz and Marlene found sleep difficult to capture. They drifted in and out and finally, before dawn, Hanz got dressed and went into the front room to stir the fire. Werner was up having a smoke and had made a pot of fresh coffee. After getting the fire going again, Hanz had a discouraging thought.

"After our escape to England, I suppose the Nazis could still invade Britain."

Werner sat in silence for a moment before he spoke. "I think Hitler has missed his opportunity. He is bogged down in Russia and now the Americans are in. The Third Reich will be defeated and the defeat will destroy Germany." Hanz began to see that Werner was more urbane in his understanding of the war. "And what are your plans?"

With no hesitation Werner said simply, "To go back." Hanz looked at him. "To go back. To find my wife. She is all I have. She is all I want."

Hanz silently admired this man, the driver of a beer truck.

The day passed quickly. It was cold and clear. The group kept the fire going and at one time or another they all took turns napping, anticipating the escape. Marlene could only imagine life without constant fear. She longed to know of Anna and hoped she would find out soon enough. As evening approached, Trey opened a bottle of Bordeaux and proposed a toast to the success of their mission and the eventual restoration of French sovereignty. By 9:00 p.m. they were all wrapped and ready.

A few minutes later, Pierre appeared and led the group down to the marina. As they positioned themselves in the boat he asked Trey and Werner to man the oars and told the Eichenwalds to sit forward. He warned that a colleague had told him the German patrol boats seemed to be more active in the past two days. The boat would have to go about 45 minutes with rowing power. Then it should be safe to use the outboard. They had a hand held battery operated search light for signaling the Sub. The code was two short and a long.

The sea had four-foot swells. Marlene felt relieved when Pierre started the outboard. His small hand-held compass kept them on the dead west bearing. Using their speed recorded on the motor and time traveled, Pierre had a rough idea of their four mile target position.

When the boat reached three and a half miles, Pierre slowed and Trey started the code flash signals...short, short, long...short, short, long. The H.M.S. Aberdeen was an attack class submarine with a crew of 80. She was commissioned in June 1940 and had seen combat only once. Her mission was to track and destroy German U-boats and protect shipping lanes for supply ships coming from the U.S.

First officer Jonathan Smithwick was on the periscope. Captain Eric Stewart was in command. As soon as Trey started the code, Smithwick picked it up.

"Captain, I'm seeing the signals about 500 meters off the starboard bow."

Stewart wanted to take another few moments for his radar officer to scan for any vessels in the area. Suddenly the radar officer spoke.

"Captain! I'm picking up a signal about 3,000 meters north-northeast moving directly for us."

The captain quickly walked to the scope.

"What size vessel? What's the rate of approach?"

Radar replied, "Small and closing rapidly."

The captain suspected it was a German patrol boat designed for rapid deployment in coastal waters. If so, it would have no more than a 50 caliber deck machine gun. British intelligence had not identified any German surface torpedo boats. He gave the order. "Surface...surface."

The captain turned to his staff seaman.

"Mackenzie, get your crew up fast and man the deck gun."
"Aye, sir!"

The deck gun was 90 mm cannon that could fire one round per second with a range of 2000 meters.

A German shore patrol had seen Pierre's boat leave the coast and had notified shore surveillance command. Shore command deployed two search craft for the chase. These boats were not equipped with radar but were headed in the general direction of the rendezvous. The second boat was about 20 minutes behind the lead craft. Pierre had cut his outboard for fear of overrunning his position. Suddenly he heard the approaching German boat.

"They've found us!"

The resistance workers had small side arms and knew the patrol boat would capture them or simply blow them out of the water. Hanz and Marlene were clinging to each other. It was too dark to see much, but the roar of the enemy motor launch was now very loud. Then the lights of the German boat were visible in the far distance and heading for them.

Suddenly, about 200 meters from Pierre's boat, the nose of the Aberdeen burst out of the ocean like a breeching whale. The wake almost capsized his boat. Everyone clung to the sides. In less than a minute, the H.M.S. Aberdeen had surfaced. Within another 90 seconds, the deck gun was manned. Mackenzie and crew began to hear the 'ratta-tat' from the German patrol craft. They were not certain if they were being fired on or if Pierre's boat was drawing the fire. The German captain quickly realized he was facing a British submarine rather than a 12 meter fishing boat. As he turned his craft to escape, his gunner began firing at the sub. The deck cannon had an electrical turret and swung to face the Germans. The 90 mm cannon then burst into action…'bam..bam..bam..bam'. It delivered four rounds in four seconds with two direct hits. One round hit a fuel tank and the patrol boat burst into flames. The explosion bisected the boat and both sections began to rapidly sink. The deck gun had done its job…the enemy swallowed by the sea.

Almost simultaneously, the Aberdeen had launched a large raft to get the Eichenwalds. Within minutes they were on the raft with Werner and transported to the sub. Hanz turned to give a triumphant wave and thumbs-up to Pierre and Trey, but they had disappeared into the night.

*　*　*

Christian Engel had been given a deferment from military service because of his position as chief of the Trauma Service at the University Hospital. It would have been unusual to place a man of his talent and experience in a field hospital. Now Christian was facing the most daunting task of his young life. He had a sense that time was becoming critical. He had no call obligation for the weekend of January 21st and decided to visit his sister in Leipzig. He had purchased a ten year old Mercedes coupe and enjoyed driving it in the country. Leipzig was about two hours from Berlin by auto.

Christian had visited Leipzig several times in the five years his sister Sarah had lived there. The city was famous for being the place where Bach lived and worked for 27 years. It was also the birthplace of composer Richard Wagner. The historical attractions were of no interest to Christian. He cared only about Anna's safety.

Sarah Engel was three years younger than Christian. She idolized him as she was growing up. She had earned a degree in economics and had moved to Leipzig for a position with the Bank of Leipzig. Before her move she held a position in marketing for Germany's largest steel producer. After the 'Night of Broken Glass' Sarah joined efforts to rescue Jews from the Nazi pogrom. Initially she helped in the emigration and relocation effort. That program had been stopped by the Gestapo. Relocation was now to ghettos and concentration camps. Sarah had never met Anna but was anxious to meet her.

Christian reached her apartment that evening and the two had dinner at a local café, one of Sarah's favorites. He was anxious to learn details of Anna's relocation. He ordered a stein of beer and a glass of wine for Sarah.

"We'er going to have to make our move soon. Anna's parents have apparently escaped Germany or at least they have disappeared. The *SS* may arrest Anna any day. One reason they have not already is that she saved the life of one of their officers a few years ago. What is the status of her documentation?"

"Just yesterday I collected her papers, so your timing is good. They are amazingly authentic looking. Thank God we have some talented people working against the Nazis. She was born in Lubeck, north of Hamburg, almost to the Baltic. She will need to study the area. I have found an open position as a nurse's aide. She can make enough to live on and can stay with me until she finds a flat, but the sooner the better. The Gestapo could easily connect me to you."

"Sarah, I can't thank you enough. You will quickly grow to love Anna as I do. In normal times she would be you sister-in-law."

Sarah nodded, "Yes, I know."

Christian had always appreciated and loved his sister, but never so much as now. He leaned over the table and kissed her cheek. "Thank God for you."

Anna sat in her apartment on a dreary Monday evening look-ing at her identity papers. She realized that her life might very well depend on her becoming Heidi Brendler. She had five days to make the transition. On Friday evening, Dr. Anna Eichenwald would dis-appear and on Saturday morning, Heidi Brendler would surface. She would cut her hair and change her look. She wanted nothing to connect Anna to Heidi. She had visited a second hand book store to find study guides to help her learn more about the history and geography of the northern most section of Germany where Heidi was born. She bought second hand clothes and shoes. She made certain to discard everything in her apartment that might connect her to Christian. She burned every note, every picture, and every scrap of paper. And she destroyed all the gifts he had given her. The Gestapo would search every inch of her apartment. Anna knew she could not remain a Jew. She must become a Christian. She would have to think, talk and act like a Christian. Only Jews were being sent to ghettos. Only Jews were being sent to slave labor camps. Only Jews were being sent to death camps.

The following day was routine. There was morning surgery and clinic. On Wednesday she would run the mid-week mortality-mor-bidity conference. It was Wednesday afternoon when she finally had time to sit down with her secretary, Theresa. Anna wanted to tell her everything but knew she couldn't. The two women had grown very close. Theresa had become a sister, mother, advisor and friend all wrapped in one person. Anna took Theresa's hand and looked down, her eyes filling with tears.

"I love you, my friend. I have learned so much from you. God bless you."

Theresa had known since the passage of the Nuremberg Laws that this day would come. Still, she was unprepared.

"When?" she asked softly. "Friday," Anna replied.

Theresa said nothing. She could only pray that Anna would be safe.

Christian and Anna had planned to meet away from the hospital early Saturday morning. He would drive her to Leipzig. When the morning arrived, it was still dark outside. Anna stood like a shadow in the gray light coming through the windows and took one last look around her apartment. No matter what happened, she knew she would never see it again. She closed the door behind her, locked it and headed down Unter den Linden. She surreptitiously dropped the door key into a storm drain and never changed her step, proceeding to the corner of Middelstrasse and Friedrichstrasse. There, she stood in the doorway to the State Library. A light mist began to fall. The few people on the street looked like ghosts in a gray world.

Christian's black Mercedes slowly passed by the arched entrance to the Library but it did not stop. He circled the block to make sure he wasn't being watched, then stopped at the entrance. The girl in the doorway got into the car.

"Good morning," she said. "I'm Heidi Brendler."

CHAPTER 14
Resistance &
The White Rose Society

As Werner Heisenberg was making his presentation on nuclear bomb feasibility to the Reich Research Council in Berlin, transplanted Italian physicist Enrico Fermi was planning a full-scale chain reaction pile at the University of Chicago. The pile would be built in the form of a sphere and made of graphite bricks. Graphite was the best way to slow the neutron bombardment from the uranium. Holes were drilled into the graphite to allow passage of rods of uranium oxide to be inserted. The entire apparatus would be housed in a wooden building yet to be built.

The 'control' of this experiment in nuclear fission would be by cadmium sheets attached to wooden handles. There were ten slots in the graphite pile where the cadmium sheets would be inserted. The neutrons released by the uranium could not penetrate the cadmium. The building would be constructed on the squash courts under the west stands of Stagg Field, the unused University of Chicago football stadium. The university had long since given up football in favor of academics.

The final piece to this potentially explosive puzzle was Arthur Compton, an experimental physicist who was co-coordinator of the nation's war research effort. The final decision to proceed with the experiment was his. The amount of potential radioactive material could be huge. None of the scientist believed a large explosion would occur, but they were not certain. Fermi did the control calculations and Compton took the gamble. Amazingly, he decided not to tell the University President, a lawyer, as he didn't believe a lawyer could understand nuclear physics.

By mid-November the assembly team, under the direction of Fermi, was working 24 hours a day, in 12-hour shifts, to complete CP-1 (Chicago Pile – One). The scientists presented a strange picture leaving the site covered from head to toe with graphite soot. They looked more like coal miners than physicists.

Finally, the colossal experiment was ready. December 2, 1942 dawned bitterly cold with a high of zero degrees F. Fermi decided to have one of his assistants control the cadmium plates by hand. One of Fermi's associates, Leona Woods, had designed a neutron release baron trifluride counter to monitor the process. All were more than aware that a war was on because the day before, gasoline rationing had begun in Chicago. There was a device that transmitted the boron readings with loud clicks so the intensity of the pile would be known instantly. The last critical cadmium plate was controlled by George Weil, a young research physicist.

Mid-morning on the red-letter day, Fermi gave the order to begin. One by one, the cadmium sheets were removed. The last one controlled by Weil was the mother-lode. Fermi was calculating the rate of increase as Weil moved the last plate out of the pile. When it was half way out, the rate of the counter increased and then leveled off. It was clear that once the final cadmium plate was completely out the, pile would go critical.

One of the physicists in attendance was Leo Szilard. Years earlier, he had the idea of a chain reaction. He had believed that under the proper circumstances, neutron release would cause an atom to split, causing further neutron release each time with a release of energy. Now his idea was becoming reality. It was Szilard, a Hungarian Jew, who had most feared that Hitler would get a bomb. He was relieved to learn that Hanz Eichenwald had defected, but he also knew there were other very talented physicists left in Germany.

Fermi was instructing Weil to remove the last cadmium plate 6 inches at a time. Each time, the chatter of the counters would increase their clicking, and each time Fermi would make new calculations with his slide rule. Finally he nodded for Weil to move the plate all of the way out. He turned to Arthur Compton.

"This will do it! The trace on the recorder will climb and continue to climb. The process will become self-sustaining."

The clicks on the counters became more and more rapid. Then they were producing a dull roar. They could not keep up with the process. Fermi raised his hand. "The pile has gone critical," he yelled.

The neutron intensity was doubling every two minutes. Left uncontrolled, within 90 minutes the pile would have melted down, killing everyone in the room.

At four and a half minutes Fermi ordered it to be shut down. For the first time men had controlled energy release from the atomic nucleus. What Ernest Rutherford had once called 'moonshine' was now reality.

The last two men to leave the pile were Szilard and Fermi. They shook hands. Szilard had hoped atomic energy might lead men away from war. Now he knew this would not be the case.

"This day will be a black day in the history of mankind," he said to Fermi.

* * *

Albert Speer was Hitler's confidant and architect, serving as minister of Armaments and War Production. It was to Speer that Werner Heisenberg made his final appeal for funds for the fission project. Speer took the information to Hitler who seemed to have little interest and even less understanding of the potential of nuclear energy. Hitler simply did not have the intellect to grasp the revolutionary nature of nuclear technology.

The fear of Allied scientists and military planners was never realized. Germany never got off the ground in any real effort to produce a weapon of mass destruction through nuclear fission. The mass destruction of human life was far greater than all of the bombs produced by all of the nations of the world, a conflagration laid at the feet of one evil man.

*   *   *

The H.M.S. Aberdeen remained submerged through most of the journey across the channel to the submarine base at Portsmouth on the southern coast of England. The Eichenwalds were shown to Captain Stewart's stateroom. They were excited but emotionally drained. Each fell into a deep sleep. Werner was exhausted as well but knew this would likely be his one and only time in a submarine. One of the officers who spoke limited German gave him a brief tour. The sub traveled at a speed of 12 knots west-northwest to the coast of England, a distance of 20 nautical miles. She followed the coastline the remaining 50 miles to the Portsmouth sound. Once in the sound she surfaced, and then went into dock.

Chaim Weizmann and his wife Vera were waiting dock-side as the Eichenwalds departed the ship. Before leaving, both Hanz and Marlene thanked Captain Stewart, Hanz with broken English and Marlene with smiles and German phrases that were appreciated if not understood. As they stepped on the dock Chaim embraced Hanz and shook hands with Marlene.

"Welcome to your new home and country," he said with his polished German. "We are relieved you are here. There is so much to discuss, but I must take you to be debriefed by the military."

Hanz smiled broadly. "Whatever it takes," he said. "We are so blessed to be free!"

Soon after, Hanz, Marlene and Werner were transported the 100 kilometers to Oxted, a London suburb. The British Intelligence Service had a facility there which included what was once a small hotel now converted into a guest house for visiting officers. The interrogations took two days. Twelve hour interviews with each person. The interrogating officers were men who had lived and worked in Germany. The Eichenwalds had no meaningful military information except for the bomb project. But Werner was very helpful to the Brits, giving them a comprehensive view of the resistance and underground operations. Werner was to have close surveillance for six months. He could pose a threat if he was in fact a counter intelligence plant. They had been able to corroborate much of his information with data already in their possession. From the beginning, Werner's plan was to return to Maria. But he also was determined to help the Allies defeat the Nazi Reich. Although they did not share this with him at the time, the British believed he would prove a valuable asset to them in forming future invasion plans. He was transported to a military installation for surveillance and six months of language school.

The Eichenwalds spent the next two weeks with Chaim and Vera Weizmann in their apartment in Laughton, a London suburb. In 1937, they had made their home in Rehovot, Israel, but because of his service to England in WWI, the British government maintained a small flat for them in England. He was an honorary advisor to the British Ministry of Supply.

Weizmann had become famous as the President of the World Zionist Organization, established in 1929. He also had been instrumental in the establishment of the Hebrew University of Jerusalem in 1925. Hanz was astonished when he learned that Weizmann was only 11 years old when he wrote "that kings and nations of the world were set upon the destruction of the Jewish people." Now the world was seeing that prophecy being fulfilled. Weizmann had no intention of trying to convert Hanz to Zionism, but as with Einstein, his goal was to get him to support the concept of a Jewish National Home.

But first things first. Chaim had spent considerable time in Germany before he became a British subject in 1910. He and Vera were fluent in German and Marlene was delighted to spend time with Vera, a woman of great intellect and charm. On their first evening together, the women became locked in conversation in the kitchen. The men sat in a small study, each with a glass of brandy.

"Well Hanz," said Weizman. "I have news! When I received your initial cable, I began the process of trying to get a Rockefeller Foundation grant for you. About two weeks ago it was approved. Beginning in the fall you will be teaching quantum theory at Cambridge."

Hanz was stunned. He sat in thought for a moment then replied, "I am amazed you could do that. And that I will be teaching in the Isaac Newton Institute. It's an overwhelming thought. We already owe you so much."

"You owe me nothing," Weizmann retorted. "I have been working for 10 years to aid Jewish individuals in academics. That is why God put me here!"

Hanz knew that Weizmann believed deeply what he had just said. He had known about

Zionism to a limited degree but was fascinated to learn more. "I would like to know more of your views of Zionism and about the Balfour Declaration," said Hanz.

"Delighted!" Chaim responded. "It is a complex subject. I'll give you my perspective. At the turn of the century, Palestine was part of the Ottoman-Turkish Empire. It was inhabited by about half a million people, mostly Muslim and Christian Arabs. There were also a handful of Jews, about 20,000. My view of our return to Palestine is on Religious grounds....that historically, the Lord gave a portion of what is known as the 'Fertile Crescent' to his people to be their homeland. It is rightfully ours by Divine decree. Others see our return to the land as a secular movement, the response of rampant anti-Semitism. This initially was Einstein's view, which he modified somewhat after visiting America."

Hanz felt his curiosity increasing. "What did he see in America?"

"Well, in his words, it was in America that he discovered the Jewish people. He said he had seen many, many Jews in Berlin and Germany, but he recognized Jewish people first in America, people from Russia, Poland, and Eastern Europe generally. People willing for self- sacrifice. They are the people we need in Palestine. People willing to sacrifice."

"I know of the Balfour Declaration," said Hanz. "Does it still have some influence?"

"To a limited extent. It expressed the formal British Cabinet position, in 1919, for support of a National Jewish home in Palestine. That has not happened. But it reminds the Brits that they owe us. Or at least they owe me!"

The Eichenwalds entered language school the following week. They were furnished a small auto by the British government, and Hanz began the challenge of trying to manage a left-hand drive. Their coded cable to Anna was returned. 'Address not found' was stamped on the envelope. There was no phone service to the continent, and the underground could not help. Three weeks into their language school, a cablegram arrived from the Swiss Embassy. Marlene was too nervous to open it and handed it to Hanz. His eyes quickly scanned the message. He read it to Marlene, "It's from Christian Engel. 'Package safely transferred sub-terrestrial.'"

"What does it mean?" asked Marlene.

"Anna has gone underground. She's safe

* * *

Sarah Engel was excited to be finally meeting Anna, whose new name was now Heidi Brendler. She had heard her brother speak often of her over the past year, but the war had severely limited travel and made it impossible for the two young women to meet. Sarah spent the morning making certain her small, one bedroom apartment was tidy. She gently placed a cushion on the daybed in the living area then gazed out the window. The apartment was located next to a park on Goldschmidtstrasse, three blocks from Mendelssohn-Haus, now a museum. The train station, the largest in Germany, was a 15-minute walk, and the University of Leipzig was only 10 minutes away.

Christian parked on a side street. Heidi had one large piece of luggage packed with all it would hold, with nothing that led to her past except her stethoscope. She could not bring herself to abandon that one possession she had prized since she was a junior medical student.

Once in the apartment the two women shook hands then embraced. Sarah was amazed at Heidi's beauty. The short, thick black hair was covered by a maroon beret, tilted slightly to one side. Her face was long and thin. Most astonishing were her aqua blue eyes. Sarah had almost called her Anna, but caught the slip before it came out. She had made sandwiches and a pot of coffee. The three sat around the small dining table. The two young women were already becoming friends. Christian could only observe and finally left the table to let them talk. As evening came, he stood to leave.

"Anna, I've got to be going now." There was no response. "Anna!"

She slowly turned to face him.

"Are you addressing me? My name is Heidi."

It was then that Christian came to grips with this charade. It wasn't a game. He knew it was a life and death issue.

"I'm sorry. Heidi. I won't make that mistake again."

The two lovers strolled to the door. After a lingering kiss and a long embrace, Christian whispered in her ear. "I love you. I will stay in touch."

He left, praying silently that God would protect her from the Nazis. Let her survive this war, he pleaded soundlessly.

The next week was busy for Heidi and Sarah. Their search for an apartment yielded a small efficiency flat only three blocks from

Sarah and a 10-minute walk from the University Hospital, Heidi's new place of employment. She had interviewed for a position as a nurse's aide.

When hired, she requested instruction for taking blood pressures and giving oral medications with supervision. She had withdrawn all of her savings before leaving Berlin. Then she burned her identity papers. Her goal was to simply vanish. The following week, she moved into the flat and began working. A part of her efforts were also aimed at putting her past where it belonged - in the past. She was now Heidi Brendler from Lubeck, near the Baltic Sea.

Leipzig had no military instillations and no munitions factories to speak of. For this reason it was not a bombing target of the R.A.F. Heidi stayed to herself although she had been noticed by more than one physician at the hospital. She realized that there was a small risk that she might be recognized by someone she had known in Berlin, but none of the surgeons there had trained in Berlin and she was most comfortable in the hospital. One Neurologist, 10 years her senior, asked her to dinner. Tactfully, she told him that her fiancé was at the Russian front and she had no intention of betraying his love. She told the man she would complain to the authorities if he persisted. From then on, he carefully avoided her.

Heidi spent hours thinking of Christian, but he only communicated through Sarah. She also received word that her parents had arrived safely in England. With each passing week the nadir of the war seemed farther and farther away. As the months rolled by, she blended into the fabric of Leipzig and the hospital. Her supervisor recognized her intelligence and even suggested that Heidi consider nursing school. She politely declined.

Sarah and Heidi spent one evening out each week, a highlight for them both but especially for Heidi. At first, she hung on every word about Christian and her eyes searched for coded messages in his letters to Sarah. They had decided against direct written communication. The Gestapo was notorious for intercepting and re-sealing mail.

Just before Christmas, 1942, the two friends acquired tickets to a Bach concert. They made dinner reservations at a small café near the symphony hall. Heidi had seen Christian only once in the eight months she had lived in Leipzig. She often found herself staring at Sarah, as she was a propitious reflection of her brother.

As much as the women enjoyed their one evening out each week, spending time in public places was frightening. They frequently saw Gestapo officers, notorious for staring at beautiful women. Heidi tried very hard not to make eye contact with them. She saw only death in their eyes.

The Erwachen Café was an intimate, almost remote little place with only 20 tables laid out in a very long room that resembled a corridor. The décor and food was Mediterranean and the café had an outstanding wine selection. The two young women sat at a table near the rear of the corridor, which gave them the privacy they wanted. On this night they noticed no military as they walked to their table, always a relief.

Heidi wanted to find out more about Sarah's faith. If Heidi appeared to be Christian it would be much more difficult for the Gestapo or anyone to see that she was Jewish. They ordered a bottle of red wine from France. It was always easy to find goods from German occupied territories. The other item of information Heidi wanted was about the resistance movement. She was not going to be content to live out the war hiding from the Nazis.

As the two women shared their Bordeaux, Heidi began pressing Sarah about her involvement in the underground.

"Sarah, I want to be involved in the resistance. The Nazis have taken everything from me including your brother, the love of my life. I know I cannot get out of the country. I don't want to die, obviously. But I won't just sit out the war."

Sarah leaned forward, noticing that there was no one close enough to hear.

"The resistance is very dangerous. If caught you will be executed, no questions asked. If you are determined, I will put you in touch with the area commander. He will decide if you can help. I have worked mostly in communications. We have a short-wave radio and are in contact with the British. We also pick-up the BBC so we know what is happening in the war. There is so much going on that is never reported in Germany."

The waiter returned for orders. Both women ordered the house specialty, grilled redfish and boiled potatoes. Heidi raised her fork and took a bite of the fish, savoring the taste and a new feeling growing inside her. She was beginning to sense more purpose for her life again. "Can you share with me about the war?"

Sarah nodded, taking a sip of wine. "Just last week the Russians launched a massive counter attack at Stalingrad and have trapped the entire German Sixth Army – 22 divisions. The winter has set in now, and it's brutal in Russia. I am certain Hitler has been defeated on the Eastern front. Oh, yes. One last thing. About two weeks ago, a British-American force, under the command of someone named Eisenhower, invaded North Africa."

The defeat at Stalingrad was disastrous for the Third Reich. The Fourth Panzer Army was given the mission of reaching and rescuing the trapped Sixth Army. They advanced to within thirty miles of Stalingrad but their attempt failed. It failed to a great degree because Hitler would not allow the Sixth Army to break out and retreat from their position. The Commander of the Soviet forces sent an ultimatum to General Paulus, the German Commander. It read in part:

"The situation of your troops is desperate. They are suffering from hunger, sickness and cold. The cruel Russian winter has scarcely yet begun. Hard frosts, cold winds and blizzards still lie ahead. Your soldiers are unprovided with winter clothing and are living in appalling sanitary conditions....Your situation is hopeless..."

The terms of surrender were honorable. All prisoners would be cared for. The wounded and sick would be given medical attention. All prisoners would maintain their badges of rank and keep their personal belongings.

Paulus radioed the text of the ultimatum to Hitler...the reply was *Surrender is forbidden*! The Russians began to pound the trapped German Army with thousands of rounds of artillery

and the slaughter was on.

January 30, 1943, was the 10th anniversary of the Nazi takeover of the German government. On that day, Paulus radioed Hitler: "Final collapse cannot be delayed more than twenty-four hours."

The Sixth Army had held their position to the last man... 'for Fuehrer and Fatherland.' At 7:45 p.m. an unauthorized final radio message was sent: "The Russians are at the door of our bunker. We are destroying our equipment."

Heidi moved to her other concern, feeling full and more relaxed after her first glass of wine. "I need to know much more about your faith. I have a vague understanding, but I would like to know more."

Sarah had not brought up the subject. She had the feeling it was something that had not been an issue between Anna and Christian. "I would be delighted. Where shall be begin?"

Heidi started the conversation. "In the Torah, the God of Israel was known as Yahweh – the Lord. Yahweh is his name in Hebrew. He is a covenant God, and made royal agreements with Noah and Abraham, then with Abraham's descendants, the Hebrew Nation. But when you pray you do not address God as the Lord; you call him 'Father'. I find that very strange."

"Your question goes to the heart of the Christian Gospel," said Sarah. "Each year, you celebrate Yom Kippur or the Day of Atonement. It's a day of fasting and prayer."

"Correct. It is symbolic of the day in ancient times when the Priest entered the Holy of Holies in the Temple to atone for the sins of the Nation. In this way each year we are restored to God."

Sarah continued. "We agree. All men must be restored to the Lord because our sin has alienated us from him. But for Christians the one who restores us is Jesus, the promised Messiah of God. His death on the cross and resurrection is our atonement, and it occurred one time for all sin for all time. Jesus is now our High Priest who gives us access to God. He has brought us into the family of God. Father has become for us God's covenant name. We are now children of God. It is natural for us to address him as Father."

"So when you attend your church, Lutheran I believe, you go to worship Jesus, not God." Sarah smiled.

"It's not exactly like that, Heidi. "We believe Jesus is God.... the second person of the Trinity...God the Father...God the Son... God the Holy Spirit."

Most of their food was now sitting on plates growing cold. They finished and ordered coffee.

"Well, this is going to require some getting used to," said Heidi. "But I would like to come with you to your church."

"Good. We can walk there together on Sunday."

*   *   *

Landis Koller was anxious to leave his job in the ball bearings factory just north of Leipzig. For the past two weeks he had worked overtime, 12 hour shifts for 14 straight days. It was Friday, January 12, 1943. Leipzig had been covered with a thick blanket of snow, the first major winter storm. Landis had promised to take Naomi sledding. At 10 years old, this was one of Naomi's favorite activities. He and his wife Gretchen had become very protective of Naomi since the loss of their first born, a son named Philip.

It had been six years. Philip was born with Down's syndrome in 1930. He was a beautiful child with the typical mongoloid facial features. Though mentally retarded, he grew into a warm affectionate little boy. He loved to cuddle and would sit for hours while Gretchen read to him or held him in her lap. Then Naomi was born when he was three. In time, he took great pleasure in holding her and rocking her. He could not say her name and instead, called her 'Omi' which became her family name.

In 1935, Landis decided to join the Nazi Party. He was not interested in politics, but believed the Nazi propaganda of 'strength through joy'. They were getting Germany out of the great depression. Jobs were being produced and wages were up. He worried when Hitler abolished most civil rights and the authority of the Reichstag but getting the country out of the depression required bold action. Landis did not agree with Nazi anti-Semitism but saw this as a minor part of the Nazi agenda.

Landis himself was handicapped. At age 13, while helping his father bail hay, his right foot was mangled in a conveyor belt. He suffered multiple broken bones in the foot and ankle and required multiple surgeries and more than two years of healing. He was left with a badly deformed foot and a fused ankle, thus, a noticeable limp. He was otherwise, a robust man of more than six feet, with sharp Aryan features and a muscular build. Before the accident he had been a star soccer player. His Nazi colleagues were sympathetic. Even Joseph Goebbels, the Reich Minister of Information and Propaganda, was left a cripple from childhood polio. Surely Hitler's ideas of 'survival of the fittest' or social Darwinism would not be applied to the German Volk. It was difficult to imagine that Hitler's dogma would in fact become official party policy.

Early in 1937, the Kollers were asked to meet with the Nazi Counsel on Eugenics. The subject was their son Philip. The counsel requested that he be placed in a home for handicapped children. The Kollers resisted. He was seven years old and had never been away from his parents. They were told he would have good schooling and would be around many other children who were handicapped. They could see him twice monthly on weekends. When he turned 12, they would have the option of taking him back home. The counsel made it clear that they did not have a choice. The facility was only 100 kilometers from Leipzig near Dresden. It was in a pastoral setting and was well kept.

When they arrived, there were about 50 children around Philip's age. There was a playground with swings and slides. They were told Philip would sleep in a dorm of sorts with 20 other children and a dorm 'mother'. When they left, Philip was busy playing and did not even notice their leaving. Gretchen could not hold her tears. Landis tried to comfort her saying Philip would be happy there. Silently he thought back to the Nazi rhetoric of a "pure Germany"...a super Aryan race.

The first few weekend visits Philip seemed very happy. He was happy to see them and gave them hugs as always. He was easily distracted by his playmates and they began to believe that this possibly was the best place for him. The Kollers met other parents who were having similar thoughts. But for an unknown reason, Landis got names and addresses of two of the other couples with children there. Then the call came, almost six months to the day of his enrollment at the home. They were told that Philip had taken suddenly ill and had died of pneumonia. He had been buried on the grounds. The following day they traveled to see his grave site. It was among three other graves, all unmarked, his the only 'fresh' grave. Even though he had been out of their home for six months, a vast emptiness began to come over Gretchen. She began to have guilt that she had abandoned him to strangers.

Over the next month, Landis reflected over and over on the word he had heard the previous year at a Nazi Party meeting. A visiting official had mentioned the problem of *Untermenschen* – subhumans. The referral at the time was to Slavic people who were Bolsheviks, enemies of the State. In a broader context, it might refer to Jews. Suddenly the Nazi agenda was becoming clear to him. Anyone who did not fit their view of the 'Master Aryan Race' was *untermenchen* - subhuman. This included Jews, Gypsies, and the mentally and physically handicapped.

Landis quickly sent letters to the two families they had met at the home. Both couples had been notified that their children had died after a brief illness. The Nazis were systematically murdering these children. Philip had been exterminated….one of many.

The abject evil of the Nazi Reich was now apparent to Landis. A feeling of despair overwhelmed him. How could he have missed what was happening? How could his countrymen be complicit in these crimes against humanity? At that moment he decided he would do all in his power to defeat Nazism and he would do it from within the Party. He would not tell Gretchen any details. He only told her he was now working to 'free' Germany. He would carry to his grave the murder of his son.

The resistance movement in the Saxony Province of Germany had been started by Dr. Karl Goerdeler, the mayor of Leipzig. He, like Landis Koller, had supported the Reich initially. But in 1936, he began to notice the brutality of the new regime, including the repression of the churches and especially the Jews. When the Nazi governor of Leipzig tore down the statue of Jewish composer Felix Mendelssohn, Goerdeler resigned. In the year following, Goerdeler organized a network of prominent anti-Nazi men who, for multiple reasons, favored the overthrow of the Reich. They worked to this end by political means, but soon realized success could only be achieved through the military.

The first and possibly most important military official in the resistance movement was Colonel Hans Oster. He was a senior officer in the Abwer (German Military Intelligence Service). During the entire war until his execution in April, 1945, he fed important information to the Allies, provided warnings to individuals being sought by the Gestapo, and helped Jews escape Germany.

Perhaps the most prominent General to oppose Hitler was Ludwig Beck, retired Chief of the General Staff. He was a friend of Dr. Goerdeler and became the leader of the entire German resistance movement. In the next two years, the multiple conspirators agreed that the overthrow of the Reich could not be accomplished unless Hitler was killed. From 1941 moving forward, the efforts of those involved was to eliminate the Fuehrer. But multiple attempts on his life failed, all for different reasons. Nevertheless, they continued.

Sarah Engel had spoken with Landis about Heidi Brendler. She explained that Heidi was a friend of her brother Christian, and strongly anti-Nazi. Koller agreed to meet with Heidi only because he trusted Sarah. It was early December and anyone committed to the anti-Nazi movement would be a welcome addition for the work the following year.

Their meeting took place at a farmhouse about 20 kilometers from Leipzig. The women were picked up and escorted to the rendezvous place on a Friday evening. Sarah had not confided to Heidi that the rules of engagement placed her at risk of being eliminated if she was thought to be a Gestapo plant. It was not an issue so Sarah thought 'why bother'.

Upon their arrival the driver escorted them into the old house. It was clean, but musty. A fire roared in the hearth and a pot of coffee was on the old wooden stove. The room was illuminated by several coal-oil lanterns. After about 30 minutes the front door opened and Landis Koller entered with another man he called Max. The women stood. He greeted Sarah with a hug and extended a hand to Heidi, who had noticed his limp. He took a cup of coffee and said nothing for about five minutes. The silence was awkward. Then he looked at Heidi, who was looking at the floor. She felt he was playing mind games with her or trying to intimidate her. Heidi raised her eyes to meet his.

His expression did not change. Then he spoke in a low voice, "Why are you here?"

Heidi felt confident and said quickly, "I hate the Nazis."

"I can see that. Why would you risk death to help us?"

Heidi's eyes flashed. "I am a Jew."

* * *

On Christmas Eve a light snow was falling. Most of Germany had a rich tradition of Christmas celebration and worship of the birth of the Christ child, but in 1938, the Reich banned singing carols and the Nativity play in schools. Christmas had been replaced with the new term 'Yuletide'. The Nazis believed that Christianity and National Socialism were irreconcilable. They wanted a completely secular society. The Catholic Church and many Protestant Churches resisted the pressure from the government, especially during Christmas.

Handel and Bach, the great composers of spiritual music, were both born in Germany the same year, 1695. For more than 200 years the world had celebrated Christmas through their music. Heidi and Sarah attended a candle-light Christmas Eve worship service. It was always a magical time for Sarah, and Heidi exclaimed the music was the most beautiful she had ever heard.

Christmas Day was a red-letter day for both women. Christian Engel made the trip from Berlin arriving about noon. He brought gifts and a plumb pudding. Heidi ran out to meet him in the snow throwing her arms around him. After their late afternoon meal Sarah decided to visit a friend from work to give the two sometime together. They had much 'catching-up' to do. Heidi decided not to mention joining the underground, and Christian did not mention the increased bombing by the R.A.F. and now the Americans. They took a walk in the snow.

"Tell me about Berlin and the hospital." Christian shrugged.

"Work is work. We are seeing more cases from the front but nothing acute. Most are young men with extremities blown off or healing chest or abdominal wounds, or those missing half their face. Fifty percent of our beds are now rehab. Berlin is somber. The Nazis will not acknowledge publicly that they have been defeated in Russia. To continue the war is insane, but Hitler is insane. The war will be fought until the country is destroyed."

Heidi looked up at him. "Amazing so few of us saw this coming. Our people were so focused on our economic recovery that we were blind as to how it was happening. I once attended a Nazi rally when I was an undergraduate. I was stirred by Hitler and his oratory. For a period of time even I believed the propaganda, but Hitler's goal was a 'master race' with the conquered Europeans made slaves for the profit of Germany. And his Europe would be 'Jew free'. So many in the academic community got out in time. And here I am hoping to just survive."

They both were in their own private thoughts as they returned to the apartment. Once inside Heidi took Christian's hand and they sat side by side.

"Christian, my people are suffering unspeakable inhumanities and are dying by the hundreds of thousands. I have been in contact with people who have been to Poland. About one year ago the Nazis sequestered 400,000 Jews into a ghetto in Warsaw. The purpose was to work them to death. After a year only 100,000 had died, so the remaining 300,000 were "resettled" to Treblinka where they were gassed and their bodies burned. Regardless of the war, my life will never be the same. You know I love you, but now my life is not my own."

As they sat on the sofa, she wrapped her arms around him and began to cry softly. Christian understood that he was losing the woman he loved, not to another man but to the idea that she must resist the evil of the Nazi Reich with all in her being.

The first weekend of the New Year, 1943, Heidi, Landis and Max traveled to Munich to meet with university students who had formed a resistance group. During their travel time Landis provided Heidi with an overview of the underground efforts in Saxony which were focused on the area between Leipzig and Dresden. Heidi shared that she wanted to use some of her savings to buy a truck that could be used in the anti-Nazi work. There were about 20 workers in Saxony, but there was no formal organization and no meetings per say. Even Landis knew the identity of only seven of the twenty. Secrecy was their talisman. Their mission was threefold: to distribute anti-Nazi material, to hide Jews from the Gestapo, and to rescue and hide downed Allied airman. The last aspect of their mission was especially critical, since a directive issued by Hitler in 1941. It stated that captured Allied airman were to be hanged. This directive was a flagrant violation of the Geneva Convention which had been signed by the Germans.

On that evening, the three from Leipzig met with three students from Munich, including Sophie Scholl, her brother Hans and Christoph Probst, a married medical student with three children. Sophie was studying biology and philosophy. Hans was also in medical school with Christopher. Heidi took an instant liking to these brave young people. As they were getting better acquainted, Sophie articulated their mission goal most eloquently,

"The 'Prince of Darkness' has blinded the hearts and minds of people so they cannot see the truth. Our goal is to reveal truth to them."

These three brave souls, along with a few others and philosophy Professor Kurt Huber, were preparing thousands of anti-Nazi leaflets to distribute at the University of Munich as well as universities in Nurnberg, Frankfurt, Stuttgart, Leipzig and Berlin. Their motivation was based on their Christian beliefs and a just cause to combat evil. Hans Scholl expanded on their plan.

"Our hope is that a true anti-Nazi movement will spring from the students. Many social movements have been student led. This could be one."

"But you are risking your lives because you are being so open in your protest," said Landis.

Sophie looked at Heidi then Landis and continued, "And Darkness covered the Earth! Then God brought forth Light into the world."

"And you represent that Light," Heidi asked.

"Exactly!" said Christopher.

The Leipzig group slept on the floor of Sophie's flat. After a breakfast of coffee and muffins they bundled 2,000 leaflets to be distributed at the University of Leipzig. Heidi gave Sophie a long hug.

"We are kindred spirits. I admire so much what you are doing. God bless you." On the drive back Heidi opened one of the leaflets and read it to the others......

It is certain that today every honest German is ashamed of his government. Who among us has any conception of the dimensions of shame that will befall us and our children when one day the veil has fallen from our eyes and the most horrible of crimes – crimes that infinitely outdistance every human measure – reach the light of day? If the German people are already so corrupted and spiritually crushed that they do not raise a hand, frivolously trusting in a questionable faith in lawful order in history; if they surrender man's highest principle, that which raises him above all other of God's creatures, his free will; if they abandon the will to take decisive action and turn the wheel of history and thus subject it to their own rational decision; if they are so devoid of individuality, have already gone so far along the road toward turning into a spiritless and cowardly mass – then, yes, they deserve their downfall...Offer passive resistance – resistance – wherever you may be, forestall the spread of this atheistic war machine before it is too late...DO NOT FORGET...that every people deserves the regime it is willing to endure.

These isolated 'antagonists' rode for the next hour in silence. Finally, Landis broke the silence.

"I'm fearful they will be caught. They are so bold...so out in the open."

Sophie Scholl was the fourth of five children, born and raised in Forchenberg, southern Germany. She was a very bright student and read extensively. After finishing secondary school her love of children led her to become a kindergarten teacher. She was also developing a deep distrust of Nazi National Socialism. Working in the Reichsarbeitsdienst (National Labor Service) was a prerequisite to be admitted to University. She reluctantly joined the Nazi organization for the required six months and entered the University of Munich in May 1942 to study biology and philosophy.

Sophie was influenced by her older brother Hans and his friends. Two of these young men had been required to spend a semester break at the Eastern front. It was there they witnessed atrocities of the SS, who herded a group of Jewish families into a field and cut them down with machine gun fire. On their return they vowed to resist the Nazi Reich. Their small band was called "die Weibe Rose". Hans and Alex Schmorell, both medical students, began composing leaflets for distribution, denouncing the Hitler Reich. Soon they were joined by two other students, Christoph Probst and Willi Graf. When Sophie learned of the group she joined as well.

Their common bond was their scathing criticism of German citizens who would not oppose the Nazis.

They were also drawn together by their shared love of music, literature and Christian worship. Hans had named the group the White Rose to reflect their purity and innocence in the face of evil.

The week after meeting with the workers from Leipzig, they turned out between 6,000 and 9,000 leaflets using a hand cranked duplicating machine. As they were placing the leaflets in bundles of five hundred, Hans said to the others, "It should be obvious that Germany has been defeated in Russia. Hitler continues to lead the German people into the abyss. We have lost freedom of speech, freedom of religion, and freedom of assembly. The people must rise up and resist this evil."

On February 17, 1943, Sophie and Hans packed two suit-cases with leaflets. Their plan was to distribute them between eight and nine a.m. the following day in the main lecture building. Students going to their 9:00 a.m. classes would pick them up to read. The following morning on their way to the University, Sophie turned to Hans. "Last night I had a dream that we got caught."

"Well, I suppose if we believed in omens we would not go."

"We have never seen Gestapo or *SS* at the University," Sophie said. "Anyway, it was only a dream."

The previous week, Hans, Alex Schmorell and Willi Graf had painted several buildings in the area with graffiti that said 'Freedom' and 'Down with Hitler'. They had expected an increased presence of the Gestapo but had seen none while monitoring the situation.

The Scholls entered the building at 8:35 a.m. It was a three story structure with an enormous atrium in the center with broad marble stairways on either side of the atrium. The atrium was sur-rounded circumferentially with broad hallways that, from the ground, had the appearance of balconies. They quickly distributed the leaf-lets in the hallways of the second and third floors. They descended the stairs to the first floor when Sophie realized she had one bundle of leaflets left in her suitcase.

"I'm going back up to the top and throw these into the atrium."

"Hurry! It's five minutes 'til nine."

Sophie ran up the two flights of stairs to the third floor bal-cony and opened her suitcase, then flung the last bundle of leaflets over the balcony. They floated down like giant snowflakes. One of the custodians noticed them and became angry since it made more work for him. He locked the large brass front doors and called the police. Sophie and Hans were anxious to see the reaction of the students and had not noticed the custodian. The Gestapo quickly sealed the exits from the building and arrested the Scholls. That same day, Joseph Goebbels gave a speech in the Sportspalast in

Berlin urging the German people to embrace 'Total War'. The speech was designed to counter the news of their defeat at Stalingrad.

Four days after their arrest the Scholls and their colleague Christoph Probst were taken to trial in the Volksgerichtshof – Peoples Court. The head of the court, Roland Freisler, was an ardent Nazi. After a two hour 'trial', with little fanfare, Freisler pronounced the three guilty of treason with punishment of death. Their sentences were to be carried out that day. As they were being led out of the court Hans looked at Freisler.

"You know as well as we do the war is lost. Why are you so cowardly that you won't admit it?"

At 5:00 p.m. in Stadelheim Prison Sophie Scholl walked calmly with a matron guard from her cell on death row to the execution chamber. As she entered the chamber she looked at the executioner who was going to bind her hands.

"That will not be necessary," she said. The matron guard looked at her.

"Do you have a final word for your mother and father?" "Ja! Die sonne scheint noch – yes, the sun still shines!"

Sophie knelt down and placed her head on the guillotine block. Then literally in a fraction of a second Sophie Scholl moved from her heroic life on earth into eternity. She was followed by her brother Hans and their colleague Christoph Probst.

Original Sketch of Sophie Scholl by Delia Hunt

Heidi Brendler received the news the following day with great sadness. It was a stark reminder that what she was doing was very dangerous business...that a mistake could cost her life. It also gave her a new determination. Her weekly dinner with Sarah was to be the following Friday. Heidi could not wait. She was more convinced than ever that the sure way for evil to triumph was for good people to do nothing.

CHAPTER 15

Normandy Invasion

By the fall of 1943, Werner Schmidt had finished English language school. He had provided valuable information to British Intelligence about the German resistance and had successfully convinced British officials of his zeal to help defeat Hitler and return to his homeland. He had applied for and received political asylum as a German National and refugee. But Werner Schmidt had done much more. He had requested to join the British Army as a special advisor on German geography and topography for preparation of the invasion of Europe, which was planned for the spring of 1944. He spent countless hours poring over detailed maps of central Germany and France. He made suggestions about bridges and places to ford rivers. After spending two months with invasion planners, he was accepted as a special advisor.

In November, 1943, Schmidt was sent to Scotland to be trained as an agent of British Special Operations Executive (SOE) - a British commando. His instruction lasted two months and included physical training, weapons use, silent killing, parachuting, demolition and field communication. Werner was intense in his training and desire to excel. He returned to London the first week in January for assignment, having received a 'superior' evaluation.

The defection of Werner Schmidt was just one of hundreds of factors important for planning a European invasion. One of the first was provided by the German Fuhrer himself. He had miscalculated that the United States would focus on the Pacific War and cast the war in Europe as a second priority. In fact, the opposite occurred. The U.S. adopted a strategy of waging war on 'Germany first'. When he finally faced the reality of America's industrial capabilities for mass production of arms, aviation fuel, aluminum, trucks, electronic equipment, and advanced radar, he was in essence, a man poking a large bee hive with a stick – up close and personal.

The impact of U.S. industry would be felt almost immediately. Millions of gallons of high octane aviation fuel went to Russia, along with 400,000 vehicles, 2,000 locomotives, and 11,000 freight cars. Russia could not have repelled the German invasion at Stalingrad, without these supplies.

A second factor was the battle of El Alamein in Egypt, which secured the Suez Canal for the Allies. The picture had been bleak for the Allies in August 1942. German Field Marshal Erwin Rommel was highly respected by the Allies and had already become a legend in the ranks of his own troops. His counterpart was British General Claude Auchinleck, who had little respect as a Commander and less ability. Churchill knew that British morale was low in England and also in the field. His solution was a new Commander, General Bernard Montgomery.

Montgomery was highly organized and brought confidence back to his troops. He also was aided by something his troops called 'swallows' - 300 American Sherman tanks, each with 75 mm cannon capable of penetrating the Panzer armor at 2,000 meters. These new tanks provided a significant advantage for the allies in the battle for North Africa.

Perhaps even more important to the Allied cause was the work at the decoding center at Bletchley Park, 40 miles north of London. It was an old estate turned code breaking center for the Allies. The team working in the code breaking center was a select group of scholars and mathematicians, including the reigning British Grand Chess Champion. Their mission was to crack the Nazi communication codes. The Germans had an encoding machine called Enigma, developed in the early 1930s. But Polish intelligence groups had broken the early cipher, which was altered every few months. The Poles shared this information with British intelligence in 1939. By that time the Germans were changing the cipher once a day, giving 150 million possible settings from which to choose. But British code breakers were up to the task. The British Navy had captured a U-boat with a new Enigma machine which aided the cause.

There was great secrecy about the breaking of the Enigma codes. In an attempt to hide the information, the reports about Enigma were given the appearance of coming from a British spy whose code name was Boniface. He had a network of imaginary agents inside Germany. In reality, there was a chain of wireless intercept stations across Britain that tracked enemy radio messages. Code breakers were now working around the clock to log and send the intelligence they were gathering straight to London. Special liaison units were set up to feed the Bletchley Park information to commanders in the field.

One of the first commanders to benefit was Montgomery. Workers at Bletchley got hold of Rommel's battle plan and successfully deciphered it. They also furnished Montgomery the location of Rommel's supply lines. When these lines were knocked out, the famous German Field Marshall was severely crippled for lack of fuel and supplies. Meanwhile the Allies were being supplied from the sea.

The Allies had placed a large number of land mines south of El Alamein at a place called Alam Halfa. The approaching Panzer tanks were severely damaged or destroyed in this mine field. Many other tanks became sitting targets for Allied fighter planes. The defeat of Rommel in Egypt was preceded by an order from Hitler *not* to fall back but to throw every gun and every man into the battle. In his years as Supreme Military Commander and Fuhrer, Hitler had never allowed a retreat for any reason. But on November 4th, at risk of being court-marshaled, Rommel saved what army he had left and began to retreat. In all, the Axis forces lost 59,000 troops due to death, injury or capture, and 450 tanks. To date, this was the most significant German defeat from a strategic standpoint. But many others were to follow.

On the same day that news of Rommel's collapse spread, German intelligence reported a large British-American armada in the Mediterranean Sea off Gibraltar. For several reasons, Hitler did not grasp the implications of the report. He was preoccupied with his failures on the Russian front and was also scheduled to deliver his annual speech to his old Nazi party cronies in celebration of the anniversary of the famous 1923 Beer Hall Putsch, the Nazi attempt to overthrow the Munich government.

On November 8, 1942, at 1:30 a.m., General Eisenhower's forces landed on the North African beaches of Morocco and Algeria. Within a matter of months, they defeated the Axis forces and secured all of North Africa including Tunisia. They would now turn their full attention to Italy, where the corrupt fascist Mussolini regime was fast crumbling.

There was great unrest among the Italian working class, and multiple strikes being waged. Benito Mussolini, who had become Prime Minister in 1922, and who formed his fascist totalitarian government in 1925, decided to leave the country. His attempt to escape with his mistress failed when he was captured near Lake Como. The following day, April 28, 1943, they were executed by firing squad in the small village of Giulinodi Mezzegra. Their bodies were hung upside-down in Milan. Six weeks later on July 10th, the Allies landed in Sicily with almost no resistance. The Italians had little stomach for a fight. Thus ended the corrupt and egregious reign of the man who called himself 'IL Duce'...supreme leader.

During the summer of 1943, the air war was significantly intensified by British and American forces. British bombing runs were generally made by night and the Americans took the day shift. The air raids were especially important in slowing the testing and production of the V-1 and V-2 rockets. These unmanned jet-propelled aircraft were named after the German word *Vergeltungswaffen* - weapon of reprisal. The Allied target was the V-1 production installation at Paenemunde and it was severely damaged in multiple bombing runs. While the German munitions and armament plants were progressively being damaged, the greatest casualty was the morale of the German people, as their homes and work places were systematically being destroyed.

About midnight on July 28th, a soft knock on the door awakened Heidi Brendler. Given the late hour, she stood at the door for a moment. She didn't move. Finally, she recognized the voice of Max from the resistance group and quickly unlocked the door. "Wait, Max. I have to get something on."

Max, unmarried, respectfully looked down at the floor. It startled him to see the body of a woman, his colleague, standing naked beneath a sheer nightgown. Heidi made no sound and moved quickly to the bedroom. She returned, tying the sash of her house coat.

"Max! It's so late. Why are you here? Do we have a problem? Do you want some coffee?"

"There's no time. We've located a downed airman and he's badly injured. We have him in a barn about 20 kilometers from Dresden. If we hurry we can reach him and you can take a look and see what you can do for him. Then we have to get him to a safer place. They're looking for him already. His 'chute was seen when he bailed out last evening."

"I'll get dressed. I'm not scheduled to work today."

In the waiting truck was 30 year old Franz Schwartz. He had met Landis at the ball-bearing factory. He was the only remaining son in his family. His two older brothers had been killed in combat and Franz had been released from the military removing him from harm's way. Heidi did not like meeting strangers in the resistance. She knew she was vulnerable to the Gestapo. The more people who could connect her to the underground, the less safe she felt. But these were risks she had to take.

She got into the truck and greeted Franz briefly. As they sped off into the night, she noticed that he had a semi-automatic weapon with the barrel pointing to the floor. He also had a large knife strapped to his left lower leg. There was no small talk. Max left the main road south out of Leipzig.

As they rode in silence, Heidi felt the reality of what she was doing. She was putting her life on the line, her own small effort to work toward the defeat of Hitler. She thought back to the time he had confronted her at the University Hospital. Now she felt even more strongly that this was a cause for which she was willing to die. Tonight, she knew she might actually have to.

Max turned west, taking small back roads to the village of Tanneberg, then due south for three kilometers. They turned back east onto a dirt road leading to the farm that housed the downed airman. The farm consisted of some 100 acres of oats and grain and the owners also ran 80 head of sheep and a few hogs. Max pulled behind the barn and parked the truck. Then he and Heidi slipped out and into the barn while Franz kept watch. Inside, an elderly woman sat beside the airman with a coal-oil lamp. The man appeared to be about 25 years old. He was dressed in a green flight suit. He had been flying fighter cover for a group of B-29's heading for Berlin. Heavy anti-aircraft flack over the Frankfurt area had damaged his wing tanks and he began to lose fuel. He realized he did not have the fuel to complete the mission so he aborted and bailed out near Dresden.

His eyes closed but he was not asleep, just struggling to deal with the pain. He had learned a limited amount of German but had never expected to use it. He opened his eyes and looked up at Heidi.

"Schmerzen haben?" she asked.

"My shoulder and ankle," he whispered.

He simultaneously moved his left hand to his right shoulder and then his right ankle. Heidi unzipped his flight suit and carefully slipped his left arm out, then gently pulled his right arm out of the sleeve. His right shoulder appeared to be out of socket.

"Posterior dislocation," she whispered to herself.

Heidi removed her shoes and sat down on his right side. Then she took hold of his right hand with both of her hands and placed her right foot into his armpit. She pulled on his arm and pushed with her foot. As the bone slipped back into the socket, the man muffled a scream.

"Better!" he managed to say.

Heidi asked for some rags and made him a makeshift sling. She took his hand and pushed it against his abdomen. "Don't move it."

He nodded.

Heidi then removed his right boot and examined his swollen ankle. She though it was probably a sprain but there was no way to know without x-rays. "Let's go," she said, replacing the boot.

They made their way to the truck. Heidi had bought it for the resistance. It had a flat bed with side rails and a back drop. Now they would see how well it would work in their efforts. German patrols were actively looking for the downed pilot. Heidi and her team would have to move him to a farm closer to Leipzig for a week or so and then get him to France.

"Help him on to the truck," Max said to Franz. "You both can lie down under the tarp. We will be traveling about an hour. If we run into trouble you know what to do."

A blanket was folded on the truck bed. Franz spread it out and helped the airman lie down. Then he lay down beside him and pulled the tarp over them. It was about 4:00 a.m. They back-tracked along the same route they had taken, staying off of the main roads. The countryside was a mix of farmland and pine forests, a soothing picture even in the dark. Heidi began to relax. She believed they were safe. They would not encounter a patrol, but then she saw the headlights. A vehicle was approaching from the west. It happened so fast they could not turn off the road or avoid the oncoming vehicle. As it got closer Max could see that it was a military truck with two occupants in the cab and two soldiers sitting on the truck bed. The truck slowed and then turned to block theircpath. The two soldiers in the back got down with their weapons. The sergeant in command climbed out of the cab leaving the driver. Max slowed to a stop and simultaneously reached under the seat and brought up a pistol. Heidi had not known it was there.

"What are you doing out at this time of the morning?" the sergeant asked. He had walked to the driver's side of the truck and placed one foot on the running board.

"We are returning from seeing our sister," Max said calmly. Then he grinned. "She just had a baby."

"Really? Well, someone around here just had an enemy pilot drop down from the sky," the sergeant replied, his grin matching Max's. "We'll need to take a look in the truck."

"Have a look," said Max waiving his left hand toward the truck bed. He simultaneously brought the pistol to the door with his right hand, holding it just below the window.

The two soldiers walked to the back of the truck. They lowered the tailgate just as Franz threw off the tarp. He sat up and fired the semi-automatic, hitting both men in the chest. The impact knocked them back 10 feet and to the ground. Simultaneously, Max raised his pistol and shot the sergeant at close range. The bullet entered his brain just above his left ear. The private driving the truck jumped out. Having left his weapon in the back of the truck, he started to run. Franz jumped down and ran after him. Within seconds there was another burst from the semi-automatic. Franz returned from the darkness.

"You okay?" he asked Max.

"Yes. Let's go!"

* * *

Heidi spent the next few weeks trying to forget the violence she had witnessed. As a surgeon she had seen firsthand the result of the violence of warfare – but always after the fact. Now she had seen a man literally blown into eternity by another man. She knew that if not for the actions of Franz and Max, she and the others would be the corpses. Hatred had turned the farmlands and pine forests, the fields of hay and oats, into killing fields, and all because of a single mad man, an Austrian no less, who had gained control of an entire nation that was not his own. Man's inhumanity to man was as old as civilization, yet still incomprehensible.

Two months to the day after she had helped the airman, Heidi was introduced to another wounded soldier, this time a German. Klaus von Stauffenberg had come to the hospital in Leipzig from the war zone in Tunisia, where he was the operations officer for the 10th Panzer Division. He was a man of astonishing gifts who had served with distinction in France and on the Russian front. In Tunisia he had driven over a land mine and suffered grave injuries including the loss of his right hand, two fingers on his left hand, his left eye and ear. He was initially seen and treated by Professor Sauarbruch in Munich then transferred to the Leipzig University Hospital for further convalescence.

Heidi was assigned to his ward, but was reluctant to get involved with a Nazi officer. She was working the evening shift and served his evening meal tray. As she approached, he smiled.

"You're very kind," he said. "I appreciate your service."

Heidi returned the smile and said, "Thank you."

Curious about his injuries, she turned to his chart and began reading. She glanced at the man. He was handsome. His facial trauma was healing well. She looked closely at his face and the patch over his left eye. The word 'dashing' came to mind.

Later that evening she made her medication rounds, leaving him as her last patient. "Good evening," she said softly as she entered his room.

He smiled. "Good evening."

As they began to talk, Heidi learned more about this war hero. It was soon clear that he had strong feelings against the war *and* Nazi anti-Semitism. He was not the usual military officer. He had a passion for horses, art and literature. He was an admirer of the work of German poet, Stefan George, whom he had met. Even with his negative feelings about the Nazi Reich, he had thrown himself into battle, the consummate professional.

One evening Heidi met his wife. She was from aristocracy. The Countess Nina strongly supported her husband's views on the war and shared her thoughts with Heidi. "He feels he must do something to save Germany," she said.

By September 1943, the wounded officer had finished his convalescence. He was assigned the position of chief of staff to General Olbricht at the General Army Office in Berlin. He had been promoted to the rank of Lt. Colonel. The first evening of his time at his new post, Olbricht asked him to dinner. Berlin was full of out of the way places, none crowded because of the bombing curfew. The two men settled into a corner table and ordered wine.

"Settled into your quarters?" asked Olbricht.

"Yes, thank you sir," said von Stauffenberg. "Nina and the children are only an hour away."

"Good! Then I'll get right to the point. We have not discussed this, but I know you are sympathetic to the cause. Hitler must be dealt with. You have knowledge of the English explosives obtained by the Abwehr."

Olbricht was referring to the Intelligence Division of the High Command. Stauffenberg was slow to respond.

"I am aware of them and feel they are capable weapons. I also feel that to save Germany, Hitler will have to be killed."

Over the next few months, Stauffenberg began to dominate the thinking of the conspirator group. He demonstrated great clarity in his evaluations and great determination. He realized that if Hitler were killed, the conspirators would have a brief opportunity to take over politically, but could only do so with the military. Soon Stauffenberg had the key men he needed including General Stieff of the Army High Command, Edvard Wagner, Quartermaster General of the Army, Erich Fellgiebel, Chief of Signal Corps of the High Command, and Paul von Hase, chief of all Berlin based troops excluding the Gestapo and SS. There were a few others like Fritz Fromm,

Commander of the Replacement Army, who seemed sympathetic but would not fully commit to any plot to assassinate Hitler.

Stauffenberg realized that there was a large piece of the puzzle still missing. The conspirators did not have a Field Marshall in the group. Several had been approached and again were sympathetic, but declined. Without Stauffenberg's knowledge, one unlikely candidate was emerging. Erwin Rommel, the 'Desert Fox' of North Africa, had been given command of Army group 'B' in the west. His army was to be the first line of defense against an Allied invasion of France. His home was at Herrlingen, near Ulm, but he was spending more than half of his time in France. He was also seeing two old friends, General Alexander von Falkenhausen, Military Governor of Belgium, and General Karl Heinrich von Stuelpnagel, Military Governor of France. Both of these men had joined the conspiracy and were an influence on Rommel. In time, Rommel agreed to join the plot but was opposed to killing Hitler. He thought it would make him a martyr. He favored arresting him and trying him for war crimes.

The final plan was based on a number of presuppositions. One, that the Allies would not demand an unconditional surrender. And two, that the Allied armies would join a new German government against Russia, which had designs on a Communist Europe. This, despite the fact that many conspirators were pro-Russian but anti- Bolshevik. But all of this was unrealistic. The previous January, Roosevelt and Churchill had met in Casablanca and agreed on a position of the unconditional surrender of Germany. Later the Russians joined them.

The conspirators had control of the Berlin Police through its Chief, Count von Helldorf. But they did not have enough soldiers to oppose the SS and the Gestapo loyal to Hitler. They realized that for success, the revolt would need to be achieved and completed within 24 hours. Too, the moment Hitler was killed, his headquarters at Rastenburg would have to be cut off and isolated to prevent either Goering or Himmler from creating another Nazi regime. So detailed plans were completed to take control of Berlin as well as instructions to the district military commanders for putting down the SS and arresting leading Nazi leaders.

As 1943 was coming to an end, the cabal was ready and in place. But by the spring of the following year, time seemed to be running out. Among other things, the Gestapo was closing in on a number of the conspirators. Many of the top generals were being shadowed by Himmler's men. Those involved were finding it increasingly difficult to meet. Rome had been abandoned to the Allies, and a European invasion through France seemed imminent.

*　*　*

Werner Schmidt spent most nights thinking of his wife Maria. He had decided not to try to contact her by short-wave communication. Any message to the German underground would have to be in code and then would have to be delivered by currier. Although unlikely, the Gestapo had classified him as an underground operative and might still be watching Maria. By January, 1944, Roosevelt and Churchill had agreed their main concern centered on the defeat of Germany rather than checking the advance of Communism. The invasion of Italy had been remarkable. In the south, the Italians embraced the invading Allies and essentially joined the fight against the Germans. The situation in the north was much different, where German reinforcements poured in. They unleashed their animosities against their Italian counterparts, executing about 10,000 Italian soldiers as 'traitors'. That fall, half a million Italian troops were placed in railway cars and shipped north to be used as forced labor for the Germans. As the Nazis quickly turned on their former comrades in arms, the German hegemony with Italy was a bitter display that German loyalty extended only to themselves.

During the build-up for the invasion of Europe, the strategic bombing of Germany increased. The targets continued to be military but there was also emphasis on transportation, mostly rail lines and communication centers. The so called 'collateral damage' included the loss of life and home. There were no cinemas, cafés, shops or newspapers operating in the major metropolitan cities. Life was chaotic, and there was the ever present danger of more bombs.

Except for an occasional V-1 or V-2 rocket attack, England was relatively safe. London was packed with thousands of support personnel. The final planning of the invasion was to be done by Supreme Headquarters, Allied Expeditionary Force, General Dwight Eisenhower, Supreme Commander. The British favored an attack from the south through Italy, but the U.S. insisted on the shortest route to Germany which was through France. Two landing sites were considered. The shortest distance across the channel was to Pas de Calais. It had the broader, flatter beaches but was the most heavily defended and fortified area of the French coast. For this reason, the alternate site of Normandy was chosen. While Eisenhower was the Supreme Commander, General Montgomery of North Africa fame was in command of all ground forces. He was in charge of actually formulating the battle plan called Operation Overlord.

Montgomery envisioned a 90-day campaign that would culminate at the Seine River. A total of 47 divisions would be committed to the effort with an initial landing force of five divisions by sea and three by air. In all, 1.4 million troops would be involved with 4,000 landing craft, 12,000 aircraft and 1,000 transports for paratroopers.

A critical part of the invasion was the development of a massive deception called Operation Fortitude. It was implemented by using a British Intelligence double cross system, literally referred to as the XX system for Roman numeral 20. Multiple German agents in England had defected or been captured. The Allies developed an entirely fictitious army group called the First U.S. Army Group (FUSAC) commanded by General George Patton. Fake radio traffic was used to convince the Germans that the main invasion would be at Pas de Calais. Other radio traffic indicated a second attack would be in Norway. A number of these 'double agents' were from the Abehr – intelligence bureau of the OKW, High Command of the German Armed Forces. The commanding officer of the OKW, Admiral Canaris, and his chief assistant, Colonel Hans Oster, were both anti-Nazi and worked against Hitler throughout the war.

The spring of 1944 was an exciting time for Werner Schmidt. He was part of a team of 20 special operatives who would be dropped by parachute the day of the invasion into the Black Forrest on the German western border. Their mission was to blow up two rail bridges that crossed the Rhine River. All of the men were fluent in German, but only Werner and one other man, Karl Zeller, had been born and raised in Germany. Karl's family had immigrated to England in 1927 when he was 12 years old. Werner and Karl would head the two teams of 10 men each. After the demolition they would rendezvous with French resistance, then work their way south to Bordeaux, a distance of over 700 kilometers. There, they would be picked up by the British Navy. All except Werner. He would leave the group and make his way to his farm near Heidelberg, 100 kilometers north of the Black Forrest. With the invasion on, the danger of encountering German military would be significantly diminished. And with the maximum effort to defend the Fatherland, Werner believed he could remain undetected at his farm until the war's end and the Allies made it to Germany. Most important for Werner, he would be with Maria.

The German army was beset with uncertainty as to the time and place of the invasion. There were 18 straight days in May of good weather and there had been no invasion. German meteorologists predicted that the first two weeks of June would bring stormy weather with rough seas. On June 4th the Luftwaffe reconnaissance flights were grounded because of weather. The morning of June 5th, Rommel set off for his home at Herrlingen to spend a night with his family. The following day he was scheduled to go to Bechtesgaden to confer with Hitler. He never made the trip.

June 5th was a quiet day. Anglo-American air sorties continued just as they had for weeks. At sundown the German High Command Headquarters received information that the BBC was broadcasting an unusually large number of coded messages to the French resistance, and that German radar stations up and down the French coast were being jammed. Eisenhower had received his own weather forecast for June 6th predicting a brief break in the stormy conditions. Late on the night of June 5th Eisenhower gave the order to "go."

June 6, 1944 dawned, and three airborne divisions, two American and one British, began to parachute into northwest France. Two hours later, five Allied divisions were landing on the Normandy beaches and the general alarm was sounded by the German High Command. After fierce fighting, on June 9th, the Allied forces were well established in France. They had secured one deepwater port to off-load troops and supplies. The Luftwaffe had been driven from the skies and the German Navy from the seas. The Allies now had the upper hand, and the German field commanders knew it.

Werner Schmidt had been in training with his commando team for more than two months. They had each done five live jumps out of a C-47 transport. The jumps were relatively low level, 5,000 ft. Their jump over the Black Forrest would be even lower at 4,000 ft. The first problem would be getting on the ground without major injury. Sprained ankles were not uncommon. Five men would carry a type of plastic explosive and one man a small short wave radio. The other four would be loaded down with water and food rations as well as extra ammunition. They were each issued a Thompson submachine gun that used 30 round clips, a 0.45 automatic pistol, four hand grenades, and an 8" knife.

The drop zone was just west of the mountains of the Black Forrest. There was a plateau between the mountains and the river giving them a clearing of 500 meters width. Their departure time was 6:05 p.m. on the 6th day of the 6th month. The estimated flight time of 2 hours and 45 minutes would place them over the drop zone at just before 9:00 p.m. The 20 men would be dropped mid-way between the towns of Baden-Baden and Offengurg, which was also mid-way between the two bridges. These rail lines were used to bring men and supplies from the Munich area to the front. It was not known if the bridges were guarded, but underground intelligence indicated they were not.

The 20 were loaded on their C-47 at 5:15 p.m. Their departure base was at Ipswich on the eastern coast of England. The flight plan would take them due east over The Haag, Netherlands, then diagonally into Germany. Major metropolitan areas would be avoided. They were counting on the confusion of the invasion to keep them unnoticed. Their altitude would be 10,000 ft. until they descended for the drop zone approach. Their departure was on time, 6:05. Both German and French underground had been informed of the mission. Two German resistance men were to be waiting in the Black Forest.

Each man packed his own 'chute' as was customary. Because of the extra equipment, there were no auxiliary parachutes. At take-off, each man snapped his ripcord line onto the cable and sat down to wait. Engine noise made conversation very difficult. But few were interested in talking. These commandos had a dangerous and difficult job. If accomplished successfully, it would ensure another nail in the Nazi coffin. As the men sat listening to the roar of the twin 1200 HP Pratt & Whitney engines, each in his private thoughts, only

Werner was truly excited. It had been more than two years since he had seen Maria. He had thought he might never see her again or at least not until the end of the war. He always believed the Nazis would be defeated, but never could have imagined being involved as he was.

The clock turned to 8:52, and the jump-master stood. He opened the double doors. The commandoes stood in two parallel lines. Each man shook hands with his opposite in line and said 'good luck' or 'good hunting'. Two of the men said 'God's speed'. On command of the jump-master and at 5 second intervals, each man bailed out. The pilot had found the Rhine River and had followed it diagonally to the Baden-Baden area. The drop zone was just east of the river. So far the mission had gone smoothly.

All of the commandoes were on the ground within seven minutes. There were two sprained ankles but no broken bones. The German resistance had been instructed by short-wave code to have two men at the drop site. One to go with each group. The identification code was 'ransom' (das Losegeld). Werner's group would go north to the bridge at Baden-Baden and Zeller's group south to the bridge at Strasburg.

The distance to each bridge was approximately 18 kilometers or 11 miles. The demolition time was set for 5:00 a.m. and the explosions would be coordinated. As they were burying their 'chutes' two men dressed in black approached from the forest. The commandoes dropped prone on the ground when one of the men called out 'das Losegeld'. Werner moved toward them and engaged them in a brief conversation. The commando groups synchronized their watches at 10:37 and started 'double-time' to the bridges.

Werner's group hugged the tree-line. He had been to the Black Forest many times as a youth and knew the area well. With his lead they covered half the distance in 55 minutes. After a 15 minute rest, they continued and arrived at the bridge just before midnight. Staying in the trees, they could see the bridge well in the moonlight. To their distress there was a guard house on the German side of the river. The river was about 100 meters wide at the point of the bridge. As Werner was scanning the structure, he was startled to notice that the bridge was double decked. It was an auto as well as a rail bridge. Fortunately, the rail portion was below the auto segment. But this would make the demolition more difficult.

They could see both guards in the guard-house. They appeared to be playing cards and one was smoking. The guards usually worked eight-hour shifts. The evening before, the underground men had noted the shift change was at 6:00 a.m., so they had time to take out the guards and blow the bridge at 5:00 a.m. as planned before the scheduled shift change. It was critical that the explosions occur simultaneously or as close as possible. If not, the area would quickly be crawling with soldiers before they could make their escape. The commandoes had all worn civilian clothes and planned to discard their packs and Thompson's in the river. They must blend into the population and they all carried forged papers. But each man would keep his .045 pistol concealed as well as his hand grenades. If cornered, they would simply fight their way out. About half of the men spoke French as well as German and each man carried 1,000 French francs. The teams would travel independently to Bordeaux and expected help from the French resistance.

Time was growing short. It would take about three hours to set the explosives. It was approaching 12:30 a.m. Werner and two other commandoes moved cautiously toward the guard house. If shots were fired the mission would be aborted. As they got closer, they could hear the small talk. These Germans felt fortunate that they were not at the front in the thick of the invasion. One mentioned that the casualty rate was expected to be at least 50 percent. Guard duty was the safest job in the army next to being a cook. This night would prove to be an exception.

Werner rolled a large rock down an embankment outside the guard house door. One guard stepped out to investigate. From behind, Werner rolled into him at knee level slamming him face down onto the ground. Werner quickly jumped on his back and placed his left forearm over the man's face and mouth pulling his head back. In the same motion he plunged his knife into the base of his neck severing his trachea and left carotid artery. The guard made no sound.

Simultaneously, the two other commandoes rushed into the guard house where the remaining guard was reaching for his rifle, propped in the corner. The first commando hit him in the face with the stock of his Thompson. The force of the blow knocked him back against the wall also knocking off his helmet. The second commando plunged his knife downward into the base of his neck, transecting his aorta as it arched out of the heart. Blood poured from the wound as the guard slumped to the floor. He took two agonal breaths and was dead. Both bodies were dragged down the embankment to the river's edge, then pushed into the water.

The demolition officer took Werner and six commandoes onto the bridge walking along the rail segment. It was a truss design with three 60 meter spans supported by two 40 foot vertical granite pillars. Each granite pillar was built on steel reinforced piles sunk to bed rock in the riverbed. These vertical structures could not be significantly damaged. They were simply too strong. The only hope was to dislodge the middle truss off of its mooring on the granite support. The charge would be placed on the 'French' side of the bridge.

By 4:00 a.m. the explosives were in place and the detonator wired and connected, the wire running 40 meters from the river's edge. All of Werner's team now was on French soil. They had said their good-by's and Werner ran along the railroad tracks back to the German side of the river.

The demolition officer would compress the detonator while his comrades waited 100 meters up stream. By 4:35 all was ready. The commandoes reluctantly placed their packs and submachine guns in the river. Werner and his resistance companion retreated into the edge of the forest but could see the bridge in their field glasses.

At exactly 5:00 a.m. the detonator was compressed. The explosion was equivalent to 1,000 pounds of TNT and rattled windows for almost two miles. The concussion shock wave was felt by Werner and his comrade. As the smoke cleared they could see that the middle truss had been blown off of the mooring and had fallen into the river. The weight of the fallingsteel truss pulled the opposite end lose as well and the entire structure now was in the river. Three minutes after the explosion the two men disappeared into the Black Forest.

Maria Schmidt had worked out a routine to care for her needs and the needs of Werner's father. She had three milk cows, a dozen laying hens, and a large vegetable garden. Her first chore was to milk the cows and then gather the eggs. Her day usually started at 5:30 a.m. June 8, 1944 was no different. She had no radio and traveled into Heidelberg with neighbors about once a month for supplies. A neighbor had stopped by the day before to share the news of the invasion. Maria had thought little of the war and had not seen one person in uniform since the night she was terrorized by the Gestapo. She had little understanding of the true meaning of the invasion, but simply thought that eventually it might bring Werner home – if he was still alive.

There were days when Maria worked the farm and talked openly to Werner as if he were there. On those days she enjoyed his company and her work-day passed quickly. But as time went on, those days were fewer and fewer. On other days she convinced herself that he was not alive. She was trying to adjust to the idea that she would not see him again and her life on the farm would be a solitary existence.

Sunrise was about 6:00 a.m. in early June and Maria always took a kerosene lantern to the barn. She placed straw in the trough for the milk cows. For a brief moment she had a feeling she was not alone and glanced around but saw no one. She picked up the milk pale, and then he spoke. "Maria!"

She turned toward the voice as he stepped out of the shadows.

"Maria!"

She looked into his face in disbelief and then dropped to her knees on the straw covered floor. She buried her face in her hands and began to sob. He kneeled beside her taking her in his arms. Now, with her arms around him, she finally believed he was not an apparition. God had returned to her the man she had loved since she was 12 years old. Once able to speak, she asked four or five questions. But Werner stroked her hair and pleaded quietly.

"I have been walking for 24 hours. Let's get some breakfast and I will tell you my story."

* * *

Ten days after the Normandy invasion Heidi was walking to her flat from the hospital after working the evening shift. As she was approaching the apartment complex a man standing in a group of trees said the word 'freiheit' (freedom). This code was used by the resistance. Heidi paused but was suspicious. She knew it could be a trap.

"It's Landis."

She walked into the clump of trees. "I must talk with you," he said.

"There's a small park two blocks from here that should be safe," Heidi whispered. They walked silently to the park and sat on a park bench. The street and the park were deserted as the Leipzig black out was in effect.

"Max has been betrayed," he said. "We found his body today. He went missing three days ago. He was shot in the back of the head and looked as if he had been tortured. If he had talked, we would have already been arrested."

Heidi paused to absorb this news. She could feel the adrenalin hit her blood stream as her heart began to pound. She had one question. "Do you feel we are out of danger?"

"Yes, but I will not contact you for a month or so. It's possible we are being watched, who knows. Stay vigilant."

He then got up and disappeared into the darkness.

CHAPTER 16
Conspiracy

By the afternoon of June 6th, American and British forces had penertrated up to two miles into

France. Hitler finally had received the bad news at Berchtesgaden. That day at 4:55 p.m. he gave what his field commanders could only view as a bizarre order. It was that the bridgehead must be "annihilated" and the beach head "cleaned-up" no later than midnight that night. Even Rommel seemed to take the order seriously and telephoned it to Seventh Army Headquarters. General Pemsel was on the other end of the line and gave a blunt reply to Hitler's order.... 'Impossible'!

On June 17th, the field marshals enticed Hitler to come for a firsthand look. They met in an elaborate bomb shelter originally for use during the abandoned invasion of England. Hitler was curt and quickly made it clear that he held his field commanders responsible for the allied successes. Rommel argued that the superior Allied Air, Naval, and troop strengths made the situation 'hopeless,' though Hitler scoffed at the notion. Rommel pointed out that fighting close to the beaches left their troops vulnerable to the heavy naval bombardments. He argued for a pull-back 12 miles out of range of the big guns and a regroup for a counter attack. Hitler would not listen to any proposal for a pull-back.

'Retreat' was not in his vocabulary. He seemed to believe that was part of his 'military genius'. The meeting lasted six hours including lunch. Rommel and the others noticed that for the entire length of the meeting, two *SS* officers stood behind Hitler watching the others. They even tasted his food before he ate.

Once again, on June 29, Rommel appealed to Hitler to face the reality of defeat on the Eastern front and now in the West. If Germany would capitulate perhaps a million lives would be saved. Rommel's reception was frosty and blunt. Germany now had "miracle weapons" that would bring victory. On July 15th, Rommel put his thoughts in a letter to Hitler. The next day he said to his Chief of Staff, General Hans Speidel, "I have given him his last chance. If he does not take it, we will act!"

Two days later, Rommel's staff car was strafed by a low flying Allied fighter. He was critically injured but survived. This was a crushing blow to the conspirators who looked to him as their pillar of strength.

For months the conspirators had needed something positive and toward the end of June they got it. Their intellectual and emotional leader, Klaus von Stauffenberg, was promoted to full colonel and made chief of staff to General Fromm, the Commander of the Home Army. Now he could issue orders in Fromm's name but more importantly, he had direct access to Hitler. Deep in the recesses of his mind he felt the coup would be successful, and a new anti-Nazi government would be established. He had even shared with Dr. Goerdeler his desire for the Allied invasion to fail. One evening, in discussing their fate, he said, "If the British and Americans suffered a bloody set-back, they might be more willing to negotiate with a new anti-Nazi government." Goerdeler agreed.

"Even though they have said they will insist on 'unconditional surrender' they might go easier on a non-Hitler government. Besides, I am certain Churchill fears a Russian takeover of Europe."

"All the more reason to move on with the plan," Stauffenberg concluded.

But the younger men involved in the conspiracy were not totally convinced. There was much more at risk than their careers. Failure would mean execution. They had to come to grips with that fact.

There were non-military members of the conspiracy as well. In the spring of 1942, two Lutheran clergymen traveled to Stockholm on hearing they might have an audience with Dr. George Bell, the Anglican Bishop of Chichester. One of the travelers was Dietrich Bonhoeffer. This remarkable man had earned a doctorate in theology from the University of Berlin at age 21. He was too young to be ordained and went to the U.S. for a year of post-graduate study. After spending time in London, he returned to Germany in 1935 to teach. Soon he became involved in forming the 'Confessing Church', a group that opposed the anti-Semitic Nazi policies. In 1939, he joined the resistance and was soon barred from preaching or teaching by the Gestapo.

On the trip to Stockholm he traveled incognito using forged papers from Colonel Oster of the Military Intelligence Office (Abwehr). His opposition to Hitler was based on moral grounds, not political. He felt he must be a witness against the tyranny of the Nazi Reich. In discussing the issue with the Bishop, Bonhoeffer provided him with a list of conspirators. But the list fell into the wrong hands and later would be used against him.

Klaus von Stauffenberg was a war hero and looked the part. He was a strikingly handsome man even missing his right arm and left eye and ear. The eye patch gave him the distinguished look of an aristocrat. On the weekends he and wife Countess Nina spent countless hours discussing the plight of their country and their efforts to change the course of history. She was never involved directly in the coup. In the event of failure, she had to survive to raise and care for their children. But she felt as strongly as her husband about the Nazis and would gladly have given her life for the cause.

Along with other issues, their discussions included the "RoteKappelle" affair (Red Orchestra). The term 'Red Orchestra' was used by the Gestapo to describe a resistance group of about 75 individuals, 40 percent of whom were women. They were headed by two men, Havro Schulze-Boysen, an intelligence officer, and Avrid Hamack, a brilliant young economist. The group collected information on Nazi human rights violations. Documented violations and Nazi secrets were communicated to foreign embassies. It was very secretive, but a group so large was dangerous.

A second group was run by agent Leopold Trepper. This group was in fact a Soviet espionage network. One of their undercover men in Belgium was caught and became a double agent trying to save his own skin. His treachery eventually led to the arrest of both Schulze-Boysen and Hamack and their wives. In all, more than 100 members of the Red Orchestra were captured, and most were executed. Hitler's orders were to have them killed by hanging. But there were no gallows in Germany. Executions had always been carried out by ax beheading. So, the hangings were carried out by strangulation of these 'traitors' with ropes hung from meat hooks. One young nursing mother was allowed to wean her young son and then was hanged.

The Stauffenbergs and all of the others exhibited bravery even beyond that of the front line troops. An encouragement to all of these brave men and women was Major General Henning von Tresckow. Born in 1901, this distinguished soldier was first in his class at Knegs Kademic (the Prussian Military Academy). He initially supported National Socialism until the Night of Long Knives in June of 1934, when Hitler personally led *SS* troops in a bloody purge against the Storm Troopers headed by his erstwhile comrade, Ernst Rohm. It was easy for the Nazi warlord to kill a colleague once he was considered 'in the way.' Rohm had been fiercely loyal to Hitler, but was a crude man and suspected of being homosexual. In the following days, many non-Nazis were murdered as well, including retired General Kurt von Schleicher and his wife. Their execution was ordered by Hermann Goering to 'settle an old score'.

It was then that von Tresckow decided to oppose the Nazi Reich. He came from a long tradition of military service and continued to serve with distinction. Over several years he was involved secretly in several attempts on Hitler's life. All failed. All for different reasons. In 1944, he was the chief of staff of the Second Army on the Russian Front. He sent a message to encourage the conspiring group in Berlin, which said in part

"We must prove to the world and future generations that the men of the German Resistance movement dared to take the decisive step and hazard their lives on it."

His letter inspired the doubters and revived the conspiracy.

It was clear that the plan's success rested directly on the shoulders of Klaus von Stauffenberg. An unfortunate incident on July 4, 1944 forced the hand of the plotters. Julius Leber was a socialist and trade-union leader. He had become a close personal friend of Stauffenberg. Another socialist, Adolph Reichwein, the Director of the Folklore Museum of Berlin, joined Leber to influence the conspirators to inform the Communists of the plot. Stauffenberg was initially cool to the idea but became convinced it might be useful to know what the Communists would do in the event the putsch was successful. So he reluctantly agreed for Reichwein and Leber to meet with underground Communist leaders. His parting words were, "Tell them as little as possible."

The meeting took place the following week in East Berlin. The Communist leaders actually knew a good bit about the plot and wanted to know more. They requested a second meeting to take place on July 4th. Stauffenberg was asked by Leber to attend but he refused. At the meeting the Communist brought a third man they introduced as "Rambo". Unknown to the Communists, he worked for the Gestapo.

These men were non-military and likely did not fully understand the risk they were taking. The Gestapo rules of engagement were egregiously harsh. There were no second chances. All of the men, Leber, Reichwein and the Communists, were arrested. The conspiracy was now in peril. Would Leber and Reichwein crack under Gestapo torture? Even brave men had limits. The ill fated meeting had indeed forced their hand.

Klaus von Stauffenberg knew that time was short. The burden of this monumental task was constantly on his mind, yet the more he thought of it, the more he was certain it must be done and certain it was worth the risk. It was not just another battle in the war. It was a way to redeem the Volk - the millions of 'good Germans' who had followed Hitler down the dark path of social Darwinism. Now Himmler's death squads were on their heels. Like wolves after prey, they had the scent and were in a frenzy for the kill.

Desperate men often make foolish decisions. The group had convinced themselves that killing Hitler would not be enough. The cabal must eliminate Goering and Himmler as well. These two were the only men who could galvanize the Nazis against them. With all three gone, the top field marshals would surely join them. There would be no choice, especially with Rommel on their side. Goering and Himmler usually attended the daily military planning conferences and it was felt that all three could be taken out with one bomb. The plotters were in possession of several of the special English-made bombs obtained through Colonel Oster of the Abwehr. All of the conspirators were in agreement - all three should be killed.

On July 11, Stauffenberg was summoned to military headquarters at Obersalzberg. His task was to brief Hitler on the supply of badly needed replacements. The night before his trip he carefully placed one of the English-made bombs in his brief case and concealed it. The plane ride from Berlin was uneventful. The bomb fuse was to be triggered by a chemical contained in a small glass vile that would dissolve the wire holding the detonator pin. Once in contact with the chemical, the wire lasted approximately ten minutes before the firing pin was released. When Stauffenberg entered the room, he noticed that Himmler was not at the meeting. After his report, he stepped out and called Berlin to confer with General Olbricht. Together they decided not to set the bomb. On his return plane trip, he could not help thinking that it all could have been over.

A disconsolate Stauffenberg returned to meet with his comrades. Each had ideas of what to do next, but none was certain. Dr. Goerdeler wanted to fly to Paris and try for an armistice that would free German forces in the West to reinforce their flagging forces on the Russian front. General Beck argued that a separate peace with the Allies was a pipe dream but continued to feel that killing Hitler to save the honor of Germany was noble. Stauffenberg agreed.

On the evening of July 16, the Stauffenbergs invited a small group of friends and family to their home at Wannsu, an hour from

Berlin. The group included Stauffenberg's brother, Berthol, who was an advisor on international law at naval headquarters, and Lt. Colonel Caesar von Hofacker, a cousin who was a liaison officer to the Western Field Commanders. Hofacker had just returned from the Western front and had two important items to report. One, the war was going poorly and second, Rommel continued to back the conspiracy. They talked late into the night and all agreed that it was critical that Germans – not the Allies – should rid Germany of their homegrown tyrant.

On the following day, Goerdeler was tipped off by friends at police headquarters that Himmler had issued an order for his arrest. Reluctantly, he went into hiding. A day later, Klaus von Stauffenberg spent the morning playing with his children and then returned to Berlin after a cheerful good-by to Nina. On the afternoon of the 19th he was again summoned to meet with the Supreme Commander to report on the progress being made in the training of replacement troops for the Eastern front. The news from the Ukraine was not good. The situation was rapidly deteriorating. His report would be given at Fuehrer headquarters at 1:00 pm, July 20th.

Just after six o'clock the following morning, Colonel Stauffenberg drove with his adjutant, Lieutenant Werner von Haeften, past Berlin's bombed out buildings and on to the airport for the flight to Rastenburg. He had worked on his report until almost midnight. In his briefcase, along with his report, was the English-made bomb wrapped in a shirt. General Beck had informed key officers in the garrisons around Berlin that Thursday, the 20th, was *the day*. The meeting would be at the "Wolf's Lair" at Rastenburg in East Prussia.

The plane was the personal craft of General Edward Wagner, the First Quartermaster of the Army and a ringleader in the plot. It was old but reliable. The pilot was instructed to have the plane refueled and ready for the return to Berlin no later than noon. The bomb would be detonated by the breaking of the glass capsule containing the chemical that dissolved the firing pin wire.

The Wolfsschanze headquarters was in a heavily wooded area of East Prussia. It was almost impossible to see from the air for obvious reasons. The area was surrounded by electrified barbed wire fences and mine fields and patrolled around the clock by the *SS*. There were three check points on the way to the inner compound where Hitler lived and worked. Since Hitler had personally summoned Stauffenberg, he was waived through with little fanfare. He and his adjutant arrived at 10:49 and had a late breakfast with Captain von Moellendorff, adjutant to the camp commander. The one person Stauffenberg needed to see before giving his report was the communications chief, General Fellgiebel. They met in the communications office and went over the final plan in detail. Fellgiebel was to notify Berlin of the bombing and isolate the compound by shutting off all communications, telephone, telegraph and radio, for three hours. He was critical to the plot's success.

At 12:07, Stauffenberg entered the office of General Keitel, the Chief of the OKW (High Command of the Armed Forces). He hung up his cap and belt. Keitel informed him that the meeting had been moved up to begin at 12:30. Stauffenberg briefed Keitel on the report and they began the short walk to the Lagebaracke (compound barracks). After taking only a few steps Stauffenberg suddenly wheeled around and said, "I left my cap and belt in the ante room."

He did it so quickly that Keitel did not have time to remark that the adjutant could get them. Once in the ante room, Stauffenberg quickly opened his briefcase and using a pair of tongs, he crushed the glass canister holding the acid and checked his watch. The wire thickness required ten minutes before explosion. He awkwardly put on his belt and cap. It took a one-armed man a bit longer to do anything. As he walked out of the ante room, he spoke to the desk sergeant.

"I am expecting an important call from Berlin. I'll be back.' When he returned Keitel was aggravated. "Hurry! You're going to make us late."

As Keitel feared, they were late. He muttered a profanity under his breath as they entered the room. The conference had begun in the relatively small room which had a rectangular shape, some 15' X 30.' In the center of the room was a heavy oak table 18' in length. Hitler sat with his back to the door. By the time the two men entered the room, about four minutes had elapsed. Detonation of the devise was six minutes away.

General Heusiger, Chief of Operations of the Army was speaking. Keitel took his usual seat to Hitler's left. There were eighteen other officers from the service branches and the SS. General Heusinger was in the midst of a comprehensive report on the central Russian front. Keitel broke in to announce the presence of Stauffenberg. Hitler glanced up at the one-armed officer and curtly nodded. For one brief moment they made eye contact. Heusiger continued.

The massive oak table had an unusual construction in that it did not have legs. Instead, it had two large vertical supports the same thickness as the table top. They were placed six feet from either end, leaving a six-foot center section. Stauffenberg took his place two seats to the right of Hitler, placing his briefcase just inside the large oak vertical support only three feet from Hitler. He glanced at his watch. Five minutes to go.

At the four minute mark, Stauffenberg leaned over to Colonel Bo Brandt, seated to his right. "I'm expecting a call from Berlin."

With that, he stood to leave the room. No one other than Brandt seemed to notice. Brandt was absorbed in looking at the map and stood to get a better view. As he stood, Stauffenberg's briefcase was in his way and he reached down and placed it on the *outside* of the large oak vertical table support. General Heusiger was finishing his report. His last sentence was, "If our army group around Lake Peipus is not immediately withdrawn, a catastrophe....."

The sentence was never finished. At precisely 12:42 pm the bomb exploded.

At that moment, Stauffenberg was standing with General Fellgiebel in front of his office, some 150 meters away. The blast was deafening. The percussion blew out all of the windows in the meeting room with smoke and flames pouring out as well. The explosion had such force that both men believed there would be no survivors. Stauffenberg immediately rushed to his waiting car and Fellgiebel hurried to call Berlin. The next task was to get out of the Rastenburg headquarters camp. Since the guards heard the explosion, all exits were closed. At the first check point, Stauffenberg jumped from the car and demanded to speak to the duty officer. He then phoned someone, or possibly no one, and turned to the officer.

"Herr Lieutenant, I am authorized to pass!"

The gate was opened then word was sent to the next check point to allow him to exit. The final check point was a different story. A master sergeant refused to let them pass. He was a career soldier and veteran of WW I. He could not be bluffed. Stauffenberg then called Captain von Moellendorff with whom he had had breakfast, and got permission to pass. His car raced to the airport. On the journey, his adjuvant dismantled a second back-up bomb, tossing the detonation mechanism onto the roadside. The airfield control had not yet received word of the explosion, perhaps because of the communication blackout.

The pilot was sitting with the engines running. In two to three minutes they were in the air. As they lifted off they noticed someone running out of the air control office. Possibly the call about the explosion had just gotten through. The Heinkel plane was relatively slow and droned through the air.

Stauffenberg and his adjuvant were in high spirits. Since the plane had no long-distance radio, they were unable to confirm the success of the mission. Stauffenberg turned to von Haeften. "It looked like an artillery shell had hit the conference room. There might be no survivors." They touched down after a grueling three hour ride. Stauffenberg raced to a phone in the airport command center and placed a call to General Olbricht, Chief of Staff of the Home Army. When he heard Olbricht's voice, Stauffenberg immediately realized something was wrong. He was having a difficult time understanding the message.

"General, you'll have to speak up!"

"He survived the blast! Hitler is still alive."

OriginalSketch of Claus von Stauffenberg By Delia Hunt

* * *

Heidi Brendler and Sarah Engel were diligent in their efforts to stay the course of the resistance work and survive the war. They were encouraged that the allies were making steady progress in the West, and by mid-August, the Red Army was on the border of East Prussia on the Baltic Sea. The capture and execution of Max had not resulted in further arrests which was prima facie evidence that this brave man had withstood the torture of the Gestapo. Heidi had been pleased to learn that the U.S. airman they had helped had in fact made it to France. But there were at least two others who had been caught and hanged. A day did not go by that she did not think of the life and death struggles of the war. Late on the night of the ill-fated plot to kill Hitler, a brief nation-wide radio broadcast was made by the Fuehrer himself. He assured the nation that his injuries were minor and his survival was confirmation that he was to continue the role 'providence' intended for him.

Several weeks later, details of the failed coup began to leak out. It was then that Heidi learned that the man at the center of the plot was none other than Klaus von Stauffenberg, the one-eyed war hero she had met and admired the previous year. She recalled his nobility and the words of his wife, Countess Nina, that he felt he must do something to 'save Germany'. Heidi also learned that he and some of the other conspirators had been executed the night of the attempt. There were times she felt like a small boat being tossed about on the ocean by a raging storm. But storms had a limited time of destruction. This war seemed to have no end.

Because of schedule conflicts, Sarah and Heidi had missed their last two weekly dinners together. It had also been several months since Heidi had heard from Landis Koller. Then one evening as Heidi was returning to her flat, she stopped by the corner market to pick-up milk and coffee. When she entered the apartment, she noticed an envelope that had been slipped under her door. She anticipated a communication from Landis, but upon opening it she recognized Sarah's handwriting. The note was brief and read, *"I need to see you tonight! Urgent!"* It was unsigned.

Heidi set the milk and coffee on the kitchen table. The August night was warm and there was at least another hour of daylight. She quietly closed and locked the door to her flat. The three-block walk to Sarah's apartment would take only five minutes. A number of thoughts flooded her mind. She anticipated an urgent mission for the resistance. As she walked, she began to feel an excitement. She welcomed another opportunity to actively oppose the Nazi Reich. For some reason Landis had decided to communicate with her through Sarah.

Heidi reached Sarah's door and knocked softly. As it opened, one glance at Sarah answered all of Heidi's questions. Sarah was in her housecoat, her eyes red from crying. Her hair was not combed. "Christian has been killed," she said quietly, her voice monotone. "His apartment was hit three nights ago by an R.A.F. bomb. I received a call from his office early this morning."

Heidi closed the door and wrapped her arms around Sarah. They stood for several minutes embracing. "Sarah, I'm so sorry....I'm so sorry." Heidi was stunned and tried to hold back her tears but could not. It had been eight months since they had seen Christian. Heidi had gradually begun to sever her emotional ties to him believing that the circumstances of the war would keep them apart. Now it would be forever.

The two young women had become best of friends and felt more like sisters to each other. Heidi went to the kitchen to heat water for tea. When it was ready, they sat at the table and did not speak. The previous months had left Heidi emotionally drained. The death of Christian increased the darkness around her. But she knew this hour was even darker for Sarah.

"I remember him from when I was about five," Sarah finally said. "He was always teasing me and hiding my toys. He would put them in places where I could easily find them and then he'd act so surprised."

Sarah smiled, her bottom lip trembling. "Over time it became a game. When we got older the teasing stopped. He became protective of me. He kept an eye on any boys that came around me until he went to University. We made a pact, Heidi. We made a pact not to be involved with Nazi Youth clubs. He was always the shining light in my life."

Heidi nodded and looked away. After a few moments of silence, she remembered her own games with Christian and the times he played tricks on her in med school and surgical training. She recalled these moments for Sarah and the hours passed quickly. Finally, Heidi glanced at the clock. She wanted to explore one more subject before she left.

"What are your feelings about Christian's death? I suppose what I mean is…what do you feel has happened to him?"Sarah gave a soft smile. "He is with God. We are, all of us, created in God's image.…with an eternal soul or spirit. He is in Paradise, the place where God resides. That is what scripture says and what I know to be true. It is a matter of faith."

"I hope you are right," Heidi responded. "He was a wonderful man." Heidi stood to leave and put her arms tightly around Sarah. "We loved him well, didn't we Sarah…and he will always be in our hearts."

Over the next few weeks Heidi spent many hours reflecting on her life. She felt blessed to have known and loved Christian and knew that she and Sarah would remain close. She was aware that the constant danger and hostility surrounding her was beginning to take its toll. She had not confided to Sarah that she was beginning to feel a longing for a homeland away from Germany, that she dreamed of a place she had never seen, a place she could only imagine, a place that had been promised.

I will go there some day!

* * *

Shortly after the execution of Colonel Stauffenberg, the Nazis' brutality toward their fellow Germans reached its zenith. Hitler had become fanatical in his determination to payback a thousand-fold, the renegades and their families. His thirst for revenge was unquenchable. He determined that the criminals would be hauled before the People's Court and tried with lightning speed. The sentences were carried out with haste and without mercy.

The first trial took place on August 7th. Multiple defendants were in the dock including Field Marshal von Witzlaben and Generals Hoepner, Stieff, and von Hase. Before trial the men were beaten and made to look as shabby as possible. The chief judge of the court was the ardent Nazi Ronald Freisler, who had tried the White Rose participants two years earlier. Freisler was a vile man prone to mawkish outbursts. He had been a P.O.W. in Russia in WWI. While there, he learned lessons in cruelty and was now anxious to inflict that same cruelty on others.

The trials continued non-stop, in the People's Court and other venues. The death toll was extensive - eventually numbering almost 5,000. Executions were carried out until the last two weeks of the war. Hitler had demanded that all those directly involved be "hanged like cattle".

Most were taken to Ploetzensee Prison and hanged with piano wire from meat hooks. Each man was stripped to the waist, their hands bound and belts removed. The executions were filmed for Hitler's viewing. As each man dangled by the wire, the weight of his body caused him to strangle and he began to have seizures as he suffocated. Their belt-less pants eventually fell to their feet leaving them naked as they died, a final humiliation.

The People's Court remained in session through the fall and winter, grinding out death sentences until the morning of February 3, 1945, when the court took a direct hit by an American bomb. Judge Freisler was killed in the devastation that also destroyed the records of most of those awaiting trial. The bombing held the fate of one conspirator, Fabian von Schlabrendorff, a lawyer who had opposed

Hitler from the start. His trial was in session, but he was not badly injured and eventually was liberated by Allied forces.

Most of the others were not as fortunate. Carl Goerdeler, the former Mayor of Leipzig, had gone into hiding three days before the assassination attempt. He was scheduled to be made Chancellor in the new post-Nazi regime. Now he was wandering between Berlin, Potsdam and East Prussia, never spending more than two nights in the same place. Hitler had put a price of one million marks on his head. One morning while waiting to be served breakfast, he recognized a woman in uniform eying him. He left without eating as she notified authorities. His attempt to escape into near-by woods was futile and he was apprehended after only a brief chase. He was sentenced to death in September 1944, and finally executed in February the following year.

Some of the most distinguished and high-profile field officers did not face trial. General Henning von Tresckow had been a consistent inspiration communicating from the Eastern front. His letter to the conspirators in the summer of 1944 gave them a reason to move forward. He had urged these men to put their lives on the line and he was doing the same. On the morning of July 21st, this distinguished general made a portentous decision not to give Hitler the satisfaction of executing him. He bid farewell to his friend and adjuvant, Captain Fabian von Schlabrendorff, who recalled his last words:

"Everybody will now turn upon us and cover us with abuse. But my conviction remains unshaken.....we have done the right thing. Hitler is not only the archenemy of Germany: he is the archenemy of the world. In a few hours I shall stand before God, answering for my actions and for my omissions. I think I shall be able to uphold with a clear conscience all that I have done in the fight against Hitler... Whoever joined the resistance movement put on the shirt of Nessus.

The worth of a man is certain only if he is prepared to sacrifice his life for his convictions."

Tresckew then drove to a nearby military rifle range and walked into 'no man's land '. He pulled the pin on a hand grenade and held it in front of his face. The explosion literally took his head off.

Lieutenant Colonel Caesar von Hofacker, a cousin of Stauffenberg, was present at the dinner at the conspiracy leader's home on the night of July 16th. He was the plotter's liaison with the generals on the Western front, and was in complete agreement that Germans should be the ones to free their country of Hitler's tyranny. That night he reported two highly significant pieces of information. He claimed that Germany's western defenses were collapsing. He also predicted that Rommel would back the conspiracy despite his opposition to killing Hitler. When arrested, von Hofacker was taken to a Gestapo dungeon in the Prinz Albrechtstrasse, in Berlin. Under intense torture he told of Rommel's agreement with the conspiracy. When Hitler read the transcript of Hofacker's 'confession' he determined that the famous 'Desert Fox', loved by the people, must die.

In the fall of 1944, Rommel was still recovering from the injuries he suffered in the July strafing. He was at his home near Ulm, due east of the Black Forrest. On September 6th, he was visited by General Speidel, his former chief of staff. The talk turned to Hitler.

"That pathological liar has now gone completely mad," said Rommel. "He is venting his sadism on the conspirators of July 20th, and this won't be the end of it."

The following day Speidel was arrested and Rommel realized his house was being watched.

Hitler wanted to avoid the scandal of arresting Germany's most popular general. So, on October 14th, two ranking officers from Hitler's staff drove to Rommel's home and presented the evidence against him. They explained that he would have a state funeral and full military honors if he took his own life. The distinguished field marshal then met with his wife. Afterward, he met with his son Manfred. "I have just had to tell your mother that I shall be dead in a quarter of an hour," he told his son. "Hitler is charging me with high treason. In view of my service in Africa, I am to have the chance of dying by poison. The two generals have brought it with them. It's fatal in a matter of seconds. If I accept, none of the usual steps will be taken against my family. I'm to be given a state funeral. It's all been prepared to the last detail. In a quarter of an hour you will receive a call from the hospital in Ulm to say that I've had a brain seizure on the way to a conference."

Rommel donned his old Afrika Korps leather jacket and with his field marshal's baton, got into the car with the two generals. A mile down the road he took their poison and was dead in less than a minute.

Hitler wired Frau Rommel:

"Accept my sincerest sympathy for the heavy loss you have suffered with the death of your husband. The name of Field Marshal Rommel will be forever linked with the heroic battles in North Africa."

CHAPTER 17
Observing a Mad Man

In October 1944, Heidi Brendler spent her energy going from day to day and trying to deal with the helotry of her life. It had been three months since she had been involved in an underground mission. Although willing, deep down she was grateful Landis Koller seemed to be ignoring her. And in reality, he was ignoring her. Since the execution of Max, he had felt the need to shield her from the obscenity of war and the possibility of capture, torture and execution.

Germany was being bombed daily. Leipzig somehow avoided the bombardment, though the ball bearing plant took a minor hit causing some damage. The people moved and worked like a ghost community. They went through the motions of life, almost in a robotic way. One exception to this was Sarah Engel. She seemed to have a limitless supply of optimism and energy. In all of the degradation, she remained indefatigable.

When she moved to Leipzig, Heidi brought two books on ancient history and the Hebrew Torah. Many nights, she read her books by candle light, seeking answers to the cataclysm engulfing the Jewish people. Information from one of the books by Flavius Josephus illuminated a time in A.D. 70, not unlike her own, when one million Jews were killed or taken as slaves by the Romans. It was a dark time for the Hebrew people. They were cut off from the Temple just as she had been cut off from the Synagogue. The Jewish people of that day had lost nationhood. The extreme darkness Heidi was experiencing seemed to parallel the nadir of that time. She now believed the circumstances in Germany represented the judgment of God on her people. She felt abandoned. She determined that when God abandons a society, holiness disappears, wisdom evaporates, and love ceases to exist. This is what Germany looked like to Heidi in 1944.

The more she read, the more Heidi came to believe that the Creator of the Universe, the One the Hebrews called *Yahweh*, was sovereign in the world. She also believed Him to be *just.* But where was this justice in light of the expanse of human suffering she was witnessing? In Hebrew, the word 'Satan' literally meant adversary. She understood Satan to be God's adversary. And yet it seemed the Lord was allowing his adversary to attack her people through a man who had once been only a down-and-out vagabond in Vienna. This man rose only to the rank of corporal in WWI. He was a derelict in post war Munich. This man, an Austrian, was now the German Fuehrer. And he personified a maniacal hatred of Jews.

Since the time of her ancient forefathers, Abraham, Isaac and Jacob, the pattern had repeated itself. God had guided and protected her people as long as they were faithful to worship Him and Him alone. When they abandoned their worship of Him, He abandoned them. The ancient text was clear. The Lord had made unconditional promises to the patriarchs. Abraham had traveled to the land of Canaan, and there, God had promised to make him and his descendants a 'great nation' and to give them the land. But Palestine, the land of the promise, was now in Arab hands, and the Hebrews were being slaughtered by the millions.

Heidi believed the promises and concluded that the abandonment was temporary. She continued to worship the Lord her God as a sovereign and just God, true to all that He had promised. Except for Sarah she was alone in Germany. She was anonymous. Her survival depended on it.

*　*　*

After the shameful forced suicide of Field Marshal Rommel, all semblance of nobility in the German military was lost. The officers who were not involved in the assassination plot were forced to stand by while their comrades were hauled before the farcical trials in the People's Court. This was possible because Hitler created a so-called 'Court of Honor' where all Army officers thought to be involved in the plot were expelled from the military so they could not receive a court martial. The Court of Honor was not permitted to hear an accused officer in his own defense. The only evidence presented came from the Gestapo. The presiding generals of this court included Field Marshal von Rundstedt, who had been relieved of several commands, and General Guderian, the renowned Panzer tank commander. Together they turned over several hundred of their comrades to certain execution after drumming them out of the Army.

The general staff, as a meaningful entity, had come to an end. The men who had stood by while Hitler murdered his colleague Ernst Rohm in 1934, who stood by while Nazi policy murdered thousands of disadvantaged children and millions of Jews, who stood by while Germans ignored the rules of the Geneva Convention and committed countless war crimes, were now just as guilty of the crimes as if they had ordered them. With the execution of their colleagues, there was no more opposition to Hitler. Many of these generals knew the evil of the man before whom they groveled. In the final stages of the war, General Guderian made this observation of the Fuehrer:

"In his case, what had been hardness became cruelty, while a tendency to bluff became plain dishonesty. He often lied without

hesitation and assumed that others lied to him. He believed no one any more. It had already been difficult enough dealing with him: it now became torture that grew steadily worse from month to month. He frequently lost all self-control and his language grew increasingly violent. In his intimate circle he now found no restraining influence."

The last meaningful effort to rid the world of the Austrian Corporal turned Supreme Commander failed by a simple act which was of ominous significance. Colonel Stauffenberg had placed the powerful bomb three feet from Hitler and exited the room with four minutes to detonation. In the next two minutes Colonel Brandt, who was sitting next to Stauffenberg, stood to get a better view of the maps on the heavy oak table. As he did, the briefcase containing the bomb was in his way, making it difficult for him to stand. It was then that he reached down and moved the briefcase to the outside of the oak table support. It was this support that took the brunt of the massive explosion and shielded Hitler from its force, saving his life.

Sadly, even at this time, the majority of the German people still believed that Adolph Hitler might lead them to victory, so complete was his hold over the German mind and soul.

CHAPTER 18
Beginning of the End

Normally fall was a beautiful time in Leipzig. The days were crisp and clear, and the nights produced a light frost. Maple and oak trees adorned the city landscape and parks were dotted with swaths of bright orange and yellow. The aroma of burning pecan and pine filled the brisk evening air. This was Sarah's favorite time of year. She loved a crackling fireplace even if her own apartment did not have one. There was an enormous hearth in the bank's lobby that filled her appetite.

Rationing kept most food items in short supply. For weeks, Sarah and Heidi had been saving some items to enjoy on a Friday evening at home. Heidi had acquired flour and yeast for fresh bread and saved a bottle of Bordeaux. Sarah had a small pot roast and vegetables. She also found a pumpkin for a pie and bread.

Heidi left the hospital about 4:00 p.m. and dropped by her flat to get her items. Along her walk she noticed a flight of geese high overhead and heard their distinct honking. She marveled at their 'V' formation, the aerodynamic flight pattern that allowed them to travel hundreds of miles without stopping. Every hour or so, the lead goose in the formation would drop back and be replaced by a fresh leader. But the leader always had the same motive – get the group safely to their destination with no malice toward any other creature. Heidi pulled her scarf tightly around her neck and thought that men could learn much from the geese.

She wanted to be at Sarah's place before 5:00 p.m. so she could make the bread. She needed an hour for it to rise and an hour to bake. The recipe was one her mother had obtained from her friend Paula Herzog at the Pumpkin Bakery. Heidi had used it only once back in Berlin when she cooked for a Jewish holiday. Over the years, she had enjoyed the fresh hot pumpkin bread at the bakery. She was hoping to duplicate that. As she walked, her thoughts drifted back to her time with Christian and the joy of loving him. It seemed like many years ago and yet, only yesterday.

Heidi looked forward to December. She was scheduled to work in the children's wing of the hospital. Being around children lifted her spirits and gave her an avenue to escape the horrors of the war. She sometimes though perhaps she should work exclusively with children if she ever returned to surgery.

She climbed the stairs to Sarah's flat. At the top, she paused and thought again how fortunate she was to have Sarah as a friend. Sarah was the only person in Germany who knew her true identity. Their times together had given Heidi great pleasure as well as a companion. Sarah opened the door.

"Well, finally here. And what is this?"

Heidi had passed a small flower shop on the way and bought a chrysanthemum plant. "I found these on the way. I couldn't pass them by…a little color to go with our feast."

"They're nice," Sarah said with a smile. "I'll take them and your coat. Then we'll get started."

Sarah loved to cook. Heidi did her part reluctantly. She managed to get the flour mixed with the pumpkin, added the yeast and covered the dish with a moist cloth. She placed the dish in the oven which she set at low heat. Sarah had already made-up the pumpkin pie filling. The bread and the pie would be baked together. Sarah had cooked the pot roast the night before so it would only require warming.

The girls enjoyed a glass of wine while the baking was completed. They both thought frequently of Christian and were now comfortable talking about him. Heidi also shared some of her current hospital experiences. "I've been assigned to work on the children's wing for the month of December. It will be a nice break from war rehab and the elderly. I wish I could work there full-time."

"Why can't you?" Sarah asked, thinking the obvious.

"Well, everyone prefers taking care of children. They are so spontaneous and refreshing. And besides, they heal and get well so quickly. If I survive this war and ever get back to being a surgeon, I would really enjoy just doing pediatric work."

"The war should be over in a few months, Heidi. We'll rebuild our country. This time next year, you'll be back in Berlin at the University. You watch."

"A mere thought, but I think it will take 20 years to rebuild, maybe even 30. You're the money girl, you tell me!"

"Well, unless we get a lot of help from somewhere, it will be 30. That's the rest of our lifetime." Sarah lowered her voice to a whisper and continued. "Thanks to the maniac Austrian Corporal."

The women enjoyed the home cooked meal, a rare treat of pot roast and fresh bread. They talked little of the war, but each woman thought about it daily. On Friday nights as a routine, the BBC provided a short-wave transmission of updates. Sarah's transmitter-receiver was in her attic. She had never used the transmitter because the Gestapo had technology to track and pinpoint transmissions. But reception of incoming signals was not a problem. Sarah listened every Friday night. Sometimes there were coded messages from the resistance, so Sarah always listened with pencil and pad in hand. Heidi was eager to listen in. This frequency was intended for Germany and was transmitted in German.

They moved to the attic just before the 10:00 o'clock broadcast. They took their coats with them as the attic had no heat. There were two sets of head phones. At precisely 10:03 the transmission began.

"This is the BBC, transmission # 104 from London. In the past three months Allied forces have liberated Holland, Belgium, Luxemburg and France. Enemy forces have fallen back to the Siegfried line west of the Rhine River. The Western Front has been quiet for the past six weeks. Of significant importance to the allied effort is the opening of a second deep water port at Antwerp. This has been accomplished with the completion of the fourth phase of the Battle of Scheldt. British, Canadian and American units have distinguished themselves in this area. Axis forces have continued to maintain defensive positions and posture. This is BBC transmission # 104, signing off from London."

Sarah turned the set off and they moved out of the attic.

"Things seem relatively quiet," she said. Hopefully it's a prelude to a major

Allied offensive."

"It can't happen soon enough for me!"

* * *

In the fall of 1944, Sarah's intuition was right. A massive offensive was being planned, but not by the Allies. The Austrian Corporal

– Third Reich Fuehrer - was determined to attempt one last desperate gamble.

August and September saw the enemy converging on the Reich in massive numbers from the East and the West. The Russian summer offensives brought their troops to the border of East Prussia on the Baltic Sea. By the end of August new attacks had claimed Rumania and the Ploesti oil fields, Germany's main source of crude oil.

In the West allied forces, including the U.S. Third Army commanded by General George S. Patton, swept across southern France. On August 23, Patton's Army approached the Seine River from the southwest, other Allied forces from the northwest, both within a few miles of Paris. On that same day, Hitler ordered his Commander in Paris, General Dietrich von Choltitz, to detonate the bridges across the Seine. These bridges were not only beautiful but were artistic historical treasures, and von Choltitz refused. Two days later Paris fell to the Allies who found that the French resistance was already in control of the center of the city. As soon as Paris was lost, again Hitler ordered the city be leveled using heavy artillery and V-1 rockets. Again von Choltitz refused.

The following day he surrendered to avoid certain court martial. Thus a defiant Nazi General was responsible for preserving one of the world's most beautiful cities. Perhaps the most important tactical advance was made by British General Montgomery who drove his Second Army and the Canadian First Army, 200 miles northeast to Brussels. He over-ran Antwerp the next day, preventing the startled Germans from destroying the Antwerp deep water port facility. Having a second deep water facility was critical for the final Allied push into Germany.

For Germany, the enemy was 'at the gates' and her leaders were forced to take drastic measures to find troops to defend the West. The previous age for military service was 18. It had now dropped to 15. By October, another half million young men were found to hurriedly supply the Nazi Wehrmacht. It had been over 130 years since Germans had fought on German soil. The last time was during the defeat of Napoleon at the Battle of Nations in Leipzig, October 1813. The 15-year old boys were greeted with stirring speeches and the grim reality of their superiors, among others, Field Marshal Model, who said:

"None of us gives up a square foot of German soil while still alive….whoever retreats without giving battle is a traitor to his people."

By the first week in September the Allied advances had ground to a halt. There were two significant problems. One, they had out run their supplies. Two, Allied leadership could not agree on a battle plan to invade Germany. Montgomery wanted to strike in the north into the Ruhr which was the industrial heart of the German Republic. He felt this blow would open the road to Berlin and end the war. Eisenhower rejected the proposal in favor of an advance on a 'broad front'. Finally, after two weeks of haggling, Montgomery prodded Eisenhower to attempt a bold plan to seize a bridgehead over the lower Rhine at Arnhem. The Rhine River was the only significant natural barrier into Germany. The code name for the attack was 'Operation Market Garden'.

The Market aspect of the plan was the use of three airborne divisions dropped behind German lines to capture and hold strategic bridges on the Rhine. The Garden portion was the use of the XXX Corps of an elite British armored formation whose mission would be to advance and support the airborne troops. In all, 34,000 men would be involved.

The plan failed, both for logistical and tactical reasons. The greatest problem was that the Eisenhower Command Team believed the German forces were spent and that their resistance had been broken. This was a false assumption. Newly appointed Field Marshal Gerd von Rundstedt rejuvenated his command for battle. A second problem was that the airborne divisions were green and not well trained. There was early success on September 17th, day one of the operation. But every day that followed brought negative results for the Allies. After only nine days, September 25th, the 1st Airborne Division received orders to evacuate back across the Rhine. To Eisenhower, this was evidence "that much bitter campaigning" remained. But he hardly was prepared for the stunning surprise in store for his forces.

December 12th saw the first heavy snowstorm in central Europe. It was a time both Heidi and Sarah enjoyed. They looked for cafés with large fireplaces to add to the warmth of the atmosphere. Sarah would have to face her first Christmas without family. Both of her parents were deceased, and now she was without Christian. It made her especially grateful for Heidi. The two were planning dinner on Christmas Day and were also planning to attend a Christmas Eve service. Even though Heidi did not celebrate the birth of the Christ child, she loved the beauty of the pageantry. To plan their time they decided to try a bistro called das Gleichnis (the Parable). It was in an old 18th century home, actually once an estate, set on a hill on Dresdner Strabe.

They took a taxi from Sarah's apartment. Leipzig had experienced only one bombing raid in three months so taxies were allowed to operate. A light snow was falling during the ten-minute ride. The Parable Bistro overlooked a large pond now iced over. The circular drive at the café was preceded by a twisting road over the fourteen-acre estate. Sarah marveled at the grounds. When they arrived, she asked the driver to return for them at 10:00 p.m. They hopped out of the taxi clutching their purses, both filled with money they'd been saving for this extraordinary night out. It was an evening they would not soon forget.

On that same evening some 200 kilometers to the southwest, another event was unfolding. The senior Field Commanders of the Nazi forces on the Western front were converging on General von Rundstedt's headquarters. They were loaded on a bus after being relieved of their side arms and brief cases. The bus drove through the snowy countryside for about an hour and then pulled up to the entrance of a deep underground bunker. As they filed into the fortress, down approximately 60 feet, they were told they would be meeting with their Supreme Commander. It was here they were introduced to an offensive battle plan that had been highly secret, one that had been in formulation since mid-September. The code name for the operation was *Unternahmen* (Operation Watch). The U.S. Military officially called it the Ardennes Offensive, but it quickly became known as the Battle of the Bulge.

The idea had been in Hitler's mind since the failure of Operation Market-Garden. The only officers brought into the planning were von Rundstedt, General Model, plus the Chief of Staff of G-3 and one aide each. Security was extremely tight. The penalty for a breech was death. The men involved remained very uncomfortable with the stress of the situation. The Headquarters charged with the operation were OB West and Army Group 3. There was blanket radio silence for the planners.

The objective was to drive a wedge between the British and American forces from the Rhine to Antwerp. The final objective was to isolate and hold the Antwerp deep water port, one of only two being used by the Allies. Hitler himself described the plan as the Field Marshals sat in stunned silence. The reason for the silence was obvious. In the summer of 1944, the combined losses on the Eastern and Western fronts totaled 1,200,000 dead, wounded or missing. An additional 230,000 troops had been placed in positions from which they could only surrender. The German military-industrial complex had become the monster it was by conquests, now all lost, including Rumanian oil, Swedish high -grade iron ore, Russian manganese, Yugoslavian copper, and Finnish nickel and molybdenum. Finally, the Allies possessed overwhelming superiority in air power, troop strength and supplies.

The overall picture was bleak but Hitler saw only the positives. Even with the heavy bombing, war materials production was down only a third. The extensive German rail and canal complex would support a major offensive, and finally he had what he believed would be his 'trump card', complete and total surprise.

His selection of the Ardennes Forest as the sector for the counter-offensive was based solely on the principle of attacking the Allies where they were weakest. The Allies occupied a line from the Swiss border to the North Sea, a distance of some 600 miles. There were some poorly defended areas. More to the point, the Allied Command was convinced that the Germans were incapable of launching a major offensive.

A major portion of the surprise was cover and deception. To the Allies there would appear to be a major build-up of forces in the Cologne area, east of Aachen, while the real troop concentration would occur under cover of darkness in the Eifel Mountains adjacent to the Ardennes. At the last moment the troop concentrations in Cologne would be moved to Eifel under cover of darkness.

The Allied Commanders awaited an enemy that would be predictable, use rational thinking and logic. Clearly, these Commanders still did not understand the decision- making process of the German Fuehrer. Hitler believed the Allies would consider the Ardennes area to be almost impassable in winter because of the rough terrain and normal heavy snowfall.

On December 14th, a female escapee reported to the 28th Infantry Division Commander that the area in the woods of the Eifel was 'jammed' with troops and mechanized equipment. She was interrogated the next day by VII Corp G-2 and sent to 1st Army Headquarters. She arrived there on December 16th. That same day, the first thunderclap of the massed German artillery was heard. Shortly after, the full-fledged counter-attack was launched by the German Sixth Panzer Division.

*   *   *

Das Gleichnis was a remarkable place by any standard. The estate was built in 1869 by a Prussian industrialist who was a relative of Wilhelm I, King of Prussia and the first German Emperor. Wilhelm had been a guest in the home as well as his Prime Minister, Otto von Bismarck. It was under these men that Prussia achieved the unification of Germany and established the German Empire. The main house on the estate contained 26 rooms on four levels. Only the first floor was used as a dining area. The grandson of the original builder was killed in WWI and the family sold the estate in 1918. In 1934 it was refurbished and became das Gleichnis.

The structure was made of light gray granite with a large circular covered porch. The stairs leading up to the main level were circular as well. The snow fall had put a thin layer of white powder on the stairs that had not yet been swept. The enormous double steel front doors were inlayed with double-leaded glass. When Heidi and Sarah entered, these unrelated 'sisters' were astonished to find themselves in a 40 foot long central atrium with a 30 foot ceiling. In the center was a circular dome filled with a fresco of multiple and suppliant angelic figures. The main dining area was on the right side of the atrium and was also 40 feet in length. There was a large central hearth and a roaring fire, which lent itself to the metaphor of tranquility in turbulent times.

The women were seated at a table to the right of the hearth, midway to the front of the building. The 20-foot-tall windows were covered with heavy burgundy brocade. All of the tables were candle-lit, and a middle-aged gentleman in tuxedo stood at the far end of the room playing violin.

"Well, this is a fantasy!" Heidi whispered. "Now we can be aristocrats."

"At least for one evening we can be," Sarah agreed. "That's if we're allowed." They ordered wine and were served an ' amuse`. Their dinner was as elegant as the surroundings. Each felt like Cinderella, only without a Prince Charming.

"You know," said Sarah, "in a few moments we have to return to sagacious reality."

"Yes, I know," Heidi replied. "And it sounds ominous."

"It is! Landis Koller has communicated to me that there may be a way to get you out of Germany. In the past two months the resistance has helped five Jews escape to France. They have been doing it near Offenburg which is directly on the front. There is a five kilometer 'no-mans-land' between the forces. The underground has been successful in making two runs, one with two people and a second with three. Heidi, it would save your life. You could join your parents."

There was a long pause.

"I'll have to think about it," said Heidi. "I feel secure here, and I don't want to leave you. I believe the war could end in a matter of months. I'm not sure it would be worth the risk."

Sarah turned very sober.

"It is worth the risk. If you are caught, you'll be sent to a work camp or worse, a death camp."

Heidi bit her lip and finally spoke. "I'll consider it. It's a difficult decision....you know.... life and death."

* * *

The counter-offensive of December 16th slammed the door on further underground operations to help escaping Jews. The troops on both sides of the front were on high alert after this unexpected attack. Following the initial penetration of the German forces, the Armies of the Third Reich had even more successes. They had caught the Allied Commanders by complete surprise. On December 17th, elements of the Sixth Panzer Army pushed to within eight miles of the U.S. First Army headquarters at Spa.

The Fifth Panzer Army was attacking to the South with its objective to cross the Meuse River. The success of the counter-offensive depended on several factors. Surprise, already noted, foul weather to keep the Allies Air power grounded, which they had, and rapid success and capture of Allied gasoline supplies. The Germans had all of these factors save one. The Sixth Panzer group came within one mile of an enormous American gasoline dump containing more than three million gallons. Stubborn make-shift resistance or good fortune or both kept the gasoline in Allied hands.

One very unusual part of the effort was called 'Operation Grief'. This clandestine chicanery was commanded by one Otto Skorzeny, a Commando of Austrian descent, fluent in German, French, and English. He took two dozen English-speaking German soldiers in American uniforms, and using stolen American Jeeps, penetrated behind Allied lines. They spread disinformation and confusion, changed road signs and ultimately tried to take control of a bridge over the Meuse River. The confusion led to massive traffic jams. As MPs began trying to locate them, road blocks were set to ask questions only American soldiers would know such as the name of Mickey Mouse's girlfriend. No one escaped interrogations. General Omar Bradley was briefly detained when asked the Capitol of Illinois. He correctly answered Springfield, but the MP thought it was Chicago.

When captured, several of the Germans were executed as spies for being in American uniforms. So the remaining Germans put on their uniforms under the American ones. Eventually, all were rounded-up except their leader Skorzeny, who avoided capture and survived the war.

The critical battle to contain the Germans was the effort to hold the town of Bastogne. Five important roads converged in this small hamlet in eastern Belgium. The path of the Fifth Panzer Army to the Meuse River led directly through Bastogne. The German battle plan was to reach the river by day four of the operation. Timing was critical. On day two they were only 15 miles from Bastogne, which had a paper thin defense. However, on that night, the U.S. 101st Airborne Division was ordered to drive all night to reach Bastogne, which they did by daybreak. But by the 21st, the town was completely surrounded and under siege. The following morning, General Heinrich von Luettwitz, Commander of the German 101st Armored Corps, sent two officers under white flag into Bastogne. They carried a surrender note to the U.S. Commander, General A.C. McAuliffe. It read as follows:

"The fortune of War is changing. This time the U.S.A. forces in and near Bastogne have been encircled by strong German armored units. More German armored units have crossed the river Our near Ortheuville, have taken Marche and reached St. Hubert by passing through Hompre-Sibret-Tillet. Librament is in German hands.

There is only one possibility to save the encircled town. In order to think it over, a term of two hours will be granted beginning with the presentation of this note.

If this proposal should be rejected one German Artillery Corps and six heavy A.A. Battalions are ready to annihilate the U.S.A. troops in and neat Bastogne. The order for firing will be given imme-diately after this two-hours term.

All the serious civilian losses caused by this artillery fore would not correspond with the well-known American humanity."

The German Commander

McAuliffe was preoccupied with his defense planning and at first said nothing. "Sir, we have to reply," his aide said.

"Aw, nuts!" was McAuliffe's response. "Sir, is that our reply?"

Without looking up McAuliffe said, "Yeah".

The aide scribbled 'nuts' on a piece of paper and presented it to the waiting German officers. When asked what it meant, the aide replied. "It means 'go to hell."

The fire fight was on. Because of the intensity of the battle, the Fifth Panzer Army could not get their divisions around the town. The 101st Airborne was fiercely holding on. The U.S. Second armored Division suddenly entered the battle from the north. On December 23rd, the weather cleared and major air support for the Americans began, including the dropping of supplies to Bastogne. The Germans became desperate and throughout Christmas day launched attack after attack. But the 101 Airborne Bastogne defenders held on.

General Eisenhower and troops – Victory in their grasp

The day after Christmas an armored force of Patton's Third Army broke through from the south and relieved the town. The two principle German Generals, Manteuffel and Rundstedt, strongly advised a complete withdrawal, but Hitler would not listen. On New Year's Day he ordered more attacks on Bastogne using troops from a bridgehead on the Upper Rhine. The Commander of these forces was none other than Heinrich Himmler who had never had a battlefield command. The other Third Reich Field Marshals thought it was a joke. The effort lasted two days and on January 5th, the Germans abandoned all hope and began their withdrawal.

Thus ended the 'brainchild' of the Austrian Corporal, the Supreme Commander. The Battle of the Bulge, also known as the Ardennes Offensive, caused 84,834 German casualties, including 15,652 killed, 27,582 captured or missing, and 41,600 wounded. American casualties were also staggering at 89,987. Those killed numbered 19,276, with 23,554 captured or missing and 47,493 wounded. The British suffered 200 killed and 1,400 wounded or missing.

The most tragic day of the battle might have occurred on December 17th, near Malmedy. There, more than 100 American prisoners were murdered by a combat group of the 1st *SS* Panzer Division commanded by Colonel Jochen Peiper. After the war, 43 of the *SS* officers responsible, including Peiper, were tried for the crime, convicted and sentenced to death. Because of concern by a group of U.S. Senators, the death sentences were commuted to life in prison. Eventually, under a general amnesty, all of those responsible were released from prison.

* * *

Heidi Brendler did not feel trapped. She had a job in healthcare which gave her anonymity. She had a very special friend, more like a sister, and in time, the nightmare of the Third Reich would be over. She was much like a person in an ocean of sharks that would by nature, rip her to shreds – or possibly not even notice her in the midst of their evil.

One of the chief pariah's was Herman Goring. He had made the Nazi purpose very clear when he said, *"This war is not the*

Second World War. This is the Great War. In the final analysis it is about whether the German and Aryan prevails here, or whether the Jew rules the world, and that is what we are fighting for out there."

Clearly the Nazis saw the Jews as an existential threat. In concurring Europe, they would also achieve racial 'purification' of Europe. To this end, they would either relocate entire populations or kill every Jewish man, woman and child upon which they could lay their hands. This policy was justified by the concept which Landis Koller had learned as *Untermenschen.* If individuals could be deemed subhuman, there was no guilt in killing them and murder was not in fact, murder. Jewish people were even sought in countries Germans only occupied and in which they had no interest, countries such as France or Holland. Even from these countries, Jews were shipped hundreds of miles to death camps in Poland.

Alexander Solzhenitsyn, Russian historian and novelist, made these observations while serving in the Red Army.

"Gradually it was disclosed to me that the line separating good and evil passes not through states, nor between classes, nor between political parties either...... but right through every

human heart....and through all human hearts."

While the fierce Battle of the Bulge was being waged, 300 kilometers due east, Heidi and Sarah were anxiously following the progress on the BBC. Heidi wanted the fighting to end but not the month of December. That would mean her time in the children's ward would also come to an end. She had not enjoyed her work as much in many months. There were days she dreamed about the children she might have had with Christian, children she now would never experience. They would have been exceptional, because he was exceptional.

The last Monday of the month was cold and clear. Heidi had gotten to the ward early to see a four-year old girl who had been admitted on the previous Friday, suffering measles pneumonia. Heidi was careful not to appear too familiar with the charts and medical records. The charge nurse was strict and an irascible Nazi. A perfunctory glance of the chart revealed the girl's temperature was down and she was taking solid foods - good signs.

By 9:15 a.m., Heidi had finished her medication rounds and was ready to give her children their baths. As she turned to walk away from the nursing station, she saw a woman who looked vaguely familiar. Then the woman spoke to Heidi.

"Dr. Eichenwald! Dr. Eichenwald!"

Heidi was terror struck. She pretended not to hear and continued walking. "Dr. Eichenwald, I'm Gretchen Stoller."

The woman stepped up to Heidi and continued.

"You did surgery on my child in Berlin about five years ago. You saved her life. Her name is Hannah…. Hannah Stoller."

The woman was smiling and waited for Heidi to respond.

"You must be mistaken," she said, forcing a shake of her head and a confused smile. "I'm Heidi Brendler, a nurse's aide."

The woman also continued smiling. "I am sorry. Do you have a twin? You look exactly like Dr. Anna Eichenwald, a surgeon at the University Hospital in Berlin."

"No. I'm sorry," she said, quickly walking away. She kept her eyes forward, wishing she had a chart to stare at. She exhaled slowly, wondering if the charge nurse had overheard. She walked quickly into the ward for bathing the children and tried not to look distressed. She put on her best smile and tucked her shaking hands into her pockets.

For the remainder of the day she had no indication of a problem. She couldn't shake the nervous feeling in the pit of her stomach and worried through every task until her shift was over. Finally, she was able to leave the hospital. She walked to the bank to look for Sarah, but she had already left for the day.

On the way to her apartment, Heidi went over every second of the encounter. She ran the words through her head verbatim, recounting it several times. She chose against entering the building and instead, decided to watch it for a moment from a distance. She didn't see anything unusual, no suspicious bystanders, no dark, unfamiliar vehicle parked nearby.

Finally, she decided to go in. As she unlocked the door all was quiet. She closed the door behind her and sat down. She was still trembling. Maybe she was a sitting duck. Maybe she was worrying for nothing. Either way, she had nowhere else to go. If she visited Sarah and was being followed, that would put Sarah in jeopardy and the Gestapo would surely find the short-wave receiver. Sarah would be arrested and executed as a spy. For these same reasons she could not approach Landis Koller. If the charge nurse had heard, it was over for Heidi.

She sat in silence for an hour. She trained her ear to the window and listened to the street noises. She heard an occasional voice in the next apartment. She heard someone walk past her door. She heard the faint opening and closing of a door down the hall. Heidi suddenly felt nauseated and went into the toilet. She splashed cold water onto her face. Another hour passed. It was just after seven in the evening when she heard the heavy boots. Someone was walking toward her door. Then she heard the knock.

"Police! Open!"

The voice was gruff and traveled like a gun shot through the first floor of the apartment. No one opened a door. Slowly Heidi stood. Then she walked to the door and opened it. Two Gestapo officers entered, a lieutenant and a captain. The senior officer turned to her.

"Anna Eichenwald?"

She opened her mouth to speak and formed the word 'yes' but she wasn't sure if any sound came from her throat.

"Doctor Anna Eichenwald?"

This time she took a deep breath and responded, "yes."

"You are under arrest!"

CHAPTER 19

Buchenwald Prison

The ride to the central prison in Leipzig was short, about 15 minutes. Anna, in handcuffs, rode in the back of the Gestapo car with the captain. She was numb. She said nothing. Once at the prison, she was searched by a female guard while her paperwork was completed. It was now almost 8:00 p.m. Her clothes were confiscated along with her wristwatch and the small diamond ring Christian had given her. She was handed a prison dress of course burlap and still cuffed, led down a long corridor through a steel door. It opened to a concrete downward stairway. At the bottom of the stairs was another steel door that opened onto a long corridor leading to a basement cell block.

The cell block consisted of 20 individual cells lined 10 on each side, each one 15' by 20' with a single cot, lavatory and toilet. The corridor was strung with four light bulbs hanging equidistant down the hallway. This was the only lighting. For reasons that were unclear, Anna was the only prisoner being kept in that area. There were no outside windows and the only door was the one through which she entered. She noticed two floor drains centered on either end of the corridor. There was a high-pressure hose mounted on the wall at the far end of it. As she entered the end cell on the right, she was given a blanket and a cup of water. It did not enter her mind that this cell block was often used to torture prisoners with the high-pressure hose.

The handcuffs were removed by a female guard and her accomplice, a tall middle-aged man she called Gerhard. They closed and locked the cell door without a word. The last thing Anna heard was the loud 'click' of the steel door being locked.

Anna lay in silence on the cot and took in the musty smell of the damp basement. As her mind began to sort out what had happened, her eyes filled with tears. She thought of her parents and happier times in Berlin. Along with her childhood friend Erin Nitschmann, she had committed to memory several of the ancient Hebrew Scripture verses. Silently she recited one from Isaiah... *'So justice is far from us, and righteousness does not reach us. We look for light, but all is darkness; for brightness, but we walk in deep shadows.'*

Anna knew the war was in its final stages. She would have to hope that the repugnant cataclysm that was the Nazi Reich would soon run its course. Surely their priority of creating a 'Jew-free' Europe was no longer a possibility as the Nazis were facing certain defeat.

She had lived through the horrors of the 'Night of Broken Glass', but she reminded herself that she had been spared arrest because she had saved the life of an *SS* officer. A Jew who had once evaded capture was now a prisoner. What kind of violence lay ahead for her?

The Wannsee Conference of January 1942, had established firmly the Nazi pogrom for the 'Final Solution to the Jewish Question'. She was well aware of the death camps in Poland and the official Nazi policy to work Jews to death. But in the midst of all of the uncertainty she held out hope for survival.

Anna drifted in and out of sleep. She was vaguely aware of what sounded like rats, so she pulled the blanket over her head. During the night she thought of Sarah. Anna had always known the likelihood of her fate, that the Gestapo would find her. If only she could say a last fare-well to her dear friend Sarah, but she knew this was impossible.

With no windows, Anna had no way to determine time. Had five minutes passed or five hours? She couldn't know if dawn was breaking. She could only confirm that she was cold and scared.

The bolt on the steel door disengaged. A short, overweight private in thick glasses walked to her cell, and then placed a bowl and cup at the pass-through. The bowl contained a boiled egg and a stale piece of bread. The cup held water. As the private turned to leave, he spoke to her.

"You will be seen by the captain in one hour."

Otto Lang had risen through the ranks of the Einsatzgruppen, the paramilitary killing arm of the SS. He had originally been part of a death squad that followed the Wehrmacht into Russia during Operation Barbarossa. Because he had shown significant leader-ship qualities, he was given a commission of lieutenant. He was transferred back to Germany after the failure of the Russian inva-sion, and believed that the war was lost. He never discussed his thoughts with anyone. Like others in the SS, he was now working in the Gestapo and had lost his taste for killing. But he intended to do his duty until the war ended. He had always been uneasy with the killing and now he was beginning to believe that he and the thou-sands involved would someday answer for it.

Lang was serving as the commander of the Gestapo unit in Leipzig when Anna was arrested. A routine communication to the

SS headquarters in Berlin was quickly followed by a request for her interrogation and transfer to the Buchenwald work camp, some 100 kilometers southwest of Leipzig near Weimar. The call had come from one of Himmler's aides. It gave Lang the impression that Anna Eichenwald was no ordinary Jew.

At 9:17 a.m., Anna was taken to the top floor of the three-story prison building and into Lang's office. He had not yet received her dossier from Berlin. As she was brought in, Lang was startled by her beauty. Even the fatigue and fear on her face could not disguise her loveliness.

"Sit," he said with a motion. "Do you want coffee?"

Anna was numb to the surprise. She only shook her head.

Lang sat down behind his desk and glanced at his aide who stood by ready to take notes. "Why are you in Leipzig?"

"To work in the hospital."

"And where did you come from?"

"Berlin."

"And your work in Berlin?"

"I was an attending surgeon at the University Medical Center."

Lang paused. "Do you have family in Germany?"

He knew she would not confirm this even if she had 50 members of her clan still there.

"No."

Again, Lang paused. "If you lie to me," he said softly, "it will go much harder on you. Have you ever been involved with the underground?"

Anna did not hesitate. Her blue eyes stared back at him, piercing and certain. "I have not," she said defiantly.

"Where did you get your false papers?"

This time Anna paused, but only briefly. "From a fellow surgeon at the University."

"And this fellow's name?"

Anna looked down. She was losing her resolve. Her voice broke. "Christian Engel."

"So he was willing to break the law to help you? And where is he now?"

"He's dead. He was killed by an Allied bomb."

Lang had no information that Anna had ties to the resistance. Still, he wanted to find out more about what she had been doing and who her friends might be. Anna was just as determined to tell him nothing. She would not connect herself to Sarah or the resistance movement.

"Who are your friends here in Leipzig?"

Anna knew the Gestapo was searching her flat even as they were speaking. She also knew there was nothing there to tie her to Landis Koller and the underground. But she felt a rising concern that there might be some kind of reference to Sarah. Had she made any mistakes? Had she kept a card or a note with Sarah's name on it?

"I kept to myself," she responded. "I was not willing to have anyone risk becoming friends with a Jew."

Lang had no way of knowing if Anna was telling the truth. He would now be forced to wait on the search of her flat and the report from interviews with those who knew her at the hospital. He was certain of one thing. He was not prepared to have her stripped naked and assaulted with the high pressure hose to try and break her. He was convinced that in the long run, this tactic would not help Germany, especially when this woman was headed to Buchenwald. He looked at her.

"That's all," he said tersely. "You may go." Lang turned to his aide, sergeant Leibbrant. "Have your notes typed and on my desk in the morning, and send a copy to SS headquarters in Berlin. A copy will need to accompany her as well."

"Ja, Captain," the sergeant replied.

He stood at attention and snapped his heals together. Anna looked at him and then at Lang. She had no idea where she was going.

* * *

Sarah Engel had a sense that something was wrong. She had tried to contact Heidi the night before. The following morning she called the hospital from her office in the bank and found that Heidi had not shown up for work. She could not risk going to Heidi's flat, but realized that if Heidi had been arrested, the Gestapo might easily connect the two women. Sarah knew she must get rid of the short-wave transmitter. She also knew that time was short. It would be too risky to contact Landis or anyone in the resistance. She had no one to help her. Then she thought about a possible exception. Sarah knew of a woman in her church who had helped a Jewish couple escape.

Werner and Maria Schmidt were the only people in Leipzig, outside of those in the resistance, whom Sarah Engel felt she could trust. Werner was the pastor of the Bethany Lutheran Church and had studied theology under Dietrich Bonhoeffer in Berlin. He and wife

Maria moved to Leipzig in 1934. They were aware of Bonhoeffer's activity in the underground, activity that had gotten him arrested. The Schmidt's had not been active in the resistance but had helped several Jewish couples escape before 1941. Werner had been very concerned about his friend and mentor. He was hoping that Bonhoeffer's life would be spared because he was such a respected theologian. Werner was also aware that the Nazis were unpredictable. Although an ardent anti-Nazi, Werner had been reluctant to speak out publicly against Hitler. He was not afraid. But he believed he could be more valuable to God out of prison than in it. There were times when he felt guilty regarding this stance. But he had made his decision.

Maria was a courageous woman. She had been arrested in 1939 for being publicly critical of the war and Nazi anti-Semitism. She spent four months in the Leipzig prison and was released through the efforts of her husband and a local bishop. Maria had once told Sarah about her experience. For the first month in prison she felt there was a great evil presence in her cell. She had prayed against the evil, singing hymns for comfort. One morning after praying through the night, she had experienced the delivery of this evil from her cell. She believed God had exorcised it. She then experienced what she later described as a 'blessed peace' in her cell.

Sarah felt that if anyone could help it would be Maria Schmidt. On her way home from the bank, Sarah took a detour and headed for the church parsonage. Maria was baking bread and welcomed her friend inside. Werner was upstairs in his study.

Briefly, Sarah explained her fears to Maria.

"Let me get Werner," Maria said quickly. "We can help. I'll put on some water for tea."

When Maria returned with Werner, the two listened intently as Sarah explained what she believed had happened. The Schmidt's had not known of Sarah's involvement with the resistance. Still, they were not surprised. Werner took Sarah's hand.

"The short-wave set must be moved tonight," he said.

"But how?" moaned Sarah. "The Gestapo is probably watching my place even now."

Maria thought for a moment. "How large is the set?"

Sarah had measured it more than once and was ready with her answer. "It is about 60 centimeters long and 20 wide."

"I think it will fit just fine in our old baby carriage," Werner said to Maria.

"You know, my dear, I think you're right."

Maria turned back to Sarah. "I'll be at your apartment in an hour to show you our six-month old grand- daughter."

"I didn't realize you had a six-month old grand-daughter."

Maria smiled, "We don't!"

The soft knock at the door was expected, but still it made Sarah jump. She opened the door slightly to make certain it was Maria. The baby carriage was old. But Maria was sentimental about such things and had used the church basement for storage of the buggy and a number of other items of memorabilia. The carriage was packed with two blankets and a small pillow. Sarah had brought the transmitter down from the attic and placed it in a closet. She was growing increasingly apprehensive. She'd been using the receiver for more than two years, but had never fully appreciated the danger involved. Now she did. Possession of a short wave transmitter was a death sentence, a bullet in the head or a public hanging.

"Maria, you should probably stay for a while, say half an hour."
Maria agreed.

"We need to get the transmitter loaded into the carriage to make certain it will fit. Then we will pray."

Sarah went to the closet and lifted the six-pound set. The women removed the pillow and blankets and placed the transmitter-receiver into the carriage. They covered it with the blankets. It made for a very large baby so they took one blanket and the pillow out.

Sarah sighed.

"If anyone looks carefully, there's going to be a problem."

The two women sat on the sofa and said little. They were thinking the same thoughts. Only the grace of God could deliver them from the evil surrounding them.

Twenty minutes passed. They prayed together, then Maria put her hands on the carriage and headed out the door. She reached the end of the street. Out of the corner of her eye she noticed a military auto with a Swastika on the side. It was parked in front of Sarah's apartment. Maria took in a deeper breath. She continued walking. She crossed the street and kept her eyes away from the auto, too afraid to look. But after only a few steps, she could no longer keep her eyes away. She looked. Two officers were getting out of the car and walking toward the apartment building entrance. Maria continued walking un-noticed.

* * *

Anna was still trying to come to grips with her arrest. She had worked very hard to conceal her true identity. Then a chance encounter had blown her cover. Ironically, this had been done by someone who had benefited from Anna's work as a doctor. The mother of the child she had helped was likely one of the minority of Germans who did not live and function in the world of Nazi anti-Semitism. Even more likely, she did not concern herself with the race of the skilled surgeon who had saved the life of her child. Unknowingly she may now have sent her heroine to certain death.

The cell seemed colder. Anna spent the afternoon on the cot, which was actually wooden cross slats on a metal frame. She placed a portion of the blanket underneath her as a cushion. Now she was focused on where she might be going. She had learned through Sarah that the death camps in Poland had been shut down. A work-concentration camp in Germany was her likely destination. At 44, Anna was in good health and relatively young. The war would be over in a matter of months. She would survive. She would see her parents again. As she lay in the cell, originally a torture chamber, she began to smile. She fantasized that she would go to England without contacting her parents and simply nock on their door. As she played this scenario out in her mind, she began to laugh.

Corporal Muller, the soldier who had accompanied her female guard, brought her afternoon meal. Muller had been at the prison for about a year. He was turning 50, an old age for a corporal. But there was a reason. He had joined the military in 1934, a year after the Nazis came to power. He was uneducated but made a good soldier except for one problem. Muller liked to drink. He eventually rose to the rank of master-sergeant and became a gunnery-sergeant in a Panzer tank as part of the 5th Panzer Division. He was in multiple battles on the Eastern Front, but was sent back to Germany and demoted to corporal after his second episode of being drunk on duty. He was given a job with little responsibility with the understanding that further problems would result in a court martial.

Muller had been married as a young man. He and his wife had a son. But within three years, his wife left him because of his drinking and took the boy with her. Muller was now a bitter man, bitter toward his ex-wife and women in general.

That evening, Muller walked slowly down the basement cell block corridor with Anna's evening meal. It consisted of a bowl of potato soup and a hard roll. As he approached Anna's cell he kneeled down to slide the tray through the slot. Anna sat up and began to walk toward the meal tray. He stood watching her, not taking his eyes off of her. She knelt down to pick up the tray. His eyes followed her back to the bunk. He continued watching her, and Anna began to feel very uncomfortable. She looked down as she finished. When she looked up, he was gone.

Anna returned the tray to the cell door and slid it through the slot. It would be collected in the morning. She hoped she would soon be transported. The lack of sunlight only deepened Anna's discouragement.

*   *   *

The knock on Sarah's door was sharp. "Police, open!" barked the Gestapo officer.

Sarah quickly walked to the door, took a deep breath and opened it. She had made a diligent search of her apartment when she feared Anna had been arrested and had burned everything that might tie her to her friend. If they knew of Christian they could connect Sarah to the two and claim Sarah knew Heidi was Jewish. The Gestapo tactic was always to intimidate, but they had to have evidence.

The lieutenant stepped into her apartment followed by his aide, a sergeant. He looked around as he spoke.

"We have reason to believe you were involved with a Jewish woman going by the name of Heidi Brendler."

"I know Heidi Brendler. I did not know she was Jewish. What makes you think she is Jewish?"

The Lieutenant did not answer the question. "How did you meet her?"

"She was introduced to me by my brother. She worked at the hospital. We attended services together at the Lutheran Church."

"And what of your brother?"

"He is dead, killed in a bombing raid." The lieutenant then tried to trap Sarah.

"Did she mention that she is in the resistance?"

Sarah did not hesitate. "No!"

"And you have no knowledge of the underground?"

"Of course not."

"We will search the apartment."

While the apartment was ransacked, Sarah sat in the front room. She and Heidi had spent many happy hours there. The lieutenant asked to see the attic. The ordeal lasted two hours. Finally, the men left, annoyed that they did not find anything to link Sarah to the Jewish woman or the resistance. For the Gestapo, people were guilty until proven innocent.

Sarah closed the door. She sat down and allowed the trembling to overtake her. Silently, she thanked God for Werner and Maria Schmidt.

* * *

Anna drifted off to sleep. She was wrapped in the blanket, quieted by the silence and isolation of the basement cell. But the loud 'click of the steel door being unbolted jarred her awake. Heavy army boots pounded the concrete floor in the distance. Anna sat up. What would bring a visitor this late?

The soldier came into view. It was Gerhard Muller. He stopped in front of her cell door but said nothing. He simply stood and stared at Anna. She did the same, standing still beside her cot. Then she dropped the blanket to the floor. Muller placed the key in the lock and opened the cell door.

"What do you want?"

Her heart was beginning to pound in her chest. Muller showed no emotion.

He walked through the door and the lock snapped shut with a click. Muller left the key in the lock on the outside. Anna began to back-up.

"You will be caught!" she cried. "You will be punished!"

Muller had no comeback. Instead, he continued walking toward her. Even in her panic, Anna had noticed the key left in the lock. She knew she must try to get to the door. She also knew there was no way out of the basement. But she might be able to lock Muller in the cell.

As he approached, Anna quickly shoved him with all of her strength. She hoped to catch him off guard. But he grabbed her forearm and slung her back up against the wall. The force of it stunned her. He grabbed both of her wrists as she tried to fight him, finally breaking her right hand free. She closed her fist, aimed at his neck and punched him in throat.

Muller was momentarily stunned and gasped for air. Anna pushed him again and lunged. He spun her around and simultaneously swung his right fist catching her on her left temple. The blow knocked her to the ground. He then grabbed her and threw her onto the cot. As Anna began to regain her senses, Muller hand-cuffed her wrists around the metal frame of her cot. Anna stared up at him. She knew he could easily kill her.

"You can," she whispered. "But if you do kill me, it will cost you your life."

"Oh," he sneered. "And do you really think the Nazis care about a Jewish whore? Muller reached to his belt. It had two leather attachments, one for his nightstick, and one holding a 12 inch bayonet.

Anna remained very still.

"That's better," he said, his breath beginning to become shallow.

Anna could smell his foul breath. It reeked of alcohol. She closed her eyes tightly and whispered, "God help me! God help me!"

Sergeant Leibbrant had remained in his office late to finish typing the report of Anna's interrogation. He did it with triplicate carbon copies. He closed and locked the door, then descended the stairs to the first floor. He glanced in the office of the night guard whom he knew to be Muller. Leibbrant, an old-school soldier, had seen action in WWI. This would be his last assignment before retiring from the military. He had attained the rank of master-sergeant and took pride in his work. It bothered him that the office was empty. Muller should have been there. Leibbrant walked around the corner to the door to the basement cell block. It was open. This was odd, he thought. It was always locked at night.

Leibbrant descended the stairs and entered the basement corridor. As he reached the last cell he knew immediately what was happening. He unlocked the cell door and drew his nightstick.

Muller, straddling Anna, was holding her shoulders as he sneered at her.

Sergeant Leibbrant, one hand on either end of his nightstick, brought it over Muller's head and pulled back, cutting off the corporal's airway. Muller began to gasp, flailing his arms wildly as Leibbrant pulled him off of Anna. Muller grabbed the nightstick trying to get air as the sergeant drug him back toward the cell door and then into the corridor. Muller was beginning to lose consciousness. The sergeant pulled him down the corridor and into a cell. He released the nightstick and Muller began coughing and gasping. He confiscated Muller's knife and nightstick from his belt and locked the door.

Leibbrant quickly walked back to Anna's cell and removed the handcuffs. He left for a few moments, and then returned with a basin of warm water and a wash cloth. He left again and returned with a cup of hot tea. Then he knelt beside her.

"Are you hurt?"

Anna bathed her head with the cloth and shook her head.

Leibbrant stood up. He pursed his lips in silence. Then he walked to the door. Locking the cell, he turned to Anna. "Not all Germans are Nazis. But all Jews are human beings."

Roland Leibbrant had been troubled by the Nazi Reich from the beginning. He was a professional, the consummate soldier. He had joined the military at 22 years of age and had survived the trench warfare of WWI. During the build-up leading to the invasion of Poland, he remained skeptical of Hitler's motives and methods. He followed the orders of his superiors, but never agreed with the Jewish pogrom.

He called in a replacement for Muller and stayed until after 10:00 p.m. to write a report on the incident. Captain Lang arrived at the prison each morning at 8:30 and Leibbrant was in the habit of getting there half an hour before him. It was especially important to brief the Captain about what had happened since one of his staff had been arrested. The briefing took about 20 minutes, then the two men descended to the basement to confront the corporal and explain the military court martial procedure. As they opened the steel door to the cell block, they were greeted by the grotesque figure of Muller. He had hanged himself with his belt from a metal beam in the ceiling. His face was deep purple, almost black, his body already becoming stiff. Both men looked at him for only a moment.

"Get him down and out of here," said Lang. "His war is over and ours will soon follow."

Master sergeant Leibbrant would not discuss the matter further. When he returned to his office he considered once again the paradox of a regime that had made it a crime to rape a Jewish woman and yet instilled a policy that would send that same woman to a concentration camp with the stated intention of working her to death.

By 1945 the vast majority of Jews in Germany and throughout Europe had escaped, been placed in work camps, or were sent to a death camp. About one third of those who died in the gas chambers were women and children. The only Jews left were the few who were successfully in hiding. That number was small, probably less than a hundred in the entire country. Captain Lang had received a *SS* communication about Anna signed by Himmler. He continued to puzzle about her significance. He would never know.

The instructions were very specific. She would be picked up and transported under guard to the Buchenwald work camp in the Thuringia Providence near Weimar. Weimar was the historical home of Germany's most renowned literary figure, Johann Wolfgang von Goethe.

Anna was kept in the Leipzig prison until the day after Corporal Muller's suicide. An *SS* driver and two guards then took her on the 100-kilometer drive to Buchenwald. She was allowed to take her coat and shoes, nothing more. She was unaware of her destination, but relieved when she realized the destination was not far from Leipzig. They drove her toward the city of Weimar then turned northwest for ten kilometers. They drove through the dense forest then came into an enormous clearing. Anna stared out the window at the conglomeration of buildings that seemed to sprawl out of nowhere. The road led to what seemed to be a central area of the clearing with a two-story structure with a large iron gate in the center of the lower floor. The central structure was painted a dark brown. Anna read the white letters painted each a foot high above the gate:

B U CHENWAL D

Jedem das Seine

Anna understood the meaning of the words in-laid below the name of the camp. "Everyone gets what he deserves!"

United States Senator Barkley observing some of the dead of Buchenwald

CHAPTER 20
An Execution and a Miracle

The Buchenwald concentration camp was established in 1937. It was designed for detaining political prisoners, most of who were, at that time, Communists. Initially, there were only about 1,000 inmates, but the camp was expanded several times to accommodate the thousands of workers needed for the nearby armament factories. All the work provided by the prisoners was forced labor and a critical benefit in the war effort.

German Equipment Works (Deutsche-Austustungs-Werk) or DAW was an enterprise owned and operated by the *SS*. Prisoners worked in these plants as well as in multiple other armament facilities, the camp work-shop and the quarry. The cornerstone of DAW was the Mabiu Factory which made components for the V-2 Rocket.

By the time Anna arrived, the camp was stretched to almost 100,000 prisoners. They were stacked into quarters four times the capacity for which they were designed. Buchenwald was a sprawling facility that swept across several hundred acres. The main camp was in the northern segment and housed the prisoners in about 180 barracks. Some of the barracks had indoor plumbing and adequate heat. But most were little more than shelters with latrines. The area was surrounded by a 10-foot electrified barbed wire fence and multiple guard towers built into the fenced structure. Each tower was staffed with three military personnel, .50 caliber machine guns, and powerful search lights.

The southern section housed the *SS* guards and administrative personnel. Central to this section was an enormous parade
ground surrounded by 18 barracks built in a semicircle. These were
positioned as spokes on a wheel with the parade grounds as the
center. Each barrack held 100 guards. The second story of the main
gate house was the principle administration area. To the right of the
administration section was the 'bunker' or camp jail. Cell # 1 in the
bunker was the 'death cell.' Here, prisoners were held before execution. Not far from the bunker was a separate building housing the
crematorium. Most of the work camps in Germany built the crematorium outside the camp and out of sight. But Buchenwald was different. It housed the crematorium in plain sight, serving as a constant
reminder that death was always close at hand. In the basement of
the crematorium was an execution chamber where men (and occasionally women) were hung from large steel hooks mounted on the
walls. There was also another method for killing. A scale and height
measure backed up to the wall in one corner. Behind the wall was a
small room that hid the executioner. A small hole was placed in the
wall and was positioned so a prisoner having his height and weight
measured could be shot in the back of the head or neck. This portion
of the wall was painted black so the hole went unnoticed.

Upon her arrival, Anna was taken to a holding room where
she sat for two hours before being joined by three other women,
each in their 30s. They were then transferred to the main camp. The
first building inside the electrified fence was a small one-story structure. As they entered they were instructed to strip. Each woman was
shaved, including their heads and pubic areas. They were then led
into another room built with a creosote shower. They were sprayed
with disinfectant, then given a uniform of striped shirts and pants.
Once dressed, the women were brought to yet another room where

they received a numbered tattoo on the inside of the left forearm. Anna was B-76083.

The camp was experiencing a typhus epidemic, a fact Anna discovered almost immediately. Typhus is carried by an infectious agent transmitted to the body through lice. Anna actually appreciated the effort to disinfect new prisoners.

Anna was now one of approximately 100 women at Buchenwald. The women were kept in a single dorm separated from the male prisoners by a six-foot fence. The dorm included two large rooms with multiple wooden bunks stacked three rows high. The center section held showers and toilets. The dorm also had a small kitchen and mess room. Meals were given twice a day and the women worked in 12 hour shifts that began at 6:00 a.m.

Two of the women with Anna were assigned to the camp brothel and the other was designated as cook. Anna was assigned to work in the Mibau V-2 Rocket facility. For the first time, she was grateful for the Nuremburg laws of 1935, especially the first law which protected German blood. Although it stripped her of her citizenship, it also prohibited her from engaging in sexual intercourse with non-Jews.

There was one central heater in each sleeping area. The building was not insulated and the high each day could reach the mid-60s. But night was another story. Temperatures dropped dramatically after the sun went down and each woman was given only one blanket. Some more fortunate souls had been allowed to keep their coats. But women who arrived in the warmer months didn't get to keep theirs. Anna noted that about half the women were significantly malnourished. She was also aware of their behavior. Most stayed to themselves and used either their first names or gave none at all.

Meals were eaten quickly. Breakfast was nothing more than a bowl of watery porridge with little taste. It was not unusual to find worms in the porridge, but given their hunger, most of the women ate them without much notice. The evening meal was typically a piece of bread and a serving of turnips or another vegetable. Given her background, Anna was aware that there was almost no protein in the diet. She knew that within a few weeks, the bodies of these women, hers included, would begin to break down their own protein, thus producing the wasted, emaciated look. Lack of vitamins would lead to mouth and tongue ulcerations. Scurvy was rare in the 20th century but common in Buchenwald. Women who became too weak to work were removed for 'rehabilitation'. Hollow eyed, they would be taken to the death room in the basement of the crematorium, hanged and cremated.

The two women who arrived with Anna and were sent to the brothel were soon noticeably pregnant. In malnourished mothers, babies are usually born prematurely. In Buchenwald it was no different – with the exception of the fact that the newborns were immediately thrown into the incinerator, alive.

As the women became more malnourished, most stopped ovulating. Anna wondered how long she could last in Buchenwald. The information from the BBC indicated the war could be over in a matter of months. Unless she became ill, she held on to the hope that she had a chance.

The day after her arrival at the camp, Anna was sent to an orientation for her work in V-2 Rocket production. The V-2 was a sophisticated weapon. It was being built from a proto-type developed by Wernher von Braun and Walter Riedel in 1936. A ballistic missile with a range of about 150 miles, it was powered by a liquid fuel engine. The fuel was a mixture of liquid oxygen, ethanol and water. The war-head was 2,000 pounds of Amatol, a mixture of TNT and ammonium nitrate.

The factory was located three miles from the main camp. It was a sprawling complex surrounded by an elaborate 12-foot fence. Approximately 800 prisoners were transported to the facility daily in 20 buses. Another 160 German workers were employed as supervisors and engineers. There were 100 *SS* guards in the plant during the day work shift. The night shift was somewhat smaller, around 50 guards.

The morning after her orientation, Anna boarded a bus with two other women and 80 men. The ride to the facility was a short one, only five minutes once they exited the main camp gate. Anne felt strange riding in the bus. She stared out into the open country feeling somewhat outside her body.

The facility she was headed toward on that morning was one of several that were being used to make components for the V-2, a rocket that had taken several years to develop. The principal developer, von Braun, received a doctorate in physics from the University of Berlin in 1934. By then, he had joined the Rocket Society, *Verein fur Raumschiffarht*. Von Braun was interested in sub-orbital flight, but funding was only available for military rockets. He developed a team of 80 engineers to design and test rockets. Eventually a production facility was built at Peenemunde on the Baltic coast.

The proto-type that was developed and test fired was called the A-4. The 'rocket' was in fact, an un-manned ballistic missile 46 feet in length with an engine thrust of 56,000 pounds and a payload of 2,200 pounds. It reached a height of 50 to 60 miles with a velocity of 3,500 mph. Since it traveled greater than the speed of sound there was no warning, no sound, only the sonic boom just before impact. It was first used in combat in September 1944, 14 months after Hitler had ordered it into production. After the first successful firing in combat, von Braun remarked to a colleague, "The rocket worked perfectly except for landing on the wrong planet."

The allies became aware of the V-2 in 1943 when a test fired missile landed at Blize, Poland, and was recovered by the Polish resistance. They shared the technical details with British intelligence. Eventually a massive bombing campaign was launched against the Peenemunde facility. This slowed the V-2 production and prevented the Germans from using it during the Allied invasion of Europe. Hitler believed the rocket could give him a 'vengeance weapon' that would possibly lead to an early armistice. Hurriedly, a massive underground production facility was constructed named Dora, near Nordhausen in central Germany. This complex weapon with thousands of component parts cost about the same as a four-engine bomber but was much less effective. Never- the-less, Hitler was determined to use as many as could be produced.

The Mibau facility produced four components; the outer steel shell, the guidance gyro system, the liquid oxygen and container, and the warhead casing. The administrators knew Anna was a medical doctor and felt she could be of use in the manufacture of liquid oxygen, which, when added to the alcohol-water mixture, provided the propellant. Anna spent a week learning how the liquid oxygen was produced and stored. Oxygen was taken from the air and run through a condenser coil to cool it down to -183 degrees C. This was done using liquid nitrogen. It was then placed in a holding tank at three atmospheres pressure to be shipped to the underground assembly facility, Dora.

During her first week in the Mibau plant Anna was startled to find out that those in the plant were given a mid-day meal. She had seen hundreds of emaciated men on her way to the bus, but those in the plant looked healthier. Now the reason was obvious. The meal was generally a bowl of vegetable soup with meat, a meal that provided protein, vitamins and calories that others in the camp weren't getting. She was specifically told not to mention the extra meal to anyone outside the facility. But it was clear to the prisoners that those who worked in the plant were getting an extra benefit.

Roland Montague could not help but notice the new woman. He was working in the French resistance when he and four others were caught in southern France. There were actually 10 men involved in the attempt to blow-up a German ammunition dump south of Paris near Orleans. There was a fire fight and six of his countrymen were killed. Of the four captured, three were sent to Buchenwald. The fourth was shot trying to escape.

Roland was an engineer before the war, trained in metal alloys. He was involved in the assembly of the missile's gyroscopic guidance system, one of forty prisoners who worked with ten German engineers to assemble and test the system. For months he had been trying to work out a method to sabotage the system, but it had been impossible to do because of the extensive testing. Just before he arrived, a worker who had been suspected of sabotage was hanged.

Roland's 18 months in Buchenwald had been a better experience than for many other prisoners, all because of his work in the V-2 plant. He was convinced he could survive the war by remaining valuable to the Germans, although he thought daily about ways in which he could possibly alter the guidance system. The only thing that brought a smile to his face was the mental picture of a V-2 aimed at London suddenly turning in mid-flight and heading for Berlin. He often thought that if he could pull it off, it would be worth the risk.

Roland felt fortunate to have been assigned to V-2 production near Buchenwald. The Germans were desperate for some way to neutralize the allied advances. The missile production was up to five per day at Dora. In 18 months, he had seen more than 7,000 men leave for Dora, none of whom ever returned. He believed they were being worked to death and then executed. There was obviously a different policy at Mibau. The plant director had apparently made a decision to get the prisoners trained and keep them alive for more production. This seemed like a sensible thing to do, and all the more since he was at Mibau.

By the third week Anna had adjusted to her routine. She worked 12 hour shifts six days a week. Sunday was a day for showers and washing clothes with the little bit of soap they were given. She had remained well. But several women had come down with dysentery. Anna knew few names but had talked on occasion to the woman who slept directly below her. Erika had been at Buchenwald for almost six years. Initially, she was not a prisoner but an employee. She had begun working as a secretary in administration when the camp opened 1937. She had a secret. Erika's maternal grandmother was Jewish. Erika was Christian and had been able to conceal her family background for years. But a change in the camp's leadership in 1941 brought a new commandant. He required a background check for everyone in administration. Erika's background was discovered. The day this came to light, Erika was arrested and made a prisoner. One day she was free, the next she was not.

One evening after the meal, Anna and Erika began talking. Erika explained why she was there and how it happened. She was interested to know that Anna was Jewish. Although a Christian, Erika was proud of her Jewish heritage. She talked of the first commandant, Karl Otto Koch and his wife Ilse. Anna could lie on her stomach and look down to the bunk below. Erika was easy to talk to and began her story.

"The Buchenwald camp was opened in July 1937. I was working in Weimer and decided to apply for one of the secretarial jobs. I knew there were about 1,000 prisoners and that almost all of them were Communists. I worked for the first commandant, Colonel Koch. He joined the National Socialist Party in 1930 and the *SS* in 1934.

In 1936, he commanded the Sachsenhausen camp near Berlin. That's where he met his wife, Ilse. He was transferred to Buchenwald when it opened and his wife got involved in running the camp. She was barbaric. She loved to abuse prisoners. Everyone called her the 'Bitch of Buchenwald'. I know for a fact that she had more than one prisoner killed."

Anna stopped her. "Killed for what?"

"All I can tell you is what I heard. She looked for men with exotic tattoos. She used their skin for lamp shades, Anna. And Colonel Koch was just as bad in his own way. He liked women. He'd trade extra pay or time off for sex. I resisted him and because of that, I was never promoted or given a raise."

The woman pursed her mouth, then sighed. "He was so cruel. He beat men...lots of them. He put them on the hanging tree."

"What is the hanging tree?" Anna asked.

"It's a large pine pole next to the bunker. They tie the men's hands behind their backs and hang them by their wrists. Their weight slowly dislocates their shoulders. You could hear them scream even with the windows closed. Over time, more of the prisoners were Jewish. Some were even POW's."

"Do you believe both Kochs had people murdered?"

"I'm sure of it," said Erika. "Ilse was having an affair with one of the camp medical doctors, Dr. Hoven. He murdered some prisoners by injecting them with phenol. It was common knowledge that men with exotic tattoos who were seen by Frau Koch were sent to the hospital...and they were never seen again. Before they left in 1941, two medical personal, one of the doctors and an orderly, were found dead under mysterious circumstances. There were some records though, that showed they were treating Colonel Koch for syphilis.

Well, after he left, the new commandant arrived...and my family secret was uncovered. As for the Kochs, like all *SS*, they should be arrested and tried for war crimes."

The women were silent for a while.

"Erika, did you see any well-known people come through the camp?"

"Several. The one who stood out to me was Paul Schneider. He got here in the fall of 1937."

"Who is Paul Schneider?"

"He was so great. He was a pastor, a member of the Confessing Church. That's the one started by Dietrich Bonhoeffer. And really, it was started to oppose the Nazis. He preached against the policies of the Third Reich and against anti-Semitism. He was constantly being warned about what he was doing. And he was even arrested one time, but was released. Then finally, he started excommunicating church members who violated congregational discipline by supporting the Nazis. He was arrested again. But they released him and told him he had to leave Germany. But he wouldn't do it. He went right back to his congregation and family. Two months later he was brought here."

"What happened then?" asked Anna.

"He started speaking out against prisoner abuse. And they put him in solitary. But he wouldn't be quiet. He preached from his cell window almost every day. God, they beat him for that. He wore this beret. And he wouldn't take it off to honor Hitler's birthday. That was April 20th. A lot of the prisoners begged him to stop preaching and to stop speaking out. Then in July he was taken to the infirmary. They murdered him by injection. That part brought everybody down. It was like a cloud over the camp, so much sadness that he was gone. I actually started thinking about leaving my job here. But the Kochs left and by then it was too late for me. So here I am, a Christian with a Jewish grandmother. I'll die here, unless the Allies come."

The weeks dragged on. Anna began to get a clearer picture of the reality of Buchenwald. It was basically a slave labor camp. Not surprising was the Nazis' flagrant violations of the Hague and Geneva Conventions which forbade nations from using prisoners of war or the incarcerated in a forced work environment. Of the 80,000 men at Buchenwald, at least half were forced to work in multiple armament plants or in the quarry. About 50 percent of the men were Jewish. Ten percent were POW's. The remaining were communists or criminals. The death rate from starvation, beatings and random selection killings was pushing 1,000 per month. Every week, a thousand men were lined up on the parade grounds and every tenth man was selected for extermination.

The *SS* officers were sometimes sadistic in the selection process. They ordered the men to number off one to ten and then called out a number. As each man realized who would live and who would die, they'd change the number and laugh.

Anna remained fairly isolated in the women's barracks, with the exception of an hour on Sunday morning and another on Sunday afternoon. She was surprised that she had so little contact with the SS outside the Mibau factory. The supervision of prisoners was the responsibility of the 'kapos' or German criminals. There were hundreds of kapos left in charge of work details and discipline. The kapos reported to the SS and kept strict and sometimes brutal control of the men in the camp.

There were only 11 female guards. All worked in the women's barracks. Women prisoners generally had more freedom than the men. They were allowed to use a walking path just inside the perimeter of the electrified fence. Anyone on the path was always in sight of the guard towers. But there was one area at the far end of the main camp where the terrain changed a bit, providing a small depression. Four of the barracks were out of sight of the guards. As Anna would soon find out, some unusual activities were taking place there.

Roland Montague had his eye on Anna from the first day he saw her. His work station on the gyroscopes was in the same section of the factory as liquid oxygen production. No conversation was allowed in the workplace, but the lunch break offered the opportunity for speaking. He had learned some German working in the French resistance and had become more fluent since his time in Buchenwald. Roland made it a point to speak to Anna within a month of her arrival. The information he had for her was important for him and could be critical for her. He had discovered that she was a physician and that she was Jewish. One Friday he made his way toward her and sat down next to her during lunch.

"Frau Doctor, my name is Roland Montague."

Anna looked up, curious at the sudden opportunity to socialize.

"Please listen very carefully. We have little time. There is an extensive underground in this prison camp supporting and protecting almost 900 children, mostly Jewish boys. The youngest is four years old, the oldest is 15. Six hundred of them are in block-66, a large windowless barracks that is unseen by the guard towers. The other children are scattered throughout the camp and are watched over by kapos. The camp elder in charge of block-66 is Julian Richburg. He's a Czech communist from Prague. His assistant is a Polish man, Beryl Yenzer. The children scattered throughout the camp are hidden and protected."

Anna's mouth dropped open. Could this be true? The Nazis went to great length to deceive their victims and others. Once a month, a concert was performed by the camp orchestra, mostly Jewish men who were musicians before their arrests. They were kept in the same barracks and allowed to practice on Sundays. Twice in the past year, the Danish Red Cross had been allowed in the camp. They were allowed to see only what the Nazis wanted them to see. On both occasions the camp orchestra played for them. Could it be that now, the Nazis were the ones being deceived?

The Germans allowed Red Cross care packages into the camp, several hundred each week. These were distributed randomly to prisoners. Anna had already noticed that many of the packages made their way to Block-66. Hundreds of prisoners and many of the kapos were determined that none of the children would die in Buchenwald. Two months previously, one of the Kapos who hated Jews had threatened to expose block-66 to the *SS*. His frozen body was found two days later by the electrified fence. The SS assumed he was trying to climb it. They didn't notice his skull had been crushed because he was wearing a wool cap.

The time had passed quickly. Roland needed to tell her one more thing. He wolfed down the soup that remained in his bowl and whispered.

"A number of men in the underground are planning a break-out. Are you interested?"

Friday nights for Anna were the prelude to Saturday, the Jewish Sabbath. It had been several years since she had been to Synagogue but she still thought of it, remembering the happier times with her family in Berlin. In those days, she and her best friend Erin would grill the Rabbi with unanswerable questions. Now Anna had little to be happy about. But she tried to focus on the one relief she could hold; Erin was not in a prison camp. Anna smiled to think of that. She imagined Erin to be a concert violinist and married with children.

As Anna lay in her bunk she was struck with the idea. She now had children to look after....900 boys. The excitement grew from the pit of her stomach and seemed to travel to her heart and her head and throughout her arms. She squeezed her hands shut and then opened them. It was a rush she hadn't felt in years. She had a purpose. Even in this hell hole there was something worth living for, something worth dying for – if it came to that. It took Anna a lengthy hour before she could finally close her eyes and sleep.

There seemed to be no apparent reason for the *SS* to be in the main camp. Anna had not seen them in such numbers since she was first incarcerated. All of the women were ordered outside and lined-up. There were about ten officers and ten guards with machine guns. The officers were questioning each woman individually. The women, about 100 in all, were in rows of 10. When the interrogations of one row were completed, they were dismissed.

Anna was in the ninth and next to last row. In row seven, one officer began shouting.

"Don't lie to me!" he yelled, slapping the woman so hard it knocked her to the ground. The woman tried to rise but another guard hit her with the butt of his gun. She screamed as they dragged her away.

Anna watched in silence. It appeared they were taking the woman to the bunker. But they were also headed in the direction of the crematorium. Anna bit her lip and turned her eyes away. She stared straight ahead. The women in line eight were now being questioned. Anna could now clearly hear what was being said. It was about the children. The *SS* had found out about the children.

Every woman was denying knowledge of any child. Anna was unsure of who actually knew of them. She herself had only learned recently of their existence, and that was because she was a doctor. There was no reason for the other women to have known.

The officers had finished with the eighth line and were moving toward hers. Did they know she knew? Had they discovered that Roland told her? Had they seen him talking to her?

Suddenly a guard stood in front of her.

"Doctor Eichenwald…it is doctor Eichenwald is it not?" Anna's legs began to weaken.

"Yes. I am a doctor."

"We have information that you have been told of children hidden in this camp. You have one chance to tell me about this. Where are they and how many are there?"

"I don't know of any children."

The officer did not hesitate. He turned his head and barked out an order. "Take her to the bunker!"

Two of the guards took her, one holding each arm. They began walking the 300 yards toward the southern end of the camp. Anna had been told it was a holding place for prisoners before execution.

There was no point in resisting. Rather than being dragged, Anna kept her head up and walked with the men. Once inside, she was led to the far end of a hall toward a large steel door. It opened to a concrete block room without windows. As the door was opened a large rat ran out of the room. Anna was pushed inside and the door was slammed behind her. The room was pitch black and she began to scream.

"No! No! Please, no!"

"Anna, Anna."

It was Erika. She was shaking Anna's shoulders. "You're having a dream!"

Anna was drenched in sweat. Her nightmare over, she looked around and tried to get her bearings.

"I'm so sorry I woke you," she said.

"Dreams here can be very frightening. It's probably not your last."

The only reason Anna looked forward to Saturday was the fact that it meant the next day would be Sunday. She was allowed to take walks on Sunday. But she was unaware of block-66. She had not seriously considered the prison break and now with a chance to help these boys she had dismissed the thought all together. She was very focused and found herself excited to see how she could be involved. She also was beginning to like Roland. It had been almost a year since she had experienced any positive feelings toward any man. There had been no man and no interest in anyone since Christian. This hellish time in history had been brought about by vapid, truculent men who had somehow captured control of an entire culture. It was more and more clear that evil men could so easily influence other men to become evil. Anna now believed that most men, maybe all of them, could be swallowed up by their own depravity. Yet even in the midst of this squalor, the toxic atmosphere of a Nazi prison camp, there were men of valor who were choosing to risk their lives for other human beings. Anna smiled thinking of Roland.

"Thank God for men of valor," she whispered to herself.

* * *

By the end of 1944, more than seven million civilian foreigners and POW's were working as slave laborers for the Third Reich. Most had been essentially kidnapped in occupied territories and deported to Germany in boxcars with little food or water and no sanitary facilities. They were forced to work in factories, fields and mines. The kidnapping operation even had a code name – 'Hay Action'.

In western occupied territories, the SS blocked off sections of towns and seized all able-bodied men and women. Workers brought from areas of Eastern Europe were rounded up in an even more shameful way. Villages resistant to the forced-labor order were simply burned to the ground and their inhabitants carted off. All of the workers were subjected to overcrowding, inadequate food, water, clothes and toilets. And for all these reasons, diseases spread throughout the camps, which served as breeding grounds for the spread of typhus and infestations of lice.

One group of men working in the Krupp Works, maker of most of Germany's guns, tanks and ammunition was kept in a dog kennel for six months. The men slept in a cubical three feet high, six feet wide and nine feet long. They entered by crawling on all fours just like the canines for which the kennels were built.

Among the unusual stories coming from the occupied countries in the West, those coming out of Denmark were the most extraordinary. This was especially true of the great Danish physicist and Nobel laureate, Niels Bohr. His father was a devout Christian and a professor of physiology at the University of Copenhagen. His mother was Jewish and came from a wealthy Danish banking family. Bohr had been awarded the 1922 Nobel Prize in Physics for his work on the structure of the atom. He was the first to propose the theory that the chemical property of an element was determined by the number of electrons in orbit around the nucleus. In 1943, Bohr received a coded message from James Chadwick in England inviting him to move there to work on nuclear fission. At the time, Bohr was skeptical of the application of atomic physics. He also felt a higher calling to aid in the protection of exiled scientists who had come to Denmark seeking refuge from the Nazis.

The Germans were dependent on Danish agriculture for food stuffs and needed the cooperation of the Danish government and indeed the entire population. A delicate memorandum of understanding existed between the Nazis and the Danish government. The Danes would continue to supply needed agricultural products in exchange for continued self-governance and the security of the 8,000 Danish Jews, most whom lived in Copenhagen. As German occupation became more egregious, there was less cooperation from the Danish farmers. Finally, things came to a head. Hitler ordered a takeover of the Danish government in Copenhagen. His real malevolence concerned his anger that the Danish Jews had escaped the 'Final Solution' of the Third Reich.

In early September of 1943, Bohr learned from the visiting Swedish Ambassador that the Danish Jews were in danger of being arrested. The following day an anti-Nazi woman working at Gestapo headquarters in Copenhagen saw orders from Berlin directing the arrest of Bohr. That night the Bohrs walked through the darkened city to a seaside suburban garden and hid until they were picked by a small boat. They were transported to a waiting fishing boat off the coast, then taken through mine fields to safety in Sweden.

The next day Bohr learned the Nazis planned to arrest all Danish Jews remaining in Denmark. He rushed to Stockholm and worked through bureaucratic channels to gain asylum for the 8,000 Danish Jews. In the interim, the Danes had taken the initiative to hide more than 7,000 Jewish people. Within days asylum was granted and almost all of those being hidden were taken across the Oresund to safety.

The Germans did not give up easily. Although Sweden was officially a 'neutral' country, Stockholm was crawling with German agents. It was evident that Bohr had played a pivotal role in the rescue of the Danish Jews. On October 2nd the offer of asylum was broadcast on Swedish radio. Hitler was furious. He sent a communication to agents in Sweden to find and eliminate Bohr immediately.

British intelligence was aware of the risk to Bohr. The next day, a telegram was sent to him by Lord Cherwell, the English physicist who had been appointed by Churchill to be the principal scientific adviser to the British government. The telegram asked Bohr and his family to come to England as soon as possible.

Bohr was the first to go. The British flew diplomatic communiqués back and forth to Stockholm on an unarmed twin-engine Mosquito bomber. It was a light, fast plane capable of flying at altitudes high enough to avoid German anti-aircraft batteries located on the Danish and northern Norwegian coastlines. The flack usually reached 20,000 ft. The Mosquito could take a single passenger seated in the bomb-bay. Bohr was fitted with a flight suit and a parachute. He was given flares to use in case the plane was hit. If that occurred, he was instructed to parachute into the North Sea and use the flares for rescue.

As the flight took off and the great Danish physicist was secure in the Mosquito bomb bay, a problem arose no one could have foreseen. Niels Bohr had an enormous head. His flight helmet with earphones simply would not fit. As the pilot climbed to

25,000 ft., out of range of the German anti-aircraft guns, he radioed for the crew to start oxygen, but Bohr could not hear the order. He soon lost consciousness. When the pilot got no response, he realized there was a problem. As soon as the plane cleared the coast of Norway, he dropped down and crossed the North Sea at low altitude. By the time the plane touched down in Scotland, Bohr was fully conscious, none the worse for wear.

A week later, Bohr's family, including his 21-year old son, Aage, followed. Bohr and Aage, a budding physicist in his own right, toured British scientific facilities and learned that the arduous effort at nuclear fission had shifted to the U.S. and was centered at Las Alamos in northern New Mexico. Now Bohr had gained an understanding of what was happening, an understanding that only his brilliance would allow. So the Danish theoretician headed a team to the U.S. Aage would later conclude that the work on atomic energy had progressed much faster than his father could have imagined. In the words of Robert Oppenheimer, head of the Manhattan Project and the development of the atomic bomb, "to Bohr the enterprises in the United States seemed completely fantastic.

* * *

On Saturday night Anna had trouble going to sleep. This was uncommon for her. The weather had been unusually warm for February in central Europe. Anna lay awake with her eyes open. She knew she could share with Erika what she was going to be doing on Sunday. But she decided against it. Erika would find out soon enough. Anna went over the instructions Roland had given her and finally drifted off to sleep.

Sunday's breakfast was the usual porridge. Anna finished it quickly. The first hour for walking came at 9:00 a.m. The daily census count would come at 6:00 p.m. All female prisoners had to be accounted for each afternoon.

About 30 women were going to walk today. The sun was shining, and the temperature rose to 40 degrees. The perimeter walkway was a little more than a four-mile loop. The women had one hour to complete it. Fifteen minutes per mile was a brisk pace, too much for all but the healthiest women.

The section of the path that remained out of sight of the towers was one section about half a mile in length. Anna began the walk with Erika and another woman. As they progressed the first mile, Anna shared briefly the information about block-66 and the children. The plan was for Anna to enter the block and remain until the afternoon walk. As it turned out, Erika had heard of a place in the prison where children were being kept, but she had no idea where it was.

The women made their way around the perimeter speaking in casual conversation. But all the while, Anna kept a sharp eye out for the barracks. Suddenly they were out of sight of the guard towers. She had been told to look for three medium sized pine trees as a tip off to the barracks location. There it was, a long flat-topped building that had no windows. There were four large roof canopies spaced equidistant from one end to the other. There was a set of double steel doors and multiple smoke stacks were scattered along the rooftop. Smoke was rising lazily from each.

Anna broke off from her two companions and quickly approached the steel doors. She knocked and a moment later, one of the doors opened slightly, then half way. A large man with a dark beard wearing a blue wool cap stood looking at her. Then he reached an enormous hand out and took her by the arm.

"Please," he said.

Beryl Yenzer gently pulled her inside and closed the door, locking it with a large steel dead bolt. His accent was heavy. In mellifluous German he spoke quickly.

"Thank you for coming. We've been expecting you."

He was a massive man, several inches taller than Anna. Yet his nature was that of a gentile patrician. She learned later that he had been headmaster of a Yeshiva in Poland.

Yenzer led Anna down a dark hallway into a small office lit by a single bulb on a cord. The walls were concrete. In the center of the room was a large oak desk with one chair and a wooden bench sat against the wall. He motioned her toward the bench. "Please sit down. Can I offer you some hot tea?"

Anna shook her head.

"As Roland mentioned, we are part of a clandestine network of men, mostly Jewish, who are protecting 900 children. Six hundred of them are in this block."

"Six hundred children are here?"

"Yes. You'll see shortly."

Julian Richburg was a precise man, a Jewish Communist who was brought to Buchenwald after his arrest in occupied Czechoslovakia in 1942. He was a thin, balding intellectual who had been a bank president. After the invasion of his country, he joined the resistance. At the time of his arrest the execution of men in the underground had stopped. The Germans were more interested in slave labor by that time and even execution of Jews had slowed. This was a change in policy that was being kept even from Hitler. It was in the camp that Richburg had met Beryl Yenzer, who had served in the resistance in Warsaw.

Richburg was a man of extraordinary organizational skills. He and Yenzer soon realized that many Jewish young men were being hidden in the camp. With at least 80 percent of the prisoners being Jewish, organizing to protect the boys was a common cause. In time, they had been able to bribe about 20 SS officers to cooperate with them. As the war dragged on, many German officers felt defeat was simply a matter of time. They began to see life after the war, life after the Third Reich.

The prison administration had no idea of block-66. Their concern was supplying men for the armament factories. The SS who had accepted bribes were also vulnerable to being exposed. In a strange way it was Richburg who had the upper hand, at least where the children were concerned. The entire effort was supported by many of the kapos who saw a chance to do something noble for a change.

The story had now unfolded as Anna listened. "May I see them?" she asked.

"Of course."

Anna was escorted through a narrow hallway that led into an enormous area some 200 yards in length. It was well lit. There in front of her were young boys ranging in age from four to 15. They had been organized into six 'squadrons' each with a 15 year old squadron leader. The majority of the boys were 10 years old or older, but 23 of them were under 10 years old and six of them were under the age of seven. The youngest boys were in the same squadron. Each squadron had been named after a bird of prey.... the eagle squadron, hawk squadron, etc. Each squadron slept in the same area and ate together. In the center of the living space was a large open area for games and recreation. Surrounding the recreation area were bunks stacked three high. The kitchen and mess hall were on one end of the living area and the toilets and showers on the other. Each of the boys except those under five had a 'buddy' to look after him. Buddies looked after each other and reported any problems to the squadron lieutenants of which there were five in each squadron.

Every morning after breakfast was 'sick call'. This was followed by 'school' which was three hours of reading, math and science. Beryl supervised the school which involved the older boys teaching the younger. After Beryl went underground, his entire family was murdered; his mother, father and three sisters were all killed at the Treblinka death camp. Now Beryl's mission was focused on saving the children. On Friday mornings, he taught Hebrew classes and on Saturday they held 'Synagogue'. The afternoons were for free time, competitions and recreation. Fifty boys were significantly ill. These were the children who would be brought to Anna.

She was still trying to absorb all she was hearing and seeing. It amazed her that an underground effort and culture of this magnitude was in existence here, especially given the fact that the purpose of its existence was to save the lives of Jewish children in a country dedicated to killing all Jews. Anna believed all life was sacred and her singular focus as a physician was to save lives and relieve suffering. As she progressed deeper into the citadel of block-66, she began to sense that it represented something almost enchanted, a safe haven from the death that surrounded it. The entire block was evocative of a Jewish home - except there were no mothers and fathers.

She was escorted to the center of the large complex where a table and a chair had been set up. using blankets draped from the ceiling, a makeshift exam room had been fashioned. The 50 boys were waiting to be seen. All activity had stopped, and all eyes were on Anna. It had been many months and for some, almost a year, since they had seen a female. A number of healthy boys suddenly felt disappointment that they had no malady that could provide them the chance to have contact with the beautiful doctor.

Many of the boys had upper respiratory infections and common colds. An eight-year old had an abdominal mass that Anna believed might be a kidney tumor. She could do nothing for him. Many of the boys had varying degrees of malnutrition.

After sizing up their medical conditions, Anna spoke with Julian about how the problems might be addressed. The Danish Red Cross was delivering care packages to the main camp on a weekly basis. They had some items only adults could use, such as coffee and tea. But some of the packages had dried fruit and chocolates. Anna stressed to Julian he should gather as many of these packages as possible for the children.

The last child brought to Anna was Eric. He was carried in by his squadron leader, Martin. Eric was near death. He was four years old and had been in block-66 for about two months. Little was known about him except that he had been significantly malnourished when he arrived. He would not eat nor speak. It was reported that he had witnessed the murder of his parents by the Gestapo. When the officers had turned to deal with him, he was gone, and it was unclear how he had come to Buchenwald.

Beryl had decided to call him Eric. Mostly because Beryl's late father's name was Eric. The child had curly black hair and dark eyes that showed no emotion. His legs were swollen, as was his abdomen. His cheeks were sunken and there were multiple sores in his mouth. Anna had never seen a child in such poor condition, but she recognized it from her medical studies. Eric had Kwashiorkor.

Anna took him in her arms. He rested his head on her chest as his legs dangled lifelessly over her lap. His form of malnutrition was the most severe. With no protein or caloric intake, the body essentially uses its own protein causing severe muscle wasting. Finally, the immune system shuts down and cannot protect the body even from normal bacterial flora in the mouth. Tongue and mouth ulcers develop which make eating painful and difficult. Eventually, these children become listless and anorexic.

As Anna held Eric she asked his squadron leader to get Julian. Anna rocked him back and forth as she contemplated how to save him. Julian arrived in minutes.

"Can we save him?" he asked.

Anna looked into the eyes of this fragile little piece of humanity.

"I think we have one chance. Call Beryl. I need both of you to hear my instructions."

Beryl arrived and Anna began.

"We need someone to get to the camp infirmary and steal a stethoscope." "What's that?" asked Beryl.

"A stethoscope is what a doctor uses to listen to the heart."

"Yes, the heart. I know what to look for."

"I need cooking oil and a large syringe, also from the infirmary. And can we get salt?"

"Yes!" said Julian.

"Good! I want you to clean his mouth sores three times daily with warm salt water. Two other things. Can we get eggs and milk... cow or goat, it doesn't matter."

"Of course," Julian said, having no idea how he was going to get it.

It was almost time for Anna to leave. One of the squadron leaders was looking out for women making their afternoon walk. He saw them.

"They're coming," he said in a loud voice.

"Notify me through Roland when you have what we need. I'll be back." With that, Anna got her coat and disappeared out the door.

The following Monday and Tuesday were routine work days. Anna was at work before 6:00 a.m. for her usual 12-hour shift. She saw Roland but they did not speak or make eye contact. Anna performed her work routinely but could not stop thinking about Eric. She knew he could not last another week. His kidney and liver function would start to shut down and he would die in a matter of days. She had held him for less than half an hour, his eyes listless and his body rail thin. But in that time he had become for Anna, her country's chance at redemption; if she could just save Eric. Although it would not bring back the tens of thousands of Jewish children who had been gassed or starved or killed in some other way, it was a start, a new beginning. The soul of Germany had died. Men were still dying daily at the hands of the *SS*. She wondered why the life of one four-year-old child could matter so much. But it did.

On Wednesday she got what she was waiting for. Roland walked past her during lunch and without looking at her, quickly spoke.

"They have what you have asked for."

"I'll be there tonight," she replied quickly.

Anna had the routine in the women's barracks down pat. Two female guards worked in 24-hour shifts. They generally stayed to themselves in their quarters, played cards and smoked. The barracks doors were locked but could be opened from the inside. They would not re-lock unless completely shut. Anna's plan was to leave her exit door slightly ajar so she could get back inside.

After supper she lay down in her black topcoat and covered herself with her blanket. The guards had completed their evening count. Anna had told Erika what she would be doing. The night was overcast and the weather had turned colder with a few snow flurries. There were four guard towers between the women's barracks and block-66. Anna's plan was to hug the fence because the flood lights from the towers were aimed at the men's barracks. In contrast, a person in a dark coat walking close to the fence would be difficult to notice. If she were noticed she would be shot as an escapee.

Anna waited 30 minutes after she saw the light go out in the guard's quarters. The women in the barracks were sleeping except for Erika. Anna got up, walked quietly to the rear door and pushed it open. She placed a small pebble at the bottom to prevent the door from completely closing.

The cold wind hit her face. She hugged the side of the building until she reached the end. Now the first guard tower was in view. Getting from her barracks to the fence would be the greatest risk. The floodlights prohibited her from seeing inside the tower. She stood for a moment and then was ready to make her move. Suddenly she froze. There were two guards on the walkway apparently making evening rounds. They had stopped to talk with the guards in the tower. Their backs were to her and she saw they might be distracting the men in the tower. Suddenly, as if some force compelled her, she darted across the walk to the fence. If she was going to be seen, she'd know it immediately.

She held her breath. But the guards continued talking. They were all laughing at something one of them had said. The guards on the walkway moved on into the cold, night air. Anna stayed about 50 feet behind them, hugging the fence as if stalking them. She moved at their pace. She no longer noticed the cold.

The men in block-66 were waiting for her. As soon as she knocked softly on the door, Beryl opened it.

"Do you want something warm to drink?" he asked after pulling her inside. "Later. Where is he?"

She followed Beryl to the interior of the block, shed her coat and without thinking, handed it to Beryl. It had been more than two years since Anna had functioned as a doctor. It was as natural to her as breathing.

Eric looked unchanged. She took a small flashlight and looked into his mouth. The ulcerations appeared less angry. The warm salt solution was helping. She took the stethoscope and disengaged one of the rubber tubes. She then covered it with cooking oil and inserted it into Eric's nose and down his esophagus. When she thought it had reached his stomach, she took the earpiece of the stethoscope with the remaining tube placed into her right ear. She looked at Julian.

"Gently blow into the tube," she said, handing it to him. "Good!"

The tube was in his stomach. She took a string and double looped it around the tube, then tied it around Eric's head. She looked at Beryl.

"I need the syringe, milk and eggs." When she had them she continued.

"Every three hours around the clock, I want you to give him one raw egg mixed with four ounces of milk."

She took a cup, broke the egg into it then filled it with milk. She attached the syringe to the tube and slowly poured the mixture into the syringe, holding it up. Gravity delivered it into his stomach.

"He'll need the tube feeding around the clock without fail," she said, looking at Julian. "And he'll need someone with him at all times to see he does not pull the tube out."

"Done," said Julian. Anna turned to go.

"By the way, where did you get the milk and eggs?"

Julian looked at Anna admiringly. "If I told you, you would not believe me."

"Fair enough," she said. Then she did something unexpected and unplanned. She walked over to Julian, put her arms around his neck and hugged him. She did the same to Beryl. Afterward, both men walked with her to the door.

"God bless you, both," she whispered. "God bless you."

The next few days were uneventful. Erika and Anna spent significant time talking hopefully about Eric. Anna anticipated that two weeks of forced feeding would be necessary before he would be able to eat on his own. As his nutrition improved, his ability to fight infection would improve. Anna had made it clear to the men of block-66 that all of the boys needed vitamins, but especially the younger ones.

The following Sunday Anna had to restrain herself to keep from running to block-66.

"Slow down!" Erika finally said softly. "They're going to see you and they will know you are up to something."

Anna slowed her pace. By the time she reached the block she was almost afraid to go inside. Would he be better? Would he be alive?

Beryl met her at the door. She was afraid to ask so she simply said, "How are the children?"

"Better. Improving."

Anna's heart was pounding. "Where is he?"

"Come with me."

Eric was sitting in a chair by the exam area waiting for Anna. He still looked frail and swollen but he was supporting himself and actually had expression in his eyes. After just four days of the high protein feedings his body was drinking in the nourishment as a suffocating man would gulp for air. He was not only getting protein and calories but minerals from the goat's milk. Anna was thrilled with what she saw. Later, she learned the men had gotten him some vitamins from the same source as the milk and eggs.

Sick call that day was down to about 25 boys. The increase in Danish Red Cross packages was improving the overall situation. Before leaving, she instructed Julian and Beryl to pull the feeding tube from Eric on Wednesday. This would give him a full week of feedings. As she left she was already anxious for her next visit.

For more than a year, a number of men in the camp underground had been working on an escape plan. Most were Jewish and two were from the French underground; Roland Montague and Pierre Oberaud.

All of the men working on the plan worked in the V-2 facility except for Ehud Katz and Chaim Nussbam. They both worked in a *SS* armament plant that made explosives, including artillery shells and hand grenades. This plant was heavily guarded and carefully monitored. In all, there were nine men working on the project. All lived in the same barracks. All had been in Buchenwald for two years and all were in reasonably good health.

The motivation behind the plan was due to several factors. They had witnessed the continual random killing of men. Eleven months earlier, two young men in their 20s had killed a guard with a knife and attempted to blow a hole in the electrified fence using a hand grenade taken from the guard. They were caught and hanged naked upside down by their ankles for six hours on the parade ground. About 2,000 prisoners were marched out to the area to watch as they were shot in the head as an example. None of the men planning the escape expected to die in camp. They were not motivated by fear, but by a desire to create turmoil. If they could get to Allied lines, all the better.

In the latter days of January 1945, something occurred that pushed their plan into action. Late one afternoon, some 700 prisoners arrived from Auschwitz. As the Russians were closing in on Poland, the Germans had begun evacuating the death camps. In early January, 60,000 men from Auschwitz were sent to various camps in Germany, some on forced death marches, some by train. Three thousand men were marched to Buchenwald with little food or clothing, all of them Jewish. Along the way, hundreds fell by the road from exhaustion. They were all shot and left by the roadside. In the final few days of the march, 10 men escaped into the forest around Weimer. The guards did not bother to chase them. It was becoming obvious that the Nazis were not going to allow their death and concentration camps captured full of prisoners to testify to their horrors. The men from Auschwitz who did escape told of enormous pits of dead bodies that were being burned to destroy evidence. There were an estimated 80,000 men in Buchenwald. The men in the underground were beginning to wonder if the Germans intended to try to kill them all before the allies came.

The head of the escape committee was Pierre Oberaud, a Frenchman who had been a police lieutenant before the war. After the fall of France, he had worked in the resistance. He was caught in December 1944, when a paid informant turned him over to the Gestapo. Now his goal in life was to escape and return to deal with the informant.

The men of barracks-12 were well organized and had come into the camp with skills. One of the men was an electrical engineer. Another had been a mathematics teacher.

Barracks-12 was located on the perimeter of the camp, only 24 feet from the electrified fence. For more than a year, the men had been digging an escape tunnel under the walkway and under the fence. They worked every night in three hour shifts with three men to a shift. They had a pulley cart on wheels for moving the soil and progressed further into the tunnel at a rate of about a foot every four or five days. The major challenge they faced was disposal of the dirt. It was moist and had a significant clay component, so the tunnel needed only a moderate amount of shoring.

The tunnel was eight feet below ground. The men who worked in the armament plant walked to work and dispersed the dirt along their one-mile walk. They would fill their pockets and drop hand-fuls of soil every 100 feet or so. Other men got rid of soil when cleaning the latrines. One of the men worked as a gardener close to the administration building and proved most helpful at disposing of the dirt.

The tunnel had been finished for more than a month. They had taken the tunnel to within one foot of the surface, 30 feet outside the fence. Their exit sight would deploy into a clump of trees if their direction was accurate. Now they needed the right time to go.

The break came when a Jewish locksmith was asked to repair the main door of the arms storage area in the south camp section. This was a separate building, a window-less concrete bunker. The walls were two feet thick and steel reinforced. The door was solid steel, four inches thick. It was built to withstand a direct hit in a bombing raid. The lock was a complex double key lock mechanism. One key was kept by the arms quartermaster for the entire camp and one was kept in the SS commandant's office. Because of this double lock system, security for the arms cash was never a concern. The lock mechanism was dismantled by the locksmith and he took it to a workshop to rebuild. While there was no lock, the bunker required 24-hour guards. A SS sergeant stayed with the locksmith while he worked on the mechanism but paid little attention to what he was doing. The work was tedious and took two days to complete. As he re-mastered the keys, he made two sets, all unnoticed by the sergeant. When the mechanism was reinstalled he left the duplicates hidden in his workshop.

The arms quartermaster met the locksmith at the bunker. The repairman got a brief glimpse inside and noted boxes of ammunition, explosives and hand grenades. There were rifles and pistols, but they appeared to be locked in separate vaults. The rebuilt lock system functioned well with the double key mechanism. The duplicate keys were safely hidden. The locksmith, a man from Warsaw named Martin Lazar, would pass the information to Roland by an intermediary.

When Roland received the news the following day, he convened an urgent meeting of the escape committee and set it for midnight. The kapo for block-12 knew of the plan but had not yet decided to stay or to go.

Some 30 men in block-12 were aware of the tunnel. They had decided not to be involved in the attempt but to take their chances staying in the camp. They believed the escapees would be tracked down and shot. They were also aware of something the Germans called 'collective responsibility.' In the past, escape attempts had led to severe punishment or sometimes even killing if it was believed that others may have had knowledge of an escape plan. The SS would interrogate everyone in block-12. Anyone who admitted to knowledge of the tunnel would be punished, tortured or killed. This practice kept the escape attempts at a minimum. Everyone knew the more men who attempted to escape, the greater chance of being caught. So it appeared the original nine who dug the tunnel would be the ones to go.

The tunnel entrance was in a small storage room adjacent to the showers. These were used only on Sundays. The nine men gathered at mid-night. Pierre Oberaud informed the other seven of the keys to the arms bunker.

"We have been given a stroke of good fortune," he said. "We have been furnished duplicate keys to the arms bunker. We can get in and get grenades and explosives but not guns, which may be best anyway. We don't want to get into a shoot-out with the guards. The *SS* does inventory once a week so we have only a few days to steal and use the explosives."

Moshe Unger, the electrical engineer, stepped in. "We will steal a case of hand grenades providing we can get the detonator pins. They may be kept separate from the actual explosives."

"We'll create a diversion by blowing up a guard tower," said Roland. "We need to be in the tunnel when the explosion goes off. And our plan is to try to kill all of the tracker dogs."

"How will that be accomplished?" asked Karl Reinhardt, the mathematician.

"Moshe has an idea to rig a delay action detonator for each grenade," replied

Roland. "Men in block-16 are next to the kennel. There are five tracker dogs in separate pens. We have saved chocolate bars to bring them into the open pens. Then we'll kill them with the grenades. The kennel explosions must be coordinated with the guard tower explosions."

"We can be several miles into the forest before they know we are missing and with no dogs to track us, we can make it," said Pierre.

"The locksmith is Martin Lazar," Roland explained further. "We owe everything to him...literally everything. The SS will go immediately for him. When he hears the explosions, he will take a cyanide pill."

"Why?" interrupted Pierre. "He can come with us."

"He is 60 years old and has no family left," said Roland. "They killed his wife and son in Poland. He has nothing to live for. It was his choice. This is his way of fighting back. They took his life when they gassed his wife and son."

Pierre finished the meeting solemnly.

"We will get the grenades in the next two days. The following night we will go." The underground in Buchenwald prison was extensive, probably in excess of 400 men. Since the prison was run by kapos, as long as the work was done and there were no uprisings, things went smoothly. It had been more than two years since any major problem had come up and more than three months since a man had been put on the hanging tree. When the prison was quiet, the only guards visible were those in the towers. That was about to change.

By this time, there were 80,000 prisoners in a facility designed for 20,000. Because of the enormous overcrowding the kapos could not keep track of all the prisoners, nor did they try. Consequently, if careful, resourceful men could get many things such as flashlights, money, cigarettes, and even knives. The major problem for the underground was that scattered among the barracks were informers who would gladly trade information for improved living conditions, extra food or a night in the brothel. There were barracks where Danish and Belgian POW's were kept with more humane living conditions. Informers sometimes tried to get transferred into those blocks. But informers were considered traitors and when discovered, they were killed. Being an informer was a dangerous game.

Karl Reinhardt was playing this game. He was a Communist from Hamburg who had been a Soviet sympathizer. He was suspected of being a soviet espionage agent but had not been convicted. When he entered the prison in July of 1943, he made a deal with the *SS* to feed them information but only information considered of major importance. He was anti-Semitic and was suspected by the underground of being a traitor. He lived in block-13, next to the block of the tunnel. He was unaware of the tunnel but knew something unusual was in the air. Two underground men also lived in block-13 and were watching Reinhardt.

The lock to the arms bunker had been repaired on a Tuesday. The following day the duplicate keys were in Roland's hands. That night, two men from block-24, next to the arms bunker, let themselves in and took a case of hand grenades. They were relieved to find that the firing pens were in the case in a separate compartment. Arms inventory was done each Sunday and there was no risk the grenades would be discovered missing until they were used. Over the next two days the one dozen grenades made their way to the men who would plant them. Five would go to the men living next to the kennels and the remaining seven to the men adjacent to the guard house tower. Karl Reinhardt suspected that an escape attempt was imminent, but he had no details. He asked another man in block-13 casually if something was 'going on'. The reply was, "Why do you ask?"

Immediately Reinhardt understood he was suspected of being an informer. He lost his composure and tried to run out of the barracks to get to a guard tower. Five men blocked the door and quickly stuffed a rag in his mouth. He was dragged to the shower area where another man was waiting.

"This is what we do to traitors," he said with an ugly grin, then quickly plunged a knife into the informer's heart. Later that night, Reinhardt's body was dragged out of the barracks and placed under a remote barracks. He would not be missed until the following evening when he did not show up for census. It took three more days of searching before his frozen body was found.

Soon, it was evident that the effort to place a delay on the firing pin would not work. The detonation pins were spring loaded. Once pulled there was a 20-second delay before explosion. Placing the explosives would not be a problem at the kennels but might prove to be a more difficult issue for the guard tower. The men attacking the tower would have to run in the open to escape, and if not successful in taking out the tower, they could easily be caught in machine gun fire. A number of men would be risking their lives for the escape of nine. None of it made sense except as a way of venting their hatred of the Nazis.

Friday, the following day, was escape day. Roland had not talked with Anna or even seen her for several days. He made a point to sit by her at lunch. As they were finishing, he looked at her.

"I will not be seeing you again," he said with a whisper.

She looked up, startled. Then she understood as she caught his faint smile. Without speaking she took his hand in hers briefly before he stood to leave.

Anna watched him go. She had enjoyed knowing this charming Frenchman whom she really didn't know at all. Her thoughts raced back 16 years to the time her father had taken the family to see Charles Lindberg land in Paris. She was charmed by Frenchmen then and by Roland now. This evil war had brought her in contact with many extraordinary and courageous people.

At midnight everyone was in place. Five men were at the kennel, each with a chocolate bar and a grenade. Four men were hidden beneath the guard tower. Two would throw their grenades into the elevated tower hut and two would set the remaining three at the base of the tower. The nine-man escape committee was in the tunnel, plus one. The kapo had decided at the last minute to join them.

Each man at the kennel made a commotion that brought the dogs out into the individual dog runs. One shepherd barked briefly before smelling the chocolate. As the dogs got busy with the chocolate bars, each man dropped his grenade over the fence into the dog runs, then ran. The kennel explosions occurred almost simultaneously and rocked the quiet camp. Martin Lazar, the courageous locksmith, quickly swallowed his cyanide tablet and was dead in seven minutes.

The four men at the base of the guard tower then went into action. Two lobbed their grenades up toward the machine gun nest. At the same time, the three grenade pins were pulled at the tower base. One of the thrown grenades crashed through the glass into the gun nest, the other came quickly to the ground. All of the men began to run as the grenades demolished the tower and killed all three guards in it. The multiple explosions in rapid succession brought all the flood lights on.

In less than 3 minutes all of the men were back in their barracks. The escape committee plus one had made their way through the remaining soil and out to freedom. They ran about a mile into the forest and then split into three groups of three, three and four. The two Frenchmen and one German went west, the other two groups northwest and southwest. Each man had buried his prison garb and put on stolen clothing. By day light they were already 10 miles from Buchenwald.

The section of the camp with the exploded guard tower was a mass of confusion and SS troops. The entire camp went immediately into lock-down. The SS commandant personally took charge of the investigation. The escape tunnel was discovered about 4:00 a.m., meaning the escapees had a four-hour head start. All of the tracking dogs were dead. Without them, the escapee routes could not be found. Approximately 100 troops were dispersed to search for the prisoners. They were in armored vehicles and on roads. The prisoners were in the forest on foot. It was going to be difficult to find them.

There were approximately 100 men in each block. Those in block-12 were out on the parade ground within two hours. The commandant lined them up by tens. They were surrounded by about 40 soldiers.

"I want details of this tunnel!" shouted the commandant. "Who dug it? Over what period of time? Every detail. You have one minute to comply. Then I will kill one man each minute until I get answers."

No one spoke. The men in block-12 understood that they were in control. As long as they did not break, they were in control. They were willing to give up their lives for this principle.

After one minute, the first line of men was ordered to turn around and kneel. The commandant proceeded to shoot one man in the back of the head each minute for 12 minutes. No one spoke. It appeared he would have to kill all of them and have nothing to show for it. Disgusted, he turned to his adjuvant. "Pick out five and get some information from them. Torture them!"

By chance the five chosen knew nothing of the tunnel. They were tortured but had nothing to give up.

Within a week, the commandant was relieved of his command and his deputy was moved up. The deputy had been the head of all of the *SS* security in the armament factories and the outlying camps of which there were almost 70. He was now in command of all of the 1,800 *SS* men at Buchenwald and the armament facilities. He was an unusual man for an *SS* Colonel, and he had no intention of bringing a reign of terror down on the prisoners in Buchenwald for doing what he knew any man would try to do.

*   *   *

Because of the lock-down, Anna did not get to go to block-66 that Sunday. She could get no word of Eric and would simply have to be patient. In the evenings she talked with Erika who assured her that the little boy was likely improving. It was nearing the end of February and spring was around the corner. What the women did not know was that the Allies had taken Hamburg and Hanover to the west and were only 100 kilometers from Weimar. So spring was coming and the Allies were as well.

The following Sunday the lockdown was lifted. It had been almost a month since Anna had placed the feeding tube in Eric. He had improved initially but she had not seen him in two weeks and she was apprehensive as she walked along the perimeter.

"He is fine….I'm sure of it," said Erika as they approached block-66.

Anna smiled but did not speak. She moved on and made her way to the door, where she knocked gently. One of the squadron leaders met her. She greeted him and briskly walked to the central area's exam room. Beryl Yenzer walked up and before he could say hello Anna immediately asked about Eric. Beryl smiled.

"I think he is looking for you."

She turned around. Eric was walking toward Anna with a smile on his face. He was still very thin but his face was starting to fill out a bit and his dark eyes sparkled. Anna dropped to her knees and the boy put his arms around her neck. He held her tightly.

"Eric, you look so much better. Are you also feeling better?"

"Yes."

"Is your mouth better?"

"Yes."

Anna laughed. "Can I hold you for a moment?"

"Yes."

She held him in her arms for a long minute. It felt as if she were holding a miracle in her arms. She rubbed her hand along his shoulder to his wrist and noticed the tattoo on the inside of his left forearm, B-6130. She was hoping this would be his only scar from Buchenwald. She was more determined than ever to do all in her power to bring all of the boys safely through the war. There were obviously more resources available than she could have imagined, and she planned to use them all.

In the afternoon she met Erika on the walkway with a broad smile. Erika returned the smile.

"So, I take it things are going well with the children."

"Very well. Eric is significantly improved, and I think out of danger, thank God. He is such a charmer. I wish you could have seen him.

"I will, and it may only be a matter of weeks!"

The new commandant had spent little time in the actual camp during his tour as deputy commandant. His duties had been in the DAW (German Equipment Works), the sprawling enterprise to make arms for Germany and money for the SS. During his first week, his orientation revealed many of the atrocities he had heard about but had not seen. He interviewed the doctors who were doing medical experiments and learned of the results of poisoning subjects with various substances and performing autopsies before sending them to the crematorium. He toured the camp and viewed thousands of starving men. Except for those working on the V-2 project at the Mibau facility, fully 25,000 men were near death, emaciated men who looked back at him with hollow eyes. The sanitation was squalid. The kapos would not use the latrines and were given access to the indoor toilets. He came across a building that had once been a horse stable. It now held over 200 starving men who had nowhere to go and nothing to do.

The new commandant was a soldier, a distinguished colonel who had fought bravely and honorably for his country. He had been wounded on the Russian front and there would be no more combat for him. By the time he had taken in the horror that was Buchenwald he was deeply depressed. There was no honor left in Germany. Now orders were to evacuate the camp before it was over-run by the Allies. But how to do it? And where were the prisoners to go? There was no place to hide thousands of starving prisoners. Most of the men were so starved and sick they could not scream. But the crimes of the Reich would scream. They would be heard from this camp and they would be heard by the world.

His thoughts harkened back to 1933, when he had decided to join the Nazi party. Expectations were high for the German Volk and there was great excitement in the air. He was disturbed by the 1935 Nuremberg Laws that deprived Jewish men and women of their citizenship. Then in November, 1938, things turned very ugly with Kristallnacht…. 'The Night of Broken Glass' when 1,000 Synagogues were burned, 7,500 Jewish businesses were destroyed and 30,000 Jewish men arrested. He knew then that it would not end well. But he was a soldier, not a politician and 10 months later Germany invaded Poland. Now the end was near.

The following week, the second week of March, he received a classified communication from *SS* headquarters in Berlin. It was marked 'urgent' and signed by Himmler. It read as follows:

> March 13, 1945
>
> From Obekommando der *SS*
>
> To: Commandant Buchenwald Camp
>
> -Orders for immediate execution of prisoner
>
> Anna Eichenwald
>
> -Confirmation to *SS* headquarters required.
>
> General Heinrich Himmler

The commandant sat in his chair trying to absorb what he had read. "Colonel, shall I have the order carried out?" asked his adjuvant.

"No. I will execute the prisoner myself today at 5:00 p.m."

March 14th was a routine day for Anna. She was counting the three days until Sunday when she would return to block-66 for a visit with Eric and to evaluate more sick boys. She did not even mind the grueling 12-hour work days making liquid oxygen. She had something to look forward to and in fact, since her loss of Christian, something to live for. The days were passing quickly. Spring was in the air. Within the next two weeks the fields and meadows that could be seen through the electrified fence would begin to burst forth in color.

In mid-afternoon something unusual happened. A SS car pulled up to the main entrance of the Mibau facility. The driver was the adjuvant to the commandant. The commander of Buchenwald was in the front seat. The rear seat was occupied by a sergeant and a lieutenant. The sergeant and lieutenant got out of the car and went into the plant. They inquired about Anna's work station. The presence of the SS brought ominous quiet and a palpable apprehension. The supervisor led them to Anna's station. She had not noticed the two.

"Anna Eichenwald?" asked the lieutenant. She was startled but turned to face them. "Yes, I am Anna Eichenwald."

"Come with us!"

Anna collected her coat and started to ask where they were taking her and why. Then she decided it must be related to her caring for the boys. She felt she could defend her involvement in block-66.

She was placed between the two soldiers in the rear of the car, which sped away. The commandant said nothing. As the car turned to the north, she realized they were going away from the camp entrance. Her heart began to race.

"Where are you taking me?"

The lieutenant did not answer. After another moment she repeated the question. "Where are we going?"

"Silence!" he said harshly.

It took Anna only a very brief moment to realize she was facing the end of her life. She sat perfectly still sandwiched between the SS lieutenant and his sergeant. The dark gray sedan with the white swastika on the door belonged to the Commandant of Buchenwald Prison, and the Colonel in the front seat was apparently that man. Initially when placed in the car she had demanded a reason, but she got only silence. She wanted to scream, but she was now finding it hard even to breathe. Night was falling and the horizon was fading into black. Through the window she watched the cold landscape grow increasingly dim. They were taking her in the opposite direction from the prison. Heart pounding in her chest, pellucid thoughts raced through her mind. She would not see her parents again; she would not see Eric again.

The end would be quick. As a physician she knew the bullet from the German Lugar would explode into her brain with unbelievable violence, much as the Nazi Reich had exploded with violence onto her country twelve years earlier. It was very cold, and she began to shiver. The landscape was becoming more remote. Her lifeless form would freeze quickly.....slowing, at least for a time, the decay that would follow. She thought back to a similar cold day in Berlin when she was officially confronted with the nightmare of Hitler's *new Germany*. So much had happened. She had always believed it would end differently.

The car traveled for six or seven minutes along the country road, then turned off onto a narrow side road that was obviously little used. After another half mile the car stopped. The lieutenant opened his door.

"Get out!"

He took her arm and pulled her out. Anna now knew she was to be shot. She felt weak as the adrenalin of fear poured into her system. She was having trouble standing. The Commandant got out of the car and turned to the lieutenant.

"I will do this. You wait in the car." The lieutenant started to argue.

"Sir, I……."

"Wait in the car," the commandant said again. Anna was looking down. Her legs were trembling. "Walk ahead of me," the commandant said. They moved away from the car.

"Dr. Eichenwald, listen very carefully. I am Ernst Bishoff. Twelve years ago, I was shot in the chest in a Communist riot. You saved my life. When I tell you, stop and get on your knees. I will fire my pistol very close to your head. Immediately fall over. Twenty minutes after we are gone walk back to the main road and follow it north about 10 kilometers. You will come to a farmhouse. They will help you."

They walked another 20 paces.

"Stop and drop to your knees," he commanded.

He drew his Lugar and put a bullet into the chamber.

"I am the one who supplied the goat's milk and eggs for the boy. We are not all evil men."

He raised the pistol and fired once. Anna immediately slumped to the ground. It was easy to do, as she could no longer stand on her weakened legs.

The following morning the lieutenant sent a communication to *SS* Berlin headquarters reading:

Anna Eichenwald eliminated……bullet to the head.

CHAPTER 21

Auschwitz

Anna lay motionless for what seemed like a very long time. In reality, it was only about 20 minutes. The wind was calm and a thin crust of snow blanketed the ground. The sun was going down, though, and the temperature was dropping rapidly. Anna began to feel cold. She decided it must be safe to try to make it back to the main road. After all, she had been left for dead, supposedly with a bullet in her head.

Anna stood up and was immediately aware of two things. She was shivering and had a dissonant ringing in her ears. In fact, it seemed she could not hear anything from her right ear. The Lugar muzzle blast had taken its toll.

She began to follow the ruts of the little-used road back to the main road. She walked at a brisk pace to try to get warm. She wondered if others had been brought to this spot to be murdered. She would never know for sure, but she suspected this was a place for murder.

It was dark by the time she stepped onto the main road. Instinctively she turned in the opposite direction from which she had been brought, hoping it was north. She was surprised at her strength. After her near death experience she wondered why she didn't feel weak. That would come later. For now, she picked up her pace. The colonel had said there was a farmhouse. And she remembered that he had mentioned 10 kilometers. Still, her mind was cloudy. Where did he come from? She remembered his surgery, the gunshot wound to the heart and the encounter in the hospital with Adolph Hitler. But she had forgotten the colonel's name. His surgery was one of hundreds she had performed. His stood out only because it had kept her from being arrested for a time.

Anna continued down the road. She walked as fast as possible but gravity seemed to be pulling her down. She thought about her survival. She'd been at Buchenwald more than two months and then suddenly she was selected for execution. She knew the former commandant would have had her killed. But he was gone and Ernst Bishoff, a former patient, had replaced him. The whole thing was bizarre.

She was beginning to tire. The cold was numbing but she pushed on, now unable to feel her feet. They felt like wooden pegs. She had no hat and her exposed face and head were draining her body of heat. But she knew that as long as she kept moving she would not freeze. The daytime temperatures were in the 30s but night could see single digits.

So the man whose life she had saved had in turn saved her. She thought of this paradox and whispered to herself, "I won't die here on a frozen road in rural Germany."

She pushed on. And then she saw them, tiny dots of light. They were gone quickly but then reappeared through the trees. She tried to run. The lights grew bigger, brighter. Another few minutes and she could clearly make out the farm house with a large barn behind it. Now she could see a fence and a chimney with smoke billowing from it. He had not deceived her. It was just as the colonel had said.

Anna's legs were shaking as she stepped onto the porch. Her hands were almost uncontrollable. She put them together and tried to knock on the door. As it opened, her eyes were met by those of a woman in her 50s. The woman's face was weathered from years of hard work and outside exposure.

"Come in, come in! We have been expecting someone."

Anna stepped into the room, a warm space with a large hearth and blazing fire. Although it was an old structure, it was pristine. The chimney was stone, the floor wide- plank pine, and there were hand sewn curtains on every window.

"I am Greta, Greta Thiele," the woman said with a smile. She turned and nodded toward a tall thin man standing by the fire. He wore overalls and had the same weathered look.

"This is my husband, Johann," the woman went on. "Here, come to the fire and warm yourself. We'll get you hot soup and tea."

Anna sat as close to the fire as possible, her nose and ears bright red. She did not want to remove her coat, embarrassed by her prison clothes. But she realized they knew she was from Buchenwald. As Johann handed her the hot tea, Anna took a sip and let the warmth settle into her system.

"How did you know about me?" she asked.

Greta sat down in a large oversized chair covered with a handmade quilt.

"We have worked in the underground for almost three years. In 1940, our only son was killed in action in France. He was 19. We have two daughters, both in Hamburg working in armament factories. We were always against the Nazis. Johann fought in WWI, which gained us nothing as a country. This is our way of fighting back. We do not kill. We work to prevent them from killing."

Anna looked up from her seat at Johann. He was standing by Greta. "Can you share how you knew I would come here?" she asked again.

"He is one of us."

"Colonel Bishoff?"

"Yes. He is my oldest sister's son. He was almost killed after becoming a Nazi when Hitler came to power. Over the next five years he became more and more disenchanted with Nazi policies. He was a good soldier, decorated for bravery. When he was wounded on the eastern front, he returned and decided to work against the Reich from within the *SS*. Fortunately, he did not join the conspiracy to assassinate Hitler. That decision represented the third time his life was spared. He is very cautious and has involved us reluctantly. We have hidden several people over the past two years, usually for several weeks until we could get them to a safer place or out of Germany. We are hiding someone now."

"A man?" Anna asked quickly.

"Yes."

"In the barn?"

"Yes. We are hoping you will be the last. Allied forces are only 100 kilometers to the west, still you never know. We have gotten some strange requests. Just last month we sent milk and eggs to Buchenwald."

"For the Colonel?"

"Yes."

Anna smiled. She finished her soup.

"You are so tired, my dear," said Greta. "Let me show you where you can sleep." Greta ushered Anna to a small room with a single bed, a table and a lamp. She gave Anna a flannel nightgown.

"Tomorrow we will burn your clothes. I have some things for you to wear. Now you rest."

Anna nodded her head and closed the door. She had not felt safe since attending a meeting at the University of Berlin when she was forced to watch a film of men being executed by hanging with piano wire. Years had passed and she still had not been able to get the images out or her mind. As she closed her eyes, a sense of calm swept over her. She thought of a time as a child when her father rocked her to sleep because she was afraid of the dark. She wondered if she could ever feel that safe again.

The morning was bright and crisp. Anna had been in a deep sleep when Greta woke her, prodding her gently.

"Anna, Anna, time to wake up."

The sleep had been the best, most peaceful she'd had in years. When she opened her eyes, a refreshing feeling rushed through her, a feeling that had been missing for the same length of time.

Greta knew of the extreme hardships at Buchenwald and the other camps. She and Johann had nursed several men back to health. Now, to help a woman would be special for Greta. Her oldest daughter was only six years younger than Anna. She easily transferred that love to Anna. She heated water and led Anna to a room where a tub of that hot water waited. Anna was speechless.

"Take as long as you wish. Your clothes are on the chair."

Anna smiled back at Greta and lowered herself into the largesse of warmth, unable to do anything but sit back and relax her body and mind.

*   *   *

Hans Ulrich had made a snap decision to join the escape committee at Buchenwald. He had been relatively safe as a kapo, the principle 'elder' of block-12, having served two years of an eight-year sentence for embezzlement from a bank in Munich. He had always been a gambler and knew he might be stuck in the post-war prison system of a defeated Germany with no advocate or way out. Court records would likely be destroyed or lost. He had skills as an accountant and could make a fresh start. He thought he had made the right decision. Now he was not so sure.

Hans was not an outdoorsman. Fortunately, his two French companions had learned much about living off of the land working in the French resistance. In a week they had made their way northwest toward Hanover a city due west of Berlin. Unknown to them, the allied forces had reached Hanover and were in a race with the Russian Army approaching from the east to get to Berlin.

The three men were staying deep in the forest. They had matches and on two occasions had built fires, once to cook a rabbit and once to cook a large bass they literally had trapped in a pond. This had been the extent of their food. The cold and exhaustion were taking a toll. They stayed completely off the roads to avoid German troops in defensive positions trying to slow Allied advances. About half a million Wehrmacht troops were deployed along a line from Lubek in the north, down east of Hamburg and Hanover, then to Nuremberg in the south. Eventually they would fall back to form a perimeter defense of Berlin.

On the evening of April 1st, the three escapees felt they could not go on. Pierre Oberaud was the strongest and thought he could make it to Allied lines, possibly in another two days. They could hear Allied artillery far in the distance. They had even seen British aircraft flying sorties supporting troop movements, but they had no idea where the Germans were, nor the Allies. Exhausted, they had to gamble. They had purposefully avoided contact with anyone. Now that must change. They decided to ask for help at the next farmhouse or cabin. The opportunity presented itself that evening.

Kurt and Fran Heirholzer had prospered during the war. Their 100-acre sheep farm had provided wool for uniforms and they had made more money in four years than in the previous 15. The economic boon had turned Kurt into a staunch Nazi. The Reich had become his religion. The war was making him rich. Any doubts he had experienced at the invasion of Poland had been washed away in a cornucopia of Reich marks. It was Kurt and Fran Heirholzer's sheep farm the trio of Buchenwald fugitives were approaching.

Hans Ulrich stepped onto the farmhouse porch and knocked. He knew late evening visitors would be unusual and possibly unwelcome. They had decided to take this chance because many in the rural areas were in fact anti-Nazi. Even so, under no circumstances would they divulge their fugitive status. They would present themselves as working in the resistance. The door opened slightly and Hans began to speak.

"Good evening, sir. We are very sorry to bother you but as you can see we are very cold and in need of help."

When Kurt saw the condition of the men he opened the door wider. Hans and Roland were shivering and pale. Pierre looked somewhat better. Fran Heirholzer was standing behind her husband.

A roaring fire was in the hearth. Nazi or not, she wasn't about to turn sick men away.

"Have them come in," she said.

As the men entered the lighted, warm room, she was startled to see their condition and also puzzled by it. She sat them down on a bench in front of the fire and gave each a cup of hot tea. She looked at her husband who remained silent.

"Where are you from?" she asked. "And why are you here?"

Hans took a long drink of tea. "We work in the underground. A week ago, we became separated from a larger group that was doing reconnaissance for the Allies. We have been trying to get back to Allied lines."

Kurt was at once skeptical, but said nothing. Their clothing was thin, not what anyone would wear in winter, even the underground. They obviously had no weapons. But he didn't want to confront them. Then he had an idea.

"My wife has a pot of lamb stew on the stove. You can stay in the barn tonight and get a fresh start in the morning. I have several old coats I can lend you."

"You are very kind," Hans replied. "A hot meal and a night's sleep will restore us. We'll be on our way early in the morning."

The men were led to the 'mud room' to wash up. As Fran Heirholzer was getting soap for the men, she noticed the tattoo on Roland's forearm through a hole in his shirt sleeve. Keeping it to herself, she moved back into the kitchen to dish the stew. Each man had a large bowl, then another. Little was said. Kurt would not feel safe until they were in the barn and locked in at that. True to his word he found three old woolen work coats for them, then led them out to the barn which was a relatively new and sturdy structure used to store winter hay and his two plow mules.

"You men have a restful night," he said, an unctuous tone to his voice. "We'll have breakfast for you then you can be on your way."

As he closed the door he locked it with a large padlock and took a deep breath. Now they were trapped.

"I have locked them in the barn," he told his wife as he re-entered the house. "They can't get out, no way. Early in the morning I'll go for the Gestapo."

"I felt something was not right about them," she said. "Then I got a glimpse of a number tattooed on the forearm of one of them. I don't think he knew I saw it."

"It doesn't matter now, they're locked in."

The fugitives were warm, dry and well fed. They were also aware of the locked door. That wasn't so unusual given the fact they were total strangers in a time of war. But they also had no intension of remaining locked in the barn. Pierre began to search for possibilities for a break out. The first thing he noticed was the timber used for the walls. It was 4 inches thick, as was the door. There were no hay loft windows or any other doors. The perimeter footings were concrete. After his inspection he sat down.

"I'm not sure we can get out. This place is a fortress."

"Are there any tools, a shovel or a hand ax?" Hans asked.

"I found an old shovel, but the handle is split. Besides, we would have to dig under the perimeter concrete footings. We would have to tunnel our way out. That might take a day or so."

The men fell silent.

"I have a solution," Hans said suddenly. "We can blow our way out."

Pierre was perturbed by the attempt at comedy.

"Yes, that's right, Hans. We'll huff and we'll puff. Look, this is no time for joking. We're locked in and he may be going for the Gestapo as we speak. Save your wisecracks...and your breath."

Hans looked at both men but he was not smiling.

"I don't plan on using my breath," he said dryly. "I have a grenade." "What! Where did you get a grenade?"

Finally Hans felt as if he was contributing.

"The elder in charge of block-24, the block responsible for stealing the grenades, was one of us. The case of grenades did not have the usual dozen. Instead, there were 13. He gave me the extra. I have kept it pinned to my belt, covered by my jacket.

Pierre stared back at him. "Well I'll be damned...an accountant turned soldier. I will give you a battlefield promotion."

"I'll take it," Hans said with a grin. "How about you call me General Ulrich?" The men were now convinced of two things. One, they had no way to escape the barn. Secondly, Heirholzer intended to turn them in. Their only option was to use the grenade and blow a hole in the barn wall. It was a significant risk. Any Nazi troops nearby might come. But it was their only chance.

None of the men knew the terrain. They needed light and they also needed sleep. Their zero-hour had to be around 5:00 a.m.

"Agreed," said Hans.

Pierre glanced over at Roland who was staring at the ground. "Roland? What is it?"

"I was just thinking of the locksmith, Lazar. We're here because of him. Okay, so 5:00 a.m. it is. We can all get five hours of sleep. I'll take the first shift."

No one had a wristwatch so the zero hour would be a guess.

Pierre took the last shift. After the meal and sleep he was refreshed and ready to get out of the barn. He decided to wake the others when he could see any sign of daylight through a crack in the barn door. As it happened, the time was 5:30 a.m.

The men decided to blow out the wall at the far end of the barn, away from the mules. They would stack bales of hay between the grenade and the interior, then each would barricade himself behind a bale at the opposite end of the barn.

Kurt Heirholzer was ready to take hay to his stock. There was less to do in the winter although today would be an exception. He gathered eggs from the laying hens but didn't enter the barn. Instead, he had a second cup of coffee. By this time Fran was up and making biscuits. They would have breakfast and then drive the 35 minutes to the police office in the nearest town. It was a small two-man office. The sergeant would likely have to call for help in arresting the escaped prisoners. It seemed straight forward. Heirholzer had walked around the barn slowly and saw nothing disturbed. He knew they could not escape the barn. He had built it himself.

By 6:00 a.m. the couple was sitting down for hot biscuits and scrambled eggs. In an instant the still of the country morning was shattered. The explosion rocked the silence, rattled the windows of their home, blowing out the rear window in the back of the house. The sound of the percussion brought the farmer to his feet.

"What the hell!"He ran quickly to get his old shotgun perched on the wall over the fireplace, his mind racing to think what could have exploded.

The grenade ripped a huge hole in the wall of the barn and immediately the three were out and racing to the wooded area about 100 yards across a meadow. Heirholzer, shotgun in hand, saw them running but knew they were too far away for him to get off a shot. As he turned back to the barn he was gripped by a horrible sight. The explosion had ignited a portion of dry hay and smoke was pouring out of the hole in the barn wall. He ran to the house to get the pad-lock key.

"The barn's on fire....get some buckets," he yelled.

He ran out to the barn, hand shaking, and had trouble getting the key in the lock. Finally the lock was disengaged. As he swung the door open the two terrified mules ran out of the burning structure. Now the entire end of the barn was engulfed in flames. The nearest neighbor was four miles away. He and his wife stood hopelessly watching as the fire consumed the entire structure. What had taken him three and a half months to build was gone in less than an hour.

Within the hour the fugitive trio was deep in the woods and three miles away. They stopped for a breather, enjoying their wool coats courtesy of one Kurt Heirholzer. Roland was the first to speak.

"From certain capture, to hearty meal, to a good sleep and warm coats," he said, raising his hand as though giving a toast. "We've had a good 24 hours."

They were still concerned about the possibility of being caught and could not have known that Kurt Heirholzer never made it to town. But they did soon learn they were only 10 kilometers from Allied lines. Pierre Oberaud was wearing a dirty white shirt which they used as a truce signal to get safely into Allied hands by that afternoon.

*   *   *

Anna soaked in the tub for almost an hour. The water was no longer warm and her freshly washed hair contributed to the cold. She dried off and donned the cotton dress and sweater. She was embarrassed to have no undergarments. Hers had long since rotted. It had been months since she had been able to adequately deal with her feminine issues. Greta was a great help in that area. As she entered the main living area of the farmhouse, she was greeted by Johann.

"Feel better?" He asked.

"Much, thank you. We had weekly showers but no soap. Soap is wonderful. I have a new appreciation for it now."

Anna was still trying to grasp what had happened to her in the past 24 hours. She had been a prisoner at Buchenwald, singled out for execution, left on a deserted road in a perfidious murder scam, then wound up in a farmhouse and a bathtub filled with hot water. Was she dreaming?

"We saved you some breakfast," Greta said, breaking Anna's thoughts. "Would you have a cup of tea?"

"Yes, for the tea and breakfast."

Anna enjoyed the tea and home baked bread as much as the bath. She was anxious to know more about Greta and Johann. Greta took Anna back through the story of their lives, how they met, their children, their simple life-style and finally, their work in the underground. Anna could imagine there were hundreds, perhaps thousands of good German people like the Thieles who were risking their lives every day. Greta did not want to inquire of Anna, but Anna did briefly share about her parents, her life in Berlin and her work at the University. She did not mention that she had saved the life of Ernst Bishoff, but she was curious to know of the man in the barn

"What can you tell me about him...if anything," she asked. "Will he be coming into the house?"

"I can tell you what I know which is not much. His name is Josef. He was brought to us in mid-January and apparently had escaped a death march from Auschwitz, a camp in Poland. When he was brought here, he weighed about 90 pounds...just skin and bones. In two months he has gained 30 pounds. He stays in the barn and sleeps in a small storage room. We placed a wood burning stove there for him and vented it. He refused to sleep in the house. But he takes breakfast and dinner with us and sometimes takes walks. He's very distant and speaks very little. We haven't asked about his experiences."

That afternoon, Anna saw him. Josef was walking in a meadow that bordered the farm. He climbed the fence that contained the sheep. She noticed that he was rather tall, about six feet and very thin. She only saw him briefly and never saw his face. Anna had heard of the death camps in Poland. She suspected the trauma had overwhelmed him.

Anna looked forward to the evening meal. She wanted to become better acquainted with Johann and Greta, and Josef if possible. It might be another month or so before they could be liberated. She was anxious to be able to return to Buchenwald to look for Eric. She had tried not to think about him too much but prayed daily for his safety.

Anna soon learned that the evening meal was a reward for a hard days work. Greta and Johann were sturdy 50-year olds who put in long days. Their living was meager but rewarding. They were sitting with Anna by the fire when Josef entered. Anna stood up to greet the man.

"Hello, I'm Anna," she said, extending her hand.

"Anna," Josef said politely as he shook her hand. He sat down on the sofa and stared into the fire. Anna stared at him. She was surprised at his youthful appearance. He had sharp angular features and a crop of dark hair, windblown and unkempt. His face was kind. She thought he might be handsome with another month of good food.

The evening was pleasant although Josef said nothing during the meal. When they finished eating he stood to leave, thanked Greta, then excused himself.

Over the next week the process with Josef repeated itself. Each day he walked, exchanged polite greetings, and disappeared after dinner. He remained withdrawn and unresponsive.

One evening after dinner Anna decided to attempt dialogue. She felt even the most grievous experience could be overcome if it could be shared.

"Josef," she said softly. "Can you tell us about Auschwitz?"

He gave no sign of surprise. "What do you want to know?"

Josef looked at the floor. His eyes filled with tears. He did not respond for several minutes.

"Are you sure you want to know?"

"Yes."

"Auschwitz...it was a place for killing. My wife and I were deported there along with our three-year-old son. We were taken in December of 1943. We had been living in a ghetto in Krakow where I was a school teacher. We were the last of the Jewish people to go. When we arrived I was separated from my family. I didn't see them again. I was given a job...the task of collecting the clothing of those who went to the gas chambers. Then I was made to move the dead to the crematoriums. I was one of the sondercommandos...the crematorium warriors. Every day thousands of innocent people... men, women, children...were thrown into the ovens. They literally disappeared up the chimney.

During my second week there, I was collecting clothes of the people killed that day. I found my wife's dress and her shoes. They were in a pile with my son's playsuit. The gas chambers...they were disguised as showers. There were holding pens where several hundred people would stand...and signs that read 'to the baths and disinfecting rooms.' Most of the time symphony music was played on loud speakers...Mozart, Bach. *SS* officers would stand on wooden towers above the pens. They shouted for everyone to remove their clothes. Of course, the men and women were reluctant to do this. If they were too slow the officers would come down and beat them. Children clung to their parents and those without parents to each other. They were told to place their clothes in neat piles so they could find them after the showers.

The people tried to comfort each other. They spoke in Polish or Yiddish. Before the gas chamber door opened, most were already dazed with fear. They knew something dreadful was going to happen. They could feel it...my god, they were standing there naked with guards ready to beat them. Of course, they were scared...how could they not know was about to happen?

I remember a young mother undressing her daughter. The child looked about two years old. Then the mother took her own clothes off. She held the child in her arms and rocked her from side to side. They were a picture of my wife and son. They were going to their deaths....naked and afraid.

The chamber doors...they were plated steel on rollers. Inside the concrete structure there were pillars, some to support the ceiling, some to hold the Zyklon-B cyanide pellets. There were shower heads in the ceiling to deceive the victims. As the doors rolled open the SS officers would scream for the people to get in. After the doors were shut, some of the officers liked to look through glass in the doors to watch them dying. Then two men with gas masks would get on top of the roof and pour the cyanide pellets into open cylinders that went into the chamber. These cylinders had perforations to allow the poison gas to escape into the chamber.

I saw this. I heard the coughing and the screaming. The people would bang on the doors. And then the screaming would stop...usually within 10 minutes or so...and then everything would be quiet. The exhaust fans would clear the chamber. Then when the doors were opened the bodies would tumble out, usually the stronger men first because they were able to claw their way to the door. Pregnant women sometimes in late term, had partially delivered their babies...the head would be expelled out of the birth canal.

Sondercommandos would pull the bodies out amid excrement and vomit. Each adult was checked by German orderlies for jewelry and gold fillings and these would be removed. Then the bodies were transported to the crematoria. This was done in large dumpsters on rails.

Most of the clothing I collected had a yellow Star of David sewn on the front of the garment. The clothes, shoes and eye glasses were all saved, obviously of more value than human lives. My job was to collect the clothing and then load the bodies into the ovens. In the last few months, to save time and expenses, many of the younger children were thrown alive into the ovens. I witnessed all of this. Auschwitz was a place for killing!"

Auschwitz was liberated on January 27, 1945. The Germans tried to destroy the gas chambers and crematoria with dynamite. Auschwitz, however, was only one of many death camps. Most, if not all of them, kept *Totenbuch* or death books. But all were incomplete and many of them destroyed. The final number of deaths has been estimated by most scholars to be between *five and six million* souls.

* * *

In the spring of 1945, the end came quickly. The 1,000-year reign predicted by Hitler for the Third Reich ended after a laconic 12 years. The fall of the Ruhr industrial area in west central Germany was key. The area was bordered by three rivers; the Rhine to the west, the Ruhr to the south, and the Lippe to the north. About 80 percent of German coal and steel production was centered in the Ruhr. Allied forces mounted a successful campaign to encircle and capture this area. In doing so, they captured several hundred thousand Wehrmacht troops. Coal was the dominant energy source for all of Germany and after the loss of the Rumanian and Hungarian oil fields, there was a critical shortage of aviation fuel for fighters and petrol for tanks.

The hope for 'miracle weapons' was a sophistry. Launching sites for the V-2 were lost with the occupation of the French and

Belgian coasts. It was true that Germany had developed a jet fighter, and that the conventional Allied prop planes were no match for the jets. But they required a special type of fuel and the few refineries for this fuel production had been taken out with precision bombing. These planes also needed longer runways which were easy to spot and destroy.

The effort to develop a successful fission bomb never materialized. After the defection of Hanz Eichenwald, Werner Heisenberg became head of the project. Heisenberg was an outstanding physicist and was made director of the Kaiser Wilhelm Institute of Physics. He may have opposed the development of an atomic bomb on moral grounds but he may also have realized that Germany would need large amounts of Uranium 235 which had to be separated from U-238, a process that was both extremely difficult and expensive. For whatever the reason, during a meeting with Albert Speer, minister of munitions, Heisenberg did not pursue development of the bomb. This, despite the fact that nuclear fission had first been achieved in Germany just four years earlier in 1938 by Otto Hahn. As it turned out, Hitler had little understanding of fission and even less interest.

By mid-March the Germans had lost another 350,000 men who were killed, wounded or captured. Hitler was desperate. In a prolonged meeting with his generals and in a fit of rage, he contemplated completely denouncing the Geneva Convention and executing all POW's. Most of his staff objected to this policy on legal grounds and as a result, it was never established. Still, hundreds of POWs perished when forced on long marches without adequate food or water.

Thousands of German troops gave themselves up as quickly as possible to the advancing British-American forces. Nazi generals and military leaders were fanatical in their reprisals. On one occasion early on the afternoon of March seventh, units of the 9th U.S. Armored Division approached a railroad bridge over the Rhine at Ludendorff. They expected the bridge to be destroyed. When it was not, their tanks poured across and drove back a weak German defense force. By the end of the day the Americans had a strong bridgehead on the east bank. Soon after, the eight officers in charge of defending the bridge were executed by a special 'Flying Tribunal' that had been set up by the Fuehrer. There were no second chances with Hitler.

Over the next few weeks, the Nazi Supreme Commander was becoming a physical wreck. His vengeance turned from the advancing enemy to his own troops and the German people. His railing against his commanders grew to a fever pitch. In meeting after meeting, he stood before them flushed with rage and trembling. He would complete his tirades with truculent outbursts at individual staff members. It was during one of these outbursts that he made one of the last momentous decisions of his life. On March 19th he issued a general order to make Germany a vast wasteland. All military, industrial, communication and transportation facilities were to be destroyed. Nothing would be left to help the German people endure their defeat.

Fortunately, before the 'scorched earth' policy was handed down, it had been anticipated by Albert Speer, Minister for Armament and War Production. On March fifteenth, he drew up a memorandum in which he strongly opposed the policy. He presented his views to Hitler on March eighteenth. It said in part:

"In four to eight weeks the final collapse of the German economy must be expected with certainty. . .After that collapse the war cannot be continued even militarily . . . We must do everything to

maintain, even if only in a most primitive manner, a basis for the existence of the nation to the last. . . .We have no right at this stage of the war, to carry out demolitions which might affect the life of the people."

Hitler was unmoved. The next day the egregious policy was handed down. It was more comprehensive than could be imagined and called for the destruction of all industrial plants, water works, gas works, electrical facilities, food and clothing stores, railway and communication installations, canals, ships, bridges, railcars, and locomotives – all of them. But the country was spared this catastrophe, in part by the rapid Allied advances and also by the adroit, almost superhuman efforts of Speer. He mobilized military personnel who, in direct opposition to Hitler's orders, raced about the country to make certain the plan was not carried out.

Once the German forces in the Ruhr were trapped, some 21 divisions, the Nazi defense front was split leaving a 200-mile gap open to the Elbe River and the heart of Germany. On April eleventh, a spearhead reached the Elbe near Magburg. The U.S. Ninth Army was now only 60 miles from Berlin.

Another significant event was occurring about 100 miles south at Buchenwald. While the Germans were preparing to evacuate the camp, they discovered block-66 and the 600 Jewish boys. On April tenth, Julian Richburg was ordered to have all children in the camp on the parade ground at 10:00 a.m. to evacuate the camp. Now that the *SS* had been made aware that children were being hidden, he had no choice. So there they were, hundreds of Jewish boys standing before the gate waiting for it to be opened. More than 60,000 prisoners, including all the women, had already left the camp. As the guards were preparing to open the gates, two U.S. P-51 Mustang fighter planes suddenly made a low-level pass over the camp.

History records the planes as coming 'out of nowhere' with roaring engines soaring at about 500 ft. As sirens sounded throughout the camp, all of the guards scattered, and the boys ran back to their barracks. That was the last time Julian Richburg and Beryl Yenzer saw uniformed German soldiers. The following day, advance elements of the American Third Army, commanded by General George Patton, arrived and drove the remaining Nazis from the camp. The American soldiers found some 21,000 starving prisoners still holding on to life in the hell of Buchenwald.

Master Sergeant Paten Johnson from Provo, Utah, was astonished when he opened the door to block-66. He stared at the faces of more than 600 Jewish boys who had been saved by two Jewish underground operatives. Within days, the international Red Cross set up a relief station to care for the Buchenwald survivors... among them a large burly man named Beryl Yenzer. He was holding a small and very frail four-year old boy named Eric.

Nuremberg was the city of the great Nazi rallies of the '30s, rallies in which Hitler would address up to 50,000 party faithful at a time, with his orotund speeches. By April 16, 1945, Nuremberg was occupied by American forces - on the same day Russian troops broke loose from their bridgeheads over the Oder River and marched to the outskirts of Berlin. On the afternoon of April twenty-fifth, patrols of the U.S. 69th Infantry Division met elements of the Russian 58th Guard Division at a village called Torgue, on the Elbe River. North and South Germany were severed, and Hitler was trapped in Berlin. The last days of the Third Reich were at hand.

In Berlin, the thunder of Russian heavy artillery could be heard. Hitler had returned for the final time on January sixteenth. His plan was to eventually make it to his mountain Villa, the Berghof, at Berchtesgaden in the mountains of Barbarossa. On April tenth, he sent his house staff but he himself was cut-off and could not join them.

Since the attempt on his life the previous July, he had grown distrustful of everyone. He was living in his bunker 50 feet below the bombed out Chancellery. He fumed to one of his secretaries.

"I can rely on no one. They all betray me. The whole business makes me sick….If anything happens to me, Germany will be left without a leader. I have no successor. Hess is mad, Goering has lost the sympathy of the people, and Himmler would be rejected by the party – besides, he is so completely inartistic….Rack your brain and tell me who my successor is to be!"

Strange, with the disastrous end staring him in the face, this physical wreck of a man was obsessed with who would be his successor, as if there would be anything to succeed to. In a bizarre paradigm, a few of his most fanatical followers clung to the hope they would be saved by a last-minute miracle. Goebbels above all embraced this hope.

One evening in the bunker, Goebbels was reading to Hitler from the History of Frederich the Great, the King of Prussia from 1740 to1786. This war hero frequently led his forces into battle personally and reportedly had several horses shot out from under him. He was admired as a tactical genius. Hitler identified with this man who had established Prussia as one of the five European powers of the day. Like Frederich, who took no pleasure from his popularity with the Volk and instead, preferred the company of his pet greyhounds, Hitler also had strained relationships with those around him - but he loved his pets.

The last portion read by Goebbels went as follows:

"Brave King! Wait yet a little while, and the days of your suffering will be over. Already the sun of your good fortune stands behind the clouds and will soon rise on you."

Hitler's eyes filled with tears. He wanted to search for the 'good fortune' that he believed would be bestowed on him.

The following day Goebbels acquired two horoscopes. One for the Fuehrer, drawn up the day he became Chancellor; the other of the Weimar Republic, composed by an obscure astrologer at the birth of the Republic in 1918. Both horoscopes had made similar predictions. Amazingly, both predicted the outbreak of the war in 1939, the early victories of 1941, and the reversals for the German forces leading up to 1945. In April they predicted temporary successes. Just as in the Seven Years' War, when the death of Czarina brought about a 'miracle' to the House of Brandenburg, Goebbels was expecting a death that could change the fortunes of this war.

Goebbels returned to Berlin the next night after yet another RAF bombing. The remains of the Chancellery and the Adlon Hotel were burning. As he ascended the steps to the Propaganda Ministry, he was approached by an aid with 'urgent news'. The aid shouted, "Roosevelt has died!"

* * *

Anna had spent an amazing four weeks with Greta and Johann. She had not only gained her weight back but had experienced a great deal of emotional and spiritual healing. She saw Josef at meals. She had worked to befriend him but had little success. She understood he might never recover from the trauma of Auschwitz. She was not certain she could recover given the same experience. And she knew she didn't have the skills or the knowledge to help him.

In long conversations with Greta, Anna told her own short history and the stories about how she had become a surgeon, fallen in love, fled the Nazis and lost Christian. With the story of Josef in Auschwitz and her own experiences at Buchenwald, she felt blessed to be alive. She did not yet know that approximately 6,000,000 Jewish men, women and children had perished at the hands of the Nazi Reich. But she knew she had designed a new goal for her life. She would find Eric and raise him as her own. She had first considered this when she placed his feeding tube in the hope of saving his life. When the boy survived, she began to love him. Was he a gift from God? Was he the child she would never have with Christian?

The news traveled quickly once Buchenwald was liberated. Within seven days Allied forces had moved rapidly to within a day's travel to Berlin. Anna felt it was safe to make the short journey to Buchenwald. Johann agreed to take her in his truck. They were now in Allied occupied territory except that Anna had no documentation of her identity.

During the 20-minute ride they encountered one Allied check point. They were allowed to pass when Johann explained that Anna had been a prisoner and was returning to look for a child. Anna displayed her forearm tattoo to the inquiring corporal, who seemed bewildered to find that human beings were apparently branded like live stock. It was also the first time Anna and Johann had traveled in open country without any sight of Nazi military. This fact alone was testimony to the truth - the war was indeed over - or almost over.

Buchenwald was different and yet the same. There were about 50 workers with the Red Cross team and a medical team from France. Their goal was to save as many of the starving 20,000 in the camp as possible. A detachment of Belgian military had been left to aid in this effort. Most of the Belgian troops spoke some German, enough to help Anna learn what she needed to know. It was quickly apparent that the children were not there. They had been sent to a holding area in Dresden, another 50 kilometers south-east of Leipzig. Anna was disappointed but not discouraged. She was able to accomplish two important things with the aid of the Red Cross. She sent word to her family and she received identity papers.

It had been more than three years since Hanz and Marlena Eichenwald had seen or heard from their daughter. They had settled onto life in England with the academic teaching appointment for their livelihood. They both spoke their new language with thick German accents, Hanz better than his wife. Hanz was highly respected in his field of Quantum physics and had been a stellar addition to the department at Cambridge.

Marlena had made a few friends among the faculty wives, but she knew that as Germans, she and Hans were eyed with suspicion when they were away from the University. They had been able to find a synagogue and had met several Jewish couples there. One man was a physician who had fled Denmark just prior to German occupation.

Not a day went by that Marlena did not think of Anna. They had heard of the death camps and work camps. Marlena prayed that Anna was alive, but deep in her heart she feared the worst. She knew about the gas chambers. She would think of this and shut her eyes and her mind to the thought of her daughter being taken there. Hanz, on the otherhand, was an optimist. He believed that Anna was alive. Perhaps she was being hidden by the underground and they would soon hear from her. A number of concentration/death camps had been in the BBC news reports. Buchenwald was on the list. Hanz paid little attention. Marlena had the names memorized.

The cablegram arrived on a Tuesday morning. It came from the International Red Cross – and from Buchenwald. Marlena did not open it. She couldn't make her hands move. She knew the Allies had liberated the camp and that there would be a death list. Was this the formal notification of her precious daughter's demise?

She sat in the main room of the flat and felt the grief descending through her body into her heart. She tried to conjure up old memories of their times together. She tried not to cry.

Hanz came home at his usual 6:00 p.m. When he walked in the door he knew immediately that something was wrong. The house was dark and he called out to his wife.

"Marlena!"

"In here," was the quiet, labored response.

Hanz walked into the room. He could not see the unopened envelope on the end table. "Do we have news of Anna?"

"Yes."

"A cablegram?"

"Yes! There on the table."

Hanz saw the envelope, unopened. "So, you have not read it?"

Marlena was silent and shook her head from side to side. Hanz quickly opened the envelope and his eyes searched the contents. Then he smiled and slowly sank down beside his wife.

"Duleiber himmel!"

Hearing her husband cry out 'good heavens," Marlena began to laugh and cry simultaneously.

"She's alive?"

"Listen," he said, "I have survived and am well….searching for my child! God is good! Will explain later. Love, Anna."

Marlena almost shouted, "Anna has a child?" She sat back slowly as the tears flowed. "Anna has a child."

The International Red Cross was overwhelmed and faced thousands of problems. Other aid agencies were on their way, but it might be weeks before help arrived. Their priority now was to save lives. It would have been a tragedy for a man to have lived through starvation, beatings, torture and abuse, only to die after the Nazis left. But in truth, many had irreversible nutritional problems, typhus, intestinal parasites, or tuberculosis. These were at least the most common problems. Close to 1,000 men needed hospitalization which was impossible. Red Cross workers were putting in 15-hour days and that was all anyone could ask.

When Anna returned to the farm, she filled Greta in on the situation at Buchenwald. There was no sign of Colonel Bishoff or any German soldiers. Greta and Johann had no money of significance but had a small savings of 500 marks hidden in the floor. They gave Anna 75 marks and searched to find her a ride to Leipzig. They belonged to a co-op of 10 dairy farmers who sent milk twice weekly to Leipzig for pasteurization. The driver agreed to take her to the center of the city after dropping the milk delivery. Anna said good-by to her dear friends and vowed she would stay in touch with them when and if the postal service returned to normal.

Little had changed in the Leipzig landscape, but everything had changed politically. The ball-bearing plant had been leveled. Other than that, things looked the same with the exception of the flags with swastikas that used to fly. These were gone, as were the Gestapo and SS. Anna reminded herself as she walked by the

University Hospital toward Sarah's apartment, that the swastika emblem had derived from Sanskrit and its original meaning was 'good luck.' That meaning would never be denoted again from the swastika. It would forever symbolize evil. But she was pleasantly surprised to realize too, that this once feared symbol of the Nazi Reich was gone and would never return.

It was about 3:00 p.m. on a beautiful spring day. Fluffy clouds drifted lazily above and flowering plum trees were beginning to bloom. Anna passed the Mendelssohn-Haus, then turned onto Goldschmidtstrasse to Sarah's apartment. She sat on the front steps. As she thought of seeing her dear friend, she began to smile.

"She'll think I'm a ghost," she whispered aloud with a smile.

Anna's thoughts drifted back to her days in the resistance, working with Landis Kohler and Max. The risks were great and so were the rewards. Many had died for the cause and none more courageously than Sophie Scholl and the students of the White Rose. Anna silently prayed that the bravery of those students would not be forgotten and the freedom from tyranny they sought would always be defended.

Anna kept her eye out for Sarah. She always took the same route home. As a slight breeze blew the strands of thick black hair across her brow, Anna realized she was beginning to think like a woman again. The clothes given her by Greta were thread bare and faded. Anna laughed to herself. At least they were better than prison garb. It was at that instant that Sarah rounded the corner and began to walk towards Anna. Anna continued sitting, knowing Sarah had not seen her, then stood and turned toward her.

They made eye contact. Sarah slowed to a full stop. For a brief moment she seemed confused. Then she let out a shriek and began running. Anna did the same. The two ran into each other's arms, both in tears. Sarah was the first to speak,

"Anna! Anna! I can't believe you're here. I can't believe you're safe, alive." Tears streamed down their faces.

"Yes, yes! Sarah, I'm safe, I'm alive."

CHAPTER 22
The Coward's Escape

The following week was a festival of non-stop chatter and laughter for the two soul- mates. Anna had only been away for some six months, but a lifetime of events had unfolded in that short time. Sarah wanted to hear everything – the good and the bad. Anna's description of the rape attempt was particularly difficult for Sarah to hear. As Anna finished the macabre tale, Sarah stared back in shock.

"So, this character hanged himself! Well, a fitting end to his life, I suppose." She sighed. "This is all so sad, Anna."

The stories continued over the hours. Anna related her life in Buchenwald, Roland, Erika, and her work in the V-2 production plant. Then she began the story of Eric. Sarah interrupted several times to ask for more details. Finally, Anna went through the chronology of her 'execution.' Sarah was stunned. Then she asked Anna to go back to the surgery on Ernst Bishoff. "How close was he to dying? How could a woman do that kind of work?"

Anna, smiling said, "Just like a man. It's a process that takes many years of hard work with long hours. Doctors enjoy taking care of sick people…there are great challenges…surgery is a particular kind of challenge. Colonel Bishoff was dying and I was there, standing between him and eternity. There was no time to question what to do. I was trained and I used what I knew. That's the story. It's not magic."

"And you saw Hitler, the evil man himself?"

"I did," Anna replied. "It was a very strange experience. Years before, as a student, I had traveled to hear one of his speeches. I felt his charisma. There were about 40,000 of us at the rally, so we couldn't really get close enough to see him. But to be in his presence, well, it was foreboding."

"Do you mind talking about your near-death experience?"

"No, there's really not much to tell. I was pulled out of work one afternoon and placed in a *SS* car. I thought I was going to be interrogated about the children, but when the car went in the opposite direction from the prison, I knew their intention was to kill me. It was a bizarre feeling. Your mind is racing, and your heart is pounding. I thought about my parents. I thought about the fact that I was never going to see them again. And I thought of you. A bullet to the head is instant death, and I thought about that too.

We went to this very remote area and I was pulled out of the car. Then Colonel Bishoff told me to walk in front of him and ordered the others to get back into the car. He started talking to me while we walked. It was like being in a dream. One moment you're sure your life is over. Then the next second, you realize you've been spared and you're not going to die. You make that switch immediately, so you don't really feel everything at the moment. I mean, it all happened so fast. Believe it or not, I'm still trying to absorb and process what actually happened out there. I do know one thing for certain. I know God protected me. Now for whatever reason, I don't know. But it wasn't a coincidence. It was supposed to turn out the way it did. I just have to figure out why."

Sarah stopped asking questions and Anna didn't volunteer anything else. She would not speak of Auschwitz. She had decided to take that to her grave.

The morning after Joseph Goebbels was notified of Roosevelt's death, he received a telephone call from the Nazi Minister of Finance, Count Schwerin von Krosigk. The fatuous former Rhodes Scholar wished to congratulate the Propaganda Minister and assure him that the death of the American President was a divine judgment. Hitler's ministers were grasping for straws as they continued reading the stars for signs against the backdrop of the Third Reich's burning buildings. The 'sign' that was most evident was Berlin. It had been reduced to rubble.

The following week, on April 20, a celebration was held in Hitler's bunker in honor of his 56th birthday. All of the old guard was in attendance, including Himmler, Goebbels, Goering, and Martin Bormann, Hitler's personal assistant. But the most nugatory one in the group was Joachim von Ribbentrop, a relative latecomer to the Nazi cause. In the 1920's he was apolitical and was extensively involved with Jewish bankers and businessmen. He met Anna Elizabeth Henkell, the daughter of a wealthy champagne producer, and they married. In 1925, he persuaded an aunt, Gertrud von Ribbentrop, whose husband had been knighted, to adopt him. This gave him the title of an aristocrat. In time, he became Hitler's foreign minister and a rabid anti-Semite. But feelings toward him were strained and he was resented by the elite inner circle. Goebbels expressed their feelings when he wrote of von Ribbentrop.

'…he bought his name, married his money, and swindled his way into office.'

Hitler had truly lost contact with reality. He told the others at the party that the Russians were about to suffer their 'bloodiest defeat'. The generals knew better and urged Hitler to leave Berlin. He refused.

Later that night two of his oldest and most trusted confidants left. Himmler and Goering made their getaway. Goering took with him millions in booty he had stolen from Jewish businesses and stored at his estate. Each man left believing that soon, Hitler would be dead. Each man also believed he would be Hitler's replacement. They never saw their Fuehrer again.

Although not allowed at the birthday party, another player in the saga had moved into the bunker the previous week. Eva Braun had met Adolph Hitler in 1928 when, as a 17-year old, she began working as an office and lab assistant for Heinrich Himmler at Nazi party headquarters. She had limited contact with Hitler until 1931, after the death of his niece, Geli Raubal. Geli was 23-years old and the daughter of his half-sister. Hitler had become infatuated with her, and in time obsessively jealous, carefully controlling who she saw and where she went. One morning she was found dead, a bullet in her head. The death was ruled a suicide but the pistol belonged to Hitler. Her death left him distraught and depressed for a while. But soon enough, he was back to politics as usual. After this, he began seeing more of Braun but he still paid little attention to her. This time she was the one infatuated. When he did not return her attention, she eventually took an overdose. He could not afford the scandal of being linked to a second suicide while his political future was still unsecured, so he bought her a villa in a Munich suburb. In time, she moved to his mountain retreat at the Berghof near Berchtesgaden and became singularly devoted to him. Evan Braun was never allowed in important political meetings and had little or no influence on his decisions. They never appeared in public together as a couple. Still, she enjoyed a privileged and sheltered life until the end, and she was determined to share his end.

On April twenty-first his last military order was given for *SS* General Steiner to lead an all-out counterattack against the Russians in the southern suburbs of Berlin. Hitler waited the next 24 hours for news of the Steiner attack, but it was never attempted. The next day he stayed on the phone calling various command posts for news of the action, but no one knew. Steiner was nowhere to be found, let alone his army.

At his last military conference on the twenty-second, his rage was uncontrollable. Everyone had deserted him. He determined that he would take 'personal command' of the defense of Berlin. Himmler called and urged him to leave Berlin. Ribbentrop called for the same reason. But Hitler's response was to call for a secretary so he could dictate an announcement to be read to the German people on a national radio hookup. The announcement - he would stay in Berlin 'until the end'.

He called Goebbels and invited the Reich Minister of Information and Propaganda, along with his wife Magda and their six children, to join him and move into the Fuehrerbunker, away from their bombed out home in Wilhelmstrasse Garden. He also called his adjuvant, Julius Schaub, to burn papers he wished destroyed.

Finally on the evening of April twenty-second, he called Field Marshal General Wilhelm Keitel and Oberkommando der Wehrmacht Alfred Jodl. Both had been at his side during the entire war. He ordered them to proceed south and take command of the remaining forces of defense. Keitel had always been a lackey and said nothing. Jodl, on the other hand, protested that Hitler was deserting his troops at the moment of defeat, and that he should not abandon them. Hitler retorted, "Well then, Goering can take over!"

General Karl Koller, Chief of Staff of the Air Force, was chosen to inform Goering. There were in effect, two messages for Goering. First, Hitler was going to commit suicide. Second, Goering was to negotiate a peace.

At 3:30 am on April twenty-third Koller flew in a fighter plane to Goering's estate at Obersalzberg, near Berchtesgaden. Thus began the short struggle for the rapidly crumbling Nazi regime.

Goering quickly reviewed a copy of Hitler's decree of June 29, 1941, stating that Goering was to succeed him if he were killed or incapacitated. Goering sent for Hans Lammers, the State Secretary of the Reich Chancellery, for legal counsel. All agreed that Hitler was now incapacitated and might soon be dead. Goering had a clear duty to assume leadership of the Reich.

That very evening, the man Hitler had called 'der treue Heinrich (the loyal Heinrich), Heinrich Himmler, was himself assuming the powers of succession. Himmler was in Luebeck meeting with a Swedish diplomat, Count Bernadotte, the vice-chairman of the Swedish Red Cross. The meeting took place at the Swedish consulate. Himmler stressed to Bernadotte that Hitler would be dead in a day or so, and Himmler wanted to communicate to General Eisenhower that the Reich was ready to surrender - but only to the Allies. RAF bombing had knocked out all power in Lubeck, so a letter was drafted that night by candlelight. Goering was less perfidious. He drafted and sent a telegram to his Fuehrer that evening to make sure of the chain of command. It read as follows:

"My Fuehrer! In view of your decision to remain in the fortress of Berlin, do you agree that I take over at once the total leadership

of the Reich, with full freedom of action at home and abroad as your deputy, in accordance with your decree of June 29, 1941? If no reply is received by 10 o'clock tonight, I shall take it for granted that you have lost your freedom of action, and shall consider the conditions of your decree as fulfilled, and shall act for the best interests of our country and our people. You know what I feel for you in this gravest hour of my life. Words fail me to express myself. May God protect you, and speed you quickly here in spite of all."

On the night the Goering telegram arrived, Albert Speer, the remarkable architect and Armament Minister landed in a small military plane on a broad boulevard near the Brandenburg gate, one block from the Chancellery. Speer was loyal to Hitler and came to make a confession that he had not carried out the Fuehrer's orders for the 'scorched earth' destruction of Germany. He expected to be arrested and possibly shot for insubordination. Much to his surprise, the opposite happened. Hitler showed no anger or malevolence. Instead, he seemed touched by Speer's candor. This may have been because of his long time affection for this man whom he considered a fellow artist.

Martin Bormann, personal secretary to Hitler and head of the Nazi Party Chancellery, had held up giving the telegram to Hitler. Bormann was a bitter enemy of both Goering and Himmler. He had always resented their positions in the party and had looked for years for ways to discredit them. He presented the Goering telegram to Hitler as an 'ultimatum' and stated that what Goering was doing was 'treasonous'. Immediately, Hitler went from complacent to enrage. He railed about Goering, stating the man had been corrupted by drugs and the fortune he had amassed from Jewish businesses. Soon after this sophistry, he did a turnabout.

"Well, let Goering negotiate the capitulation all the same. It doesn't matter anyway who does it."

Then just as quickly, after being prompted by Bormann, Hitler dictated a telegram informing Goering that he had committed 'high treason' and normally would pay with his life. But because of his long history of service he would only be forced to resign all of his authority and positions in the Reich. Then, on his own and without Hitler's knowledge, Bormann ordered the immediate arrest of Goering by the *SS* in Berchtesgaden.

On April 24, the last two visitors to the Chancellery bunker were summoned. Hanna Reitsch was a test pilot. She had tested many of the experimental planes for the Luftwaffe and had become a close friend and lover of General Robert Ritter von Greim, who was to be appointed Commander of the Luftwaffe. Two days later the two comrades-in-arms flew a light single engine plane into central Berlin. As they descended, they were under heavy fire from Russian anti-aircraft installations and von Greim was hit in the leg. Reitsch took the controls and landed on the same boulevard where Speer had come in. They made it to the Fuehrerbunker where von Greim received medical attention. While his leg wounds were being bandaged Hitler entered the room and asked if von Greim knew why he had been called.

"No, my Fuehrer."

Hitler then began his harangue as his face became red and his eyes bulged. "Because Hermann Goering has betrayed and deserted both me and his fatherland. Behind my back he has established contact with the enemy. His action was a mark of cowardice. Against my orders he has gone to save himself at Berchtesgaden. From there he sent me a disrespectful telegram. It was an ultimatum!

A crass ultimatum! Now nothing remains. Nothing is spared me. No allegiances are kept, no honor lived up to, to disappointments that I have not had, no betrayals that I have not experienced, and now this above all else! Nothing remains. Every wrong has already been done me. I immediately had Goering arrested as a traitor to the Reich, took from him all his offices, and removed him from all organizations. That is why I have called you."

Two days later on the 28th, the radio listening post of the Propaganda Ministry picked up a transmission from the BBC. It was a dispatch from Stockholm. The news was of the secret negotiations of Himmler to surrender the German Army to Eisenhower. To Hitler, this was the cruelest blow of all.

Reitsch and von Greim had flown into central Berlin believing they would likely die there. They had obtained cyanide ampoules in the event of a worst-case scenario. But now, everything had changed. Hitler came to the pair and exclaimed in haste, "A traitor must never succeed me as Fuehrer. You must get out ensuring Himmler does not."

Now the two pilots would be putting their lives on the line once again for their Supreme Commander. Reitsch and von Greim were the stuff of legends. The general, who had just been made Germany's last Field Marshal, was a Bavarian by birth. He served in the artillery corps in WW1 only to transfer to the air force in 1915. He was spectacular as a fighter pilot flying two- seater bi-wing aircraft. By war's end, he had 28 kills. He was awarded the *Pour le Merite* (Blue Max) and the Bavarian Military Order of Max Joseph. This medal made him a knight or *Ritter* – a title of nobility. He was now Ritter von Greim.

In 1933, Goering had asked him to help rebuild the Luftwaffe, and he eventually began training fighter pilots in secrecy. He met the diminutive Reitsch in 1938 when she began flying the Focke-Achgelis Fa61, a fully controllable helicopter. Although married, von Greim was attracted to Reitsch and they became fast friends. The following year Reitsch was critically injured when she crashed a prototype of the rocket-propelled Messerschmitt Me 163. She spent five months recuperating and at that time, von Greim spent much of his time with her. She was awarded the Iron Cross First Class and their friendship morphed into a permanent bond.

As they waited for the cover of darkness, Hanna exclaimed to her companion, "I was prepared to die with the Fuehrer. When we flew in I thought it would be our last flight."

"War is not only treacherous but totally unpredictable," he replied. "Now I am the Field Marshal of the Luftwaffe, but I have no Luftwaffe. Our mission is to arrest a traitor to our cause, not die for the Fatherland. So it has all come to this."

Hanna stroked his head. "What is honorable?" she asked. "We are still serving the Fuehrer."

She leaned over and kissed his forehead. There was only silence and the two slipped deep into thought. They both knew their time was short. Their only regret was not having a future together. The previous year she had learned of the prison camp atrocities from a friend who was an air attaché in Sweden and had decided not to share this information with Robert. He was a soldier first and last. She wanted to spare him the discouragement she knew would befall him if he was to learn of this.

Darkness settled in and they made their way to the Tiergarten strip where their plane awaited. It had been only lightly damaged and was now refueled. The Russians were only blocks away but the strip had been kept secured by a German brigade. He was helped into the small craft and she followed. Quickly, she went through her pre-flight checks and snapped on the ignition switch. In seconds the engine was roaring. There was no time for a warm up. She pushed the throttle and they were off. Russian soldiers were taken by surprise. Thinking that Hitler might be escaping, they fired small arms fire at the plane as it began to disappear into the darkness. But it was a futile effort.

Their orders had been to fly to Plon, near the Baltic. Von Ritter turned to Reitsch. "Take us back to Munich. I am the Field Marshal of the Air Force, not a policeman. I have no intention of trying to arrest Himmler."

Munich was now in Allied hands and the two were arrested just after touchdown. As they parted, they were allowed a final embrace. They would never see each other again.

Later on the same evening, Goebbels had located a municipal councilor who was fighting with a unit only blocks away. Sometime between 1:00 and 3:00 a.m., Eva Braun was awarded for her loyalty to Adolph Hitler, who formally married his mistress. His secretaries described the ceremony as a "death marriage". On the marriage certificate his bride signed Eva B, then crossed out the B and signed Eva Hitler, born Braun. Joseph Goebbels and Martin Bormann signed as witnesses.

The wedding party and guests retreated to Hitler's private apartment for a breakfast celebration complete with champagne. Sharing in this celebration were his secretaries, cook, remaining generals, and Dr. and Frau Goebbels. Goebbels recalled his own wedding when the Fuhrer was his best man. Hitler spoke of his dramatic life and National Socialism, both now about to end. There was a short reception. But it was in fact, a farewell line and only Hitler made his way to say his goodbyes. He awkwardly addressed each person mumbling a 'thank you' for their service. He passed cyanide ampoules to both of his secretaries in case they decided to die with him in the bunker. This act of sophistry was just another illustration of a man who had lived his life impervious to reality.

Guests melted away, some in tears. Finally, Hitler himself left to meet with one of his secretaries to dictate his will and testament. It was almost 5:00 a.m. when the leader of the Third Reich began to have recorded what he referred to as his 'Political Testament'. It was divided into two parts. His appeal to posterity and his direction for a successor. The first three paragraphs are as follows:

"More than thirty years have passed since I made my modest contribution as a volunteer in the First World War, which was forced upon the Reich.

In these three decades, love and loyalty to my people alone have guided me in all my thoughts, actions, and life. They gave me power to make the most difficult decisions which have ever confronted mortal man....

It is untrue that I or anybody else in Germany wanted war in 1939. It was wanted and provoked exclusively by those international statesmen who either were of Jewish origin or worked for Jewish interests."

He continued the lie that he had proposed a peaceable solution to the British before he invaded Poland. He stated that this solution was rejected because England wanted war and had been influenced by international Jewry. And he placed sole responsibility for the war, the loss of blood and treasure, and his own reprehensible murder of six million Jews – on the Jews. He essentially reverted back to his days as a young man in the beer halls of Munich. It was there he began to curse Jewry for all the ills of the world. It was there he began to hone his skills as a demagogue and chart a course for his ephemeral journey of malevolence. He repeated lie after lie regarding Germany's lack of responsibility for the war. He also attacked his own military, especially the Army and its officer corps, whom he held responsible for the loss of the war. As a narcissistic, borderline psychopath, he was not able to comprehend the impact of the decisions he alone had made that led to the downfall of National Socialism and Nazism.

Next, he turned to his successor, first expelling former Field Marshal Goering and former Reichsfuehrer Himmler from the party, stripping them of all offices. Then he appointed Admiral Doenitz, the ranking officer in the Navy, as President of the Reich and Supreme Commander of the Armed Forces. He listed the men who were to have prominent positions in the government, stressing that above all, the government was to resist international Jewry. His pathologic pre- occupation with anti-Semitism was his dominant thought until his death.

As with his marriage document, Goebbels and Bormann were co-signatories of the document. His will was brief and explained his decision to marry. He left directions for all of his possessions to go to the party or the state. Finally, he stated his fate:

My wife and I choose to die in order to escape the shame of overthrow or capitulation. It is our wish that our bodies be burned immediately in the place where I have performed the greater part of my daily work during the twelve years of service to my people.

Dawn was breaking over the capitol as he went to bed. Russian artillery was being fired at almost point-blank range. In his eyes, his 'Political Testament' had formed a new government, and he instructed Goebbels and Bormann to leave the capitol so they might join it. Bormann was determined to carry out the order. He had never intended to share in the death of the man to whom he had devoted so much. Goebbels on the other hand took the opposite tack. For the first time, hewould disobey a direct order from his beloved leader. A future in Germany without Hitler was no future he was willing to share. He had walked 'arm in arm' with the Fuhrer to perpetuate the myths of National Socialism. Every success he had experienced he owed to Hitler. To desert him now in his greatest hour of need would be the greatest treason.

Bormann had been appointed a de facto General Secretary of the Nazi Party. His intent was now to survive and at the same time, prevent Goering from becoming Hitler's successor. To make certain this would not happen, he sent a follow-up radio message to the SS office at Berchtesgaden:

"If Berlin and we should fall, the traitors of April twenty-third must be executed. Men, do your duty! Your life and honor depend on it!'

This was an order to murder Goering and his Air Force staff, whom Bormann thought were under arrest. Unknown to Bormann, Goering had persuaded his captors to join him. Rather than arrest him, they joined him and retreated to a castle in Bavaria he had inherited. As it turned out Goering now had no ambition to rule the crumbling Nazi empire. The Nazi and SS chain of command was unraveling, along with everything else in the Third Reich.

Admiral Doenitz had been appointed President of the Reich, a fact of which he was unaware. The principle consideration now was to get Hitler's 'Political Testament' document delivered through Russian lines to Doenitz. Three separate messengers to act independently were chosen for this difficult task. They set out at noon on April 29th. Making their way through the Tiergarten they successfully slipped through three separate Russian mobilization points. But the men grew increasingly preoccupied with their own safety, a fact that overshadowed the capricious mission for a defeated country. Eventually they all got through. But it was too late to be of any benefit to the Admiral, who in fact, never saw them.

* * *

The last two weeks of April brought spring to Leipzig in vivid color of pellucid beauty. Flowering dogwoods, cherry and peach trees were abundant. In the parks, white and pink azaleas dominated the landscape. Anna and Sarah were now reacquainted with one another and had even been able to frequent one of their favorite restaurants. After Nazi troops vacated the area, Sarah re-claimed her short-wave transmitter and once again began monitoring the BBC.

One evening they were listening to the short-wave traffic from England. It was a ham- radio operator from Cambridge, seeking information about a relative in the British military. Sarah broke in and with her limited English said, "This is Leipzig, Germany…over."

"Hello Leipzig, this is Cambridge…greetings to you…over."

"Do you speak German…over?"

"Negative to that…over."

Sarah took a deep breath. "We seek to speak with Professor Hanz Eichenwald, Cambridge physics…over."

"I work at the University…will contact and set rendezvous for tomorrow…2100 hours…over."

"Copy that…talk tomorrow…over and out."

Anna was trying to absorb the news. The chance to speak with her parents was something she had not even considered. So much was happening so quickly. She was still focused on trying to find Eric but was afraid that with the passing of time, it would become more and more difficult. She believed he would be well cared for with Beryl, but had to consider that Beryl Yenzer would eventually return home to Poland. She also was sure that he would take Eric. If he didn't, Eric would be orphaned in Germany along with thousands of other children. Either option might make it impossible to find a four-year old with only a first name and no known living relatives.

The war was rapidly ending, but Anna had no money. She could not travel until a peace agreement was fully established and in effect. Sarah did have a small amount of savings and offered it to Anna, but Anna would not accept it. Sarah had already done enough. Anna was deeply grateful but had come to believe she had no future in war torn Germany. Where she would go was still unclear to her. But she had no stomach for a reconstruction effort in a country that had assisted or stood quietly and inexcusably by, as an entire segment of its citizenry was all but destroyed.

The following evening could not come fast enough. Anna spent the morning trying to read. In the afternoon she passed the time by walking to the University Hospital. She had intended to visit the children's ward where her identity had been uncovered but as she climbed the stair, she changed her mind. It would serve no useful purpose to confront the nurse who had turned her in to the Gestapo. Anna had sometimes imagined the look on the woman's face if she were ever confronted. But Anna tried to dismiss the thought. It wasn't noble and she didn't want to fall into the emotional trap of revenge. The Nazi Reich was now a thing of the past. She too, had to put this behind her.

She turned and walked back down the stairs. Because of the war, the world would never be the same. Neither would her world. She had to find a way to make a new beginning. Reliving the horrors of the Reich would only hinder that goal.

That evening, when the clock turned to 8:00 p.m., Sarah and Anna began to monitor the short-wave traffic. It had picked-up enormously now that the Allies had advanced deep into Germany. Before an hour had passed, they heard what they were waiting for.

"Hello...hello...Cambridge England to Leipzig...over... Cambridge England to Leipzig...over."

"This is Leipzig...over."

Then in fluent German the transmission continued.

"This is Hanz Eichenwald...for Anna...this is Hanz Eichenwald for Anna...over."

"Vati, Vati! Das ist Anna...das ist Anna...over."

"Anna...Anna...your voice is clear...you sound wonderful... are you well...over."

"Yes...yes...I am well. Christian's sister is caring for me...she is here with me...over." "Anna....it's your mother...hello...over"

"Hello...hello...mother...so good to hear your voice...over."

"Yes, yes...the same for us. Tell us about your child....over."

"He is a boy whose life I saved in Buchenwald....over."

"So he is not your own child....over."

"No, no... he is not my child, but I want to find him...over."

"Do you know where he might be...over."

"I think...I hope he is at the Red Cross refuge center at Dresden...over."

"Can we help...can we send money...over"

"Yes..yes...I can use some money...Sarah will explain how to send it...over." Sarah explained how to transfer funds via cablegram to her bank in Leipzig. Then reluctant goodbyes were said.

As they signed off Sarah felt envious of Anna. Sarah had no immediate family left in Germany. She thought how strange that this Jewish woman whom she had grown to love so deeply had a bright future ahead and a loving family waiting for her. She had no one. But she dismissed those thoughts when she looked at Anna's eyes and the tears that ran down her face. Any thoughts for herself quickly vanished.

The following day the Eichenwalds transferred 1,000 pounds to Sarah's bank. With rising German inflation, it translated into 50,000 Reich marks, a sum that would be more than enough to cover Anna's living and travel expenses. The past 24 hours had indeed been remarkable for the Eichenwald family. And the following two days would hold events that would close the final on the most destructive war the world had experienced.

*   *   *

Dr. Joseph Goebbels followed the dictation of Hitler's final testament with one of his own. The final portion was recorded as follows:

"In the nightmare of treason which surrounds the Fuehrer in these most critical days of the war, there must be someone at least

who will stay with him unconditionally until death . . . . I believe I am thereby doing the best service to the future of the German people. In the hard times to come, examples will be more important than men. . . .

For this reason, together with my wife, and on behalf of my children, who are too young to be able to speak for themselves and who, if they were old enough, would unreservedly agree with this decision, I express my unalterable resolution not to leave the Reich capital, even if it falls, but rather, at the side of the Fuehrer, to end a life that for me personally will have no further

Value if I canno spend it at the service of the Fuehrer and at his side.

The decision of Joseph and Magda Goebbels to murder their children was the apogee of their blind fanatical commitment to Hitler and Nazism. He had been caught up in the mystique of Adolph Hitler from the beginning. The involvement of his wife Magda was a somewhat different story.

Magda was born Johanna Maria Magdalena Rierschel in Berlin in 1901. Her mother and father were divorced three years later and at age five she went to live with her father in Cologne, then eventually to Brussels. Her mother remarried and later, Magda moved with them back to Berlin. When she was 17, she met a wealthy industrialist who began to court her and the couple married when she was 20. They had one son, Harald Quandt. She and husband Gunther grew apart. Because of his work as an industrialist, they spent little time together and divorced in 1929.

Magda joined the Nazi party September 1, 1930. She was infatuated with Adolph Hitler. But the man who was destined to lead Germany to destruction was focused on politics and had no interest in a relationship. A year later, in December 1931, she married Dr. Joseph Goebbels. Hitler remained close friends of the couple until the end. Although Joseph had many affairs with many other women, Magda stayed with him and they had five daughters and a son.

During the early part of the war, Magda was completely supportive of the effort. She entertained wives of visiting dignitaries and became thought of as the 'First Lady of the Reich'. In later defeats, she began to doubt Hitler and his judgments. The last two weeks of April, she became resolved that she would die with her husband, but the issue of her children was difficult. One evening after she had put them to bed and the bombing had stopped, she finally spoke of it to her husband.

"Joseph, I fear for the children. They will live in a country with little future. We are hearing of the atrocities being committed by the Russian troops. They are raping our women, looting and burning our villages. Our oldest, Hiega, will be abused. She will be at their mercy."

"I will not leave them to the Russians," he said as he kissed her forehead. "They will go with us. There is no other way. You must understand this and be brave. Do you understand?"

She slumped into a chair and nodded. "Yes. There seems to be no other way."

The following day, Magda Goebbels sat down and wrote a letter to her eldest son by her first marriage. He had become close to his stepfather, Joseph, and she wanted him to hear of their fate from the family. Her farewell letter was hand written.

"My beloved son! By now we have been in the Fuhrerbunker for six days already – daddy, your six siblings and I, for the sake of giving our national socialistic lives the only possible honorable

end…you shall know that I stayed here against daddy's will, and that even on last Sunday the Fuhrer wanted to help me to get out. You know your mother – we have the same blood, for me there was no wavering. Our glorious idea is ruined and with it everything beautiful and marvelous that I have known in my life. The world that comes after the Fuhrer and national socialism is not any longer worth living in and therefore I took the children with me, for they are too good for the life that would follow, and a merciful God will understand me when I will give them the salvation….The children are wonderful….there never is a word of complaint nor crying. The impacts are shaking the bunker. The elder kids cover the younger ones, their presence is a blessing and they are making the Fuhrer smile once in a while. May God help that I have the strength to perform the last and hardest. We only have one goal left: loyalty to the Fuhrer even in death. Harald, my dear son – I want to give you what I learned in life: be loyal! Loyal to yourself, loyal to the people and loyal to your country….Be proud of us and try to keep us in dear memory…."

On the afternoon of April twenty-ninth, possibly the last news from the outside reached the bunker. The death of Il Duce, Benito Mussolini, was communicated to Hitler. Mussolini and his mistress, Clara Petacci, were trying to escape to Switzerland when caught by Italian Communist partisans. They were arrested and two days later were executed. She was given the option of leaving but refused. That night their bodies were taken to Milan where, the following day, they were hung upside down for public display. Finally, they were cut down and put in a gutter before being buried in unmarked pauper's graves.

At the situation conference at noon on April thirtieth, Hitler, Bormann, Goebbels and the others learned that the Russians were within a few blocks of the Chancellery. Hitler had given his chauffer,

Erick Kempka, an order to deliver 200 liters of gasoline to the Chancellery garden. As this was being accomplished, the Fuehrer and Eva Braun bid farewells to the secretaries, staff, Dr. Goebbels, General Krebs and Burgdorf. Once again Hitler mentioned the cyanide to his secretaries to avoid the Russian brutality. Then Hitler and his new bride retired to his private quarters. Bormann and Goebbels waited in the hallway to the entrance. In a few moments a single pistol shot was heard, then silence. They entered the quarters to find Hitler dead on the floor from the pistol shot to the brain through his mouth. Frau Hitler was slumped on the couch having taken a potassium cyanide capsule.

No words were spoken. Hitler's valet and an orderly draped the bodies in army blankets and carried them up the stairs to the garden. They were placed in a bomb crater and soaked in gasoline. They waited for a lull in the artillery bombardment and lit the funeral pyre. Goebbels and Bormann stood at attention and offered the Nazi military salute, Heil Hitler. Whatever ceremony was intended, it didn't happen. The artillery shelling commenced.

Bormann and Goebbels realized that Admiral Doenitz likely had not yet received the testament message, so Bormann sent a radio message informing him that he had been appointed President of the Reich. But Bormann did not mention Hitler's death. The reason for this remains unclear. Thinking Hitler still alive, Doenitz replied to Hitler that his loyalty to the Fuehrer was unconditional and that he would fight on to honor Germany.

They had a last ditch plan to save the remainder in the bunker. The Chief of the Army General Staff, General Krebs, spoke Russian, having spent some time in Moscow as an attaché. They sent him to General Chuikov of the Russian High Command to attempt a negotiated agreement for safe passage of those in the bunker. Chuikov refused, demanding an unconditional surrender of all troops immediately. By 3:00 p.m. on May first, Goebbels carried out his last act as a Nazi. He sent a radio communication to Admiral Doenitz that Hitler was dead, and his 'Testament' was on the way.

That evening, Frau Goebbels sought out *SS* physician Helmut Kunz. It was time for her to carry out the unthinkable. She was trembling as she entered his office.

"Are you certain they will not know?" she asked.

"I am certain," he told her. "I will give each an injection of morphine that will make them essentially unresponsive. You are to tell them it is medication to help them rest so the bombing will not disturb them. They will need a good night sleep for their journey out of the war zone in the morning.

"Very well. We will give the injection to Heiga first, she is the oldest."

As they entered the children's sleeping quarters Heiga was reading to the others, a tale published in 1937, written by an Englishman named Tolkein and translated into several languages, including German. The central character was a dwarf named Bilbo Baggins, a Hobbit. As they entered the room Heiga read, 'All that the unsuspecting Bilbo saw that morning was an old man with a staff. He had a tall pointed blue hat, a long grey cloak, a silver scarf over which his long white beard hung down below his waist, and immense black boots.'

"Children," Magda interrupted, "I hate to disturb your reading, but Dr. Kunz has some medicine for each of you so you can get a good night's sleep. We are going to be leaving the war zone in the morning, and you will need your rest."

"Is it a shot?" the youngest child asked. "I hate shots."

"Yes, it is, but it doesn't hurt much. Heiga will be first and show you how to be brave." Each of the children received an injection of morphine. There was no crying. Within 15 minutes they were all sleeping. The lights had been turned off and the door closed. Magda re- entered the room with six capsules of cyanide. There was a small lamp on a table in the corner of the concrete bunker room. She paused and looked at her six children, all of whom would die before dawn. They would never see another day. She began to sob. She had convinced herself that there was no future for these beautiful children, and that any future at all would be a horror for them. She began with Heide, the youngest. She stroked her hair as the tiny four-year old lay peacefully sleeping. Gently, Magda opened the child's mouth. Wearing a rubber glove, she crushed the capsule in Heide's mouth and closed the child's lips. She repeated the process with each child, finishing with Heiga, the eldest.

Magda Goebbels then sat down in the corner and sobbed uncontrollably. She shook her head in disbelief that it had come down to this. There had once been beauty in the Reich. Now, there was only death and destruction.

She waited for 10 minutes, all the while, carefully observing each child. They were all dead. She took a long, last look, then left the room.

Joseph Goebbels was waiting in the central area of the Fuherbunker. He did not speak but took his wife's hand to walk with her to the stair entrance. He had donned his military coat, hat and gloves. They bid farewell to several friends then ascended the stairs. His adjuvant, SS Hauptsturmfuhrer Gunther Schwagermann was in the garden with a can of petrol. He turned to make certain the jerry-can was full when Goebbels fired his pistol into his right temple. Magda had swallowed an identical ampoule to the ones that had taken the lives of their children. She was dead in about six minutes. Their bodies were placed in a bomb crater, covered with petrol, then set afire.

The death of Goebbels ended the tragic life of a man who sought a dramatic spotlight but had no meaningful self-identity. Indeed, his value as a man was totally determined by Adolph Hitler. Goebbels desire for self-exaltation had ultimately led to the macabre murder of his own children.

Later that evening, shortly after 10:00 p.m., those left in the bunker, including Bormann and Hitler's physician, Dr. Stumpfeffer, tried their escape through a Berlin subway tunnel. Simultaneously, a program of symphonic music was interrupted by an emergency announcement. After a military drum roll the announcer read a statement:

"Our Fuehrer, Adolph Hitler, fighting to the last breath against Bolshevism, fell for Germany this afternoon in his operational headquarters in the Reich Chancellery. On April 30 the Fuehrer appointed Grand Admiral Doenitz his successor.'

Truth was never a tenet of Third Reich operations, so the lie that Hitler had fought 'to the last breath' was in keeping with such a tradition. This broadcast was followed 20 minutes later by a second announcement from the new Reich President, Admiral Doenitz, who knew that German resistance was at an end.

Bormann and the *SS* doctor followed the subway tunnel. When they emerged, they encountered a German tank. They crouched closely behind the tank hoping to follow it to safety. But the tank took a direct hit from Russian artillery and both men were killed.

On May fourth, the surrender scenario began. All forces in northwest Germany, Denmark and Holland surrendered to English

Field Marshall Montgomery. The next day the troops north of the Alps, principally the German 1st and 19th armies, capitulated. Finally, in a little red school house at Reims, where the Supreme Allied Commander Dwight Eisenhower made his headquarters, Germany surrendered unconditionally. The day was Monday, May 7, 1945. All hostilities stopped at midnight on May eighth. There had been almost continual bombing and fighting on the European continent since September 1, 1939.

Although hostilities had stopped, there were issues that still had to be settled. The Doenitz government, established by Hitler on April twenty-ninth, was dissolved by the Allies on May twenty-third. All of its participants were arrested. Heinrich Himmler was in the vicinity of Flensburg on the Danish border. He had been dismissed from the Doenitz government on May sixth. The following day he tried to contact the Supreme Headquarters Allied Expeditionary Force (SHAEF) to request Eisenhower appoint him Minister of Police for a post-war German government. He proposed to exchange his service for immunity from prosecution for war crimes.

Himmler's proposition was a delusion of incredible magnitude. His crimes exceeded all in the Reich with the possible exception of Hitler himself. Perhaps they are best represented by circumstances surrounding the assassination of his top assistant, Reinhard Heydrich, the acting governor of Bohemia and Moravia, the portion of Czechoslovakia incorporated into the Reich. On May 27, 1942, his car was attacked by Czech resistance fighters. A bomb was thrown into the open auto. Heydrich was seriously injured but not killed. However, he developed a bloodstream infection and died eight days later in a Prague hospital. The killers were pursued but not immediately caught. They were hidden by Czech nationals.

Early on, Hitler and Himmler had decided to unleash their wrath on the community and declared to kill all men over the age of 16 in any village suspected of harboring those responsible. On a tip they converged on the small town of Lidice, 22 kilometers west of Prague. June tenth was their day of revenge and 192 men of the village were rounded up and shot. The 184 women of the town were then separated from their children and sent to a concentration camp. The 88 children were transported to a center in Lodz, where most of them eventually died. The village of Lidice was then burned. No buildings were left.

In a desperate attempt to escape, Himmler shaved his moustache, placed a patch over one eye and put on a private's uniform. He had false identity papers which were in such perfect order that a British sergeant at a check point became suspicious. He was arrested and on May twenty- second was recognized. He was stripped of the uniform hoping to separate him from any concealed poison. The following day he was being interrogated and was to be examined by a British physician. He bit down on a cyanide capsule hidden in his mouth and his life was ended.

All in all, more than 30 Nazi officers were tried by an International Military Tribunal. Most were convicted of war crimes and a number received death sentences. One of those sentenced to hang was the second in command in the Reich, General Fieldmarshal of the Luftwaffe, Hermann Goering. He was the only high-ranking Nazi officer who had amassed a personal fortune looting Jewish homes and businesses. He was also the most prominent figure in the Nazi hierarchy to sign the order to implement the 'final solution of the Jewish Question'. He made an appeal to the court to be executed by firing squad rather than by hanging, generally reserved for common criminals. The court refused. The day before his scheduled execution he took his own life by swallowing a cyanide capsule that had been smuggled into his cell.

Thus, the four Nazi leaders most prominent in the development of the murderous Reich - Hitler, Goering, Goebbels and Himmler - all died by their own hands, cheating the hangman. In life they had plotted and codified the execution of millions of men, women and children. In death they took a coward's path, refusing the judgment they had earned.

＊　＊　＊

Beryl Yenzer could hardly believe the war was over. The word spread quickly throughout the Red Cross refugee camp in Dresden. The camp was a series of 700 tents, each holding about 60 individuals, mostly men from the labor camps in central Germany and most of whom were emaciated. Some would not recover. For every 100 tents there was a central area for dining with latrines and showers. In the vicinity of each mess hall was a gasoline powered generator to run cold storage facilities for food and large hot water heaters for the showers. A hot shower was a luxury none of the men had experienced in five years. The International Red Cross had made a decision that hot water might boost morale in a way nothing else could.

The camp also held more than 1,000 children. Most were orphans and most were Jewish. The young men from Buchenwald made up a large portion of this group. The care of the children was a priority of the Red Cross workers. The task of re-patriating tens of thousands of refugees was enormous and would take months or even years in many cases. Relief workers from Switzerland, France, Britain, the U.S., Canada, Australia, and New Zealand poured into Europe.

Many of the great cities had been almost completely destroyed. Most prominent were Warsaw and Berlin where millions were now homeless. The ruin of the physical infrastructure was devastating but the nadir of economic collapse was worse. One of the harshest consequences was food shortage. The effort to prevent massive starvation was the greatest challenge.

Beryl Yenzer resided in a tent adjacent to the children's section at the camp. The boys in the camp knew him well and the workers soon learned to utilize the skills of the former schoolmaster. He continued to keep Eric with him and when entering the camp had registered Eric as his son. Eric and the other boys had felt the dissonance lift as soon as they were transported out of Buchenwald. In one day, the fear was gone. They were treated with kindness. Most still realized they were stranded, but now they were stranded in a safe place among people who seemed to care about them.

Beryl faced great uncertainty, but he was no longer under a death sentence. Still, his family was now only a memory and he understood full well that there would be no Jewish community left in Poland or much of anywhere in Europe. There were very few adult Jewish survivors of the Nazi oligarchy and probably less than 3,000 children across the continent. There would be no children to teach in Poland and there might not be work of any kind. But he was not discouraged. He would find a way to survive and provide for Eric. To that end, he was determined to leave the camp as soon as possible. He wanted to go home. But Poland was now occupied by Russia and the Bolsheviks allowed little personal freedom. Most people worked in state-controlled jobs. Beryl was also concerned that the Communists might make it difficult for Jews to practice their faith. The worship of Yahweh had been built into the fabric of his life. Now he also had the responsibility of a four-year old boy. His desire was to teach Eric the Jewish traditions of Rash Hashanah, Yom Kippur and Passover, as his father had taught him. But he was not sure if he could do it in a communist state.

He had studied to become a Rabbi as a young man, which led to his position as the headmaster of a Yeshiva. Now that they were safe, he spent many hours trying to sort out the meaning of what had happened to his people, or to consider if there was any meaning left at all. He questioned where the justice of God had been in a time and place of such grave human suffering. He wondered if God had abandoned the innocent, those he considered God's own people. He wondered if God had lost control.

For thousands of years the Lord had worked in the lives of his people and in the lives of the Patriarchs, and had never abandoned the Jews. God had not abandoned him or the boys. In fact, God had preserved thousands of his people and almost all of the boys in Buchenwald. At heart, Beryl believed in the justice of God even in the face of great human suffering. But the Nazi pogrom had brought about unimaginable death and suffering. Now he had questions he had never asked himself about the omniscience of the Almighty.

He thought back to the story of Job who faced the great enigma of being a godly man, but a man who underwent great suffering. Job had questioned God. Beryl recalled the Lord's words to Job.

Where were you when I laid the earth's foundation? Tell me if you understand. Who marked off its dimensions? Surly you know. Who stretched a measuring line across it?

Have you ever given orders to the morning, or shown the dawn its place. Have you comprehended the vast expanses of the earth? Tell me if you know all this.

What is the way to the place where the lightning is dispersed, or the place where the east winds are scattered over the earth?

Who endowed the heart with wisdom or gave understanding to the mind?

Will the one who contends with the Almighty correct him? Let him who accuses

God answer him!

Beryl, like Job, had no answer. He could only trust that the Creator of the Universe had control of all history and was working in history, even using men's evil intentions. In spite of all that had happened, Beryl had not lost his trust in the God of his forefathers who had delivered his people from Egypt and him from Hitler's death camps. Human suffering had occurred throughout history, and God was still God. Job's understanding was now Beryl's understanding. The Creator of the Universe is sovereign, and His ways are not our ways. His plans are not our plans. Beryl had memorized several Psalms as a boy and recalled one of his favorite verses, even after the years of turmoil and emotional pain.

"Yet I am always with you; you hold me by my right hand. You guide me with your counsel, and afterward you will take me into glory. Whom have I in heaven but you? And earth has nothing I desire besides you. My flesh and my heart may fail, but God is the strength of my heart and my portion forever."

CHAPTER 23

A Desperate Search and VJ Day

By now, Germany was a shell, the paradigm of a dead carcass. Most of her larger cities were in ruins. Leipzig and those cities which managed to remain physically intact were nothing more than defined boundaries in which emotionally scarred people existed. The circumstances in which the German people now found themselves were difficult to comprehend, if not impossible. In retrospect, it would eventually be easier for them to see how this had occurred rather than why.

In 1918, the Kaiser was forced to abdicate his so-called throne. Massive inflation and unemployment was followed by rioting and civil unrest. Almost by accident, Germany became a republic. For the first time in almost 1,000 years, Germany had no king. They were like sheep without a shepherd – until one emerged, one who would lead them to slaughter and eventual cataclysm. Given the man's legendary power and charisma, he emerged quite subtly, bearing a name few people even knew. But exponentially, his power and influence widened. Suddenly the sheep were trapped in an economic nadir. That's when they began to listen. And in time, their shepherd's voice was the only one they could hear. The sophistry of his reasoning and the repulsion it should have warranted was lost in their desperation. Fear turned it into a symphony. But now, the music was dead, and the piper had been paid.

Sarah and Anna had miraculously avoided the conflagration, although Anna had been much closer to the flames. These two women were fortunate and well on their way to emotional recovery. Sarah was focused on rebuilding her devastated country. Anna, on the other hand, was looking for Eric.

By the first week of June, three weeks after the Nazi surrender, a sense of peace was beginning to invade what had been chaotic for so long. Sarah had contacted Landis Koller to see if he could help Anna in her effort to reach Dresden.

It was a warm Wednesday evening when he pulled up to Sarah's apartment in a truck that looked vaguely familiar to the women. As he stepped out of the truck, Anna and Sarah ran down the apartment stairs to greet him. With a wide grin he embraced them. They were comrades-in-arms. They had fought together and escaped death together. Landis was invited inside for coffee and pastries. As they made their way up the stairs, he looked back at the truck.

"Do you recognize my transportation?" he asked, looking at Anna. "It survived the war!"

She replied laughing, "It looks remarkably good, as do you."

Anna had felt strangely attracted to this brave man. She thought at the time it was the danger they had gone through together. She had not thought of him in many months, but was pleased to see him and surprised that the attraction was still there.

"How are Gretchen and your children?" she asked as they entered the apartment. He turned toward her and smiled. He had known her as Heidi Brendler. Now she was Anna.

"Thank you for asking. They are well. As with most Germans we are trying to pick up the pieces...to put out lives back together."

The three colleagues sat in the front room and enjoyed their refreshments and the conversation. Landis had lost track of Anna and was not surprised by her stories of Buchenwald. He had heard of the labor camps and knew of the cruelty. But he was astonished by the story of her 'execution' at the hands of Ernst Bishoff.

"Sounds like divine intervention, doesn't it?" he said, looking at Sarah.

Landis now had no job. The ball bearing plant had been destroyed. He told the women he was hoping to find work in the re-building effort. His wife's parents were farmers about 100 kilometers north of Leipzig. He knew he could move his family to their farm but was too proud to ask. Still it was a possibility. His goal was to get his children into university. He was fascinated to learn that Anna was a surgeon. This beautiful woman with the raven hair and blue eyes had actually been a teaching surgeon at the University of Berlin. *Remarkable*, he thought.

They spent hours recapping their histories – the scrapes with the Nazis and the upcoming plan to get Anna to Dresden. Landis was pleased to be able to help. After all, Anna had given the truck for the resistance effort. Without her generosity he would have no transportation. He offered for her to drive.

"You survived the Gestapo and now you want to commit suicide?" she asked with a laugh.

Early on Saturday they set out for Dresden. There was one military check point outside of Leipzig and there, Landis got directions to the Red Cross camp. Since Germany's surrender the travel security had relaxed significantly. They were pleased that Leipzig was allied occupied. They had heard the Russians were harsh taskmasters.

Just before reaching Dresden they encountered a Russian check point indicating they were entering Russian occupied territory.

All of Poland, the Czech Republic, Eastern Germany and East Berlin were controlled by the Russians. Here, there was a notable change in atmosphere. The troops were less co-operative and more suspicious. The travelers were questioned in detail about their business in Dresden, their destination and estimated time to be spent there. Anna was relieved when they were finally on their way again.

Dresden was the baroque capitol of the German State of Saxony. Before the war it had been the fourth largest city in the country, a cultural center that sprawled out from the banks of the Elbe River. The architecture and multiple green parks had given it the title, Florence on the Elbe. But Dresden had been made a military-industrial complex with more than 100 factories to support the war effort, employing 50,000 workers. Many were slave laborers brought in from Poland and Czechoslovakia. In February 1945, Allied planes dropped 4,000 tons of explosives in four separate raids. There was mass destruction of the city and an estimated 40,000 casualties.

Anna and Landis were directed to the refugee camp northwest of the city near the village of Kaditz. As they crested a hill, they had a view of the massive 100-acre complex sprawling along the river. From the hill top the white tents looked like mushrooms in a valley of green. They seemed endless. Anna was apprehensive, her heart pounding. She was trying not to get her hopes up.

The camp was just five kilometers from the Dresden airfield which had escaped destruction only because it wasn't a military facility. Twice weekly, 25 tons of food and supplies was flown in from England. There were some 10 other refugee camps set up in central and eastern Europe as well, since tens of thousands of refugees were making their way back to their homes and families. Bus transportation was being set up between the major metropolitan centers of Europe and economic aid was coming in. But it was in woefully short supply. All of the major economic powers of the world had been involved in the war, and all but the U.S. had no reserves and the U.S. was still fighting Japan.

Just after noon, Landis pulled the truck up to the make-shift administration tent. It was actually one of three tents that held about 40 aid workers overseeing the camp. The central tent held the Red Cross emblem on top. Portable wooden flooring had been placed on the ground to keep dust or mud to a minimum, depending on the weather. The tent ceiling leaked significantly when it rained. There were standing electric fans strategically placed to keep air circulating.

Anna and Landis were asked to take a seat with more than a dozen others who were making efforts to locate missing loved ones. After an hour's wait, a middle-aged Swiss woman came to get them. In fluent German she asked them to come into her cubicle. As registrar of the camp, she was responsible for tracking everyone on the premises. She sat behind a large table set between oversized filing cabinets. Anna and Landis sat across from her. The woman smiled faintly but her voice was tired.

"So how can I help you?" she asked.

"We are looking for a young Jewish boy named Eric," said Anna. "He would be about four or five years old. He is an orphan."

"Do you know his last name?" "No, I'm sorry. I don't."

"There are about 1,200 children in the camp," said the woman. "I can go through the roster but it will take some time."

Without speaking further she opened a file drawer and placed a thick folder on her desk and began scanning the names. After a few minutes she spoke without looking up.

"Here is an Erick Konipinski. He is listed as age 10." She continued her search. "Erick Rabii. Listed as age 13." She scanned another ten pages. "There are no other boys named Erick."

Anna looked down for a moment. Then it occurred to her.

"Could you look for two adult names? Julian Richburg or Beryl Yenzer?" There were 40,000 men in the camp, but the names were alphabetical. The woman handed Anna a stack of papers with names and gave another stack to Landis. They both began scouring the lists.

"Here he is!" Anna cried out. "He is with Beryl Yenzer. Landis, he is here!" She handed the sheet to the woman.

"There is an indication that they have actually left the camp.... just last week," the woman said.

"Left? Are you certain?" "Yes. Quiet certain."

"Is there any indication of their destination?"

The woman again looked at the sheet, then pulled out another file of people who had left or died.

"Poland. It seems they went to Poland."

Anna was crushed. She knew finding them in war ravaged Poland would be impossible. It could take years to conduct such a search.

"Landis, let's go back," she whispered.

As they stood to leave, Anna paused at the door. "Thank you. You have been very helpful."

* * *

Enrico Fermi and Robert Oppenheimer met in 1926 when Oppenheimer traveled from the U.S. to study physics at the University of Gottingen. The two became friends along with other notable men including Werner Heisenberg, Wolfgang Pauli and Edward Teller. Oppenheimer had an exceptional intellect. He completed his PhD. at age 22, under the direction of Max Born, the noted German mathematician and Director of Theoretical Physics at Gottingen.

Eventually Oppenheimer accepted a teaching professorship at Cal-Berkley. His career was interrupted when he was diagnosed with mild tuberculosis. He traveled to northern New Mexico to recover and fell in love with the high desert country. He had wide ranging scientific interests including theoretical astronomy, quantum field theory, nuclear physics and spectroscopy. After returning to Berkley he worked with and became close friends with Earnest O. Lawrence, the principle developer of the cyclotron.

Later, Oppenheimer developed the first world class center in the U.S. for theoretical physics. His esteem as a physicist grew, along with his reputation for being an eccentric. A tall, gangly man who was rail thin with sharp features and blue eyes, his demeanor was almost disarming, but women found him charming and attentive. At parties, he was often the center piece, engaging to anyone and everyone simultaneously. But on a personal level he remained aloof and detached. He did not read newspapers or periodicals and, in fact, was unaware of the great stock market crash of 1929 until several weeks after it happened.

Oppenheimer began to change in 1936. Deeply disturbed by the Nazi treatment of the Jews and aware of the effect the depression was having on his students he began to develop an interest in communism. He became involved with communist sympathizers and in the summer of 1939, met his future wife, Kitty. A petite, brown-eyed beauty, she was involved in communist activities. Her late husband, Joe Dallet, had been a communist party official before meeting his death fighting in the Spanish Civil War.

In October 1942, Oppenheimer met a man who would radically alter the course of his life. Earlier that year, General Leslie Groves had been appointed the director of a highly secretive project aimed at developing a nuclear explosive device - an atomic bomb. In 1941, the Army Corps of Engineers took over the project. Groves was an engineer by training and had overseen the construction of the Pentagon. The central office of the North Atlantic Division of the Corps of Engineers was in Manhattan. Groves named the project 'Manhattan Engineer District' which was later shortened to the Manhattan Project.

Groves' first priority was to find a scientific director. He considered several people but it was Oppenheimer who impressed him the most. Groves considered the man to be the one true genius of the group.

To be sure, Oppenheimer was a brilliant theoretician. But he had virtually no experience leading any scientific project and certainly no project of this magnitude. Still, Groves looked to Oppenheimer to lead. During their first extended visit, Oppenheimer stressed the need for a central laboratory where the best minds could freely attack and discuss multiple problems, many of which had never even been considered. Groves saw the idea of a central lab as an excellent one and now believed he had the man to run it.

There were two principle objections to this brash young physicist – his association with the Communist party and the fact he was not a Nobel Laureate. Several of the men he would be overseeing were Nobel Prize winners. However, Groves thought both objections were bogus. He presented Oppenheimer's name to the

Military Policy Committee and there were objections. No one could come up with a better candidate.

Oppenheimer proceeded to pull together some of the best minds the fields of physics and chemistry had to offer. The only man who turned him down was Linus Pauling, a pacifist. The rest, all world class leaders in their respective fields, accepted. The group was an international mix, some of them Jewish scientists who had escaped Europe. Among those was Leo Szilard, the avuncular Hungarian physicist. In 1933, Szilard was struck by the idea that an element might be found, if struck by a neutron, could emit two neutrons and thus sustain a chain reaction. Under the direction of Enrico Fermi, a sustained nuclear chain reaction had been achieved in Chicago.

In June, 1942, eight physicists working with Oppenheimer at Berkley had determined that a fission bomb was feasible. The calculations for 'critical mass' of the fissile material was to be worked out. The next question was how to find a suitable location for a laboratory. Groves and Oppenheimer settled on an obscure site in northern New Mexico – Los Alamos.

The goal had always been to find a physical location that could be guaranteed safety from both domestic curiosity and foreign attack. This was not so simple a place to find. Groves had scoured the western part of the country and at one time, toyed with the idea of Jemez Springs, New Mexico. But he and Oppenheimer both rejected it in the end. Transportation would be a problem and the area was too confined by canyon walls.

It was Oppenheimer who finally suggested Los Alamos. The site of a boys' school, the Los Alamos Ranch School sat atop a mesa overlooking the Rio Grande Valley and the Sangre de Cristo mountains. The hilltop was isolated and yet easily accessible by routes that could be controlled. Another plus was the landscape itself. The area was dotted with canyons that could serve as excellent test sites. The War Department approved it. When the academic term ended in 1943, Los Alamos swapped its boys for bomb making.

The other major project sites chosen were Oak Ridge, Tennessee for the production of uranium-235, and the Hanford site near Richland, Washington for the production of plutonium-239. The chemical element plutonium had been discovered in 1940 by Glenn Seaborg working at Cal-Berkley. It had been kept a secret and its isotope, Pu-239 was developed as a fissile fuel for a nuclear bomb. A fissile substance was something that was stable and would undergo fission, the release of huge amounts of energy when bombarded with neutrons, in accordance with Einstein's equation $E = mc^2$.

Los Alamos served as the epicenter of bomb production. A part of its charm was its beauty and isolation. It was the perfect irony. The efforts at Los Alamos were centered on developing weapons of mass destruction. But the land tucked quietly beneath the mesa served as the ancestral homeland and sacred grounds of six of New Mexico's northern pueblo nations. Here, people had lived simple lives for hundreds of years. Eschewing technology and urban lifestyles, the people of the pueblos spent their days in communal fashion, their lives revolving around family and traditions. They were farmers and pottery makers. They baked bread and celebrated feast days. They believed all of nature to be sacred. It was in this pastoral setting that the Manhattan Project was launched.

The mesa was only about 25 miles west of Santa Fe. Oppenheimer called the location a dream come true, and several times he stated that the two things he loved most in life were physics and the high desert of New Mexico.

The men and the families of Los Alamos lived a confined existence. Security was an obsession. They had no telephones, no bright lights, no night spots or outside contacts. They all had one postal box, # 1663, Santa Fe. Their leisure activities were limited to fishing and mountain climbing, soft ball and poker, and of course, their own parties. The scientists did have one outlet - the house at Otowi Bridge. There, just a few miles below Los Alamos and adjacent to the San Iledefonso Pueblo, a woman named Edith Warner ran a small tea room. Oppenheimer, Bohrs and many of the other nuclear scientists could remove themselves from the tensions inside the laboratory and sit quietly in conversation, viewing the high desert vista and feasting on Warner's specialties - spicy tea and chocolate cake. But for the rest of families of Los Alamos, there was no getaway. Only the tiny community and each family's home. They found their own reprieves. Lots and lots of babies were born at Los Alamos.

The Oppenheimer's moved to Los Alamos in March 1943. By April, the first wave of new residents had arrived. The orientation lectures were given to the scientists by Robert Serber, a physicist who had worked with Oppenheimer at Berkley. The gist of these lectures was that there would be no compartmentalization of information. Everything would be shared. Most of the men were not fully aware of the mission of the project until they got there. Over the next twelve months the remainder of the collaborators arrived.

One of the last to set foot in Los Alamos was Enrico Fermi, his wife Laura and their children. Life on 'the hill' as it was called, was soon known as mesa life. The mixture of citizenship and birthplaces was broad. They were both Machiavellian and convivial to their core. But not everyone was enamored with mesa life. When Leo Szilard first saw Los Alamos, he is known to have said, "Nobody can think straight in a place like this....everyone that comes will go crazy!"

Enrico Fermi – nuclear physicist who engineered the first 'chain reaction' Chicago Pile-1

Quickly, Robert Oppenheimer morphed into a powerful, unctuous leader. The power of his intellect and personality convinced everyone around him that their hard work could accomplish something nothing else could - the shortening of the war and the saving of thousands of lives. But these men of science soon became aware that saving lives would cost lives. They were in the business, at least indirectly, of massive death and destruction.

In September, 1944, as substantial progress was secretly being made at Los Alamos, the American and British Combined Military Chiefs had set a time table for ending the war in the Pacific.

Tentatively, it was 18 months after the defeat of Germany. Central to that goal was the invasion of Japan. Major General Curtis LeMay had command of the 20th Bomber Command, based in India with forward air fields in China to reach targets in Japan. Fuel supply for the missions was being flown over the Himalayas. But it wasn't working. Every gallon of fuel used for the bombing missions required 12 gallons to fly the fuel from India to China.

The U.S. had a better option, but one achieved at a high price. The Mariana Islands in the archipelago in the north-western Pacific, was a volcanic group that was for the most part, uninhabited. The southern section was occupied by the Japanese military and was invaded, island by island, by the U.S. Marines. The island of Tinian was selected as the ideal place to build the support air fields for the B-29 Superfortress to be used to attack the Japanese mainland. The B-29's began arriving in the Mariana Islands in October 1944. They were there to begin precision bombing of key enemy indus-tries. Along with precision bombing, efforts were also being made to accomplish what was referred to as 'incendiary' bombing, meaning the goal was to set large areas of Japanese cities on fire. Most of the structures in their cities were made of wood.

LeMay was given command of the B-29's in the Marianas. He was a tough, two- fisted man who hated failure. And he felt he was failing. But it was not for lack of effort. Six out of seven days weather was an issue over the Japanese mainland. Japanese radar installations on the island of Iwo Jima were giving the mainland early warning of the U.S. attacks, and the 29's were flying into 140 mph headwinds. This caused the engines to overheat. Finally, enemy fighter-bombers from Iwo Jima began attacking his bases.

Iwo Jima was a mass of volcanic ash only seven miles square. A large volcano, Mt. Suribachi, was on one end. The Japanese understood the strategic importance of the island and defended it with 20,000 troops dug in to 5,000 pill boxes, bunkers, tunnels and caves. American writer and journalist, William Manchester described the intent:

"They meant to make the conquest of Iwo so costly, that the Americans would recoil from the thought of invading their homeland."

Washington was deeply concerned and gave serious consideration to the concept of 'sanitizing' the island using poisonous gas. Neither the U.S. nor Japan had signed the Geneva Convention prohibiting such use. Still, Roosevelt would not agree. He believed world opinion would turn against America.

After a week of heavy naval bombardment, the invasion began on February 19, 1945. It was the only battle during the war in which U.S. casualties exceeded those of the enemy. Of the 60,000 troops committed by the U.S., 27,909 were killed or wounded. Of the 21,000 defenders, an estimated 20,703 died, either having been killed or due to

suicide. Only 216 were captured.

It appeared that bombing the mainland combined with a naval blockade would not bring an end to the war. Thus, another plan became an option.

Dozens of men played key roles in the development of the atomic bomb. They all were instrumental in supplying various pieces to the puzzle. A central component was the Frisch-Peierls memorandum, developed in March 1940, and kept highly secret. Working at Birmingham University, Otto Frisch and Roudolf Peierls made new calculations detailing the critical mass required. It was estimated to be about a pound of enriched uranium-235. The previous amount was thought to be several hundred pounds, a much harder achievement. This led to the formal effort by Britain in the following year, to establish a bomb project, code named the MAUD Project. Eventually the MAUD Project was combined with the Manhattan Project and moved to the U.S. At that time, James Chadwick, who had discovered the neutron in 1932, moved to Los Alamos to head up the British delegation. Before its move to the U.S., the MAUD Committee's code name for their bomb was 'Tube Alloys.'

In late August 1943, Churchill and Roosevelt met in Quebec City, Canada and hammered out an agreement of non-proliferation between their two countries concerning nuclear weapons. They agreed never to use this agent against each other; not to use it against a third party without each other's consent; and not to communicate any information about 'Tube Alloys' to third parties except by mutual consent. This agreement established a combined Policy Committee to oversee and coordinate weapons development.

The following November, Chadwick invited Otto Frisch, the nephew of Jewish physicist Lisa Meitner, to join his team in New Mexico. In less than a week, Frisch was made a British citizen and was on his way. He was briefed by General Groves in Washington D.C., then was boarded on a train for New Mexico. Frisch was driven the 75 miles from Albuquerque, then he and a colleague were met on the mesa by a tall, emaciated looking man smoking a pipe. The man reached out to shake hands and said, "Welcome to Los Alamos and who the devil are you?"

Oppenheimer had become an iconic leader of the lab. Hans Bethe, head of the Theoretical Division of the bomb project would later say the following:

"He knew everything that went on in the laboratory, whether it was chemistry, or theoretical physics or machine shop. He could keep it all in his head and coordinate it. It was clear also at Los Alamos that he was intellectually superior to us."

It was evident from the beginning that only one test of the bomb would be possible. Sometime before the summer of 1944, Oppenheimer code-named the test and the test site. He called it Trinity. In clarifying why this name was chosen, he explained that he was influenced by a John Donne poem expressing the idea that dying ends in death but could result in resurrection - the bomb was a weapon of death that might also redeem mankind. The paradox of the bomb was an ever-present thought of the scientists.

The site chosen for Trinity was in the Alamogordo Bombing Range, some 200 miles south of Los Alamos. Immediately, work began to build reinforced concrete camera bunkers, two 100-foot towers, and miles of communication wire with optics and expensive seismic instruments to measure blast. One of the towers was at ground zero and would suspend the test bomb. The other was 800 yards south of zero. It was filled with 100-tons of high explosives which were detonated to test the blast monitors. There were ionization chambers and instruments to reveal the explosive yield radiochmeically. The various teams had the bomb physics well in hand by November 1944. Oppenheimer set a tentative target test date of July 4the of the following summer.

As weapons grade plutonium-239 and uranium-235 were being delivered to Los Alamos, the 'Target Committee' held their first meeting in Lauris Norstad's conference room at the Pentagon. Their objective was to select four target options within the guidelines of the B-25 range of 1,500 miles and the essential of visual bombing. They were briefed by the top Air Force meteorologist who informed the group that June brought the worst weather to Japan. This meant he could only forecast a good day for bombing operations 24 hours in advance. Target selection would consider only cities that had not had previous significant damage and places that would most adversely affect the will of the Japanese people to continue the war. It was also critical that there be no POW camps near the targets.

By the end of May 1945, enough plutonium had been shipped to Los Alamos to begin critical-mass experiments. Theoretical bomb design calculations were being finalized for configurations. The uranium bomb was code named 'Little Boy' and the plutonium bomb 'Fat Man'.

The detonation device for the plutonium bomb was much more complex than the device for uranium. Thus, 'Fat Man' would not be used before testing it first. In the meantime, plans were made to ship 'Little Boy' to the Pacific by sea. Because of the complexity of devising the detonation details of 'Fat Man', Trinity was pushed back to July 16. In compliance with the Quaker Agreement, the Combined Policy Committee met in Washington on July 4th, and the British officially gave their approval to use the weapons against Japan.

The sudden death of Franklin Roosevelt on April 12th jolted the scientists in New Mexico, particularly Oppenheimer and the Americans. Without the bold vision and trust of Roosevelt, the Manhattan Project would never have begun. He had remained a talisman of support and was steadfast in his encouragement to the team. Oppenheimer scheduled a memorial service for the following Sunday and opened it to the entire community. Shortly after midnight on Saturday, a steady snow began. By morning the mesa was adorned with a blanket of white frosting. The theater was packed. Oppenheimer was eloquent.

"When, three days ago, the world had word of the death of President Roosevelt, many wept who are unaccustomed to tears, many men and women, little enough accustomed to prayer, prayed to God. Many of us looked with deep trouble to the future; many of us felt less certain that our works would be to a good end; all of us were reminded of how precious a thing human greatness is.

We have been living through years of great evil and of great terror. Roosevelt had been our President, our Commander-in-Chief and, in an old and un-perverted sense, our leader. All over the world men have looked to him for guidance and have seen symbolized in him their hope that the evils of this time would not be repeated; that the terrible sacrifices which have been made, and those that are still to be made, would lead to a world more fit for human habitation....

In the Hindu scripture, in the *Bhagavad-Gita,* it says, 'Man is a creature whose substance is faith. What his faith is, he is.' The faith of Roosevelt is one that is shared by millions of men and women in every country of the world. For this reason, it is possible to maintain the hope, for this reason it is right that we should dedicate ourselves to the hope that his good works will not have ended with his death."

Harry Truman was now president. He had known almost nothing of the Manhattan Project, and now the awesome burden of this most terrible of weapons was directly on his shoulders.

With the war in Europe won, all focus was on the Pacific Theater of Operations. Truman had agreed to meet with Stalin and Churchill in the Berlin suburb of Potsdam. He wanted to know the results of Trinity before facing Stalin so the meeting was put off until the week of July fifteenth. Trinity was set for July sixteenth.

In the two weeks leading up to Trinity, the tension at Las Alamos became palpable. Silently, men asked themselves, 'what if the bomb fails?' 'What if the two billion spent and the employment of over 100,000 is all for naught?'

Everything hinged on the implosion device for the plutonium. The detonation of 'Little Boy' had never been an issue. There was great confidence in that design. But 'Fat Man' was another story. The uranium bomb would be set off by a 'gun assembly' that was simple in concept and operation. But plutonium fission could not be started by the same mechanism. It required a more violent start – in essence, an explosion to produce the explosion. It had never been done. It was all theoretical. The mood at Trinity was gloomy.

The evening of July fifteenth everything was in place. The plutonium bomb had been lifted by a giant crane and was suspended on the 100-foot tower. Later that night the bomb would be armed. The shot was set for 4:00 a.m. the following day. Oppenheimer was standing at base camp with Cyril Smith, the head of the metallurgy division. As the sun was ducking behind the mountains, Smith heard him say, "Funny how the mountains always inspire our work."

Fat Man would be fired through cables from the S-10000 control bunker. About 2:00 a.m. a fierce thunderstorm hit base camp and dumped several inches of rain in one hour. Then the storm evaporated. But since everything depended on the weather, the rain delayed the shot until 5:30 a.m. Several men had veto over the timing, but all agreed on the delay. A B-29 was to fly directly over ground zero at 30,000 feet to get data on the blast effects at that altitude.

The main viewing site was at Compania Hill some 20 miles away. A number of physicists and Trinity staff were there. A short-wave radio broadcast the countdown. Everyone had eye protection so they could look directly at the flash. The final 10 seconds were automatic...four...three...two...one...zero.

The fission multiplied its energy over one millionth of a second, generating millions of degrees and millions of pounds of pressure. The initial hot sphere was cooled to about half a million degrees in a ten-thousandth of a second – then the shock wave formed. It moved out like a water wave expanding from a rock thrown into a still pool. The fireball formed and over the next 10 to 15 seconds its buoyancy took it up thousands of feet. All of the men witnessing Trinity were profoundly affected. Oppenheimer's response was laconic. He described the moment:

"We waited until the blast had passed, walked out of the shelter and then it was extremely solemn. We knew the world would not be the same. A few people laughed, a few cried.

"Most people were silent. I remembered the line from the Hindu scripture, the *Bagavad- Gita*: Vishnu is trying to persuade the Prince that he should do his duty and to impress him he takes on his multi-armed form and says, 'Now I am become Death, the destroyer of worlds.' I suppose we all thought that, one way or another."

Robert Oppenheimer and Gen. Leslie Groves at ground zero Trinity blast site

Churchill, Truman and Stalin at Potsdam to discuss using the A-bomb

On that same morning in the pre-dawn hours, the *USS Indianapolis* was loaded with 'Little Boy' and the gun assembly. By 8:30 a.m. she was steaming under the Golden Gate to the open sea. Her destination - the island of Tinian, South Pacific.

The week-long Potsdam conference had started the day before. The purpose was to explore conditions for a Japanese surrender. The general feeling was that Japan was desperate. But American Secretary of War, Henry L. Stimson, noted that with the mountainous terrain and their plethoric patriotism, the Japanese might fanatically resist surrender and prefer to fight to the death. When news of the Trinity success reached the U.S. delegation, their outlook changed. They debated privately about how to tell Stalin. But in fact, Soviet espionage agents had already informed him of the results. The final Potsdam Declaration demanded unconditional surrender from the Japanese, which they initially rejected with a policy of silence.

The Tuesday that Truman mentioned the bomb to Stalin, General Groves drafted the historical directive for its use. The directive was sent for approval to the Secretary of War and Army Chief of Staff George C. Marshall. Groves requested and received permission from Marshall to brief General Douglas MacArthur who, as yet, did not know of the bomb. On July twenty-sixth, the *Indianapolis* arrived at Tinian. That same day three C-54 cargo planes took off from Kirkland Air Force Base in Albuquerque with separate pieces of 'Little Boy' assembly. Two more departed with 'Fat Man's' plutonium core and initiator.

Kantaro Suzuki, Prime Minister of Japan, held a press conference to officially reject the Potsdam Declaration. That night the five C-54's arrived at Tinian and three newly modified B-29's departed Kirkland, each carrying a 'Fat Man' high-explosive preassembly.

In a final attempt to avoid horrific death and destruction, the Scientific Panel of the Interim Committee was asked to consider some type of demonstration that might change the minds of the Japanese government. Ernest Lawrence, Arthur Compton, Fermi and Oppenheimer met at Los Alamos the weekend of June sixteenth. Working late into the night, the four masterminds of physics looked at a number of options. In the end, they could not envision a 'demonstration' that might persuade the Japanese to end the bitter conflict. Exploding a bomb without any damage would not likely serve as enough evidence to the Japanese that the U.S. and Britain would in fact use it on them. It would be viewed only as a threat. There were those who would disagree. Years later, many would argue that the killing of innocent people as a means to an end was always murder.

On July thirty-first, 'Little Boy' was ready. It was too large to load into a B-29 with the normal ground clearance, so a pit was dug in which to place the bomb before loading it. Practice runs had been completed. The crews had seen film of Trinity, so they believed they had some understanding of the power of the bomb. On Thursday, August 2nd, three B-29's arrived from New Mexico with preassembly cargo for 'Fat Man'.

Now the mission waited on weather. The following Sunday, Guam reported that weather over the target cities should improve on the following day. At 2:00 p.m. on August 5th, General LeMay confirmed the mission would take place on August sixth. Paul Tibbets would fly the mission. He named the plane the *Enola Gay*, his mother's name. She had encouraged him to join the Air Force.

It was 2:45 a.m. on August sixth, when Tibbets eased the brakes of the *Enola Gay* for takeoff. She carried 7,000 gallons of fuel and an 8,000 lb. bomb. In all, she was almost 15,000 lbs. over weight. The plane used most all of the 10,000 ft. runway before liftoff and stayed at low altitude to save fuel. Within 10 minutes the crew crossed the northern tip of Sipan at 4,700 ft. By 3:00 a.m. two airmen entered the unheated and unpressurized bomb bay to arm 'Little Boy'. It was a balmy 72 degrees F. At 5:52 as they approached Iwo Jima, the crew climbed to 9,300 ft. to rendezvous with the observation and photography planes. They then took a dead reckoning to the primary target, Hiroshima, Japan.

Little Boy exploded at 8:16 a.m., just 43 seconds after leaving the *Enola Gay.* The explosion rocked everyone's preconceived ideas about its strength. At its epicenter, the temperature was an estimated 5,400 degrees F. Everything within 500 meters of ground zero – from people to animals to vegetation - was vaporized. Records were burned in the blast, so the death toll is not exact. However, it is estimated that Hiroshima's population was between 350,000 to 400,000 residents. The initial death toll was estimated at 70,000. That number increased to 140,000 by the end of 1945. The death toll due to burns, radiation and infection would rise again, and claim another 160,000 in the aftermath. Five square miles of the city were destroyed, leaving less than half of the 76,000 buildings still standing.

In the days that followed, millions of leaflets were dropped over 47 Japanese cities to get information of Hiroshima to the Japanese people. But the government remained eerily silent.

The assembly of 'Fat Man' continued. On August eighth it was loaded onto a B-29 named Bock's Car and dropped on August ninth at 11:02 a.m. on the city of Nagasaki. Five days later, Emperor Hirohito spoke to his ministers telling them he now felt the Potsdam Declaration was acceptable. He did not mention the atom bomb but said, "I cannot endure the thought of letting my people suffer any longer. A continuation of the war would bring death to tens, perhaps even hundreds of thousands of persons. The whole nation would be reduced to ashes. How then could I carry on the wishes of my imperial ancestors?"

*   *   *

Anna remained deep in thought as Landis drove the 100 kilometers back to Leipzig. She was disappointed but beginning to believe that emotionally she must move on. Life had been a struggle since losing Christian and the labyrinth of survival she'd been walking. She had never had the time to actually grieve the loss of him. She wondered now if she had perhaps transferred her love for Christian to this little boy she had saved. Her life with Eric would have meant life with a child – a life she would never have with Christian. Once again, she would have to detach herself from her dreams. But she felt empty. She had no more reserve, no more building blocks to reconstruct the citadel that had been Anna Eichenwald.

It was almost dark when the truck pulled up to Sarah's apartment. Landis got out and rounded the cab to open the door for Anna. She had taken 30,000 marks with her. She gave it all to Landis. Although he tried to push it away, Anna insisted. She knew it would be enough to support his family for a few weeks while he looked for work.

Anna looked up at Landis and began to feel a deep sadness. Her eyes filled with tears and she wrapped her arms around him holding him tightly for a few moments. How she missed having Christian's arms around her. The sadness moved from her thoughts of Christian to those of her own people and to some degree, her ravaged country. She kissed Landis on the cheek.

"I will miss you."

His eyes followed her as she disappeared into the apartment. He briefly thought of the first time he met her in the farm house, this remarkable Jewish woman who wanted to fight the Germans.

Sarah had a communication from Anna's parents. It contained information about a program that was being set-up by Chaim Weizmann, the Russian-born Zionist who had helped her parents and so many others escape Nazi Germany. The program provided transportation for survivors of *der Volkermordanden Juden* - the genocide of the Jewish People. Immigration to England or the United States was now just a formality for individuals with relatives in those countries. Although more difficult to achieve, immigration to Palestine was also possible.

Within two weeks Anna was on a train to the north of France where she would be ferried from Calais across the English Channel to Dover and ultimately, a joyous reunion with her mother and father. Anna Eichenwald had miraculously survived the war and the Nazi pogrom of her people. She would not see Germany again.

CHAPTER 24
Home but not Home

It was an unusually clear day when Anna stepped onto the ferryboat at Calais. She could just make out a suggestion of white across the English Channel. The White Cliffs of Dover were always the last thing visible when leaving England and conversely, the first when arriving. Tropical seas had once covered England and Europe, inhabited by marine invertebrates with shells composed of calcium carbonate. When the waters receded and the ice age tidal forces eroded the land, some 135 million years ago, the remains of these shells and the sediment they left behind created a striking mountain of chalk rising in some places, 350 ft. high.

Anna had only read of the English Channel. She knew of the daring evacuation of British and French troops across the channel early in the war. Now crossing it for the first time she began to mentally trace all that had happened since she had last seen her parents.

The ferry was now under full steam. Staring out at the water, Anna absently opened her purse again to touch the refugee documents and the visa that would allow her entry into the U.K. Satisfied the papers were still there, she continued staring into the water. At her feet was her one small suitcase packed with all she owned in the world.

Anna's thoughts were interrupted as she realized some of the passengers were beginning to make their way to the front of the boat. She was one of some 200 people on this journey. The ferry hadn't been in operation since 1939, when Poland was invaded.

Service had now resumed and was making two trips a day. The restoration of peace led to the restoration of freedoms that took many forms.

Anna moved to the bow and looked into the deep blue of the channel. The bow center was slicing through the sea forming a wake of foam. It was mesmerizing to watch the ocean water being parted. She raised her gaze and the white cliffs were now gleaming in the bright sunlight. She was unaware of their history and knew nothing of the miles of hidden tunnels within the cliffs, tunnels that had been created during the Middle Ages. These tunnels were used in the defense of Britain during Napoleon's reign that ended in his final defeat at Waterloo in 1815. More recently the tunnels had been expanded under Dover castle and used as a military command center by Admiral Sir Bertram Ramsey, the man who had directed the miraculous Dunkirk evacuation.

Hanz and Marlene Eichenwald planned to take the train from London to Dover. It had been three and a half years since they had seen their daughter. Although Anna was now 44 years old, Marlene still saw her as a gangly 12-year old who once placed her raven hair on top of her head in an effort to look older than she was. What had happened to the time? More importantly, what had happened to their world? Now they were in a new country speaking a new language.

Marlene had been unable to sleep. She finally got up at dawn and heated water for tea. A university car came for them at 8:00 a.m. for the trip to London's Victoria Station where they boarded the train to Dover. Two hours later they arrived. They took a taxi from the Dover station to the ferry docking site and waited. The ferry was scheduled to arrive at 12:05 p.m.

Hanz brought journals to read but he never opened them. Instead, he bought two cups of coffee and returned to sit down beside his wife. They had been together almost 46 years. Silently he thanked God that this day had finally come. Neither of them spoke. They quietly sipped their coffee. With every swallow, they vowed to contain their excitement. Neither of them wanted an emotional melt-down.

The docking hour finally arrived and Hanz and Marlene found themselves with more than a hundred others moving toward the sign that read 'Customs Entry'. Another smaller sign read, 'stand behind this line,' and a lone customs official stood by to ensure the sign was obeyed. Through a large series of glass windows they could see the ferry slowly approaching. Straining against the crowd, Marlene pushed her way to the window to get a better view but to no avail. She turned to the customs official. "How long does this process usually take?" she asked.

"About an hour, depending where you were in line."

Upon disembarking, each passenger was subjected to questioning and a check of the documents they carried. Some were on visitor visas, most were permanently emigrating. The time seemed to drag. Marlene strained her eyes, searching from figure to figure. But the sea of faces melted together in an undistinguishable mass. Marlene began to worry. What if Anna hadn't boarded the ferry? And then suddenly, there she was. A smile creased Marlene's face and she whispered out loud, "Anna! Thank God."

Marlene turned to find Hanz who was standing toward the rear watching the drama unfold. He had seen her as well. The same smile spread across his face and he began to nod. "Yes, I see her," he mouthed to his wife.

The rope was disconnected for each individual or family as the case required. Finally, it was Anna's turn. She walked briskly into her mother's arms. There were no dry eyes. Even her father, the professor and linear thinker, had trouble keeping his composure. Their daughter who was 'dead' was alive. She had been lost and now she was safely home. The family was reunited and speaking their native German.

An elderly Polish couple who had left their farm north of Warsaw just before the 1939 German invasion was waiting to board the ferry. They were observing the joyous reunion and wondering if they would find their grandson who had fought in the underground. They wondered if their farm was still standing. But that wouldn't matter if they could find their only remaining relative alive and well.

The Eichenwalds left the ferry terminal arm in arm. Anna turned for one last glimpse. She was to begin a new life with a new language. Her life as a German Jew would be only a memory. The emotional pain and scars would heal just as so many of her patients, even those with invasive surgeries, had healed completely over the years. This had always been a mystery to her.

*   *   *

In the year to come, Anna Eichenwald's world would change dramatically. So would the world in general. In a move unprecedented in history, a winning country involved in a bloody and prolonged conflict would make an effort to rebuild the countries involved in the conflict, even those counties that had been defeated as enemies. The effort in Europe became known as the Marshall Plan, named after U.S. Secretary of State George Marshall, who helped devise the plan. Although noble, it was not totally altruistic. The plan called for massive economic aid for most of the countries that had been involved in the war. Its purpose was to create a stronger foundation for the democratic countries of Europe, leading to a bond among allied states that would resist the new menace of communism. The plan was a noble one, the motives behind, not so much.

Within two years of European peace, a new conflict would emerge, one of ideologies. It would be a struggle for the minds of people. Democracy and free market economy would be pitted against the millions of disciples of Karl Marx, who along with Friedrich Engels wrote the Communist Manifesto. Completed in 1848, it suggested a pathway for the working class, the proletariat, to overthrow the bourgeois or ruling classes. It argued that capitalism as an economic model would eventually be overthrown by communism and result in a classless society; one in which there would be no private property, and an obfuscation of individual rights.

The Russian Revolution of 1917 had led to the downfall of Nicholas II, the last Czar. Soon after, he was executed by the Bolshevik leaders along with his entire Royal family. The coup d'etat was completed with a civil war and the communists took control of the Soviet Government. Vladimir Lenin, leader of the Bolsheviks, died in 1924 at age 53. An assassination attempt left him with a stroke that eventually took his life.

The vacuum of power was eventually filled by Joseph Stalin, the General Secretary of the Communist Party. He brazenly elevated himself to dictator through the killing of millions of his own countrymen. His tactics were political purges of repression, persecution and execution to gain control. It was not unlike the strategy that Hitler used a few years later. Now with Hitler gone, Stalin's goal was to impose Marxist ideology on as much of Europe as possible.

Anna and her family indirectly benefited by the Marshall Plan, as did most people in England because that country received the largest share of the $17 billion in aid. The economies of every European nation were stabilized, but none more than England and France. In the months that followed, Anna's interest turned more and more toward stabilizing her own future and finding a way to re-establish her calling as a physician and surgeon.

While Joseph Stalin was helping the Bolsheviks overthrow the Czar, another Russian, Chaim Weizmann, was laying the foundation to establish a state of a different kind. During WWI, while serving as acting director of British Admiralty Laboratories, he developed a friendship with Arthur Balfour, who had been Prime Minister from 1902 to 1905. As Foreign Secretary, Balfour was influential in supporting Weizmann's Zionism, the desire for the establishment of a Jewish State in Palestine. A 1917 document, known as the Balfour Declaration, was a government paper that set a policy to "view with favor" the establishment of a national home for Jewish people in Palestine.

This British policy was, to a great extent, in recognition of the contribution made in 1914 by Weizmann toward the winning of the war. But the issue of a Jewish state had always been controversial. The careful wording of 'Jewish home', rather than 'Jewish State' was one example of the mendacious tone of the document. In the 1920s, the area was occupied predominantly by Arabs. Ancient manuscripts as well as Old Testament Scripture referred to the land as Canaan. In more modern times, the Christian community generally called it the Holy Land, and non- Christians referred to it as Palestine.

Jewish and Arabic cultures have common ancestral heritage. Each held Abraham as their patriarch. The Biblical story recounts Abraham as having married Sarah. The couple had no children. But

Sarah was promised one by God. As Sarah grew older and beyond child bearing age, she no longer believed the promise and persuaded Abraham to take her Egyptian maid-servant, Hagar, as his wife to ensure an offspring for their family. He did. Hagar then gave birth to Ishmael, a male child, who became the 'father' of the Arabic race. But several years after Ishmael was born, Sarah became pregnant and gave birth to Isaac, the child that had been promised. He became the 'father' of the Jewish race.

Although the ancestral heritage begins here, the evolution of the Arabic and Jewish people was quiet different, even antithetical in many respects, leading to a modern day nadir of existence and co-existence.

Their languages, Hebrew and Arabic, evolved from the same ancient Semitic language. The earliest known written form of Semitic languages, cuneiform script, was developed about 3,000 BC. Hebrew and Arabic ancestors were called *Semites.* The term is derived from Shem, one of three sons of Noah. Shem's descendants became known as Semites. In the 19th century, individuals prejudiced against Jews were called anti-Semites. Because of this modern colloquialism, the Arabic ancestors of Shem are no longer referred to as Semites. That term is now used only in reference to the Jewish race, and principally as a negative connotation, one denoting opposition to the Jewish people.

The dispute over the land of Palestine dates back to antiquity. The first Hebrew temple was built in Jerusalem by King Solomon in 957 BC. The temple was destroyed in 586 by Nebuchadnezzar, king of the Babylonian Empire. It was re-built on the same location, the Temple Mount, in 516 BC. Most Jewish citizens in Israel had been exiled to Babylon, but were beginning to return by 530. The prophet

Daniel was among the exiled group. In scripture, the book of Daniel details his experiences during his Babylonian captivity.

The rebuilt temple was renovated by Herod the Great around 20 BC but was completely destroyed 90 years later by the Romans occupying Palestine. When this temple was destroyed in 70 AD, the majority of Jews living in Palestine were driven from their homeland and scattered world-wide. This process, the Diaspora, was actually the second Jewish Diaspora. The first occurred when they were exiled to Babylon.

The Zionist movement was both political and religious. The idea to re-establish a Jewish homeland was initiated in 1895 by Theodor Herzl, a journalist. The term Zionism evolved from the tradition that Mt. Zion in Jerusalem was the location of the ancient first temple. Zion now refers to the entire city of Jerusalem.

Herzl was born in Budapest in 1860. He moved with his family to Vienna in 1878 and in time, became greatly influenced by the wide spread anti-Semitism in Europe. A case in point is the Dreyfus case that occurred in France in 1899. Alfred Dreyfus, a captain in the French military, was convicted of spying for Germany. Soon after his conviction it was determined that French intelligence officials fabricated evidence against him, principally because he was Jewish. Eventually he was vindicated and reinstated as an officer.

Chaim Weizmann, a well-known biochemist, was the leading Zionist in England. As early as 1903 he was demonstrating his passion for establishing a Jewish homeland in Palestine and a Hebrew University in Jerusalem. His motivation was not based on the suffering of his people. He simply had a yearning for the Jewish people to become a nation in their ancient home of Israel – at that time, Palestine. He enlisted as many important and influential people as he could to support the idea of a Hebrew University, including Albert Einstein and Hanz Eichenwald. The cornerstone for the University was laid in 1918 and the doors opened April 1, 1925.

Palestine was known in the Hebrew Bible as Canaan, part of the Fertile Crescent, and a land with a discordant past. In the sixth Century BC, a group of people in Eurasia began to dominate Eastern Europe and central Asia. They had a common language, Turkic. The Roman Empire was in decline as was the world influence wielded by the ancient Greeks. While the spread of Christianity was ongoing, a portentous event occurred in the Arabian city of Mecca. The prophet Mohammed was born and became the central human figure of the religion of Islam. The term 'Islam' is derived from the Arabic verb *Aslama* meaning to surrender or submit. According to Islamic tradition, at age 40, during the month of Ramadan, Mohammed received revelations from God and continued to receive them until his death in 632 AD. These revelations and his preaching formed the book of Qur'an, which literally means 'the recitation'.

Over the next 1,000 years, the Turkic speaking people gradually began to dominate Eastern Europe and central Asia. They became known as Ottoman Turks, whose predominant religion was Islam. These were the successors of the eastern Roman Empire, also known as the 'Byzantine' Empire. Thus, the administrative rule of the 'fertile crescent' changed from a Christian dominated land to one dominated by Islam.

The influence and rule in Palestine is a review of a study in the history of the world. Rule was transferred from Hebrew, to Persian, to Hellenistic Greek, to the Roman Empire during the time of Christ. Then it went from Byzantine to Islamic. The Ottoman Turks maintained control until the end of WWI, but they lost it because they had chosen to support the Germans. That support led to the turnover of Turkish rule by the British in 1920.

The League of Nations then stepped in to determine mandates for all territories controlled by states that had been defeated in WWI. The mandates accomplished two things. They removed the sovereignty of the previously controlling countries and transferred control over territories to victorious, individual Allied powers. The mandate for Palestine was given to the British. It included land from the Mediterranean Sea east to Arabia. The part of the territory known as 'Trans-Jordan' later became the country of Jordan. Territorial boundaries for British Mandate Palestine were finalized in 1923 and established territory west of the Jordan River to the Mediterranean as land to be set aside for a 'Jewish homeland'.

Arab leadership repeatedly objected and pressed the British for the right to establish a representative government in the area. But the British rejected the principle of majority rule and insisted the Arabs accept the terms of the Mandate which in effect denied Arabic control over the government of Palestine. England was a democracy and it would seem would favor democratic rule. So, parenthetically, the reasons for rejecting majority rule were unclear.

In 1920, the Jewish population of Palestine was about 20 percent of the total. By 1940 it had grown to 33 percent. The Hebrew community was known as the *Yishuv*. Arabic citizens resented the influx of Jewish immigrants and Arabic reprisals on the Jewish communities soon began. In response, the Jews created the *Haganah*, a para-military organization designed to retaliate in kind.

The differences between these two neighboring groups expanded well beyond religion. The Jewish literacy rate was 86 percent, dwarfing the Arabic rate of 22 percent. The Jews gravitated to urban areas - the Arabs remained a rural people. The Jews also began to develop industrial and educational institutions including the Hebrew University in Jerusalem. The Arabs, mirroring the farming traditions of their ancestors, had none.

As hostilities escalated, the British began making attempts to control the violence. The official British policy was to deny entry of European Jewish immigrants. Since before the war, Zionists had been organizing illegal immigration efforts and rescued thousands of individuals escaping the Nazi holocaust. Most were smuggled into Palestine on rickety boats crossing the Mediterranean. Some were lost, including one vessel holding 800 passengers. It was sunk by a Russian submarine in the Black Sea.

By the war's end, there were approximately 250,000 Jewish refugees stranded in camps scattered across Europe. The British policy against Jewish immigration was unpopular in England as well as the U.S., and with international pressure mounting, the British decided to hand the problem over to the United Nations. Eventually the U.N. Special Committee on Palestine drew up a plan for partition - separate Jewish and Arabic states. The plan placed Jerusalem under international administration. It was accepted by the U.S. and the Soviet Union but opposed by the U.K. and all Arab states. Many Jewish citizens in Palestine supported the resolution, but many did not. Menachem Begin, a powerful Zionist politician was quoted as saying,

"The partition of the homeland is illegal. It will never be recognized. The signature by institutions and individuals of the partition agreement is invalid. It will not bind the Jewish people. Jerusalem was and will forever be our capital. The Land of Israel will be restored to the people."

The U.N. resolution to partition Palestine was passed by the U.N. general assembly on November 29, 1947. The British in Palestine, however, refused to implement the plan and declared they would withdraw from the region on May 15, 1948. The day before, Israeli Prime Minister David Ben-Gurion declared Israel to be a sovereign and independent nation. The nation was immediately recognized by the Unites States and the Soviet Union. However, recognition by most other nations remained a highly controversial issue and was withheld pending further developments or action.

* * *

Cambridge, England was a storybook setting for anyone, and this was especially true for Jewish immigrants who had been trapped by a helotry that now seemed like a bad dream. The physical beauty of the countryside would match anything in Europe. There was almost never snow and instead, frequent days of rainy skies. To Anna, every day of freedom from tyranny was a day of sunshine. She spent weeks enjoying the company of her mother. Marlene Eichenwald would have made an exceptional 'oma' or grandmother, and Anna would have been a good mother herself. But circumstances did not allow this. Still, the two women, one with the genetic imprint of the other, saw their blessings in life as a quid pro quo of a blessing they did not have.

Marlene was still youthful looking at 66 years old. To others who enjoyed their company, she and Anna seemed more like sisters. Most of the wives of the men in the physics and mathematics departments had welcomed Marlene into their circles. They were gracious toward Anna as well with traditional English decorum. Anna had a gift for languages and was quick to pick up English phrases and colloquialisms.

Anna had requested permission to attend Surgical Grand Rounds at Guy's Hospital each week. Her request was accepted, and she was now part of a group run by the Royal College of Surgeons. Taking the train into the city was a treat and she often combined the trip with sightseeing. She befriended a number of those attending and eventually was asked to make a presentation of her surgical procedure on Ernst Bishoff and the follow-up of her experience with him at Buchenwald. The room was packed. All in one day Anna became highly respected and admired.

There was only one woman in all of England who was a member of the Royal College, Abigail Brightman. She was born in Ireland but moved to Edinburgh at age seven when her father became Professor of Medieval History at the University of Edinburgh. She attended the undergraduate school there and then medical school. She went on to become the only female orthopedic surgeon in England. With a special interest in children's developmental problems, she was in demand as a surgeon and a speaker. Her colleagues affectionately called her Abby. Tall, with reddish hair and a ruddy complexion, she had a ready smile and was pleased to meet Anna. The two became friends within a few, short weeks and often sat together at the meetings.

In the fall of 1946, after one Wednesday session, the two left the conference hall. "Anna, next week, how would you like to stay for a dinner out and sleep over at my place?" Abby suggested. "Then you can catch the train back on Thursday."

"Sounds great," Anna responded, delighted at the invitation. "I can't turn down an offer like that. I've taken some day trips to see the sights but haven't had dinner in the city yet. I'd love to do that. Thank you."

"Then it's all set. See you next week. We won't do anything too fancy, just a pub for fish and chips."

Anna had virtually no social life. She spent time with her parents and that was it. She wanted to work but hadn't been able to qualify for British credentials unless she re-trained in their system. She had decided not to spend more years training with superiors over whom she had more experience. It was simply not a possibility for her. She slowly began to realize how displaced she was.

"I'm a woman with no home country," she thought.

The week passed quickly until she was on the train back to London. The Grand Rounds topic was a case presentation and review of a problem she had only read about, management of tracheo-esophageal fistula in the newborn. It was a devastating problem and most children did not survive.

Abby did most of her work at Guy's Hospital. Her flat was only five blocks from the hospital and 15 blocks from Victoria Station. It was a two-story walk-up with the main living area on the first level and two bedrooms and a bath on the second. The building bordered a small park with a central fountain of running water that gave a pellucid tranquility to the area.

Abby and Anna had more in common than surgery. They both enjoyed the symphony and both had been in love. Abby's love was a barrister she had met through a friend. He had made a marriage proposal but had wanted Abby to cut back significantly on her work, something she was not yet willing to do. So everything for the couple was on 'hold'. Anna shared her stories of Christian and their time together during their surgical training. She fondly recounted some of his pranks.

"So where is he now?" Abby asked innocently. Anna looked down.

"I am so sorry."

"War is tragic," Anna replied. "For everyone."

Abby had a number of friends who had gone to war, some of whom had given their lives. She hadn't really thought much of the suffering on the enemy side. She had simply felt that since Germany started the war, they deserved what they got. Now, obviously, Christian did not fit that template.

The evening out was extraordinary. Despite the ten-year age separation, both women were youthful and vibrant. The pub was typical British fare. It was furnished in rich mahogany, with low ceilings and a black and white tile floor. Large booths that actually had doors gave the guests an unexpected feeling of privacy.

They talked about the war and the Nazi Reich. The subject moved to their youth and tales of growing up, Anna as an only child and Abby with two older brothers. Finally the conversation turned to their futures. Abby wasn't hesitant to give her opinion.

"Anna, you are well trained and obviously very capable. You need to be somewhere to utilize your skills. Would you ever return to Germany?"

"Never! The German economy is in a shamble anyway and the country has been destroyed. It will take my lifetime to rebuild. Even after what happened to the Jews, there's still a lot of hatred, Abby. I believe many people would allow it all over again if they could."

"What about America?"

"I would face the same problem professionally there," Anna replied. "And I have no desire to go to the states. But I have been thinking about something for the past few months. I've been thinking about Palestine."

Abby practically shouted. "Palestine?"

"Yes. It's a place where I can be useful. I can have a new beginning. My people are going there and making new beginnings for themselves. I could too."

"But from what I have read, if the British leave there's going to be fighting with the Arabs. It could be very dangerous."

"That's true. But with what I've been through I don't give a lot of thought to personal danger. I'm probably not a true Zionist, but I do believe that God promised Canaan…or Palestine…to us, to the Jewish people. Now may be the time in history when God provides us that homeland, something we have not had for 2,000 years. If that happens, I'd like to be part of it. Possibly my life will yet count for something."

After a long silence, Abby finally spoke. "Well, those are not plebian thoughts. You are not an ordinary woman or even an ordinary physician. If you decide to go, you will have an impact….of that I'm certain."

*　*　*

It was a warm spring day, April of 1948. Anna was in Plymouth, England waiting to board the H.M.S. Darcy, destination Palestine. Through the efforts of Chaim Weizmann, Anna had been appointed an attending surgeon at the Hebrew University Hospital in Jerusalem. She was to spend six weeks in a Tel Aviv hostel for orientation to Israel, as yet not a country. She had said her good-byes to Hanz and Marlene. Both were now sixty-seven years old. They were sad to see their only child go but understood she had her own life to live. God had brought her through the holocaust, and for that they would be eternally grateful.

Anna felt an excitement she had not experienced since her days with Christian. It had been almost three years since she had left Germany. England was beautiful and she had been well received. But it was not her home. Anna longed for a home.

The ship was a 20,000-ton vessel that had been used as a troop transport in both world wars. It was a converted tanker that had been commissioned in 1895 as part of the British merchant marine fleet. Altogether, there were 748 Jewish immigrants who had traveled from all over Europe to begin a new life. Anna had agreed to serve as the ship's doctor for the five day journey. The voyage was being funded by the international Zionist Society. Each immigrant or family would be assisted financially until they were settled into employment. Among the group were teachers, farmers, laborers, musicians, architects, engineers, bankers, lawyers, rabbis, nurses, one physician and a chemist. Anna was especially pleased that there were 178 children in the group. A new country would need strong young people to survive.

The journey would take them along the coast of France to the coast of Spain and Portugal, then east through the Strait of Gibraltar, gateway to the Mediterranean from the Atlantic. The Strait is only eight miles wide at its narrowest point, separating Spain and Gibraltar on the European continent from Morocco on the African continent. Gibraltar was a British territory ceded by Spain to Britain in 1713 under the Treaty of Utrecht. Since that time, Great Britain had maintained sovereignty over the territory. The ship would sail east past the northern tip of Tunisia and the southern tip of Sicily, then continue east south-east to Tel Aviv.

The trip was uneventful. Only a handful of the passengers had ever been on the open sea, and the weather was nice, the seas calm. To a person, the excitement was palpable. Anna stood on the bow as they passed Gibraltar. She could just make out the Union Jack flying above the rock fortress that overlooked the Strait. Unlike Gibraltar, Anna was aware of the laconic British influence over Palestine, whose history dated back well over 3,000 years. After the Hebrew exodus from Egypt, Joshua led the people into the land that had been promised to Abraham by the Lord hundreds of years earlier.

In the ensuing millennia, time and again, foreign powers invaded the Jewish homeland. The Assyrians, Babylonians, Persians, Greeks, and Romans all conquered it. Until 70 AD, it had always reverted back to a Jewish land known in Hebrew as Evetz Yisrael. But after 70 AD, most Jewish occupants were driven from their land. The Byzantine Romans controlled the land for 600 years, then they were driven out by Muslims, the last being the Ottoman Turks. At the end of WWII control was shifted to the Allies and the British assumed command over Palestine. Now the British were leaving.

Even with all of the violence and blood-shed over the centuries, the Jews had always had a presence in Palestine. The longing for a homeland was constant. For generations, Jewish men, including those who had no chance or even the desire to return to Palestine, would pledge to each other at the end of their Passover Feast – "Next Year in Jerusalem!"

As the H.M.S. Darcy steamed the Jewish immigrants toward Tel Aviv, each of the 748 passengers had a single goal – to join their 600,000 Hebrew brothers and sisters in reclaiming their land. But 1.2 million Arab Palestinians were just as determined to prevent this.

Their own ancestors had lived in Palestine for seven centuries, and for the most part, they had lived a peaceful co-existence with their Hebrew neighbors. They knew they were not responsible for the murder of six million Jews in Europe, and had a history of treating the Jews with respect and compassion. But an uneasy peace was now being kept by 100,000 British soldiers. And these soldiers were scheduled to leave on May fifteenth.

Almost five months before, on the night of November 29, 1948, in Flushing Meadows New York, the U.N. General Assembly had voted to partition Palestine with a Jewish sector and an Arab sector. Jerusalem, with its highly charged religious shrines, would be under international control. This solution to the creation of a Jewish homeland was not satisfactory to either the Jews or the Arabs. The vote by the U.N. had been highly charged, but it wasn't close. The U.S. had levied diplomatic pressure in favor of partition. But while America was pushing for unlimited Jewish immigration to Palestine, the U.S. Congress had prevented a relief bill for Hebrew immigrants to even come up for a vote, maintaining the Jewish immigration quota into the U.S. at 4,767 annually.

Still, news of the U.N. vote for partition was welcomed in the Jewish sectors of Jerusalem. It resulted in a wild celebration that lasted through the night. The celebration began with the mournful bleating of a *shofar,* the ram's horn trumpet. Scripture holds that this same kind of trumpet was used 2,400 years earlier by Joshua and his army to bring down the walls of Jericho. But all was not merriment. As they waited for news of the vote, men of the Haganah, the Jewish paramilitary defense force, listened to their leader, Yitzhak Sadeh. When asked of the vote he stoically said,

"I do not care. If the vote is for us, the Arabs will make war on us. If the vote is against us, then it is we who will make war on them."

The men in the room grew grimly silent. Either way they would face death.

As synagogues opened for all night celebrations and thousands of Jewish young people danced arm-in-arm in the streets, one curious observer watched from the third-floor balcony of his hotel room in Tel Aviv. Captain Abdul-Aziz Kerine, of the Syrian Army, would be boarding a plane later that day at Lydda Airport. His mission was to travel to Prague where he planned to buy 10,000 rifles and 1,000 machine guns for the planned Arab answer to the celebrations.

The morning of April seventeenth found Anna in her favorite place on the Darcy. She enjoyed standing on the ship's bow letting the wind sweep her hair back off of her forehead. This was the only place where a passenger could observe the dolphins darting in and out of the sea in front of the ship. They danced through the water as if in a race. Anna watched them, cognizant that today was the fifth day of the voyage, the day she had anticipated for the past 18 months.

She squinted her eyes against the wind and the bright sunlight reflecting off of the water's surface. Then as the clock moved to mid-morning, she saw it. The Mediterranean coast of Palestine began to appear on the horizon. Within a half-hour, the port city of Tel Aviv was in view. Anna and her fellow passengers were going home.

Tel Aviv had grown up out of the ancient port city of Jaffa. Its name was taken from the Old Testament book of Ezekiel. A 'tel' is an archaeological site or mound where layers of ancient civilizations are found. Aviv is the Hebrew word for 'spring' or 'grain'. So the literal meaning is 'hill of spring', symbolic of renewal.

Anna could feel the flood of emotion sweeping over her. Since 1933, her people had been placed at greater and greater risk. They were all considered *'untermenschen'* (subhuman) and treated as such. Now there was a significant chance they would have a homeland. She whispered to herself the Yiddish phrase 'mazel tov' which means good fortune. After so much heartache, so much suffering and death, 'mazel tov'.

The docking of an ocean-going vessel is time consuming. The tugs met the ship about two nautical miles from the dock and slowly guided her in. The entire process took almost three hours. The first immigrant set foot on Palestinian soil at 4:47 p.m. that day, and thus began a rather arduous customs process. Tight security was imperative despite the fact that all of the immigrants had been carefully pre-screened. Sabotage was always a possibility, even with a British presence.

Each of the immigrants had indicated a desire to remain in Palestine indefinitely. Like Anna, most were displaced from their country of origin for many different reasons. Virtually everyone had made the decision not to return in favor of a new life in Palestine.

The hostel set to house the group was a series of dormitory-like buildings, four in all, on a campus three miles from the dock. Single women and men occupied individual buildings. The other two were for families or orphaned children. Each building had a mess hall and meeting rooms. Orientation lectures were given each morning of the week. But afternoons were free time.

Anna found Tel Aviv was a bustling place. It was rapidly becoming the economic center of Jewish Palestine. The climate in this portion of the 'fertile crescent' was arid, even hot compared to the wet, cooler temperatures in England. Here, the constant easterly ocean breezes kept the coastal city pleasant and the low humidity made life comfortable. No one really minded the heat. Tel Aviv was dotted with gardens that held a wide variety of plants and trees. Anna's favorites were the palms and bougainvilleas. The skies were crystal blue. Without the haze that comes with humidity, the colors seemed more vivid to her. On occasion an early morning fog rolled in, but always, it burned away by mid-morning.

Many factors bound the ménage of Israel together, but none more than their language. Anna had studied Hebrew as a youngster but had never had the need to speak it. Thanks to a 19- year old lawyer's son form Poland, Jewish Palestinians spoke Hebrew. David Green immigrated to Palestine in 1906, left to study law in Turkey, moved to New York City, got married and returned to Palestine in 1920. He changed his name because there was nothing 'Hebrew' about Green. He adopted a Hebrew name that meant 'son of a lion cub'. The man, David Ben-Gurion, then became the editor of a Zionist trade paper and was committed to the Hebrew spoken word. He also became Israel's first Prime Minister.

Over the next three weeks Anna plunged into the history of Jewish Palestine, its customs, strengths and weaknesses. She became convinced that 'the Holy One of Israel' had brought her to this land. When Anna needed or wanted a deeper understanding or a reminder of her blessing, she would look inside her left forearm. The tattoo read *B-76083*.

In the evening, Anna often took a bus 12 blocks to the central market across from the ocean. It was a food bazaar of fresh vegetables, fish, flowers, baked goods, baskets, clothing and much more. She was falling deeply in love with this land and her people and felt herself basking in the joy of freedom and the security of sovereignty. She always looked forward to the bus ride. It gave her the opportunity to study the people and their faces. She saw in them, a reflection of what she herself felt.

One evening Anna caught the bus about dusk. She had discovered that she enjoyed the market most when the cool ocean breezes of the late afternoon caressed the shoppers. The bus was two blocks from the market when her eye caught a figure that looked strangely familiar. She peered intently as the bus made its stop. When it began to roll again she jumped from her seat and ran to the front.

"Stop the bus, please. I must get off!"

Anna bolted from the door, running, her eyes searching the crowd. Then she saw him. The large man with the black beard she had seen from the bus was suddenly in front of her. She was sure she knew who he was.

"Beryl!" she called out.

The man turned toward her with a startled look. "Beryl, its Anna. Anna Eichenwald."

Without speaking he reached out, placing his massive arms around her. "Anna, Anna, you are safe, you are alive. We thought you had been killed." He stepped back to look at her.

"You look wonderful. Let me look at you."

Anna's eyes filled with tears as she looked into his face. She was almost afraid to ask. "Eric? What happened to Eric?"

"Why, Anna. He is standing behind you. He went to get ice cream."

Anna turned and found herself looking into the eyes of a tall, thin boy with black curly hair and dark eyes. He had a slight smile and looked at Anna as if he should know her.

As she realized this child, the one she had worked so tirelessly to save, was now safely with her in Israel, she whispered, "Ja! Die sonne scheint noch – yes, the sun still shines!"

Donald Hunt is a retired vascular surgeon. His academic passion was not centered on chemistry and biology, but in history. After retiring, he traded his scalpel for a pen and began research to produce a historical novel. He saw the five decades from 1900 - 1950 as most critical in shaping both the world of science and the fulfillment of the promise of Genesis 12:7. He and artist wife Delia live in the Texas hill country.

Author Don Hunt

A P P E N D I X

Historical figures, their chapter appearance and importance:

Adolph Hitler – Chapter 1

An insignificant Austrian corporal who served in WWI and rose to power in Germany in 1933. His goal was to concur and control all of Europe and rid these lands of all Jews. He predicted a 1000-year reign of the German Third Reich. It lasted 12 years. Rather than face trial for his war crimes, he took his own life and had his remains burned.

Albert Einstein – Chapter 1

The world's most noted theoretical physicist who published papers detailing his theories of special relativity (1905) and general relativity (1915). He was a German Jew who left just before Hitler came to power He was awarded a Nobel Prize in physics in 1921 for his discovery of the photoelectric effect.

Matthias Erzberger – Chapter 2

A German Catholic politician, murdered by terrorists because he had signed the armistice ending WWI.

Walter Rathenou – Chapter 2

The highest ranking Jewish official in Germany assassinated by those who blamed him for defeat in WWI.

Sir Isaac Newton – Chapter 3

English physicist who described the laws of gravitational forces controlling planetary orbits in our solar system He devised the math to prove his theories we know today as calculus.

Max Plank – Chapter 3

A German theoretical physicist who developed quantum theory (also known as quantum mechanics). This theory describes the nature of the smallest scales of energy levels of atoms & subatomic particles. He was awarded the 1918 Nobel Prize for this work.

Field Marshal Hindenburg – Chapter 4

Commander of German military, second half of WWI. Elected President in 1925 and re-elected 1932. In poor health, he was pressured into appointing Hitler as Chancellor of Germany in 1933.

Karl Marx – Chapter 5

A German born in 1818 and the son of a Jewish lawyer. He lectured at the University of Berlin, but was forced from Germany because of his radical views. In 1848 with Friedrich Engels, published the Communist Manifesto.

Charles Dawes – Chapter 6

An American banker responsible for developing a plan to pull Germany out of a severe inflationary spiral post WWI.

Arthur Schnabel – Chapter 6 b. 1882 in Austria. He was a classical pianist considered a great interpreter of Beethoven & Schubert. He was best known for performing the complete cycle of 32 Beethoven Sonatas.

Charles Lindbergh – Chapter 6

American aviator famous for being the first to cross the Atlantic flying solo non-stop from Long Island, NY to Paris. He gained fame winning the Medal of Honor for his feat. His plane, the Spirit of St. Louis is on display at the National Air and Space Museum.

Joseph Goebbels – Chapter 6

A German Nazi and Propaganda Minister for Hitler. He was an ardent supporter of Hitler, fully advocating the extermination of all Jews in Europe. After the defeat of Germany and death of Hitler, he and his wife, Magda, poisoned their six children with cyanide and committed suicide.

Heinrich Himmler – Chapter 6

As a leading member of the Nazi Party, he was the principle architect for the "Final Solution" to rid Europe of all Jews by extermination. He served as head of the State Secret Police (Gestapo) and a paramilitary organization – Schutzstaffel or SS.

Ernst Rohm – Chapter 6

As an early supporter of Hitler, he headed the Storm Battalion or SA in the 1920's and early '30's. They were the 'street thugs' who battled Socialists and Communists. Under Rohm's leadership the SA became more powerful and a threat to Hitler. He was executed by Hitler's order in July, 1934.

Lise Meitner – Chapter 7

Austrian born physicist who was a professor at the K-W Institute in Berlin in '30's. She helped discover the process of nuclear fission (splitting the atomic nucleus). She was dismissed from her teaching position because of the anti-Jewish Nuremberg Laws.... Born to Jewish parents in Vienna in 1878, she became a Christian in 1908 at age 30, and fled Germany to Sweden in 1938.

Otto Hahn – Chapter 7

A German chemist working jointly with Lise Meitner, furthered the work of Italian physicist Enrico Fermi, to bombard Uranium with neutrons seeking to 'split' the Uranium nucleus. In 1938 he accomplished this feat, opening up to the world, nuclear energy. He was awarded the Nobel Prize in physics / chemistry in 1944.

Niels Bohr – Chapter 7
b. 1885 a Danish physicist who made foundational contributions to the structure of the atom and subsequently to quantum theory. He was awarded the Nobel Prize in physics in 1922. He worked tirelessly to support scientists escaping Germany. In 1943 he fled the Nazis to England with his family.

Hermon Goering – Chapter 7
The second most powerful member of the Nazi Reich. He was the Commander-in-Chief of the Air Force (Luftwaffe) After the defeat of Germany in 1945, he was convicted of war crimes and sentenced to death by hanging. He committed suicide by ingesting cyanide the day before his scheduled execution.

Leo Szilard – Chapter 7
b. 1898. A Hungarian physicist who conceived the nuclear chain reaction. In 1928 and 1929 he submitted patents for a linear accelerator and a cyclotron. In 1939 he drafted a letter, signed by Einstein, to be presented to President Roosevelt supporting the building of an atomic weapon, what became known as the Manhattan Project.

James Chadwick – Chapter 7
b. 1891. British physicist awarded the 1935 Nobel Prize in physics for his discovery of the neutron (a subatomic particle). In the later stages of WWII he was head of a British team working in New Mexico on the Manhattan Project.

Winston Churchill – Chapter 10 b. 1874, served as British Prime Minister, 1940-1945. In the years before WWII he stressed rearmament to counter the growing threat of Nazi aggression. He replaced Chamberlain as Prime Minister in May 1940 and is widely credited with stabilizing the war effort to defeat Germany. He was also an accomplished writer of history winning the Nobel Prize in Literature.

Benito Mussolini – Chapter 10
b. 1883, Italy. A politician who served as Italian Prime Minister 1922-1943. He developed a one-party Italy to join Germany to concur Europe. Italy joined the war effort in June 1940 after the fall of France; however Italian forces were defeated on every front. He was deposed as Prime Minister in 1943. He attempted to flee to Switzerland in 1945 but was caught and executed.

Enrico Fermi – Chapter 10
b. 1901 Italy, one of the few physicists who excelled in both the theoretical and experimental arenas. He left Italy because his wife was Jewish. He created the first nuclear reactor, the Chicago Pile-1. The reactor went 'critical' on December 2, 1942, demonstrating the first human-created, self-sustaining chain reaction.

Neville Chamberlain – Chapter 10
b. 1869. Prime Minister of England 1937- May 1940. In 1938, he signed the Munich Agreement conceding the German-speaking portion of Czechoslovakia to Germany. Trusting Hitler was fatal as Germany invaded Poland Sept. 1st 1939 and two days later England declared war but were woefully unprepared. Eight months later he was replaced by Churchill.

Franklin Delano Roosevelt – Chapter 11 b. 1882, known as 'FDR' served as the 32nd President of the U.S. from 1933 – 1945 (death). He took office in what is known as the Great Depression (economic). His reforms began an upturn in the economy. But entering WWII after the Japanese attack on Perl Harbor was an even greater boost economically. His death in April 1945 elevated Harry S. Truman as the 33rd President of the U.S.

Chaim Weizmann – Chapter 11
b. 1874 in Russia the third of 15 children to Jewish parents. At 18 he went to Germany then Switzerland and earned a PhD. in organic chemistry. Eventually moving to England, he became a lecturer at the University of Manchester. He was an ardent Zionist (one who believes the Jews had a homeland in Palestine) In 1948 he moved to his new country of Israel and became her first President.

Joseph Stalin – Chapter 11
b. 1878 in Russia, he became a communist revolutionist and was active in the 1917 Civil War. He soon rose to political power under his mentor Vladimir Lenin. When Lenin died, Stalin took control of the country and began a brutal program of ethnic cleansing having millions of his countrymen killed or starved. His armed forces drove the invading German army out of Russia and back to Germany.

Gen. Erwin Rommel – Chapter 12
b. 1891, German Field Marshall known as 'the Desert Fox.' As a highly regarded tank Commander, he became a legendary war hero to the German people. He began to believe the war could not be won and joined the plot to assassinate Hitler. When caught he

was given the choice of a cyanide pill rather than the humiliation a public execution. He was given a 'hero's funeral' for the people.

Leona Woods – Chapter 14 b.1919, an American physicist who was the only female working on the team that built the first nuclear reactor (Chicago Pile-1). With her mentor, Enrico Fermi, she also worked on the Manhattan Project. Eventually in 1962 she became a professor of physics at New York University, NYU.

Albert Speer – Chapter 14
b. 1905, German architect who joined the Nazi Party in 1931. He was Hitler's chief architect and became the Reich Minister of Armaments and War Production. He was tried at Nuremberg for war crimes and accepted moral responsibility, but insisted he was ignorant of the Holocaust. He served his full 20-year sentence in a West Berlin prison.

Dwight Eisenhower – Chapter 14
b. 1890. American five-star general who served as the Allied Commander of all forces in Europe. His leadership was considered critical for the defeat of Germany. In 1952 he was elected the 34th President of the United States. One of his many accomplishments was the building of the Interstate Highway System.

Dr. Karl Goerdeler – Chapter 14
b. 1884, German politician who was elected Mayor of Leipzig in 1930. As a devout Christian he strongly opposed the anti-Semitic policies of the Nazi Reich, and worked tirelessly to bring about the downfall of the regime. He joined the plot to overthrow Hitler (he favored a forced resignation rather than execution). After many months on death row, he was executed by hanging 2 February 1945.

Sophie Scholl & Hans Scholl - Chapter 14

All students at the University of Munich, Sophie studying biology, the men, medical students. They were members of The White Rose Society, a non-violent resistance group opposing the Policies of the Third Reich and violence against Jews caught at the University distributing anti-Nazi leaflets, February 1943, they were given a mock trial and executed that afternoon. Sophie, who read and studied Augustine, said on the way to her death, "How can we expect righteousness to prevail when there is hardly anyone willing to give himself up individually to a righteous cause? Such a fine sunny day, I have to go, but what my death matter, if though us, thousands of people are awakened and stirred to action?"

General B. Montgomery – Chapter 15

b.1887, British General who commanded the British Eighth Army in two major campaigns in North Africa. He commanded all Allied Forces at the Invasion of Normandy (Operation Overlord). On 4 May 1945 he took the German surrender at Luneburg Northern Germany.

Claus von Stauffenberg – Chapter 15

b. 1907, a German military officer who saw action in the Invasion of Poland (1939) and the Soviet Union (1941). In North Africa, April '43, his vehicle was strafed by an Australian fighter-bomber and he lost his left eye and right hand. By 1944 he was fully committed to a plot to remove the Fuhrer, and by mid-July he decided to personally kill Hitler. In a meeting of almost all high-ranking officers, he placed a very powerful bomb which exploded after he left to take a telephone call. Four in the room were killed but Hitler survived. The following day four conspirators including Stauffenberg were executed by firing squad.

Dietrich Bonhoeffer – Chapter 16

b. 1906, German Christian theologian who was a key founding member of the Confession Church, a movement that rose in opposition to government sponsored efforts to unify all protestants into a pro-Nazi Reich Church. Through contacts in the Abwer (German Military Intelligence) he worked to oppose the Nazi anti-Semitism. By1941 he was forbidden to either speak publically or publish, although taught in and ran an underground seminary. He was arrested in April 1943 spending 18 mo. in a military prison, then moved to a high security Gestapo unit. In April 1945, just two months before the war's end, and after a final Sunday worship, he was executed. His last statement, "This is the end – for me the beginning of life."

Alexander Solzhenitsyn – Chapter 18

b.1918, Russian novelist & historian who called attention to the atrocities of communist Russia, both in their government and penal system. He was arrested in 1945 for his criticisms and given an 8 yr. prison sentence. In and out of prison he wrote multiple novels and in 1970 was awarded the Nobel Prize in Literature. He was expelled from the Soviet Union in 1974 and immigrated to the U.S. where he lived for 20 years. In the U.S. he implored the West not to "lose sight of its own values." After the fall of Communism he returned to Russia to live out his life.

Robert Oppenheimer – Chapter 20

b. 1904, American theoretical physicist who served as Director of the Manhattan Project (development of the A-bomb). He was considered a genius among many. He made many important contributions especially in the fields of astrophysics and quantum theory. He was an eccentric "left-wing intellectual", a brilliant researcher, and the founder of modern theoretical physics in the U.S.A chain smoker; he died of throat cancer at age 62.

Martin Bormann – Chapter 22
b. 1900, German who joined the Nazi Party in 1927. In a short few years, he gained acceptance into Hitler's inner circle, becoming his personal secretary who approved legislation, and controlled all domestic matters. He strongly supported the persecution of Christian Churches and favored harsh treatment of Jews. After attempting escape from the Soviet military, on May 2, he committed suicide.

Harry Truman – Chapter 23
b. 1884, the 33rd President of the United States, he was catapulted to lead the free world after the death of FDR. Amazingly, he knew almost nothing of the Manhattan Project. Germany had surrendered, Japan had not. Truman was to meet with Churchill and Stalin at Potsdam, a suburb of Berlin, to draw up surrender terms for the Japanese. The actual test explosion of the bomb was scheduled for the following day. The explosion was a "spectacular success", if foreboding. The Japanese refused the surrender terms, and the President decided to use the bomb. Two were dropped on the Japanese homeland, days apart. In the days following, the war in the Pacific ended….called V-J Day.